ROCK-A-BYE BABY

A Charlene Taylor Mystery #2

Luke Murphy

ROCK-A-BYE BABY
A Charlene Taylor Mystery #2

www.authorlukemurphy.com

FIRST EDITION Trade Paperback
ANM Books

June 2019

ISBN: 978-1-7753759-6-8

Cover designed by Casey Snyder Design: www.caseysnyderdesign.com

Praise for *Rock-A-Bye Baby*

"Rock-A-Bye Baby has everything—a haunted protagonist, heartfelt emotion, and a twisty, thrilling plot. A scorcher of a follow-up in a promising series." —David Ellis, *New York Times* bestselling author of *The Last Alibi*

"Murphy has cleverly crafted a riveting crime thriller, with a hefty dose of white-knuckle suspense. Entertaining and enticing to the very last page." —Cheryl Kaye Tardif, bestselling author of *Submerged*

"Rock-A-Bye Baby is an exquisitely told thriller, full of surprises and terrifying moments. Murphy is a gifted storyteller who keeps the tension crackling throughout the heart-stopping journey. The protagonist Charlene Taylor drives the story to a very satisfying and unexpected ending." —Kristina Stanley, bestselling author of the Stone Mountain series

For Elsie and Kathleen: Grandmothers are the best, and I had two very special ones. I miss our games together.

Acknowledgements

The most important people in my life: my family—Mélanie, Addison, Nève and Molly.

I'm the first to admit that this novel was not a solo effort. I've relied on many generous and intelligent people to turn this book into a reality. I'd like to thank the following people who had a hand in making this novel what it is today. I'm indebted to you all.

(The Conception) I need to thank the creative and very brilliant:
Mrs. Joan Conrod
Ms. Lisa Murphy
Mrs. Tracy Davis
Mrs. Nancy Arant Williams
Ms. Susanne Lakin

(The Research) For their professional expertise, knowledge in their fields and valuable information, thanks to:
Ms. Joanna Pozzulo (Institute of Criminology and Criminal Justice)
Keith MacLellan M.D.
Officer Laura Meltzer (Las Vegas Metropolitan Police Department)

Any procedural, geographical, or other errors pertaining to this story are of no fault to the names mentioned above, but entirely my own, as at times I took many creative liberties.

And last but not least, I'd like to thank you, the reader. You make it all worthwhile.

Book I

Mind Games

Chapter 1

Charlene Taylor sped onto Mount Olympus, gunning the engine. The old Volvo bellowed with each shift. Less than a hundred yards from the crime scene, she killed the headlights and coasted to a stop on the shoulder of the road, a row of luxury homes directly in front of her. The lashing rain fell even harder, beating her windshield as the wipers' steady rhythm struggled to keep up.

She waited and watched, looking for anything out of place. A shiver coursed through her, though she didn't know whether it was due to the cold November rain or what awaited her.

The radio squawked, startling her; dispatch was finally answering the call. The radio crackled with responses. Knowing that backup was on its way, she felt somewhat relieved…but only somewhat.

Dispatch had used the reverse 911 system to alert neighbors, making sure they stayed in their houses and kept their doors locked. It looked as if it had worked. Houses on both sides of the street appeared deserted.

Charlene continued to scope the area. Her cell phone chimed, and she pulled it out of her pocket.

"Taylor, I know what you're thinking!" her partner, Detective Larry Baker, shouted into the phone. "Don't do anything until I get there. Don't even think about—"

She hit the end button and switched the ringtone to vibrate.

Police procedure dictated that she should wait for backup, but it wasn't her style to sit around and wait. Who was she kidding? She wasn't waiting. Her adrenaline was already kicking in.

She shut off the engine, got out, and drew her standard-issue Glock 22. After checking the clip, she crossed two soggy lawns. Chilly water squished into her shoes as they sank into sodden earth.

Nothing looked out of place in the neighborhood. No hazard signs. Still no sirens or flashing lights. LAPD average response time was 7.8 minutes, but up here, in the hills, it might take longer.

Was this *his* plan? Was this why *he'd* lured her up here with *his* clues?

Charlene stepped onto a cobblestone walkway and followed it between white marble pillars to a set of oak double front doors. She gripped the brass knocker and banged, listening as the noise echoed in the silent night air.

After counting twenty seconds, she checked around the outside edges of the door. No signs of forced entry.

She proceeded around the back, sweeping the ground with her flashlight. No shoeprints. No broken windows or anything else amiss. Of course, the violent rain would've washed away all trace evidence, if there had been any.

Thunder cracked overhead.

She returned to the front, using the knocker again but followed up with a firm rap. "LAPD, open the door!"

Where was her backup?

Going in was the wrong decision, one she was trained not to make. Procedure demanded that she: secure the area and wait for backup. She had always tried her best to play by the rules, but, as usual, the Celebrity Slayer dared her to break them. Why did he have this effect on her?

Ignoring her better judgment, she twisted the knob. Locked.

She had to get inside. Now. She knew the Celebrity Slayer—knew his inclinations. That's what scared her. He had tipped her off to *something*.

Charlene pulled a set of lock picks from her pocket and worked the door, a skill she'd acquired from her father. Once she let herself inside, she quietly closed the door.

She searched the walls for a light switch, then flicked it, but nothing happened. Had the storm blacked out the neighborhood? She couldn't remember if lights were on in nearby houses or not.

Fear crawled up her already-tingling spine. She listened for movement in another room or overhead—a squeaky door or creaky floorboard.

She shone the small light around the ground floor, methodically searching the corners. Nervous energy swept over her, and she bit the inside of her cheek, a Taylor trait that surfaced in an emotionally-charged situation.

She crossed the marble-tiled floor, taking a long hallway and entering the main room through an archway. It led to the stairwell, with a wide, curving staircase. She stayed close to the side of the stairs as she climbed, avoiding the middle, where most of the creaks would likely come from.

Upon reaching the top step, she moved to the landing and stopped. Waiting, gun pointed. Every crack, every creak, had her flinching, poised to fire. The gun swung from right to left, primed for an attack.

As her eyes readjusted to the darkness of the space, she sidestepped down the hall, gun extended, checking and clearing each room. She was drawn to the master bedroom. Always the bedroom.

The upstairs was quiet, deadly quiet, except for the ticking of a clock and the low hum of central air-conditioning.

Before entering the room, Charlene crouched just outside and stuck her head in. The blackness limited her vision, until her eyes could adjust. She stepped in tentatively, moving through the bedroom with caution, the only noise her short, shallow breaths. The back of her neck was soaked with sweat.

The scent of stale, metallic flesh assaulted her nostrils. She drew closer to the four-poster bed, its drapes pulled and tied, and saw the chenille bedspread soaked in red. *Sick.*

Her foot kicked something, and she stumbled slightly. She flashed her light to the floor and spotted a body surrounded by a pool of blood. The frail drug addict had been sliced from throat to pubic bone.

She clenched the small flashlight between her teeth and held her breath as she searched for a pulse. None. The woman lay awkwardly, her satin robe flung open, revealing the ragged cut from a serrated blade. Her soft, milky white skin was now a mangled mound of flesh.

Charlene trailed her hand along the floor, and rubbed blood through the tips of her fingers—still warm. The victim had died only a short time ago. Was someone still in the house?

She stood and let out a breath, swallowing, stifling the urge to vomit.

After checking each upstairs room again, Charlene returned to the body and knelt. She made sure not to touch the victim again—the body was the most significant piece of evidence in any case. It never lied.

She squeezed her eyes shut, feeling the sting from hot tears of rage. A vibration on her hip brought her hand down instinctively. She hit the Talk button.

"Hi, Charlie."

Him.

Charlene couldn't speak; her throat tightened, but she didn't end the call either. She choked on her breath, her stomach turning in knots.

It couldn't be him. She had watched it happen in front of her own two eyes, months ago.

"I've missed you, Charlie."

"You're dead," she whispered, her voice frail.

Charlene mentally processed the crime scene around her, registering facts before her colleagues arrived. But there would be no clues, no evidence. He was too smart for that. But there was no mistaking who had performed this heinous act—Darren Brady.

"Did you miss me, Charlie?" The killer let out a soft chuckle.

Charlene remained on the floor, like a lost child, seated with her legs crossed. Sirens approached the house, accompanied by the squeal of tires and car doors slamming. The police were too late.

She punched off her phone and stood, then crossed the room and opened the French doors that led to the second-floor balcony overlooking the front entrance. The bright-red flashing lights cascaded across the front lawn and into the upstairs bedroom as two more cruisers pulled up.

She let out her breath—the life of a cop. She had seen so much bloodshed in her short LAPD career. There were no days off. No wonder she had no social life to speak of, and her family life was on the rocks. She missed her dad.

The detective was about to call down to the troops, when a noise caught her attention. A light creak, barely audible, like a footstep behind her. Before she could turn around, a hand clamped down on her shoulder—

Chapter 2

Charlene jolted awake, her chest heaving, sweat glistening on her naked body. She threw off the damp sheets, kicking them away in panic, and rolled onto her stomach, tasting the salty dampness from her pillow.

She reached down and checked the time on her iPhone; it must have fallen from her hand onto the hardwood floor when she'd dozed off: 11:34 p.m. She shook her head, rolled off the futon and onto her feet, then slipped on a pair of men's boxers.

Charlene made her way to the bathroom and splashed cold water on her face. She looked in the mirror and shook her head again, this time for different reasons. She was thin, her rib cage visible, not as athletically fit as she had once been, and prominent bags lingered under her eyes.

But it wasn't the physical changes that bothered her the most. She could handle them, because she had always been a motivated, hardworking cop who could will herself back into shape. No, it was much more than that.

After emptying her bladder, she stumbled back to the futon in the living room, her eyelids heavy, and threw herself down. She reached for the prescription bottles that waited tauntingly beside a bottle of warm beer on the floor.

Propranolol. Benzodiazepine. Fluoxetine. Paroxetine.

It had been months since her final showdown with Darren Brady, aka the Celebrity Slayer. Ever since that night, she'd been on a steady diet of antidepressants prescribed by Dr. Gardner, the LAPD psychiatrist. Sleep was now elusive.

She'd taken two months off after the ordeal, upon doctor's orders, to recover and recuperate. She thought she was fine. In her mind, that night had only made her stronger—the intense confrontation, the near-death struggle with one of the most brutal serial killers in LA history. She had survived to tell about it, believing she had put it behind her. Until the flashbacks and nightmares started a couple of weeks ago. Why now?

She hadn't told anyone about them, because if she did, she'd probably lose the promotion she had worked so hard to earn. The late Darren Brady simply would not leave her subconscious. As hard as she tried to eliminate her former LAPD colleague's image from her mind, he still consumed her thoughts; apparently her scars were only superficially healed.

Brady had been a psychotic killer, someone who'd ruined her life, and yet she couldn't stop thinking about him.

During the daytime she was fine, but the darkness haunted her. She wasn't eating consistently, and her sleepless nights came in waves. Many people worried for her—loved ones, friends, and family. But there was only one person who could help her.

The doctor diagnosed it as PTSD, common among military veterans, brought on by a traumatic event. She had visited her own personal war in hell.

She had attended a month of psychological debriefings after the incident, a series of interviews meant to directly confront the event and share her feelings with Gardner and to help structure her memories of the event so that she felt more in control. She bullshitted her way through those, as she had done most of her life, learning strategies to avoid her father's constant disapproval of her lifestyle. But Gardner had still prescribed the drugs, and she kept refilling the vials.

She continued weekly meetings with Gardner, but she had been cleared for full duty the previous month. It felt good to be back doing what she knew and loved. It felt real, and took her mind off other things. During the day.

Charlene checked her phone for missed calls, hoping that Andy had called while she slept, but he hadn't. Andy, her on-again, off-again boyfriend, had permanently turned their relationship to "off" a few weeks after the Celebrity Slayer sequence of events.

She didn't blame him. She was a basket case throughout the entire ordeal.

The relationship had probably ended long before that, but Andy had felt the need to stick around to support her after everything that happened, but eventually they both agreed to move on. She couldn't say she was disappointed, because she hadn't put in the effort to make it work.

She hadn't been easy to get along with while battling demons and knew that he deserved better. She didn't think she would care that much, but at night the loneliness seeped into her bones, and she missed his comforting presence.

Darren Brady had turned her life, her whole world, upside down.

She remembered the scene. Brady, someone she'd trusted as a cop, hovering over her, two hands holding a knife to her chest, ready to thrust down with a vengeance. She was seconds away from the plunge of the blade when her new partner came in and shot Brady point-blank.

Since that fateful moment, her professional life, her career, soared, while her personal life went in the opposite direction. She received accolades, high fives, back pats for bringing down the man known as the Celebrity Slayer. But her boyfriend had left, her family grew distant, and she hadn't slept in months.

There was no doubt in her overtaxed mind that Officer Darren Brady had been an integral part of her life—a game-changer. He had killed her father and had cleverly positioned himself in Charlene's life after her promotion to detective.

The Celebrity Slayer had become a household name, an LA serial killer who fed off the media's attention. He had a hunger for B-list celebrities, torturing and mutilating them for the fun of it. A complete psychopath, who couldn't tell the difference between reality and fantasy.

But Brady was gone. She was sure of it.

So then why couldn't she sleep at night?

"I had a dream last night."

She hadn't slept much after waking from the dream. This early-morning session had snuck up quickly.

Charlene lay on a stiff leather couch-like chair. She had grown so accustomed to it that she no longer noticed the stiffness it sent to her shoulders and lower back, or how the scent of expensive leather drifted to her nostrils. She closed her eyes, her breathing steady, as Dr. Gardner had instructed her.

On the drive in, she contemplated telling Gardner about the dream. If he thought she was on her way back down, cracking even the slightest bit, she'd be in for another leave of absence—and maybe lose everything she'd worked for. She decided to tell him it was the first time she'd had the dream and see how it played out.

Gardner sat on a chair behind her, Charlene forever aware of his presence. The aroma of his cologne, a combination of spicy herbs, softly scented the air. His calm breathing, the smooth scratching from the stroke of his pen on the notepad—were sounds she no longer noticed.

Her weekly visits with Gardner had been consistent since her father's murder. Although they originally had been department-ordered, she continued to see the LAPD psychiatrist long after being reinstated for full duty with the Robbery-Homicide division.

"Tell me about it." Gardner's soft voice had a hint of a rasp.

The man oozed confidence, his vast knowledge was the product of years of practice, honing his craft, studying patients, and reading up on the latest treatments in the field of psychology and medicine.

His reputation preceded him. Gardner was acknowledged as one of the most intelligent men on the LAPD staff, a highly sought-after commodity—a psychological-consultant for serial cases. He had worked with the Celebrity Slayer task force to help bring down the madman, but, in the end, Charlene had uncovered the truth and baited Brady to his demise.

As she lay there now, it was hard to believe that her own father, the late Martin Taylor, Grade III Detective and Sergeant II on the LAPD, had considered Gardner as a possible suspect as the Celebrity Slayer.

Charlene told Gardner about the dream. "Me against him. He won."

"But in reality, you won." His voice—pitch, volume, rhythm—never changed.

"Then why do I feel like I lost?"

"Most of the time dreams bring more questions than answers."

"That's helpful." He was used to her sarcasm.

"Why do you think you're dreaming about it, now?"

Gardner was a professional at misdirection, as Charlene assumed most psychiatrists were. He constantly answered her questions with his own. He would circle a topic repeatedly, allowing her to answer her own questions in her own time. Although effective, she sometimes wished he would just give her the answers, instead of pressing her to discover them on her own.

She opened her eyes and stared at the library of books on the shelves in front of her. Some old, some new, hardbacks and paperbacks. Books on psychology, psychiatry, neurology, sociology, and every other "gy" that existed. The titles and covers were now memorized—she'd been staring at them for so long.

After a long few minutes, without a response from Charlene, Gardner added, "You and Darren Brady shared a strong emotional connection. You worked together, closely, and a bond was formed when he saved your life. You trusted him, and, subconsciously, you probably felt that you owed him."

True, she was emotionally attached.

"I was lied to, cheated, hunting the same man I was working with, and I had no idea."

After a pause he said, "None of us did. You know it as flashbacks. In the medical world, we call it involuntary recurrent memory, a psychological phenomenon in which an individual has a sudden, usually powerful, re-experiencing of a past event or element of a past event. We have to determine why it is happening through your dreams and why now."

Suddenly she straightened, turned around, and looked at the psychiatrist. "Are you saying that I was so obsessed with Darren, that I needed the emotional connection with the Celebrity Slayer so much, that I am subconsciously reaching out to regain that link?"

Gardner was silent.

She stood and shook her head. "That's pathetic."

"Not necessarily, Detective." Gardner extended his hand for her to sit back down. She did, but this time facing the psychiatrist.

He went on, "We all need an outlet. We all need to feel necessary, to feel that there is something out there that pulls at us. Everyone makes connections to different things."

"I'm a fucking mess."

"You're normal." Gardner scribbled on his notepad and then checked his watch. "How do you feel about Darren Brady?"

He'd never asked her that question before. In all of her sessions since the Brady incident, Gardner had never once asked her how she felt about him. An extended silence hung in the air, and, this time, she knew he was waiting her out.

"He was a cold-blooded killer."

"He also saved your life."

True. If Brady hadn't found her in time, Sean Cooney, the man who had been one half of the Celebrity Slayer duo, secretly killing alongside Brady, would have killed her. But Charlene always wondered how much time Brady had let pass during that whole scene. Had he hoped to watch Cooney rape her? Had he waited just long enough, let her fear for her life, before finally killing Cooney?

She was now at a loss for words. Hot tears burned her eyes before she blinked them away.

"I think this was a productive session. We're getting deeper, even closer, Detective. You have a good week and stay safe."

After Charlene left the office, Dr. Edward Gardner picked up his phone and punched in numbers.

"Captain Dunbar, it's Dr. Gardner. I'm checking in as usual after my weekly session with Detective Taylor."

Although Gardner was bound by doctor-patient confidentiality, he was obligated to keep department heads updated on current personnel-related matters if he felt a client was a threat to herself or other law enforcement officers.

"How is she, Doctor?" Dunbar had a gravelly smoker's voice.

"Progressing, but I'm worried. She may have had a setback. From our talks, I'm afraid that she's showing signs of what we call repetition compulsion."

"What exactly does that mean?"

"It's a psychological phenomenon in which a person repeats a traumatic event or its circumstances over and over again. This includes reenacting the event or putting oneself in situations where the event is likely to happen again. This 'reliving' can also take the form of dreams, in which memories and feelings of what happened are repeated, and even cause hallucinations."

"English, Doc."

"I'm worried that Detective Taylor will continue to put herself in positions of vulnerability to dangerous situations. She will put not only herself in harm's way but anyone else who is working with her. Although it hasn't happened yet, you'll need to keep a close eye on her."

"What should I look for?"

"You and her partner are around her every day. Look for the repetition of behavior or life patterns that put her in danger over and over again."

"I'll talk with them when they come in. Thanks, Doc."

Gardner hung up and shook his head, doubting the captain would talk with Charlene Taylor. Most superiors avoided such discussions at all costs.

What he hadn't told the captain was that Taylor might have been in love with Darren Brady, as sick and irrational an idea as that was. But it wasn't totally out of the question; he'd seen it many times.

It was a form of the Stockholm syndrome or capture-bonding, in which the hostage expresses empathy and sympathy, and develops positive feelings toward their captors, sometimes to the point of defending them.

Although Taylor was never technically kidnapped by Brady, the cat-and-mouse game that she and the serial killer had engaged in brought her closer and gave her a personal connection with him that she otherwise wouldn't have had.

Dr. Gardner would have to take care of it himself, or Detective Taylor would continue to live on the edge, walk the line, until one day she fell over or jumped. And who would she take with her?

Chapter 3

Special Agent Matt Stone sat in his brother's patrol car when he intercepted the AMBER Alert. Like most cops who heard such reports, Matt's blood ran cold.

AMBER stood for "America's Missing: Broadcast Emergency Response," named after Amber Hagerman, a Texas girl who'd been abducted and killed near Dallas in 1996. The alerts were established to publicize child abductions.

He turned to face his brother, who was driving. "Let's take this."

Jake nodded, flipping on the cherries and siren. He picked up the radio. "Car seven, we're on our way."

As the car accelerated, Matt spoke out of the corner of his mouth. "So much for a vacation."

They arrived at a red-brick colonial to find three patrol cars already on the scene. "You lead, Jake. You're one of them."

"They're your friends too, Matt. Or have you forgotten that?"

Matt nodded. "I know. But I'm the only one without a uniform, and I'm outside my jurisdiction, unless I'm invited in."

Even in his hometown, surrounded by people he knew and had worked with, Matt was ever aware of the animosity between FBI and local law enforcement. Some of his former friends had taken it personally when he jumped ship from the local to the federal level.

They took their time approaching the house. Matt scanned the street, his eyes probing, wondering if the kidnapper stood among the dozen onlookers attracted by the sight of police cruisers and flashing lights. Most of the mob had out their iPhones and in ten minutes news would have spread—via Facebook, Twitter, and texting. So much for discretion in today's technology-driven society.

He saw local cops knocking on doors of neighbors' houses, canvassing the area.

Jake noted, "It's a pretty safe-looking area."

Matt didn't respond. He didn't know a thing about the case, but it was never too early to start investigating until he was fully informed.

While his brother entered the house, Matt stayed back and checked the outside lower-level windows. He looked for disturbances in the flower beds or newly laid sod and assessed the back doors, which were locked from the inside with no evidence of tampering.

He went back to the front, opened the door, and heard the usual din that accompanied a full-on police investigation. Inside he made his way to the living room, where a petite woman sat slumped on an L-shaped sofa holding a tissue to her nose. She had tear-stained blue eyes, and mascara-stained cheeks.

She was surrounded by cops, and Matt knew that somewhere in another room the child's father was undergoing the same line of questioning. The locals ran it by the book, debriefing the parents separately, making sure their stories checked out.

All too familiar.

In forty-nine percent of kidnapping cases, the parents, or other family members, were somehow involved. They would undergo an in-depth background check with every facet of their life thoroughly looked into.

As a special agent for the FBI's Behavioral Analysis Unit, trained by the best of the best, Matt stayed back from the crowd and studied the mother, monitoring her actions. Even at the age of thirty-two, Matt had analyzed all kinds of criminals.

"The parents' names are Stephanie and Mike Wilson," Jake whispered, returning to the room still scribbling on a notepad. "Their little girl, Allie, was taken from the park a few hours ago."

"A few hours ago? That's a long time to wait before calling it in."

"I thought so too."

Matt, close enough to listen in, kept his eyes trained on a grief-stricken Stephanie Wilson, she babbled incoherently, repeating the phrase, "It's my fault. I should've known."

Matt thought she looked genuine.

He said, "Issue a statewide alert, but make sure they don't know it's coming from me."

Jake nodded. "We got a good description of the kidnapper."

Matt pressed his lips together, unconvinced. "I doubt it."

He left Jake in the living room and walked through the house and spotted the child's youthful-looking father in the kitchen leaning against a tiled island, surrounded by uniformed officers taking notes.

The angry father shook his head. "This is bullshit. Get out there and find my daughter!"

Cops spoke in low tones, trying to calm the man's frayed emotions.

Matt was sure the officers had asked about enemies, acquaintances, or other possible suspects, and he'd make sure Jake could get a copy.

Jake met him at the bottom of the staircase. "It's done. What now?"

"I want to take a look around."

"Why here? The girl was snatched at the park."

"I know—we'll get there, but I want to get a feel for the family. A house can answer questions a family won't."

Jake nodded. "I'll give you some time."

The inside of the Wilson home was well maintained, expensively furnished—the epitome of a happy, financially sound family home. Three bedrooms, two bathrooms, spacious kitchen, extended living room, and a formal dining room.

As Matt turned the corner and put his hand on the railing to climb the stairs, the Denver chief of police, Janice Salinger, descended, on her way down toward him. He froze on the bottom step. The chief stopped in midstride and glared at Matt. He could feel her cold stare dissecting him.

The chief's recently cut brown hair was shoulder length, and a splash of makeup covered smooth skin and fine cheekbones. She wore a charcoal-colored pantsuit and a white blouse.

Through clenched teeth she hissed, "What are you doing here?"

"My job," Matt replied firmly, not giving an inch.

"This isn't your jurisdiction, Agent." Her reply was sarcastic, her gaze relentless.

"I thought I could help."

"We don't need your help. We can handle this. I know that we're just a small, bumbling group of oafs to the FBI, but we're actually damn good at our jobs."

Matt opened his mouth, but she cut him off.

"Officer Stone, why don't you take your brother home, where he belongs?"

Matt turned and saw Jake standing behind him, his mouth hanging open in embarrassment.

Jake nodded. "Yes ma'am."

The chief continued down the stairs, brushing past Matt, intentionally shouldering him into the wall. Matt kept his balance, moving aside to give the angry woman a wide berth.

Once she was gone, Matt patted his brother on the shoulder. "Wow, she hasn't gotten any happier, has she?"

Jake grinned. "I'm sure it has nothing to do with you."

"That was a long time ago."

"Not to her. You guys went through a lot together, and she hasn't been able to turn the page. You should talk to her."

"Does she look like she wants to talk? I've done everything I can to reach out to her, but she doesn't want my help."

"Can we go now?" Jake sounded anxious.

"Just give me a minute." Matt turned and continued up the stairs.

"Matt."

Matt spread his fingers on one hand and raised them. "Five minutes."

He climbed the steps to the second level, passing what looked like a shrine to baby Allie, the couple's only child. Framed pictures lined the wall in sequence by age.

Allie Wilson was a beautiful baby—with a full head of dark hair, a round face, brown almond-shaped eyes, and a pug nose—just like her mother.

The chief's words rang in Matt's ears. He didn't want to be caught at a DPD crime scene for long and get Jake in trouble with the boss, but as a federal agent, every scene tugged at Matt's heart strings.

He knew the procedure, knew that from here on out, until they received a ransom demand, the Wilson family and their home would be under twenty-four-hour surveillance. All incoming and outgoing calls and mail would be carefully monitored.

Matt heard footsteps on the stairs and saw Jake's head appear, looking edgy. "Are you ready yet?"

"The Wilsons certainly have money, but not enough to warrant a kidnapping for ransom."

Jake asked again, "You ready to go?"

"Not yet. Look, I don't want to get you in trouble, but this is my job. When your guys are done, ask Mrs. Wilson to show you around the house. I need to talk with her alone."

Jake shook his head. "That can't happen. The chief is still downstairs, looking pissed, and she'll be more than happy to take it out on you. Or me."

"I'm a Fed, trained for this exact scenario. The earlier we can get ahead of it, the better it will be for this family and their baby. That little girl is all I care about."

Jake nodded and headed downstairs.

Matt spent the next five minutes in the yellow-and-blue-painted baby's room. The crib sheets were neatly folded, and stencils of clowns and balloons decorated the walls. On a nearby changing table were the requisite baby supplies. Nothing unusual there.

He could hear light footfalls in the hallway and stepped out just as Stephanie Wilson and Jake reached the landing.

"Mrs. Wilson, I'm Agent Stone." Matt stretched his hand out, and she accepted it. Her grip was weak, her hands cold and shaky. "I know this is difficult, but would you mind if I asked you a few questions?"

"But I just answered some."

"I know, Mrs. Wilson, and I understand how hard this is, but I'm not with the local police."

She looked at Jake and then back at Matt, and he answered her unasked question.

"I'm a criminal personality profiler with the FBI."

"The FBI?"

"Yes." He removed his badge and credentials and held them out for her inspection. "This is my job. I've been trained to handle these kinds of situations."

She frowned. "Do we have time for this? Shouldn't we be out looking for Allie?"

"This is the best chance we have. There are already a vast number of people searching for your daughter."

She gave a tired nod.

Jake turned away and whispered to Matt, "I'm gonna go stand at the top of the stairs."

They entered the baby's room, where she picked up a framed picture of Allie and squeezed her eyes shut. She began to tremble. "I'm sorry."

"It's okay." He paused. "What happened?"

She nodded. "We were taking a walk in the park, like we do every other day. Usually we go with my neighbor, Sandy, and her son Noah, but they couldn't make it today."

"Why not?"

"Her husband's car wouldn't start at work, and she had to go pick him up."

Matt stuck his head out the door frame. "Jake."

Jake met his gaze.

"Check to see why the neighbor wasn't with Ms. Wilson today."

Jake nodded and left.

She continued. "Allie loves our walks. It's the only chance we get to go outside." She forced a smile. "Look, I've answered all of this. Why are we wasting time?"

"How was today's walk different than any other day?"

"Other than being alone, it wasn't any different. We walked the same route to the same park and sat on the same bench as we do every other weekday."

Matt made a mental note of this. People who followed regular routines made for easier targets because of the repetition. Their day could be studied and anticipated.

"When did you know that your neighbor wouldn't be joining you?"

She hesitated, as if thinking. "It was right before we left, because I was on the phone with my husband when she called. My husband calls at two o'clock every day."

"So Mike knew you were going alone?"

"Yeah. He wanted us to wait until he got home, but by then it's suppertime." She closed her eyes and tears rolled down her cheeks. "I'm so stupid."

Matt shook his head. "No, you're not. You did nothing wrong."

She pulled away from him and walked to the window, looking out at the police cruisers parked in her driveway. Neighbors stood outside their homes watching.

"Tell me what happened at the park."

Her eyes remained fixed on the chaos outside. "We rested for a few minutes at our usual bench. Allie slept in the stroller, while I read a magazine. I guess I lost track of time because when I looked up, the park was empty. We'd just started back out on the path when I noticed a thin man in a black sweat suit jogging toward us."

"Describe him."

She closed her eyes. "Average height, mustache, long brown ponytail, white headband, dark sunglasses, and what looked like brand-new sneakers."

He wrote fast, trying to keep up. "Brand name?"

"I'm not sure. He wore dark gloves, which I thought was odd considering the weather." Her eyes were still closed. "The jogger slowed near us. Then he looked at me and said, 'Good evening, ma'am.'"

"Any accent?" Matt understood that most people couldn't hide their dialect.

"Lazy—Southern maybe. But I don't know for sure." She opened her eyes.

"Did he say anything else?"

"Small talk. Weather, that kind of thing. He was nice enough, but for some reason, I felt apprehensive. He kept looking around."

"Mother's intuition?"

She looked at him. "You think?"

Matt nodded. "You sensed danger for your baby. Did he seem nervous, anxious?"

She shook her head. "Not at all. He was calm, normal, friendly." She brought a small, shaky hand to her face and swiped at a tear.

"Go on."

"He started to fuss over Allie, about how beautiful she was. He was sincere, and... I don't know, maybe I warmed up to him. He asked her name and I told him. What a fool I was. I don't know how often I've heard parents tell their kids not to talk to strangers, and there I was, opening up to a complete stranger on the street."

"You didn't know."

"He began making baby noises, and Allie responded. Then he asked for the time—"

Matt waited her out.

"When I looked down at my watch, a wet cloth covered my mouth and nose. I panicked, and started swinging at him, but he was strong." She continued through her tears. "I felt weak, sleepy, but I fought it. I couldn't let him win. I had to protect Allie." She paused and inhaled loudly. "I kept thinking if I could only cry out, but before I could do that, he restrained me, and I have no memory of what happened after that."

She would be tested, but Matt was sure the cloth had been soaked in chloroform, which would have rendered her unconscious.

"I was scared, but more afraid for Allie. I tried to scream, before I realized there were thick bushes that would've prevented nearby drivers from seeing me."

Her vocal cords would have been paralyzed by the chloroform.

"Do you or your husband have any enemies? Anyone who would want to harm you or your family? Someone from the past? Someone you never thought could do this?"

She frowned. "No!"

"Have you noticed anyone suspicious, maybe around your home or when you're out and about?"

She shook her head.

"Have you received any letters or phone calls since the abduction? Any means of communication from the kidnapper?"

"No. We already told the police this. We haven't heard anything from anyone."

"Tell me about your husband."

Her eyes grew wide. "What about my husband?"

"Has he changed since Allie's birth?"

She abruptly scowled, yelling. "Why the hell are you wasting time here? I've been over this."

Matt heard voices and the sound of feet on the stairs. Without another word, he slipped into the master bedroom, exiting that way, avoiding the rush of cops who stormed the baby's room.

It took Matt less than a minute to find Jake, and he glanced around, but didn't see the chief. He grabbed him by the arm and they hustled through the living room, where the Wilsons now hugged on the couch. Stephanie looked at Matt but whispered in her husband's ear, while pointing. The man's stare was unwavering as he eyed Matt.

Matt turned on his heels and almost walked into the chief of police, which would have knocked her over. He stopped abruptly before contact. She had been walking and talking with a man in a plain beige suit, probably a DPD detective.

"I thought I told you to leave!" Her loud, threatening voice boomed, and her face reddened. Most of the cops in the room had stopped to watch.

Matt nodded. "Let's go."

As he stepped onto the sidewalk, the front door opened, and Mike Wilson waved to Matt.

"My wife tells me you're with the FBI?"

Matt nodded, surprised. "Agent Stone."

The two men shook hands. Matt noticed the chief of police watching from the front window, unsmiling.

"I wanted to speak to you alone, because I don't want Steph to think I'm the reason our child is missing. I heard you ask if we knew anyone who might do something like this. Well, I know someone—a man at work."

"What man?"

"He was stealing money from the company, and I caught him. I got him fired."

"Why couldn't you say that in front of your wife?"

"His name is Frank Manning. He swore he'd get me back. I didn't tell Steph because I knew she would only worry, and now that I didn't take him seriously, she might blame me for the kidnapping. I couldn't live with that. I never thought Frank would do anything like this, though."

Matt jotted the name down on his pad. "Do you have contact information for this guy?"

"I can get it for you."

Matt nodded. "I'm glad you sought me out. I'll check this guy out. If you hear from the kidnapper or if your wife happens to remember anything, call me."

"Do you think we'll get her back?"

"This is what I do."

"That's not what I asked."

Matt didn't respond.

"Do you have any children, Agent Stone?"

The question caught Matt off guard, forcing him to swallow a lump in his throat. "No, sir."

"My wife is the youngest of four girls. Her sisters all have large families. Family is everything to us. Please find our baby girl."

Matt held out his business card. "My cell number is at the bottom, and I can be reached 24/7."

Jake was already sitting in the car when Matt got in. "So, formulate a theory yet?"

"It's early. I'd like to take a closer look at the Wilsons. Was there tension with a new baby in the house? Did the husband still get the same attention from his wife? Was there jealousy? The mental strain of a newborn can put stress even on a healthy relationship."

Jake nodded. "That it?"

"Check for known sex offenders and pedophiles in the area."

"You think—" Jake couldn't finish the sentence.

Matt shook his head. "No, I don't, but we need to check. Contact all local shoe stores. See if you can track down receipts for white high-top sneakers sold recently. I know it's a long shot, but Stephanie Wilson thinks they looked new."

"What are you thinking?"

"I don't get a parental abduction vibe. No ransom call. This is only the beginning. In the meantime, let's head back to the precinct. I need to see what CSI found in the park. I also want to swing by the crime scene—that's if it's been kept intact."

"Don't step on any toes, Matt."

Matt punched his brother on the shoulder and grinned. "Cross my heart."

Jake started the engine. "You think you guys will get involved?"

Matt understood "you guys" to mean the FBI. "Probably. But for now, I'll let your team handle it. Whatever they intend on doing, though, they'd better do now, because that critical forty-eight-hour window closes fast."

Chapter 4

Charlene had an ear pinned to the door, her eyes checking the narrow third-floor hallway, her Glock unholstered. She bit down on her bottom lip, her only focus on the infrequent bursts of racket inside the apartment.

The deteriorating complex, located in LA's "Skid Row" near downtown, had seen better days. The building, a one-time prominent LA landmark, now housed the unemployed and crack-dealing pimps. The odor emanating from the doorway made her cringe in disgust.

The hallway doors, at one time painted yellow, were peeling and covered with graffiti.

"What the hell are we doin' here, Taylor?" her partner whispered. She was close enough to smell Larry's sour cigarette breath.

"Our jobs." She glanced at her watch: 11:46 p.m. Over half an hour had passed since she'd intercepted the call.

"This isn't our bust. You're not Dirty Harry." Sweat trickled off his brow.

She ignored him. *What* are *you doing here?* asked a voice in her head.

This wasn't her case or even her jurisdiction, and yet she headed the pack, led the charge. This wasn't even an LAPD case, but cops were cops; they all played on the same side.

She had just returned home from the bar, when the notification burst over the police scanner, and her gut instinct kicked in.

A disturbance call, by an annoyed neighbor, gave a credible description of Phoenix Walker, a fugitive who'd recently escaped prison and eluded capture by US marshals.

She leaned back against a wall, surveying the row of tense faces protected behind shields—the LAPD SWAT Team.

Larry whispered, "Let's get outta here and let SWAT do their job." But she wasn't ready to let it go.

They'd cleared the hallways on every floor. This could go two ways: either a full-blown shootout or a foot chase, if the suspect had an alternate method of exit. Either way, Walker would be ready for them—he wouldn't go back to prison without a fight.

Charlene nodded to the SWAT leader. The short, heavy-set man, already prepped, waved the two detectives to the back of the line.

Two uniformed men sporting bullet-proof armor and face shields ran to the front of the line holding a battering ram. The leader motioned the countdown.

Three, two, one…

With a thrust, the ram shattered the door, scattering wood splinters in every direction. Angry female screams of Spanish profanity followed, echoing along the hallway, and a baby cried.

"LAPD! Freeze! Everyone on the ground!" SWAT stormed the apartment, leaping over remnants of the shattered door. Charlene followed them inside, her gun drawn.

"Taylor."

Larry's large hand came down on her back, his grip on the fabric of her jacket, but she pulled loose.

Without warning a shotgun went off, letting loose an ear-splitting blast, that sent Charlene to the floor, and the bullet made a basketball-sized hole in the wall behind her. Chunks of drywall and plaster fell into her hair.

She got into a crouching position, waiting for a signal to advance. She looked back to see her partner sprint for the staircase. Knowing SWAT had this, she turned and followed him.

More deafening automatic gunfire clattered as SWAT returned fire, freezing Charlene in place. The woman inside continued to scream, and the baby still cried.

From somewhere nearby a radio squawked. "Suspect is on the fire escape. Repeat, suspect is outside the building."

Charlene grabbed her radio. "Larry, he's outside." She waited for Larry's response, but it didn't come. She tried again, "Larry, repeat. Suspect is heading your way."

She sprang to her feet and sprinted down the stairs, taking them two at a time, her heart thumping against her chest, the heels of her boots loud in the empty stairwell. As she pushed the back door open, a piercing alarm erupted, and her adrenaline level soared.

Once the door closed, she found herself outside, in a dark alley. She tried to open the door again, to give herself light, but it had locked from the inside after closing.

"Man down." Another voice sounded on her radio. The perp was picking them off.

A SWAT member lay unmoving on the ground behind the van. She bent down, switched the gun from her right hand to her left and checked his pulse. He was still breathing, but his pulse slowed, and blood pooled around him on the concrete. She drew a deep, shaky breath.

A noise in the back made her jerk her head up. She switched her gun to her strong hand and followed the sound.

The dark alley seemed foreboding, and her nostrils flared from the stench. She used her phone light to sweep the alley, her gun pointed in front of her. The concrete-block walls were covered in spray-paint graffiti, and the garbage bins overflowed.

Two buildings down, a homeless man slept under a green Army jacket, set up against the block wall.

She cautiously headed down the alleyway, inspecting the openings for hiding places.

"Okay, Cop, drop your weapon or you're dead."

She froze, looking around. The words were filled with rage.

The voice came from behind a large dumpster at the end of the alley, not far away. She tiptoed to the corner of the metal bin and peeked around it, flattening herself against its sidewall.

A solidly-built man with a shaved head and shaggy whiskers held a sawn-off shotgun. In the dim overhead light she could see that his shirt was drenched with sweat.

Walker.

Her stomach flip-flopped. She took a moment to shake it off.

She craned her neck to see past the man, where Larry stood blindsided, uncertainty etched on his face. Her partner released his gun, letting it fall to the concrete with a clank.

Only seconds later Walker approached Larry, kicking the weapon into the grated sewer. When he looked around to make sure they were alone, she leaned back before he could see her.

They were a long way from where the pursuit had begun, too far for SWAT to reach them before it ended badly. She was too close to the fugitive to use her radio to call for help. One sound, and he'd end Larry's life.

She leaned past the Dumpster, trying to decide her next move. A sharp blow from the butt of the shotgun caught Larry just under the rib cage. His legs buckled, and he wheezed for breath. Then the fugitive hit Larry with an elbow, sending the bulky detective to the ground, where he lay, no longer a threat to anyone.

Charlene bit the inside of her mouth, trying to control her breathing. She felt numb, and sweat stung her eyes. She swiped them away with her shirt sleeve.

The gunman sneered again, obviously enjoying the pain he inflicted. "Good-bye, Pig."

It was now or never. She stepped out and shouted, "LAPD, freeze!"

The man did indeed freeze, but he didn't turn around or drop his weapon.

She shouted, "Drop your weapon, and do it now!"

The man remained motionless.

Larry screamed, "Shoot him, Taylor!"

The fugitive stuck the barrel of the gun against Larry's temple. "I'd think about that, if I were you, Taylor."

"Don't be stupid, Walker. This won't end well for you." Slowly he turned to face her, wearing a knowing grin.

Charlene stood twenty-feet away, staring into the madman's eyes, remembering the words she'd read in the file about his violent past. Walker would pull the trigger without thinking twice and live with no regrets.

"I'm not going back to prison."

He moved toward her, with the barrel of the gun swinging through the air as if in slow motion. She had just about enough time. She aimed her weapon and squeezed the trigger.

Then she heard the sound of a body folding and falling to the ground. She waited until her heartbeat found a regular cadence, and stepped closer, gun still drawn. The perpetrator lay at Larry's side, his eyes locked open in shock and a line of blood trickling from the corner of his mouth.

Larry looked at her, a tense expression painted on his face. Then he gave her a slight nod.

Neither of them was in the mood for a crowd, so Friday night at the Irish Times was just what they needed.

The silence was deafening with both detectives still mentally reviewing the incident. After their brief statements to other cops in the LAPD Central precinct, they were quick to realize what they needed. They weren't sticking around to talk with IAG.

They slid into the last two vacant stools at the end of the bar where the bartender set a bowl of trail mix and two napkins in front of them.

Larry stuck two fingers in the air. "Two beers."

The bartender left, and they waited quietly until he set their drinks in front of them. Larry took a sip. He stared at the mirror behind the bar, quiet.

Once the adrenaline rush faded, Charlene's arms felt heavy. She closed her eyes, the image of the gunman burned in her brain, and the smell of gunpowder still lingering in her nostrils.

She pulled a scuffed-up LAPD badge out of her pocket and placed it on the top of the bar in front of Larry. It must have fallen from his pocket when he'd been hit with the shotgun.

Larry looked at the badge sitting on the bar but didn't reach for it. "I almost died tonight."

"I didn't mean for that to happen." *Unintended consequences.*

"Thirty years on the job, and I've never come that close. But you saved my life tonight."

"I owed you one," she answered, trying to lighten the mood, remembering how Larry had saved her life not so long ago when he'd killed Darren Brady.

Larry managed a slight nod and took another drink.

He looked tired, frazzled, his grey hair mussed and his light-colored shirt still dark with dried sweat stains. There was a black smudge on his cheek and a butterfly bandage above his right eye, where he'd taken the blunt force trauma earlier in the evening. His eye had already started to discolor; it would be a dark bruise.

Charlene looked at her own haggard reflection in the mirror. Her jaw-length dark-blond hair was tussled and the white parts around her blue eyes were bloodshot. She rarely wore makeup, but that wouldn't have made a difference.

She asked, "How's your head?"

He touched the bandage. "I'll live. But there goes the modeling career."

His attempt at humor failed miserably.

An off-duty cop, who Charlene recognized, strolled by and slapped her on the shoulder.

"I heard what happened tonight. Nice job, Chip."

Charlene faked a smile. "Thanks."

It wasn't the first time she'd taken someone's life, either directly or indirectly, but it didn't get any easier. Even if the people she chased were all bad, it still didn't feel right to determine whether someone lived or died.

When the cop walked away, she muttered, "I hate that nickname."

"They call you that because you're so much like your father, a regular 'chip' off the old block."

Charlene nodded and knew that to be partially true, but she understood that most of the male cops called her that because of the 'chip' on her shoulder.

Larry didn't make eye contact when he spoke. "Why were we there tonight?"

"Just doing my job. You chose to come."

He frowned. "You called me. I wasn't about to let my partner go in there alone. And don't give me that shit about it being your job. That wasn't our bust."

"I thought I could help."

"Bullshit." His voice was loud, and when a few patrons looked over, he shook his head apologetically. Then he whispered, "You're unnecessarily putting yourself in harm's way.".

"I'm not going to apologize for how I do my job."

"Why are you still putting on this tough-guy act? Who are you trying to impress? I know you're a great cop. We all know. Maybe better than your father. Stop acting like a cowboy."

The partnership had had a rocky start, but Charlene believed Larry had finally started to accept her for who she was—a capable detective, a legitimate investigator, and a reliable partner—not a woman who rode the coattails of her famous father—as most everyone else assumed.

"I'm doing my job the only way I know how."

"It seems like more than a job to you. It seems like a goddamn unhealthy obsession."

Her eyes burned with tears that threatened, but she wouldn't give Larry the satisfaction of wiping them in front of him.

"You're taking this job too seriously."

"It is serious, Larry, and I'm good at it."

"No one is denying that. We're all proud of the way you handled the Professor case. Your pops would have been proud too."

It felt like years ago, but, in fact, it had only been months since she'd attempted to arrest Detective Adrienne Jackson for murder. Even though Jackson had been guilty of murdering two men, had an indirect hand in the suicide death of a young woman, and admitted her guilt, her fellow colleagues in the department had a hard time accepting Jackson's fate. She was one of them, LAPD family.

Charlene understood what would happen when she put Jackson under the microscope and accuse her of murder, but she did her job the only way she knew how—honestly, diligently, and to the best of her ability.

That Jackson had been accidentally killed in the arrest had not gone over well with LAPD.

Charlene didn't say anything, but she heard Larry take in a big breath of air and exhale loudly.

"Forget it. So, what was the outcome tonight?"

"The woman was killed in the cross fire. But the baby wasn't hurt, and Child Welfare has been called in."

Charlene felt regret that the arrest had killed a woman and orphaned a child. She knew how easily life was lost.

He asked, "Is IAG going to be up your ass?"

Internal Affairs Group was responsible for investigating department corruption as well as policy violations. They also looked into police shootings.

She shook her head. "I don't think so. It was a justifiable shoot. The lieutenant's pissed because this wasn't even an LAPD case. Tomorrow morning, I'll have to make my report."

Another bout of silence ensued.

"Thanks, Taylor."

Charlene knew that was hard for Larry to say. "Like I said, I owed you one. Plus, I'm not ready to break in a new partner just yet."

They both took another drink.

"Everything okay?" A man of few words.

Charlene looked at Larry, recognizing the concerned expression on his face. Ever since her father's death, he had stepped in and been more than just a partner. Since Larry was her father's former partner, friend, and a pallbearer at his funeral, it was as if he felt obligated to watch over Charlene—as more than just partners.

She'd been off work for months, and hadn't exactly stayed in touch with him, so he had no idea what she'd been going through.

"I've been good."

He didn't know about her mild case of PTSD, a secret shared between Charlene and Dr. Gardner, and she wasn't ready to tell Larry.

"Don't bullshit me. After what you've been through, that close to death not once but twice, in a span of days, I don't believe you. And not just that, the psychopaths that you went head-to-head with were monsters. Not many people would be able to recover from something like that."

Charlene took a drink and stared into her mug, swooshing around the liquid at the bottom before draining it. The remnants of those battles hadn't been forgotten.

"I've been having dreams about Darren." She didn't glance at Larry, afraid of how she would react when she looked into his face. Instead, she scratched at a piece of debris on the side of her mug.

"What kind of dreams?"

"Celebrity Slayer dreams. I've been reliving the scenes that Darren left in his wake. The scenes we found, that he lured us to."

"I thought you got over that."

"They've started again."

Larry nodded, but she discerned an odd look she couldn't decipher.

"I'm not sure why I can't get it out of my mind."

"It's surreal, like something from a movie. Brady, the Celebrity Slayer, one of the most disturbed serial killers this country has ever seen."

He had taunted Charlene, baited her with phone calls and notes. Brady thought that he and Charlene shared some deep, sick feelings. He even admitted he'd been in love with her, and in the end, it had ended in bloodshed.

"I don't know. I'm sure it's just something I'll get through. 'Time heals all wounds'—right?"

Larry didn't answer. He took another drink and grimaced.

"What is it? You hurting from tonight?"

He shook his head. "I need to tell you something."

He looked somber, unlike himself. He just didn't talk like this— rarely serious, never anything personal or sensitive. Something was bothering him, and she wasn't sure she wanted to hear it.

He took a deep breath and let it out. "Brady is alive."

She frowned, unsure if she'd heard correctly. "What?"

He repeated, "Darren Brady is alive."

The words hit her like an unexpected gut-punch. She felt a chill; a cold shiver crept down her spine. "What do you mean?"

"I mean, he's not dead."

"But I saw you shoot him. I saw it with my own eyes. I might have been drugged and out of it, but I remember it like it was yesterday."

He nodded. "I did shoot the son of a bitch, and it felt good pulling the trigger. When I got downstairs and saw you on that metal table, and Brady standing over you with the knife in the air, I was afraid that I was already too late. I took aim and fired without thinking."

"That's right, and you didn't miss. I remember Darren's body thudding hard against the back wall."

Larry nodded again and then took a drink. He wiped his mouth. "Yes, but you don't remember what happened after that, do you?"

"Not a clue."

"I called it in. The medics got to the house in minutes, and while two EMTs wheeled you upstairs and outside, another two tried to revive Brady."

She still couldn't process this new information. How could it be?

He drained his mug then banged it on the bar, startling her. "I stood back and watched the whole thing."

After a pause he added, "There's no way to know how long Brady had been without oxygen. It was twelve minutes since I shot him, but there was no telling if he died immediately."

"But he was dead." The words came out of her mouth, but she didn't realize she'd said them out loud.

Larry shook his head. "I'm no doctor, but I watched those medics work on Brady for a long time, and I asked them about it afterwards."

She shook her head, unable to believe it could be happening.

He held up his index and middle finger to the bartender. "Two more." Then he turned back to Charlene. "Once they stopped the bleeding, they started CPR, and then used a goddamn defibrillator on Brady. When that didn't work, they injected him with epinephrine, directly into the heart."

"Adrenaline," she whispered.

"Like a goddamn video game. Remember when John Travolta jammed that needle into Uma Thurman's chest in *Pulp Fiction*? Insane."

Charlene was silent.

"Then they rolled him out, administering more medication every few minutes, trying to keep that bastard alive."

"Why did I not know about this?"

"They kept it out of the media and press. Brady has no family, so no one came asking. As far as anyone knew, I killed the Celebrity Slayer that day."

The bartender set two new mugs of beer in front of them.

Charlene took a long pull. "Who knows about this?"

"Only a handful of people, and they're all above our pay grade."

She processed the new information at high speed, but it didn't compute. All this time, she thought Brady was dead, the Celebrity Slayer threat gone. Is that why the dreams haunted her sleep? Did her psyche know he was still alive? Impossible.

"Where is Darren now?"

"He's in an induced coma. They put him under, the day after the shooting. They have him in a secure wing at Cedars-Sinai Medical Center. There's no name on his chart. They call him John Doe."

"Why would they go to all that trouble for a psycho?"

He shrugged. "No idea. Maybe they want to experiment with his brain or something."

"This is crazy. Darren's alive."

"I wanted to tell you. It killed me not to. The lieutenant thought it would be easier for you to move on if you thought he was dead. But I've been watching you. You aren't moving on."

"I want to see him."

Chapter 5

The sports section of the *LA Times* was folded on her desk, but she didn't bother looking through it. The Dodgers, Charlene's favorite baseball team, had made the playoffs but had been eliminated early, beaten by the New York Mets in the National League Divisional Series.

She clutched a Dodgers stress ball and squeezed it.

"I thought you could use this." Larry handed her a black coffee, steaming in her blue and white Dodger mug.

"Thanks. I assume you fed the coffee fund?" She arched her brows, but she already knew the answer to that rhetorical question.

Larry shrugged. "I didn't have any change on me." He plopped down at his desk. "You look spiffy this morning."

She had on a black turtleneck shell, black slim ankle pants, and a color-block moto jacket. She said, "Can you look this over and tell me what you think?"

She had spent the entire morning filling out the report on the "police shooting" incident last night. It wasn't the first time she'd ever shot at anyone, but the paperwork was always nuts.

Larry swiveled in his chair and pushed out from his desk, then rolled over to Charlene's desk. He slid a pair of reading glasses from his breast pocket and slipped them on. He ripped the sheet from her grasp and read in silence, his eyes and lips moving.

As he read, she asked, "When can I see Darren?"

He looked at her over his bifocals. "I'm working on it." He went back to reading.

Charlene leaned back in her chair. Later in the morning, she had a meeting with Internal Affairs. She'd heard whispers that there would be backlash over the incident and someone would be coming down hard on her, as an example. There had been no reprimand handed out, yet.

Larry was unusually quiet, and she had to wonder if he knew something. She trusted him and was sure that he would have divulged whatever he knew.

She couldn't lie to herself. She'd been walking the edge for some time and knew it. She was Martin Taylor's little girl and had taken advantage of that. She knew there were things she could get away with, not breaking, but bending the rules nevertheless, just because of her dad.

She was fighting a losing battle in a male-dominated field. Many men on the force felt threatened by her after she received her promotion at such a young age, and now that her father was gone, she had to be extra careful not to step on toes.

Larry looked up from the document and nodded. "Looks like you've covered all the bases."

"Good, because I have to meet with IAG to give my version of last night's events."

"Want me to walk over there with you?"

Charlene shook her head. "No, thanks. They're giving me my own personal escort."

Larry snorted. "Sweet guys. Do you know what you're going to say?"

"The truth."

"Then let me help you with the truth."

Larry had undergone the same scrutiny when he'd shot Brady, so he would know exactly what she should expect.

They huddled at her desk, and he went over in detail what IAG would ask and what she should say. They would be looking for inconsistencies, flaws in her story, making sure she'd followed proper procedure.

Just as they finished, two men approached her desk. They were dressed in plain dark suits and wore hip holsters.

"Detective Taylor." The husky guy was still sweating from the outside heat, even in the air-conditioned office. "I'm Detective Burton. This is my partner, Detective Donahue. We're from Internal Affairs. We were told to come and accompany you to the interview."

Larry gave her an imperceptible nod. She got up and followed the two IAG detectives past the captain, who stood just inside his office door, staring at her. She thought she detected a hint of sympathy in her captain's eyes, but he had never been one to show it.

They left her office and took a long hallway to the elevators. No one spoke as they waited for the next elevator to appear.

The new LAPD headquarters was a five-hundred-thousand-square-foot structure with ten floors, both underground parking and a parking structure, and a four-hundred-seat auditorium.

The elevator took them down to the ground level, and from there they walked the block to the administration building that housed Internal Affairs.

They entered the office building and took the elevator to suite 304. Then they led her to a small, sparsely-furnished interview room and motioned for her to sit down. A DVD recorder stood on a tripod in the corner facing the table, and she knew that this video was linked to another room where others could watch it remotely. Who would be watching her interview?

Once she sat, the men removed their suit jackets, hung them on chairs, and took their seats. Donahue pulled a pile of papers over in front of him and picked up a pen. He started filling out a form.

Charlene broke the silence with a question. "So it's just the three of us?"

He nodded. "Our inspector will review our notes once we're done."

"And watch the video feed?"

Burton gave Donahue a look and turned on a recorder, speaking out loud. "Initial interview with Detective Charlene Taylor, conducted by Detective Burton and Detective Donahue." He gave the day's date and the date of the incident.

Then he turned to Charlene. "In your own words, Detective, please tell us what happened last night."

She told them everything from the start to finish: hearing the call come over the scanner, being close to the scene, following her instincts, the first one at the scene, locking down and sealing the perimeter, and then waiting for backup. She spoke fast, nearly word for word what Larry had said, knowing he would've been proud.

"Where were you before hearing the call?"

Charlene was prepared for the question, but it still made her squirm. She was sure they had already done their homework, so she followed Larry's lead.

"I was off duty—just got off work, so I went to a bar."

"What bar?"

"You mean you don't already know?"

"Did you have a drink?"

"What else is there to do at a bar? Of course, I had a drink."

The detective jotted something down. "How many drinks did you have?"

Now they both looked up from the table and stared at her. Charlene was sure that in a bar as packed as it had been that night, no way would the bartender have been able to remember how many she'd had.

"I had two drinks, maybe three."

"So two or three?"

"Two."

"Two what?"

"Two beers."

"Liquor?"

She shook her head. "No."

Again, they scribbled. Charlene could feel the heat rise in her face and hoped it didn't show. She dabbed a line of perspiration on her eye brow and bit her lip.

"How long were you there?"

Charlene shrugged. "I'm not sure exactly. Can't remember what time I left work. LAPD detectives don't punch a time clock."

They got the jab, shaking their heads. "Just answer the question."

"Maybe an hour."

"Are you on medication, Detective Taylor?"

"Prescription drugs from my doctor."

"What kind of drugs?"

"I'm sure you already know."

The agents looked at each other, wrote notes, and then continued. "How long were you home before responding to the call?"

"Maybe an hour."

There was no way for them to prove any of this, unless they started questioning her neighbors. Charlene lived in a complex, and she didn't even know the neighbors. She liked it that way.

She pulled nonchalantly on the neck of her shirt, feeling suddenly overheated.

"So you had two or three drinks within an hour's time before going to a scene with a loaded gun."

"It wouldn't have made sense to take an empty gun." From the looks on their faces it was clear they didn't appreciate her joke. She shook her head. "I had two drinks, and I'm not sure about the time. It could have been longer."

The IAG detective flipped through the stapled pages and spoke out loud. "Detective Baker said that you guys ended work at seven, then responded to the call shortly after eleven."

Larry had been generous with his timing. "That sounds about right."

"So then between seven and eleven, a four-hour span, you consumed two alcoholic beverages?" The detective looked at her as if for confirmation.

Charlene nodded.

"I'm sorry, Detective, body language isn't confirmation."

"Yes." Charlene pronounced the word sarcastically. "I had two drinks in four hours."

Charlene tramped into the office forty-five minutes later and sat down beside her partner.

Larry looked up from his computer. "How did that go?"

"Better than I expected."

He nodded. "IAG is a pain in the ass, but they're just doing their job. I'm sure you did fine."

As Charlene was about to say something, the captain walked out of his office and called her over. His deep sandpaper voice always put her on edge, but Dunbar knew his job and treated her fairly. He was short and burly, and his tie never matched the rest of his clothes.

She entered the office and grabbed a chair. The captain closed the door and returned to his desk.

"I'm giving you some time off."

Right to the point. "What? What did IAG say?"

Dunbar shook his head. "I haven't spoken with them. This is coming from me. I'm doing this for you?"

"For me?"

"Let's be honest—you've been through a hell of a lot since joining this division. That Anderson case was a disaster, and after everything that went down with Brady and Cooney, I want you to take all the time you need to get past it."

Sean Cooney, former cop and Darren Brady's partner, had come this close to killing Charlene, and she would've been dead if it hadn't been for Brady, AKA the Celebrity Slayer. Yes, it had been one bizarre case.

"I already had time off, Captain."

"Take more."

"How much more?"

"Give me your badge and gun, Detective." He reached out and opened his hand.

"My badge and gun? What for? What is this? Is this coming from you, Dr. Gardner, or IAG?"

"This is coming from me. We can write it off as stress-related."

"Then why do you need my badge and gun?"

"Look, Taylor, IAG is going to be crawling up your ass for the next little while if you don't make yourself scarce. This is just a precautionary measure."

She didn't like it but she knew he was only trying to protect her. She got up and removed both guns—her Glock, and the Smith & Wesson in her ankle holster. Then she handed them both, along with her badge, over to the captain.

She looked him in the eyes when he took them from her. "I didn't do anything wrong."

"You and I know that, and we'll make sure IAG knows it too."

Charlene left the office and joined Larry, who was still playing games at his desk. She blew air from her cheeks.

He asked, "What are you gonna do now?"

She frowned. "You knew?"

He scratched his curly grey hair. "When you were with IAG, the captain called me in for a talk."

"Did you tell him I know about Brady?"

"Hell no. He'd have my balls if he got wind that I told you that. But we both think this is a good idea for you."

"Come on, Larry."

"You need a break, kid. You barely took one after the Brady deal. I've seen cops go through what you have and never recover. I'm worried about you. Your pops would want me to watch out for you, and I think you need this."

Was there any point in arguing, in fighting this? She concluded that there was not.

She hesitated, looking around. "I still want to see Darren."

Larry sighed audibly. "I know you do."

"Are you sure you're up for this?"

Charlene hadn't yet sat down in the passenger's seat of Larry's car, when he started questioning her.

"No," Charlene answered without looking over at him.

"You can still change your mind. Brady's not going far."

Charlene rubbed her eyes. "Larry, this guy changed my life in a matter of weeks. He killed my father and had me chasing shadows trying to track him down. Brady was all that consumed my thoughts for a long time. I still think about him."

Larry put the car into gear and pulled away from her apartment building.

The evening traffic had thinned out as he turned onto Beverly Boulevard and steered the vehicle toward Cedars-Sinai Medical Center, passing rows of palm trees and young women in skimpy summer shorts and bikini tops.

They rode in tense silence, with Charlene running scenarios in her head. What would she do when she saw Darren Brady again? The man had turned her life upside down. He was dead. She'd just started to get over it, or so she thought.

She opened and closed her fists, and rubbed her sweaty palms against her pant legs, her anxiety rising.

Larry pulled up to the front of a beautiful glass and chrome structure and stopped the car there, unconcerned about being towed.

Cedars-Sinai was one of the largest nonprofit academic medical centers in the US.

Charlene followed Larry through the front doors, toward the elevators. They stepped inside, and Larry pressed the button.

"Brady is being held in a secluded room on the far side of the wing."

Charlene didn't respond. She was so focused, so anxious, that her senses worked in overdrive: The faces were indistinguishable, as she avoided eye contact with the people who surrounded her.

Mentally, she wasn't sure how prepared she was to come face-to-face with a ghost, a man who was supposed to be dead and buried.

A young uniformed officer stood guard outside Brady's door. There was no one else in the hall.

Larry held up his shield. "Take a break, Officer."

"Yes sir." The baby-faced officer nodded and looked pleased to have a break.

Charlene wondered about security. How much taxpayer money was being spent to protect one of the city's most notorious serial killers in recent history?

"Are you ready for this?" Larry asked one more time.

She nodded but could see the pleading look in his eyes. Her veteran partner had done nothing but try to protect her since she had become part of the Robbery-Homicide division.

Larry pushed open the heavy wooden door, and the first thing Charlene noticed was the odor that assaulted her nostrils. It was a smell normally associated with infection.

Brady had been bedridden for months, so there was a good chance that he had bed sores and other lesions that accompanied immobility, even if the nurses had constantly turned him.

Charlene stepped inside and closed the door behind her. Then, she saw him lying on a narrow single bed—and she couldn't stifle an involuntary shudder. But now he appeared small, as if he'd lost a great deal of weight.

Her heart dropped; she was frozen in place.

Larry was halfway to the bedside when he turned around and frowned. "Do you want to leave?"

She swallowed the lump in her throat. "Coming."

She took a single step forward, toward the comatose serial killer.

Other than the weight loss, Brady didn't look much different. His curly brown hair had grown longer, but his face, now pale and gaunt, had been shaved clean. His right wrist was handcuffed to the bed rail.

He didn't appear to be in pain. In fact, he gave the impression of being in a deep sleep. Numerous wires were hooked up to monitors beside the bed.

Brady's heartbeat had a steady, normal rhythm. A breathing tube, connected to a ventilator, extended into his open mouth and down into his windpipe, providing him with an air supply.

Charlene stepped up to the bedside, close enough to touch him. She shivered. "Can he hear us?"

"The doctor said no."

She leaned in close to Darren's face, close enough to see his eyelids twitch, and she stepped back instinctively. She was sure they twitched.

She checked with Larry. "Did you see that?"

"See what?"

"His eyes moved."

"You sure?"

"Yes."

"I didn't see anything."

"Larry, I'm not an idiot. I know what I saw."

The room door slammed shut, and Charlene jumped, reaching for her shoulder holster that was no longer there. She turned to see an East Indian doctor in his mid-thirties, wearing a white lab coat and a stethoscope around his neck.

"Hey, Doc," Larry greeted the young physician.

"Detective."

"This is my partner, Detective Taylor."

The doctor smiled. "The Detective Taylor who took this guy down?" He pointed at Brady.

Charlene nodded.

"What's his condition, Doc?" Larry asked, nodding toward Brady.

"No changes. Comatose and unresponsive. The patient cannot move or respond to stimuli."

"He just moved." Charlene, without hesitating, pointed at Brady's face. "His eyelids flickered."

The doctor squeezed his lips together. "That's doubtful."

"I saw it with my own eyes."

The doctor approached the bed and, using a light, lifted Brady's eyelids and shined it into them. He checked both eyes, and then dropped the light into his coat pocket. "As I said, there's no change. He's still in a deep coma."

"What are his chances of pulling through?" Larry asked, as if attempting to veer away from Charlene's discovery, which neither man in the room seemed to believe.

"Don't trust everything you see on soap operas. In reality, coma survival rates are fifty percent or less, and fewer than ten percent of people who come out of a coma completely recover from it."

Charlene asked, "How are you treating him?"

"There's no treatment that can cause someone to come out of a coma. We're giving him supportive care only. Coma patients are susceptible to pneumonia and other infections. Because he's been in a coma for such a long time, he's receiving physical therapy to prevent long-term muscle atrophy. Nurses also move him on a regular schedule to prevent bedsores."

"So there's no way to know when he'll come out of it?"

The doctor gave her a bored look. "Detective, there's not even a way to tell *if* he'll come out of this. Excuse me. I have to finish my rounds." He left them.

Charlene shook her head in disgust. "Do the taxpayers in this city know that they're paying to keep this scumbag alive?"

Larry nodded. "Have you seen enough?"

"Yeah, let's go."

"Thanks for the ride."

Her partner pulled the car over, as close to the apartment steps as he could, and came to a stop. They hadn't said much during the car ride back. She was still pissed that he had kept her in the dark about Brady and worried that if she opened her mouth, something inappropriate would come out, as it usually did.

She opened the door and stepped out onto the ground.

"Hang on, Taylor."

She looked back at her partner.

"I want to talk to you."

Charlene slid back inside and shut the door.

Larry ran his hand over the side of his face. "What are your plans?"

"What do you mean?"

"In case you've forgotten, the sergeant has your badge and gun."

She hadn't forgotten about the humiliating episode but hoped to put it out of her mind. "My mom wants me to fly out to Denver with her to visit Jane for Thanksgiving."

She had originally said no but now had nothing keeping her in LA.

"How is that beautiful sister of yours?"

She rolled her eyes. "Still married."

"Too bad she wasted herself on that guy, when she could have had me." He finger-combed his thinning hair and grinned.

Charlene snorted, and it felt good to laugh. She needed it.

"How's the baby?"

She now beamed, the darkness of the night suddenly disappearing. She pulled out her iPhone and thumbed through photos, then handed it to Larry.

He whistled. "She's a beauty." He handed back the phone. "I'm worried about you."

Charlene looked at him, but Larry didn't look back. "I know, I know. I'm living dangerously, putting my life on the line. Yada, yada, yada."

"I'm not just talking about work."

"I'm fine. I'm a big girl."

"You're living on the edge. This take-no-shit attitude is getting old. You need to let us help you."

"I'm just going through a rough patch."

Larry shook his head. "This started a while ago, even when your dad was alive. We both saw it escalating, and we knew that someday you would eventually blow."

"What are you talking about?"

"Trying to prove yourself to everyone. Trying to be your dad. Trying to show the world how tough you are. We know you're tough. We know that you'd still be one hell of a cop, if you followed your head more than your heart."

"You're always saying that after all I've been through, it's amazing how far I've come."

"I haven't seen many other female cops who beat up their suspects."

She turned away from him, feeling annoyed.

"That's right, I know about it. This is the LAPD, not the Catholic Church."

The incident Larry referred to happened back when Charlene was a street cop, on a house call, only to find a small girl with bruises all over her tiny, fragile body. Charlene had sent a message to the girl's father that had nearly gotten her suspended or fired. What she didn't tell Larry was that she still kept close tabs on that family.

She didn't respond, but he continued unsolicited. "When's the last time you had a meaningful relationship?"

"You mean with a man?"

"I mean any kind of relationship—men, or even your family."

"What about Andy?"

"You call that healthy?"

"I'm not interested in a relationship. I have other things in my life."

Larry nodded. "Book that flight, kid."

Charlene took that last sentence as the end of the conversation. She opened the car door and stepped out, then closed it and watched Larry drive away, the red taillights fading in the distance.

Dropping her head, she trudged up the stairs toward her apartment. She slid the key into her doorknob and noticed that the door wasn't locked. She always locked it, no matter what.

She slid the door open slightly with her foot and listened. Something was moving in the back. She reached for her hip but found no help there, because they were in the top drawer of the sergeant's desk.

She slipped inside and stepped down the front hall, then peered around the corner, but didn't see anyone. She heard clamoring in one of the closets...the most important closet in the apartment.

She grabbed her autographed Kirk Gibson Louisville Slugger from just inside the front door and moved toward the closet, pulling the bat back, ready to swing.

Standing just outside the closet door, she had just swung the bat back, when Andy stepped out. He turned, squealed and sighed out loud.

"Jesus, Charlene, what the hell are you doing?"

She dropped the bat to her side. "Me? What the hell are you doing here?"

"I'm done, for good this time."

"Stop overreacting."

But it didn't surprise her. She and Andy hadn't been good for a while.

She hadn't seen him in some time, but he hadn't changed. Always impeccably dressed: Armani suit and leather Cordovan wingtips. He had a new haircut, shaved around the ears and longer on top, and had let blond stubble grow on his face.

"I'm taking the few things that I left here. Where the hell are all of your clothes?"

"Scattered around."

"What did you do to your closet?"

"I rearranged it."

She had done just that, months ago, when starting to investigate her father's murder, removing everything inside: clothes, bags, shoes, sports equipment, and the chest of drawers. The rest of her tiny apartment had been a dumping ground, but the empty closet had made the perfect work space.

She had arranged her father's files and tacked city maps to the wall. She set up a filing cabinet with case details, photocopies of every paper from her father's murder file, as well as every Celebrity Slayer murder. The file cabinet was overflowing with reports, crime scene photos, handwritten notes, autopsy protocols, and interview transcripts. A desk and chair added to the clutter, along with a laptop. A lot of drunk, sleepless nights had been spent in that office.

If anyone had ever caught wind of what she'd done, there'd be hell to pay—reprimands, suspensions, CUBO citations, and definitely an Internal Affairs Group investigation, if not a dismissal. Darren Brady had helped her sneak out files—it was complicated.

Andy shook his head. "You're sick. You need serious help."

"I'm sorry you feel that way."

"Are you through?"

She really wasn't.

He continued, "You'll never change. You're incapable of loving anyone."

"You're wrong." *Was he?* She wasn't so sure.

"I've wasted years waiting for you. You're a wreck, and you'll never change because you won't let anyone get close to you. You're great at throwing up fences."

He tossed clothes into an Adidas bag and headed for the door.

"Andy," Charlene called out.

Andy turned around. "What?"

When she looked into his eyes, she recognized that this was finally "it." The funny thing was, it didn't really bother her.

"Nothing."

He turned and walked out the door.

She went to the kitchen window and looked out into the parking lot, where Andy's BMW sedan idled. He got in and drove away, without looking back up at her window.

Once his vehicle had vanished, she sat down at her laptop, logged on, and purchased a flight to Denver. She would call her mother in the morning to surprise her with the news.

Then she checked the time. It was still early enough to call.

Few things these days brought a smile to Charlene's face, but this new routine she'd started a while ago was one of the bright spots in her life, one of the few accomplishments she could feel good about.

She punched the programmed number into the phone and waited.

"Hello?" A child's voice—shy, but excited at the same time.

"Hi, Lauren."

"Charlene!" The girl screamed, followed by a delighted giggle.

She'd met the seven-year-old girl a year earlier when she was still a cop, working the streets. She and her partner had responded to a 415, domestic disturbance call, and stumbled upon Lauren, a little girl who lived with her mother and stepfather.

Charlene had spotted signs of physical abuse on Lauren, but, with no positive proof or witnesses, the city had yet to act on those allegations.

Still pissed off about the whole situation, Charlene had vowed to watch out for Lauren and keep tabs on the girl's family.

At least once a week, she made a conscious effort to either stop by the house or call Lauren, even though her stepfather had threatened to press charges against the police department or file a restraining order against Charlene. And she always had a little present for Lauren, usually a book or small toy.

Lauren's parents no longer answered the phone when Charlene called. They recognized her number from the call display and let Lauren answer. Which was fine with Charlene. The less she had to deal with Charles Lefebvre, the better. He had a way of getting under her skin, and she didn't trust herself around the sleaze-ball.

"How are you, sweetie?"

"Great." She could hear the smile in Lauren's voice. "Mrs. Valleau said that I can bring your book to school to show the class."

"That's great."

Mrs. Valleau was Lauren's third-grade teacher, whom Charlene had already met. She'd asked Lauren's teacher to keep an eye on the child, watching for signs like a change in behavioral patterns or exposed marks on her body.

The strength of the little girl amazed her. Whatever went on at home, Lauren always had a smile on her face. So far, Lauren's stepfather had stayed true to his word, but Charlene watched him closely.

"When are you coming over again?"

"It won't be for a while. Remember when I told you my sister was going to have a baby?"

"Yes."

"Well, she had a girl."

"What's her name?"

"Martina."

"That's a pretty name."

"I'm going to see Martina, so I'll be gone for a while. But when I get back, I'll come by to see you. And maybe I'll have something for you."

"Another book?"

Charlene smiled. "Maybe."

"Okay. Have fun, Charlene."

"Bye, Lauren."

Even after the crummy day she'd had, talking with Lauren allowed her to go to sleep on a high note.

Chapter 6

Abigail put on her gloves before opening the door and stepped inside. It was quiet.

"Joshua." she called out. There was no response. After checking the surroundings outside, she closed the door.

He usually stood at the door, waiting for her to give him even the slightest bit of attention. But this time he wasn't there. She wasn't happy about this at all. It was time, once again, for her to remind Joshua of his place in their partnership.

The mastermind looked out the window. No one had followed her, that was a certainty. She'd been cautious, beyond paranoid, having done it a number of times, and had yet to slip up. Mistakes would not be tolerated.

The only thing she saw outside was the dark-blue sedan Joshua had personally rented under a false name, which no one could trace back to either of them.

She traipsed through the house and found Joshua in the corner of a room, knelt in a crouch, eyes closed, his hands covering his ears. He rocked back and forth making soft mewing sounds.

He had reverted to his "safe" position. Ears covered, eyes closed, blocking out the world and everything evil it represented. He'd actually been ordered to this position many times as a child. After a scolding, a reprimand, or doing something wrong, he'd been forced to stay in the corner for hours, alone, to think about his behavior. They called it his "reflection time."

When Josh put himself in this "place," he saw and heard nothing around him. He would not have picked up the motion sensor alarm, planted underground on the path a mile from the cabin, activated when her vehicle had driven over it.

Right about now she knew that his temple throbbed, the voices in his head growing exponentially louder. His eyes were closed, and a deep searing pain probably burned them. She could see the intense pain on his face from his anguished expression.

Then she spotted the baby, on the couch, less than ten feet from where Joshua knelt. It wasn't near the edge—at least he had wrapped her up and kept her safe. Her anger pushed to the surface.

She couldn't stifle the anger she felt. "What the hell is that baby doing here?"

Joshua sprang to his feet, his eyes popping open, and surprise registering on his face. "Abigail, when did you get here? Welcome home."

"Why it that baby there?" She pointed at the infant squirming and making faint squeaking sounds. The baby's crying is probably what set him off.

"Sorry."

He rushed to the baby, picked it up, and left the room.

The *Denver Post* was folded on the table, and Abigail picked it up when he came back into the room, empty-handed.

Joshua pointed to the newspaper. "It's just like you said—there's not a single word in there about the kidnapping."

"Of course, the cops don't mention anything, because they're trying to unnerve us." She snorted. "It's not working, is it?"

He shook his head, but his facial expression lacked confidence.

She strode toward him, before she spoke. "You do understand the consequences if you lose control, right?"

"Yes." He refused to look at her.

He had never been able to say no to her, and she liked that.

He took the paper from her, closed and neatly folded it, and then set it on the table, smoothing the wrinkled creases. Then he reshuffled the magazines, making sure they lined up on the coffee table, from largest to smallest in size.

"You're sure you didn't leave anything at the scene? Hair fibers? Shoe prints? DNA?"

"Positive. You've taught me well."

Indeed, she had. Joshua was OCD, meticulous, to the point of paranoiac precision. With the amount of preparation and surveillance needed, it took weeks to prepare—working days, nights and weekends. He was the model protégé.

"How are your headaches?"

"Good."

A lie—she saw it in his eyes. He could never keep the truth from her; she could read him like a book.

His daylong headaches had clearly returned and grown more intense over time, which worried Abigail because she couldn't be around him 24/7. She had too many people to answer to and too much going on.

But she could use his weaknesses for leverage, as she had done for years.

"I thought I told you not to touch the baby."

"I'm sorry. I just wanted to hold it. It was crying." He lowered his head into his hands, moaning softly.

She didn't let him acknowledge the babies as anything other than "it." She couldn't allow him to get too close, too personal, because she knew what would happen. A weak-minded person like Joshua could ruin everything for her.

She went to him and wrapped her arms around his shoulders. "It's just the two of us, Josh. It's always been that way and it always will be. You know I love you, right?"

"I know."

She held him gently, rubbing his back for a few rare moments, and then pulled away and strode toward the couch.

He said, "You look beautiful today."

Abigail stopped at the wall mirror, admiring herself, then swiped her bangs back into place and touched up her lipstick.

"What a day. Get me a drink and then come and sit down." She held up the keys to the liquor cabinet.

He grabbed them and rushed to the kitchen. She could hear him unlock the bar and remove the bottle of Belvedere and Cointreau. The fridge door opened, followed by the clanking of ice in a glass.

She lay down on the sofa, rested her head on a cushion, and closed her eyes. She sat up when he entered and reached for her drink.

"Did you take your medication," she asked.

"Yes, ma'am."

"Sit behind me. You know how I like it."

"Can I have a drink?"

"Sit," she snapped. Sometimes the only way to get through to him was to be firm, but she also knew how to finesse him when required.

He obeyed, massaging her temples as she sipped at the martini and moaned playfully. She felt a stir in the crotch of his pants against her back.

"I can feel your hardness. Stop it," she hissed, knowing how to manipulate Joshua, a typical man.

He swallowed slowly, taking deep breaths, but the erection wasn't weakening. Too easy.

"Tell me about it," she demanded.

"You would have been so proud. She never saw it coming."

"I've taught you well. But you've always been an expert at disguises. You have to be, with the number of cities you've lived in, avoiding the law all this time. I don't know how you keep up with all your names."

The compliments would keep him going, for at least a while, because she didn't hand them out regularly.

"No one would ever suspect I could pull off such a brilliant plan."

"Your plan?" She puckered her lips but didn't look at him.

"Sorry."

He was learning. "Make them think you're weak when you're strong." She turned around, rubbing his midsection, gently brushing against his penis. "I want the details. I want to feel her pain."

He swallowed, his Adam's apple bobbing. He breathed rapidly, and his upper lip trembled.

"Make me feel it."

He recounted the event's beginning with the "chance" encounter in the park.

Abigail massaged the goose bumps on her bare arms, shivering with excitement. She gripped and squeezed his manhood harder with each detail, sensing that he was close to climaxing.

When his narrative ended, she gasped, shuddering in orgasmic pleasure.

"Don't stop. Describe her reaction again."

She slid closer to him, fondling him gently. She massaged his hair, breathing warm air on his neck, noting that his short hair was now damp with perspiration.

"The woman was terrified, panic clearly etched on her face. She tried to scream, tried to claw at me, kicking and flailing. She helplessly watched me take the baby before drifting off."

Abigail leaned back on the sofa, fully satisfied, picturing the helpless mother—the pain, tears streaking down her face, pleading for mercy.

She pulled a vial of pills from her purse, then shook the orange container, the capsules rolling against the plastic. "Here, baby, you've earned these. Only a half dose, though. You still have work to do tonight."

He ripped the bottle from her hand and dry-swallowed two pills.

He asked, "Do you want another drink?"

"No." Moderation was key. She couldn't have alcohol on her breath, and couldn't take a chance that her judgment would be impaired.

Just then the baby started to cry loudly.

Joshua said, "I think she's probably hungry."

"So what do you want me to do about it?"

They both left the room, entered an adjoining one, and went over to the crib to look down at the squirming infant.

She asked, "What's its name?"

"Allie Wilson," Josh said with a smile. "Isn't she per—"

Before he finished his sentence, she struck the left side of his face hard with the back of her gloved hand. He instinctively started and grabbed his cheek, now fiery red and burning.

"You goddamn fool," she screamed. "*This* baby was *not* part of the plan. Do you want to ruin me? You know how much this means to me…to us. We have a design to follow. This could blow the whole process. Now it has to change."

His eyes started to water. "I'm sorry. I just—"

"Stop crying. How many times have I told you that emotion is for the weak?" Shit, time to comfort him, by sweetening her voice. "I'm sorry too, baby." She wrapped her arms around him, kissing his neck gently. "I just want this to be perfect for us."

"Me too." He lowered his head, looking at the floor. "I promise I won't be bad again. I'll stick to the plan."

Charlene kept the lights off, following the soft sounds as she gently lifted Martina from the crib, handling the baby as if she were a porcelain doll. She couldn't believe a human could be that tiny, that delicate, that flawless.

She tucked Martina into her arms and sighed with pure satisfaction. The whole scene was perfect—the feel and baby smell of her niece, and the quiet calm of the night.

Martina squirmed slightly, nudging Charlene's breast.

"Sorry, babes, you'll starve on that. Let's go find your mommy."

"I'm right here." Jane's voice broke the dark, coming from the doorway as a dim night light turned on.

Charlene handed the baby to her sister, then watched Jane sit down and, with practiced speed, position the baby to nurse.

"Well, good night."

"Charlene, wait. Why don't you sit with us?" Jane's eyes smiled. "I won't be going anywhere for a while. Unless you're tired from the flight?"

Charlene pulled a small children's bench next to her sister and sat down.

"Did she wake you up?"

Charlene shook her head. "Nah. I'm a light sleeper. I never know when my pager might go off or the phone might ring." Plus, she hadn't slept well in some time, but she wasn't about to mention that.

Jane looked amazing for someone who had just given birth. Her long brown shoulder-length hair was straight and shiny, held back with a headband. Her body was practically back to her regular size four and hidden underneath a cute printed nightdress. Motherhood definitely agreed with her.

Jane asked, "Did the Dodgers win today?"

Charlene half-snorted. "The Dodgers have been done for a month."

Baseball, actually sports in general, had never been Jane's thing. That was Charlene. But her sister at least made an effort, which Charlene appreciated.

"Sorry."

Charlene chuckled. "That's okay."

Jane's eyes narrowed in concern. "So how have you been?"

"Good."

"Sorry I couldn't be there for you when all that stuff happened."

Charlene pointed to the baby in her sister's arms. "You had your own stuff going on."

Jane struggled to find words. "First Dad, and then that."

Jane and their mom still couldn't talk about the Darren Brady incident.

The truth was, Charlene had never been close with her father, despite their mutual occupation and hobbies. She hadn't been the model daughter or sister and accepted that. She got up and crossed the room, then started looking through baby clothes in Martina's closet. She didn't want to have this talk with Jane.

"I managed."

"You always seem to. I know you're independent and I respect you for that. But it's okay to reach out now. You know that if you need anything—"

"I know, Jane. Thanks."

Martina wiggled uncomfortably, and Jane got her refocused by tracing her fingertips over the baby's cheek, humming softly.

"You're really good with her."

Jane smiled. "I always doubted my parenting skills—thought I wouldn't know what to do."

"You're a natural."

"Thanks."

Charlene wasn't up for the girl talk.

After some time passed in silence, and Martina settled, Jane asked. "Are you seeing anyone?"

"No time."

"Listen, I know you're all about your career, and that's great. But you need to make time for yourself. What about at work? There must be a few classy, good-looking guys there." She paused then batted her eyelashes, "You know, I've always had a thing for a man in uniform."

Charlene winced. "I'd never date a colleague. The department frowns on that sort of thing."

Jane removed Martina from her nipple and held her upright, her belly against Jane's chest then tapped the baby's back. "Have you been taking care of yourself?"

That was just like Jane. Her sister was referring to Charlene's drinking but wouldn't come right out and say it. Charlene was ever aware that Jane and their mother didn't approve of her profession and lifestyle.

Charlene shot Jane a look. "What did Mom say?"

"It's not just Mom. I'm worried too. We're all worried. You have so much potential."

"Untapped potential—that's all I am, right? I know Mom hates my job, even more since Dad's death." Her voice rose, so she calmed herself so as not to startle the baby. "I'm not you, Jane. I don't want a Norman Rockwell life, the perfect family, the pretty little house with the white picket fence. I'm a cop, and I'm damn good at it. I wish everyone would just leave me alone."

"Charlene, wait—"

Charlene left the room. They'd passed a bar on the ride from the airport. If she hurried, she could still make last call.

Chapter 7

Charlene opened her eyes and blinked several times. It was still dark outside, the room a solid black, and it took a few minutes for her eyes to adjust. Once they had, she checked her surroundings, unsure of where she was, until last night came crashing back.

Talking with Jane. Arguing. Getting mad. Storming out. Drinking at a nearby bar. Turning to the bottle. Things she always promised herself she'd never do again.

Why did she constantly go back to that place, then turn to alcohol? As if it soothed all of her troubles, when it didn't. Just when she thought she had it kicked, old habits found their way back into her life.

Every emotion sent her to the bottle: anger, sadness, loneliness. Charlene admitted she had a problem, but receiving help and getting better were easier said than done.

She had it under control, or so she thought, until Darren Brady walked into her life. But hadn't he always been there? Lurking? Waiting? Biding his time? Ready to pounce.

But isn't that what all failures did? Blame someone else for their problems? Always find a reason to go back to that place they'd promised never to revisit. She had all the excuses: lousy love life, non-stop job, reckless lifestyle, personal trauma. She was tired of feeling sorry for herself.

She checked the time and pushed herself up on her elbows, listening for movement from within the house, but all was still. Even the baby slept.

There was no way Charlene would fall back to sleep, so she sat up on the edge of the bed and shook her head. The room moved slightly, or at least felt like it did. A throb began at the base of her skull; soon last night's drinks would physically haunt her.

Rising to her feet, she held the bedpost until she found her balance. Trying her best to avoid creaky floorboards, she tiptoed to the corner of the room where her suitcase remained open. She removed workout gear and got dressed in the dark.

She brushed her teeth in the hallway bathroom and went downstairs. While everyone else slept on, she opened the front door and stepped out onto the concrete landing.

The morning was brisk, but not cold. Her breath was visible in the chilly Colorado air—perfect running weather.

She slipped the buds into her ears, pressed Play, and listened to the vibrating beats while doing a quick stretch before taking off at a light trot.

She wasn't sure which direction to go, just knew that she needed to clear her head and sweat off the hangover. Darren Brady consumed her thoughts.

Ever since Larry had told her that the man was still alive and she saw it for herself, she could think of little else.

Darren Brady, the reason that she was a mess. Maybe?

It was no secret to anyone that her family had never accepted her lifestyle. Maybe it was because she had a perfect sister, who had dreamed of becoming a wife and a mom from day one. But that wasn't Charlene.

She liked to have fun and enjoy life, and had no regrets.

She had surprised everyone when she'd followed in her father's footsteps—the screw-up daughter enrolling in the academy. No one saw that one coming. Now, she couldn't see herself doing anything else.

A lot of people had questioned her actions, and she still wasn't sure why she had chosen to be a cop. Was it to be closer to her father? Did she want to make their relationship right? Those within earshot were always ready to voice their opinions on the subject.

But maybe "the life" had chosen her. Everyone said she was born to be a cop.

At the next corner she hesitated, almost stopping. Her skin prickled—not a good sign.

Was someone there? Why would anyone be out here in the dark, this early in the morning? Jane lived outside the city of Denver, where there was no business district and very few houses.

Though it might be just a simple shadow, it looked like a human form, someone wearing dark-colored clothing.

As Charlene picked up her pace from a light jog to a medium run, the shadow seemed to drift. It was no longer clearly visible, but she was sure someone had been there. When she arrived at the exact spot where it had been, she saw nothing.

Empty. Weird.

Was she paranoid? Was Darren Brady tugging that hard on her nerves? Her usually accurate cop instincts rarely let her down.

She shook it off, chalking it up as paranoia and the darkness of an unfamiliar place. She continued for another twenty minutes before turning around and retracing her steps back to the house.

Dawn had broken, and the sun shone brightly by the time she got home. Her wet bangs clung to her skin. Even with the cool morning, her clothes were damp and sweat dripped down the loose tendrils that had slipped from her ponytail. Yet the sun felt warm on her face.

She stretched at the end of the driveway to cool down, and then walked toward the house. Richard's car was gone, Jane's the only one left in the parking space. Jane's husband was an architect in downtown Denver, made good money and, from what Charlene could tell, was a good husband and father and a standup guy.

She entered the house and heard voices in the kitchen. The smell of freshly brewed coffee floated to the front room.

Her mother and sister leaned against the kitchen counter, talking, and the minute Charlene stepped into the kitchen, both women grew quiet. Worry etched her mother's wrinkled face.

Jane asked, "Did you have a good run?"

"Great. It's really pretty out here."

Jane smiled. "Not exactly the hustle and bustle of big city life that you're used to, huh?"

"Not quite."

Her mother held up the coffee pot. "Want some coffee?"

"Yes, please."

Charlene sat down at the table, pulled off her damp outer shirt and set it on the chair beside her.

"Want breakfast?" Jane set a steaming mug of black coffee on the table in front of Charlene.

"No thanks."

"You gotta eat, Sis."

"Maybe later."

Charlene took a sip, and the warmth worked its way through her body. The run had helped clear her head. She no longer had a headache and actually felt half human now. She was accustomed to pushing through the hangovers, and it wasn't a good thing.

"What time did you get home? I didn't hear you come in," Jane said.

"I'm not sure. I tried to be quiet so I wouldn't wake anyone, especially Martina. I'm sure your sleep is limited as it is."

Without a word, their mother walked out of the kitchen.

Charlene asked, "Is she okay?"

"She'll be fine." Jane sat down at the table beside Charlene. "She's just a worrier."

Charlene took another sip and looked at Jane over the top of her coffee cup. Jane stared into her own mug and played with the diamond on her ring finger, a clear sign of tension. Charlene hated seeing her sister like this, because she discerned that she was the reason her mother was upset and because of it, Jane was uncomfortable in her own home. Again, the screw-up daughter.

Charlene swallowed the coffee in her mouth and took a deep breath. "I'm sorry."

Jane set her cup down and licked her lips. "It's okay. It's my fault. Your personal life is none of my business. I'm just worried about you."

Charlene put her hand on Jane's, which trembled. "I know, and I'm fine."

"You're sure?"

"Yes."

"Well, as long as you're happy."

"I am." *Liar.*

There was nothing more to say, and Charlene was thankful when a low muffled whimper sounded from the corner of the room. She turned to see a bassinet for the first time, swinging gently back and forth.

Jane had just pushed herself to a standing position, when Charlene touched her shoulder.

"Do you mind?"

"Of course not, you're the godmother."

Charlene rose from her seat and approached the bassinet. She peered over the edge and saw a smiling Martina squirming. Charlene lifted her niece out of the basket and snuggled her tightly, breathing in the fresh baby scent—powder and lotion.

Charlene smiled. "Hello, baby girl."

Charlene dropped down on a chair, and when Martina looked up into her eyes, she calmed. That smile sent a shiver through Charlene and a sensation of warmth into her heart. At that moment, there was nowhere she would rather have been.

One little girl made Charlene forget all her problems.

Meeting her sister's gaze, Jane winked. "You up for shopping today? A little retail therapy?"

"Absolutely."

"Hey, girls." Their mother's voice came from the living room. "Come and see who's on TV."

Charlene was carrying the baby, accompanied by Jane when they stepped into the living room, where their mother leaned back on the cushions of an off-white L-shaped sofa. The sixty-five-inch plasma TV was turned to 9NEWS—Colorado's News Leader, the local NBC Denver affiliate.

Without looking at them, their mother said, "Look who shopped in downtown Denver yesterday morning."

Charlene watched as Senator Jaqueline Bloomfield stepped out of Ashley Schenkein Jewelry Design, one of the most expensive high-end jewelry stores in the city.

Jane tilted her head. "Wow, fancy."

Charlene nodded. "I think she can afford it."

Charlene wasn't into politics, not even close, but Jaqueline Bloomfield had already made a name for herself in her first term in office as a US senator of the state of New Mexico. But more than just politics drew Charlene to the senator.

The news anchormen and cameras, which loved her, closed in on Senator Bloomfield as she moved down the street.

Bloomfield was luxuriously well-dressed and stood coatless wearing an air of casual elegance in the morning sunlight; her tanned, lean arms, narrow hips, first-rate muscle tone, and flat stomach suggested obsessive workouts.

She was the kind of woman—confidently fighting in a male-dominated vocation—who Charlene strove to be. She felt much like the senator, trying to get ahead despite men knocking down both her and her ideas on a regular basis.

Bloomfield slung a Louis Vuitton bag over her shoulder, pulled the brim of her sun hat down, and slipped on a large pair of dark Chanel sunglasses. The hat was a feeble attempt at a disguise by the senator, ever aware that people watched, and all knew exactly who she was.

"Must be tough living like that," Brenda Taylor said. "Under the microscope 24/7, always on constant surveillance, the camera on your every move."

Jane smirked. "I'm sure she enjoys every bit of her celebrity status. I know I would."

Bloomfield smiled graciously, waved her hand as the crowd gathered, while people snapped pictures. Her courteous smile and surefooted stride showed signs of confidence as she made her way along the sidewalk, window-shopping the various boutiques.

Her head of security whispered something into her ear and she nodded, continuing to walk, ignoring the long black stretch limousine that followed behind her, surrounded by security people that did their best to remain out of the public eye, but stood out in their black suits, dark shades, and ear-phone mics.

Then the news crews moved in. "Senator Bloomfield, Senator Bloomfield!"

Before the media got to within twenty-feet of the senator, her well-trained guards formed a ten-foot wide human barrier, limiting access. She held up her hand, motioning for the press to stop.

Charlene focused on Bloomfield's head of security, the man standing in the middle, directly in front of the senator. Without trying he conveyed intensity and looked as if he'd be happy to settle any score with brute force.

Reporters held the cameras high over the heads of the security team as bulbs flashed. They tried to shove microphones and tape recorders inside the perimeter as the senator spoke, but were unsuccessful.

"Please, people." The senator flashed a trained beauty-queen smile. She looked each reporter in the eye, knowing they hungered for a quote. She had always been a reporter's dream, giving them direct quotes, controversial headline stuff.

"Senator." One reporter raised her hand. "Can you tell us about the new bill you've proposed to Congress?"

The senator grinned. "I'm sorry, but I have nothing to say. You'll hear my comments at the press conference after the vote. Until then, I have nothing to add."

"Why are you in town?"

The senator had never stopped walking, only slowed slightly—a clever politician tactic, conducting an interview on the move. That way she couldn't be surrounded by the media.

"I'm meeting with Senator Black at his Denver Metro office later today. The senator's legislative aide has been kind enough to squeeze me in to discuss the latest budget resolution."

"What about the rumor that your office is being investigated for your campaign's discretionary spending?"

The senator removed her sunglasses and bit down on the stem as the camera zoomed in and focused on her face. She glared at the reporter but ignored the question, and Charlene shivered at the intensity of the stare.

"I also have a lecture scheduled at Colorado State University in a few days, so I will be staying in the city. That's all I can say for now."

Her agents made a path through the reporters, a lane to the limo. The driver opened the door and the senator stepped inside, the head of security following close behind. The door closed, separating the senator from the noisy crowd.

Charlene looked at Jane, trying to give her best "puppy eyes" impression. "Did she say something about speaking at Colorado State University in a few days?"

"Tickets? I'm on it." Jane jumped to her feet and ran from the room.

Matt stood back as a plain-clothed DPD detective questioned Tina Allen and her husband on the couch, two empty tissue boxes on the mother's lap. The call had come in this morning: another baby taken in the middle of the night.

He'd already explored the house.

He drew in a deep breath and then growled in frustration. He couldn't remain in the background much longer.

They were questioning the couple in what was called the "great" room. Both the great room and foyer soared up two stories. Built-in cabinets flanked the fireplace of the room with a view of the open-rail staircase that led upstairs.

Tina Allen was a beautiful woman with thick black curls.

Matt felt compassion for the heartbroken woman as he watched the interview. "What do you remember from last night?"

She shook her head. "Mark was out, playing his regular poker game. He goes every week, while I stay here with Jonathan." She stopped, hesitated, then swiped a tear with a balled-up tissue.

Another family with a routine.

Seeing the look on her face, Matt stepped in to ask, "What is it?"

"A man."

"What man?"

"A man came to my door, introducing himself as—" She seemed to be thinking. She put a hand on her chest. "Colin. He had a name tag. He was with Resolution Research and Marketing."

Matt snapped his fingers at a nearby uniformed police officer. "Call the company. Ask if they sent anyone out here and if they have a Colin working for them." He turned back to the woman. "Can you describe him?"

"Nice-looking. He wore a suit, dark-colored with a red tie. He had a briefcase and a clipboard. He claimed that my neighbor, Mrs. Sturgeon, sent him over."

Matt nodded to the Denver PD detective who was leading. "Go see the neighbor. Find out what she knows about this guy."

"I'm doing the questioning here."

Matt's voice rose a decibel. "Do it." Turning back to Tina, he asked, "What did he want?"

She shrugged her narrow shoulders. "He said his company conducted personal in-home surveys to determine the level of security efficiency for children in the neighborhood."

"And you let him in?"

"Of course. It was about my family."

Matt squeezed the pen in his hand, to keep himself from commenting on the stupidity of her remark. "So, what happened?"

"He asked a bunch of questions about neighborhood safety. He checked things off his list and took notes. I even filled out paperwork. Then he left."

"That's it?"

"That's it."

"What kind of car did he drive?"

"I'm not sure."

"So, nothing else happened. Did he ask about the baby? You? Your husband?"

She shook her head. "No. He didn't even see Jonathon. My son was sleeping upstairs in his crib."

Mark Allen rubbed his wife's knee and pulled her closer to him.

Matt turned to her husband. "What about you?"

Grief had stripped his face of color.

"I checked the crib when I got home this morning, and the baby wasn't there. So I went to our bedroom, and when I didn't see him with my wife, I woke her up."

The front door to the house slammed shut, and the other detective came back into the room. Everyone turned and waited for his report "The neighbor said this guy went to her house first, and when she found out it was about children's safety, she sent him over here. He had asked if any families in the neighborhood might be interested in child safety. He drove a small blue car."

Matt sighed. "A blue car? That's it? Make? Model? License plate number?"

"That's it."

He nodded then asked Mrs. Allen, "Can you describe this guy?"

"Nice. Friendly. I did the survey, we drank tea, and then he left."

"And you didn't hear anything after that?"

"No." Her voice rose defensively, as if she had had enough of answering Matt's questions.

He blinked back his fear, afraid of where this case was headed.

Two hours later, Matt worked at his brother's desk at the precinct, jiggling the middle drawer. It didn't surprise him that it was jammed tight and the top of the desk was littered with papers. Normally he would laugh at his brother's messiness, but today he was rushed. Another call had come in just after they left the Allen house. Another baby had been abducted. The DPD didn't have the manpower for this.

He finally got the drawer open and unearthed a pen and notepad. Even though Jake was only a DPD officer and didn't have a computer or even access to the detective files, he'd been able to get what his brother needed.

Matt looked around to make sure he wasn't arousing suspicion.

He located the brown accordion folder and pulled it from the bottom of the drawer. He removed a sheaf of papers and studied the file, shaking his head, stunned at the similarities between this case and the kidnapping cases in New Mexico six years earlier. It was happening again, and this time the Fed was right smack-dab in the middle of it.

He knew better than to make assumptions, but in his heart, he was certain the cases were linked. The modus operandi—methods and techniques—were identical. Matt flipped through pages of facts: three kidnappings, the second last night and third just this morning.

Last night's kidnapping report already had the locals in a frenzy, when, a mere twelve hours later, another report came in. There was no downtime between kidnappings this time.

The kidnapper, or kidnappers, were speeding things up.

Unlike most kidnappings, there were no requests for ransom. The snatches had been clean, leaving no evidence, clearly the work of a pro or someone who'd done it before. What were their intentions?

But just like six years ago, Matt couldn't explain the motive. And the fact that not one of those children had ever been found not only scared him—it bewildered him.

Local law enforcement rarely welcomed the FBI into their investigations, because it appeared to question their ability to get the job done. Matt understood their defensive posture, but they had to work together, keeping their eye on the goal—to return the lost children to their families, alive and well.

So after the first kidnapping, as a personal favor, Matt had not notified his colleagues in Washington—instead he let the locals do their job, handle the case, until he felt they needed outside help.

A familiar voice in the back room startled Matt, and he automatically ducked low, below the top of the desk, in case the owner of the voice came into the room. Matt saw the chief of police come around the corner and walk by without looking over. She didn't like Matt, and this was the last place he wanted her to catch him.

Once she was gone, he turned back to Jake's notes.

Jake had the reports from interviews with witnesses, crime scene notes, and details of his own on-duty work. Everyone in the department was doing what they could, but it just wasn't enough. Finally, after victim number three, Matt had to make the call. The DPD had exhausted every investigative tool at their disposal and still had no leads. Kidnapping was a federal offense—and a death penalty offense in Colorado—and it was time to call in the pros.

He used the phone on his brother's desk and called the direct line to his senior agent in charge.

"Marshall, it's Matt. We have a situation in Denver."

"Go on."

"Three babies kidnapped in less than a one-week span."

"Are they connected?"

"Looks like it. Looks like New Mexico."

A long desolate silence hung in the air, and Matt knew he had just caught a senior agent off guard, which never happened. The better part of a minute passed before the agent spoke.

"Three babies? Why am I just hearing about this now?"

Matt explained that the locals wanted the first crack, and he hadn't wanted to step on toes.

"I'm listening," the AIC responded in a resigned tone.

Matt thumbed through the file, trying to be as detailed as possible. He knew his chief wouldn't act without being properly briefed.

"Just like New Mexico, they occurred leaving only one witness every time. But each time, the witness description has differed in height, weight, age and appearance."

"Same guy, wearing multiple disguises?"

"That's what I think, but we can't rule out a team."

"Go on."

"Again, no parents were hurt though there was opportunity."

"Tell me about the victims and their families."

Matt could hear his boss typing as he spoke. "They're all from above-average income households."

The agent cut in. "Money's usually the motivating factor. In most kidnapping cases the children with the highest risk of exposure are those from wealthy families."

"But not here. And there have been no ransom demands, ever."

"I see."

"Two boys and one girl."

"No gender bias."

They completed each other's sentences now. Matt continued, "Two of the children are Caucasian and one is African American."

"Race isn't an issue. Could these new ones be *random* kidnappings?"

Matt shook his head, aware that his boss couldn't see him. "I don't think so. We're not trained to believe in randomness. All the babies were born at the same hospital, Rose Medical Center Pregnancy and Childbirth. Last year alone, the hospital attended to thousands of births."

"What about doctors? Any matches?"

"None. Each mother had her own family doctor attend the birth."

"I agree these two cases are similar enough to warrant an investigation. I'm sending Smith out there ASAP. Meet him at the private airstrip connected to Denver International and escort him to the FBI field office there, so he can head up our new command center."

"Sir, I know I missed out last time around, and this isn't my expertise, but this is my turf and I can help. I know the area and the people, and I have a personal connection to the DPD. We both know this case isn't just about these three babies."

No answer.

Matt realized his boss's reserve meant he was analyzing the information, sorting through his tangle of thoughts, but the silence frustrated him.

Finally, the agent responded, with reluctance in his voice. "Well, we *will* need a profile. You can stay on until we decide to pull you off. I'll notify the Investigative Support Unit."

"Thank you, sir."

Matt hung up and checked his watch. He had seven hours before Smith's arrival. Normally, Matt would be working with the field agent in Denver, and Washington wouldn't bother sending anyone unless absolutely necessary.

For many reasons, this case had been given priority status.

He opened the notepad and wrote.

Parents	Child
Mike and Stephanie Wilson	Allie Wilson
Mark and Tina Allen	Jonathon Allen
Peter and Liz Bailey	Mason Bailey

In all serial cases, whether kidnapping or murder, the key victim was usually victim number one. The igniter. But how was Allie Wilson connected? Did Mike and Stephanie Wilson know the kidnapper? He would have to investigate that family more, and be far more thorough in his research.

He had work to do, a profile to start, but he saw Jake enter the precinct with his hands full.

"I know we have a lot to do, but I got us lunch." Jake held a grease-stained McDonalds bag and a white plastic bag. He handed Matt the plastic bag. "What kind of cop eats sushi?"

Charlene wasn't a religious person by nature, but not because there hadn't been a valiant effort by her mother to shove the church down her throat as a kid. She "did her time," attending church every Sunday morning at her mother's request, because in her mother's eyes it was the right thing to do. But once she was old enough to make her own decisions, church had been struck from her to-do list.

That afternoon she stood on the front steps of the Cathedral Basilica of the Immaculate Conception on Logan Street in downtown Denver, staring at the front doors. It was her mother's desire, to visit the famous landmark that had been built in 1906. She'd been talking about the church for weeks.

"Shall we go in?" her mother asked, wearing a look of excitement that Charlene hadn't seen there in quite some time.

She looked at her sister and Jane winked, aware of their mother's eagerness. They opened the doors and stepped inside, and the heavy doors slammed shut behind them. The inside of the church was pristine.

After listening to her mother, Charlene knew all about the church. The altar, statuary, and bishop's chair were all made of expensive Italian marble. A total of seventy-five stained-glass windows let in wonderful colored light. It had a vaulted ceiling rising sixty-eight feet above the slightly sloping nave.

Charlene held back as Jane and her mother blended into a crowd of tourists strolling through the church, led by a guide. She could see them talking, their mother admiring the fine architecture and sharing her knowledge of the church and its doctrines.

She hesitated, feeling strange. It wasn't the first time she'd ever been in a church, but now, it felt different—odd. She wasn't a spiritual person, and with her job, some of the things she'd seen made it hard to believe that God really existed.

She moved through slowly, keeping a distance from her family. She felt as if she were in a trance, floating, and, if she'd been even a little religious, she would've said say she had a spiritual moment.

She stopped in front of the Altar of Virgin Mary and stared into the statue's eyes, as if entranced. The woman looked sad and lonely. She shuddered, feeling a jolt in her bones. The darkness threatened to take her over, flashes of blackness dodging in and out of her psyche.

The confrontation with Darren Brady came back unbidden, in snapshot images. She vividly envisioned herself strapped naked to that metal table in Brady's basement, and Darren standing over her with a knife raised high above his head, getting ready to pierce her unprotected chest.

When the images disappeared in a flash, she blinked, certain that she'd seen a teardrop leak from the statue's eye, and when she reached up to touch her own eyes, they were wet with tears.

Without warning she wobbled then lost her balance and had to use the wooden rail to steady herself, regaining her equilibrium.

Crazy. Why was she feeling this way? Was it a sign, an epiphany? A sign of what? She didn't believe in this crap, so why was it happening to her? What was it trying to tell her?

"Charlene, are you okay?"

Jane and her mother suddenly appeared beside her, looking worried. A choir of elementary school children, had started singing in chorus, up in the loft section at the back of the church. They sang the hymn "I am the Resurrection," and the sound reverberated throughout the massive sanctuary.

Charlene tried to speak, but her throat tightened with emotion. "I'm fine. I just need some air."

She left the church without turning around.

Chapter 8

"Huh." The agent in charge from the Colorado unit, Sam Cahill, grunted in the passenger seat of their department-issued SUV.

Cahill was of medium height, his prematurely grey hair rigid with cowlicks and had a nose that dominated his face. He had a high forehead, and his jowls sagged.

Seeing the look on his face, Matt asked, "What's wrong?"

"The FBI has never sent *me* anywhere in a private jet."

Matt exhaled but didn't respond as the FBI's private jet taxied toward them.

Cahill sighed aloud. "From what I hear, Smith is the real deal—the complete package."

Matt nodded.

"Are the rumors true?"

Matt stared out the windshield. "It depends on what you've heard."

Matt had never worked directly with Agent Nicholas Smith but remembered him from the original case. The man's reputation and venerable past preceded him. Smith had over twenty years under his belt working kidnapping cases, was agent in charge of more than one hundred kidnapping cases, many of them high-profile. He also had a high rate of success, and was rumored to have integrity, loyalty, and was deeply devoted to the FBI.

"I heard he cracked. Hit the bottle hard."

Matt still didn't look at Cahill but couldn't refute the statement. The agent had heard a lot too—maybe rumors, maybe fact. He didn't work close enough to Smith to know for sure, but he never put too much faith in gossip.

Matt *had* heard that Smith put his heart and soul into the earlier kidnapping cases, and it hadn't just torn him apart but also destroyed his marriage. Stories were rife that once his family had abandoned him, he lived out of a suitcase, always packed, awaiting the call for a new case.

He'd been called in to Albuquerque, where three babies had been kidnapped. And he'd watched as that number turned to seven, before it just stopped…inexplicably.

Few suspects and even fewer leads had driven the man crazy, because there were no ransom demands, and the children never surfaced again.

Matt frowned. "Oh yeah?"

"Yeah. They say he's changed. I can hear the whispers from Denver. The New Mexico case broke him. I heard he's become obsessed, unable to let it go. People say Smith lost his wife and daughter over that case. She couldn't live with him anymore, so she took their daughter and left. From that time on, he spent night and day at the bureau, never went home and rarely slept. The word is that the case is still eating at him."

Matt shrugged. "Sounds as if you've heard a lot." He had heard the same things.

"I also heard that OPR investigated him."

The Office of Professional Responsibility, in Washington, was the equivalent of Internal Affairs for police departments across the country. They investigated FBI-related incidents involving agent conduct and misconduct. They were known for their long interviews and massive amounts of paperwork.

Matt said, "Nothing came of that."

"Why do you think they sent Smith?"

"He volunteered."

"Really?"

Matt nodded. "That case has torn at Smith's soul for the last six years. There's no way he could walk away from it. Every person who works in law enforcement has at least one case that dogs them, and this is his. Do you have one?"

"Yeah," Cahill admitted. "I was a rookie when we had a case much like this one."

Matt's cell phone rang, and he unclipped it from his belt. "Stone."

"Matt, it's Jake."

"What's up?"

"Just calling to tell you not to come to this new scene. The chief just asked about you. I don't think she wants to run into you."

"Thanks for the heads up. I'm at the airport to pick up my senior agent from DC, so we're in knee-deep now, whether Salinger likes it or not."

"Okay, I'll see you at the apartment tonight."

Matt hung up as the plane came to a stop near their vehicle and the door slid opened. They exited the car. Matt removed his black sunglasses and squinted into the dazzling Denver sunlight.

Smith stepped out of the plane, stood on the top step, and smoothed out the creases in his trousers.

Cahill whistled. "Nice suit."

To Matt, except for the two-thousand-dollar Armani suit, Smith looked like a rookie who hadn't grown accustomed to the FBI lifestyle. He'd changed.

His black hair was now salt and pepper, thinning and disheveled, and he had dark bags under his bloodshot eyes. He was a short, with feet too big for his small body.

With a briefcase in one hand and a laptop case slung over his shoulder, Smith trudged down the air stairs looking at his iPhone, texting with one hand.

"Stone." No sign of emotion on the agent's face.

"Agent Smith." Matt picked up the strong, fresh scent of mouthwash and wondered if the senior agent had taken a drink during the plane ride.

Smith switched the briefcase to his left hand and shook Matt's. Matt was about to introduce Cahill, who stood there with a dumb smile on his face, but Smith swiftly rounded the car, all business.

His voice was a monotone. "You can get me caught up during the ride."

It was a forty-minute drive from the Denver International Airport to the Colorado Bureau of Investigation in Lakewood. During the ride, Matt discovered that Smith fit the stereotypical profile of the average FBI agent. Most people felt compelled to talk when silence took over, but not Smith. He said little, only interrupting Matt's thoughts with pertinent questions about the case.

Matt brought Smith up to speed on everything that wasn't already in the file. Smith stared out the window during the drive, a bundle of nervous energy sitting in the passenger seat. The tension put Matt on edge.

When they arrived at the field office, Matt parked across the street. He had to run to keep up as Smith strode with a purpose, head up, toward the FBI building.

Cahill's windowless office was like a walk-in closet. A rectangular desk had been cleared, and ten files, from six years ago to the present, lay scattered across a nearby table.

There was no hint of amusement on Smith's face when he spoke. "I hope no one is claustrophobic."

Matt looked over at Cahill to see if they should laugh, but apparently Cahill wasn't sure either, so they didn't.

Smith ordered, "Get me a map of the city." Cahill left the office.

"My gut tells me these cases are connected, and it's only the start. I trust my instincts." He eyeballed Matt. "But I also trust you."

"Thank you, sir." Matt felt honored that Smith thought so highly of him.

Smith put up his hand. "I remember your inauguration. You're a competent agent with a knack for profiling—intelligent, capable, and a skilled investigator who never takes shortcuts. Actually"—Smith hesitated—"I wished you'd been part of the crisis management team back in New Mexico. I pleaded for you, but I was outvoted because of your inexperience."

"I won't let you down."

"The fact that I've been flown here, rather than a younger, newer agent with a fresh set of eyes, should tell you it's being taken seriously."

"We won't fail this time."

Cahill entered the office with a giant paper map of Denver, and thumbtacked it to the drywall.

"What do you know, Agent Cahill?" Smith sat down at the table and meticulously organized the case files in chronological order.

Cahill fed them the information he had, most of which the agents already knew.

When he had finished, Matt spoke. "Wouldn't you agree that this case is directly linked to New Mexico?"

Neither man said a word, only nodded in agreement. There was no point in arguing otherwise. The MOs, signature aspects, and case linkage were identical.

Matt continued, "I think we should start with the first child kidnapped six years ago. That's the starting point, the 'stressor.'"

"Goddamn it." Smith pounded his fist on the table. He looked at Matt, a hint of agitation in his eyes. "You don't think I've done that? I've studied, examined, and worked this case from every angle for six years. I've exhausted every possible lead, turned every stone, and followed every clue and I've still found nothing. These kids are gone, vanished. We need to focus on the latest victims while it's fresh, before leads grow cold and we lose them entirely."

As time went by, the case dragged on and momentum was lost.

Silence filled the space after the outburst from Smith. The man looked on edge, and Matt wondered if he was capable of handling an investigation of this magnitude. But that wasn't his call. If FBI superiors believed in Smith's capabilities to run this operation, then he was in no position to question that authority.

"Okay," Matt conceded. "We know seven babies were kidnapped back then. Why seven? Now, six years later, another three. If these are in fact the same kidnappers, then where have they been for the last six years?"

More silence.

Finally, Cahill spoke. "Are we sure it's seven?"

"I'm positive." Again, Smith's tone held a hint of annoyance. "I've been searching the NCIC database for the last six years, and then I went as far back as ten years ago. I found no similar cases of infant kidnappings anywhere. And I've checked them all. I've also worked with Interpol, but as far as they can tell the kidnapped babies haven't surfaced internationally either."

"If the International Police haven't seen them, then where have the kidnappers been for the last six years? Why come back now?"

The question hung in the air.

Matt changed directions. "We know seven children were taken the first time. Now there's three. If the kidnapper's agenda hasn't changed, then there will be four more babies kidnapped before this is over. Last time, seven children were taken in a one-month span. Now the time table has been ramped up. They're much more confident now. These three children"—Matt held up the files—"were taken in less than a week." He looked at Smith. "Instead of going through these old files again, why don't you tell us your procedure from the first time around? Who were the suspects? What was the evidence?"

Smith took a deep breath. He didn't need his notes. "I worked my ass off on that case, tracking down every person involved, securing initial interviews. Then following up, I conducted intense background searches, but we found little in the way of evidence to lead us to a suspect. We ran checks on employees from the hospital where the babies were born— nothing. We dug into the parents, looking for potential enemies— nothing. After the first kidnapping, we even went so far as to get warrants to bug the parents' home phones and cars, but they all cleared the checks."

"Who would grant such a warrant with no evidence?" Cahill asked.

Smith ignored the question with a roll of his eyes.

Matt cocked his head in deep thought. "You did have a person of interest though, didn't you?"

Smith nodded. "Susan Harper. A nurse at the hospital. The original person of interest but weak at best, and in the end, it didn't go anywhere."

Cahill asked, "Witnesses?"

"Useless. Seven different witnesses identified seven different men—of different heights, weights, and ages—absolutely impossible. And it sounds like our three new witnesses all have a different take on the man who kidnapped their children."

"That's true," Cahill said.

Matt helped out. "Rich families are always a target. In most cases, money is the ultimate motivation but not in this one. In the United States alone, almost two thousand missing-children reports are filed each day. The majority of children are taken by a family member or an acquaintance. Only twenty-five percent of kids are taken by strangers."

"Most abducted children are killed within the first three hours, but this case is different. Apparently, these children are still alive. No bodies have ever been recovered. We even posted the baby pictures across the country, hoping for leads. To sum it up in one word, ladies and gentlemen, what we have here is a big fat nothing."

The men sat silently, studying the paperwork—the victims' photos, the jumble of wordy reports, and a list of family members' names. If Matt had entered the room with these two brilliant men with a hint of hope, it had vanished with what Smith had just said.

"I'll put on coffee." Cahill left the office.

Smith rubbed his hands nervously. "There is one thing I came up with." His look was intense—serious—, his icy reserve hardening the already stale mood. "It's a long shot, but I could be right. God, I hope I'm not."

"What is it?" Matt asked, moving to the edge of his seat.

He saw a flash of fear in the older man's eyes. "I'll tell you when Cahill gets back."

It was late when Abigail left her brother, but she had another life to get to. She'd made sure to Joshua took his regular dosage of meds and a little extra something to remind him who ran the show.

Following the unlit, unmarked dirt driveway, she kept the headlights off and let the car roll down the hill in neutral. She'd been to the cabin so many times that no beams were needed; she could drive it blindfolded.

The beauty of the cabin was its seclusion. There were no marked roads in the surrounding area. The place was entirely off the map, and if you didn't know it existed, you'd never find it. She'd actually forgotten about it until Joshua reminded her years earlier.

He had been in a good mood tonight, and why wouldn't he be? The plan was running smoothly, right on schedule. Under her tutelage, Joshua had come along nicely. But no matter how good things were, she never lost focus and never stopped fearing the worst. Things could turn quickly, and she always had a contingency plan ready to deal with any eventuality.

Joshua wasn't a problem. All men could be controlled by the one thing that was always on their minds. That part was easy. She had always had a gift for that.

But Joshua was different. It took more than just sex to get her way.

She knew what to say, what he wanted to hear. Josh always waited for praise, a pat on the back. People like her brother needed their egos stroked. And she was a master at it. She'd been managing people of lesser intelligence for a long time. The power of persuasion was her forte.

Joshua couldn't be allowed to act as he had before. She couldn't risk the failure of this new plan. Last time was lucky—she'd been able to talk some sense into him—but if it happened again, it could mean trouble.

This was the end of the line for Joshua.

It took twenty-three minutes to get to the main highway. She turned on the headlights and pulled onto the paved road, setting the speedometer at the sixty-five miles-per-hour speed limit and punching cruise control.

The last thing she needed was for some rookie cop to pull her over or have her plates run and have to explain herself. What was she doing out here? How would she ever talk her way out of that?

She'd left the babies in good hands. Unlike her, Joshua had always been the caregiver. She despised the little brats—couldn't believe she'd ever wanted children of her own. He would take care of them, but it was her job to make sure he didn't get too close.

She turned the radio on and switched to 710 KNUS, Denver's number-one source for breaking news. There was no mention of the kidnappings. It made sense—there was no point in causing a city-wide panic. Yet. When the news leaked, all hell would break loose.

The FBI wouldn't have any more luck than they did before—she was sure of that.

Ten minutes later she pulled the car into an outlet mall closed for the night, parking next to a pay phone she'd never used before—not that many of them existed anymore. Prepaid cell phones couldn't be fully trusted, with all the signals that could be traced.

She dropped coins into the slot and mouthed the number she'd committed to memory. She punched in the numbers on the phone pad, difficult with gloves on, but necessary. She held the receiver away from her ear and mouth to avoid DNA from saliva and hair.

It was answered after only one ring. "Yes?"

"It's me. Everything's on schedule. There shouldn't be a problem."

"Good. The deadline has been moved up." The thickly-accented male voice asked, "Can you handle that?"

"Of course, I can." She'd been totally unprepared for this, but she knew not to raise her voice or question his authority. Obviously, this sudden change would alter their plans. She didn't dare ask for the new date; he would tell her when he was ready.

He repeated, "Can you handle it?"

She had no choice; it was either the deadline or the consequences. "Yes."

"Good."

She added, "One thing has changed."

"What's that?" The man sounded upset, tense. "You already have half my money. You'd better not let me down."

She understood completely. He didn't like changes, unless he made them.

She hesitated, and her pulse quickened. Her mouth was dry. "I'll include one more package, but that means the price just went up."

"You just have the merchandise. I'll have the rest of the cash."

She hung up without saying good-bye and checked her watch, making sure she hadn't stayed on the line for more than fifty seconds. Anyone could be listening, monitoring, and she never took unnecessary risks.

Now that Agent Smith was back and the FBI called the shots, she couldn't be too careful.

She got into the car and pulled out of the lot, resetting the cruise control. She liked to travel at night—preferred it. There would be no sleep—still too much to do and too much on her mind.

Matt sank into his chair, speechless. He felt a cold chill creep into his bones.

He and Cahill tried their best to digest what Smith told them. They looked at each other, at a loss for words. Could it be possible?

Matt had never heard this theory before. Never heard whispers throughout the bureau. Was this just some cockamamy theory Smith concocted on his own?

He understood that when cops hit a wall in terms of evidence, the route they took was to develop theories and then try to prove them. But was this one even a possibility?

He wanted to question Smith, but the agent had moved on without a second thought, as if the idea he'd just delivered was nothing new.

"Let's go over the three latest crimes—the kidnappings here in Denver. Describe them for me."

Matt checked his watch and rubbed his eyes then picked up the first file, still trying to get his bearings. "Allie Wilson was our first, abducted last Friday afternoon. Three months old, daughter to Mike and Stephanie Wilson." He threw the file onto the table in front of Smith. "Mother and baby were immersed in their normal routine, at the same park they go to every day, when they were confronted by a male, a Caucasian of medium size, with black hair and a mustache, who was jogging in the park. The man proceeded to knock out the mother with chloroform and take the baby. The mother normally goes to the park with her neighbor, but on that day the friend begged off due to car trouble. As you can imagine, the CSI report yielded little. The kidnapping had been clean—no transfer or hair fibers on Stephanie Wilson. A visit to the crime scene provided even less."

Smith frowned. "That's worrisome."

Cahill picked up the thread. "The kidnapper struck in broad daylight, had been calm and collected with no signs of remorse. The abduction was well planned—in a wooded park with the perfect amount of concealment that offered no chance for a defensive intervention and no witnesses other than the mother."

He paused for a breath before adding, "I spoke to the mechanic who'd been called about the car owned by Wayne Sterling, Stephanie Wilson's neighbor. He told me that a plug had come unhooked and just had to be plugged back in. You'd have to know about cars to know that."

Matt nodded. "I doubt that wire unplugged itself. This guy is smart. It probably means the person responsible for the kidnapping had gone to Sterling's place of work and dislodged the plug without being detected. I checked video cameras around Sterling's office, but no feed would give us a good view of the car or anyone hanging around it."

Smith held up a finger. "Says here there was a person of interest."

Matt nodded. "Frank Manning. I interviewed him."

"Anything there?"

Matt shook his head. "Not our man. Manning doesn't fit the type of person who would kidnap a baby. He's a family man, married for thirty-one years, three adult children. No prior record and at his age he's probably not capable of pulling off something as dramatic as a kidnapping."

"He just got fired," Cahill pointed out. "That's something."

Matt shrugged. "Being fired is a stressor, but Manning doesn't fit the bill. Plus, he has a solid alibi and, judging from my initial interview, Manning harbors no ill will toward Mike Wilson and has no reason to snatch the man's child."

Smith leaned back, quiet.

Matt picked up the next file. "Jonathon Allen, taken last night. Four months old, son of Mark and Tina Allen." He handed Smith the file. "The father was at his regular Tuesday night poker game. Mother was home alone with the baby. When the father came home from the poker game around two a.m., he checked on the baby, only to find the crib empty, and then woke his wife when he realized the baby wasn't in bed with her. From our interview with the mother, the only thing out of the ordinary was a man who came to the door claiming to be with Resolution, Research and Marketing, which is a local market research company. From her description, the man went by the name Colin, a Caucasian of medium build, with brown hair and a goatee. We've followed up with the company, and there is no one there by the name of Colin, and the company isn't running any surveys in the area. Mrs. Wilson answered a short survey, but we believe the man was actually the kidnapper, scoping the inside of the home. The baby was in his crib when she went to bed around nine p.m. and she never heard anything after that. We're still looking into it, including background checks."

"So, he checked out the inside of the house before sneaking back while the mother slept."

"But the perp would have had to be quiet so as to not wake her. That wouldn't be easy to do. It takes skill and practice."

"What about a plate number from the vehicle? Surely one of the neighbors saw something?" Smith's voice was strained, with a hint of impatience.

"Many of the neighbors saw a vehicle, a small blue car, but it didn't raise any suspicion. Most people can't tell the difference between makes and models. Certainly no one thought to take down a plate number. One of the neighbors said she had even talked to the man, and he seemed friendly."

Matt grabbed the third folder. "Mason Bailey, nabbed this morning. Four months old, son of Peter and Elizabeth Bailey. The mother said there was nothing out of the ordinary. She went for her usual Wednesday morning golf lesson. Took Mason out to the car, got him strapped into his car seat like every other morning, and then went to the garage to get her golf clubs. It took her several minutes to retrieve them. She didn't notice the baby was gone until she got to the day care to drop him off."

Cahill made a face. "How is that even possible?"

"Baby seats face the back seat, so parents in the front can't see them."

"What time was that?" Smith asked.

"About nine thirty. We checked with the clubhouse pro at the golf course, and Elizabeth Bailey has been taking ten a.m. lessons every

Monday, Wednesday, and Friday for the last three weeks. This is still fresh, so we don't have much yet."

Smith looked at Matt. "What's the one factor that connects them all?"

Matt knew that Smith was testing him. "They all followed a routine."

"Exactly—easy targets. Let's talk about the witness statements."

"Flashbulb memories," Matt said "A lot of emotion surrounding these events."

"A lot of good that'll do." Cahill's sarcasm was thick. "They all identified different men."

Matt tilted his head. "I think it's the same man." He had their attention now. "I think he wore a disguise and could have been wearing lifts to throw off his height."

Just before the midnight hour they'd moved the task force into another room, getting away from Cahill's cramped quarters. Matt's head felt heavy and his neck tight from exhaustion and frustration.

At one o'clock he looked around the table, noticing his partners, Smith and Cahill, didn't look any better than he felt. Sweat soaked through their shirts; they reeked of body odor, and the stuffy air in the room smelled of stale coffee and cigarettes—which Cahill smoked against the wishes of his teammates. The table where they worked was already littered with papers, Styrofoam cups, and plastic Chinese take-out containers.

Smith stood. "Three babies. Two boys and one girl, two Caucasian and one African American, all from middle-to high-income families in different areas of the city. They're all only children, which could be significant. The kidnapper never hits families with more than one child, same as in New Mexico. Other than that, he uses no pattern to choose his victims. The Wilson baby was the first, so that would be a good place to start. We need to know why these babies were chosen."

After establishing an investigative strategy, they spent the next couple of hours sifting through paperwork, witness transcripts, crime scene reports, analysis documents, photos, and evidence. Then they'd worked the phones and internet, looking for leads and patterns.

Smith, the meticulous note-taker, had a notebook full of writing. All Matt wanted to do now was go home, take a long, hot shower, and jump into bed. Exhaustion had set into his bones, and his eyes were red-eyed, tired from reading. He needed fresh air to clear his mind.

It was as if Smith read his mind. "Let's wrap it up. At this stage, we're all tired, and we won't accomplish anything more by being here. Let's pick this back up in the morning. I assume there's a cot set up as I requested?"

"We got you a hotel room," Cahill replied hesitantly.

Smith gave the agent a cold stare and an impatient headshake. He snapped, "I asked for a cot."

"Back room." Cahill jerked his thumb toward the end of the hall.

"Good."

Matt studied Smith. His eyes were bloodshot, and the vein in his forehead throbbed. Matt wondered just how much Smith would actually sleep, if he slept at all.

"See you in the morning." Cahill turned away.

"Wait. Remember," Smith said. "First thing tomorrow we'll have DPD send teams to all the neighbors to ask if they've seen anyone new or unfamiliar lurking in the area. This guy had to have scoped these places for weeks in advance, following their routine, and chances are he didn't wear the same disguise he wore during the crime."

Cahill nodded and made his exit, leaving Matt alone with Smith. He was about to say good-bye, but Smith spoke first.

"We'll need a profile." The three agents, during the meeting, had confirmed and all agreed that it was the work of more than one kidnapper, though the exact number was unknown. "Agent Marks did one six years ago, but I want your opinion. I need to know what we're dealing with here."

Matt nodded.

"Good. I'll see you back here in a few hours. Get some rest. And that theory I mentioned earlier doesn't leave this office."

They shook hands and Matt left the building, checking the lock on the way out. He got in his car and started the ignition, sitting motionless, slumped behind the wheel, the facts of the meeting still running through his head—Smith's words turning over in his brain.

Didn't look like this was a nightmare he'd waken from anytime soon.

She awoke to a car door slamming. Sitting up, Charlene looked around through glazed eyes, still groggy. She was on the couch, in the living room, with the lights and TV still on.

When had she fallen asleep? She was alone, so her mother must have slipped off to bed. The time on the TV showed 1:14 a.m. The second rerun of *Pale Rider* played with the sound turned low.

The night came back to her. They babysat Martina while Jane and Richard went out for their first date since the baby's birth. Her mother had complained because Charlene had chosen Clint Eastwood westerns to watch, a taste in movies inherited from her father. Being the "son he never had" meant taking an interest in the classics.

Then she heard a faint knock, almost imperceptible.

Had it really been a knock, or was it the stiff Colorado wind banging against the house? Had she even heard a car door slam? Charlene lay back down, her eyes half open, trying to regain consciousness.

She waited several minutes, for Jane and Richard to come in, if the noise she'd heard had been a car door.

Another knock at the front door. This time loud enough to discern.

Charlene didn't hear footsteps. Her mother must have been completely out, in bed. Were Jane and Richard even home yet? They would have woken her if they'd gotten home, wouldn't they?

She sat back up and stared at the door. The outside light, running on a motion sensor, had clicked on, so someone, or something, had activated it. Jane and Richard had a key; they wouldn't need to knock.

In the countryside, away from the city of Denver, there was no traffic. Had someone broken down or put their car in the ditch?

She got up and peered through the peephole but saw nothing. She opened the door slightly, keeping the chain latched but found no one. Then she unhooked the chain and opened the door wide, stepping out onto the porch to survey the front yard. No car.

A gust of wind picked up, almost knocking her over. As she reentered the house and closed the door, she heard a noise in the kitchen that startled her, and made the hairs on the back of her neck stand on end.

"Mom?" she called out. No response.

Charlene cautiously stepped into the kitchen, moving toward the back of the house.

The kitchen was dark, the only light coming from the back porch, which shone through the open door. The wind banged the back door against the wall. She frowned then closed the door and latched the lock, studying it, looking for signs of forced entry that only a cop would look for. Did Jane usually keep the door locked?

This was ridiculous. She was a cop, and a tough, independent woman. The only reason she walked on pins and needles was Darren Brady. If he hadn't re-entered her life, everything would be fine. But now, just the thought of him made her act totally out of character.

She turned on the kitchen lights and searched the room methodically, checking the door again. When she shut off the lights, she heard footsteps on the oak staircase.

Her mom had finally woken up. How would she explain this foolishness to her?

But when she returned to the living room, her mother wasn't there, and the footfalls fell in the upstairs hallway, on the floorboards above her. The baby monitor on the coffee table emitted a scratchy sound. She perceived static movement, someone in the baby's room.

She took a deep breath to calm her nerves. Probably just her mother checking on Martina. But when she heard heavy breathing over the monitor, she brought her right hand to her hip, but her gun wasn't there.

Where was it? Charlene lost her fight with panic and turned into the instinctive cop she was.

Without caution to danger, she hurried up the stairs, taking them two at a time. When she flicked on the nursery light, her niece lay in the crib, awake but squirming. Charlene let her breath out and picked up the little girl, hugging her gently.

A loud thud came from downstairs.

With the baby in hand, Charlene tiptoed down the carpeted hallway. She stood outside the closed door to her bedroom, planted her ear against the door, and listened. Nothing.

She nudged open the door and slipped inside, then turned on the light. With Martina in one arm, she bent and used her free hand to rummage through her duffel bag, but her backup gun wasn't there.

Shit. Had someone come in and taken it? She looked around the room for anything that could be used as a weapon, but came up empty.

She picked up the bedside phone—dead. The line had been cut. What about her cell phone?

After reentering the hallway and retracing her steps to the staircase, she stood at the top of the stairs, peering down into the darkness. The lights and TV had been turned off, and the only sound was her own rapid breathing.

"Mom?" She chewed her lip, trying to make sense of it.

No answer.

What was going on? Where was her mother? Should she hide or go downstairs, confront whoever was down there? But Martina was in her arms. She wasn't leaving this baby alone.

She couldn't decide what to do—why was she being a wimp?

She sidestepped down the stairs, holding Martina's head to her chest. Once her eyes adjusted to the darkness, she noticed the television was still turned on but had been overturned—the thud she'd heard earlier.

She stood motionless, listening for the slightest hint of a sound. She spotted her cell on the coffee table, about twenty feet away. If she could get to her phone, then she and Martina could find a place to hide and wait for the police.

"Hi, Charlie." The voice came out of the darkness.

Dread shimmied down her spine. She turned in the direction of the voice. She couldn't see him, but his presence lingered, watching her.

"Who are you? What do you want?" No question who it was. Only one person, other than her father, called her that name. But how could it be?

She gripped Martina tighter, taking backwards steps, hoping not to draw attention to the baby. She scanned the room frantically for a weapon, anything useful that could protect them. But she knew that her only option was to flee.

"Don't worry, Detective. I'm not here for you. I'm here for her."

Then the Celebrity Slayer's face appeared out of the shadows, hitting the ray of moonlight that glimmered through the window. His was a truly gruesome triangular face, like nothing she had ever seen before. She closed her eyes and turned away, repulsed.

She took a step to run away, but a hand came down on her shoulder blade. His sharp nails dug into her skin. Her legs felt heavy, and her feet like concrete blocks. The faster she tried to move, the slower she went.

She closed her eyes, hoping her fear would subside, giving her the strength to move on and protect them.

Then his other hand tapped her cheek.

"Charlene."

Her eyes shot open. Jane stood over her, and Richard held her shoulder.

"Charlene, wake up."

Her eyes opened wide now. She trembled, still dazed, and noted that her hair was drenched from night sweat.

"You were screaming and shaking." Worry lines etched Jane's face.

Charlene blinked, taking a minute to gather her wits. She wiped away a strand of hair out of her eyes, taking slow deep breaths.

She gasped, "Martina."

"I already—"

Charlene raced up the stairs, with her sister and Richard on her heels. She ran into her niece's room and flicked the light on.

Martina slept peacefully in her crib.

Jane arrived seconds later. "I already checked on Martina and she's fine. What's wrong with you?"

Charlene swallowed hard. "Just a dream."

Chapter 9

Friday morning, early. A new day, but old news. Matt stormed through the unfamiliar house—but it was the same story, second verse.

He was running on fumes after pulling the all-nighter with Smith and Cahill. He rubbed the sleep from the corners of his eyes, tried to hide a yawn, and squinted his way through a house that triggered the same eerie recurring feelings: sadness and doubt.

Another crime scene—cops were running in and out, cell phones ringing, a photographer snapping photos, feet thumping overhead, the murmur of voices in the corners as techs and law enforcement did their work.

In cases like these, hope was always a thin thread they all clung to.

Matt went from room to room, but there was no sign of a disturbance—not that he expected it. Another clean hit.

When they'd received word, Smith, rather than going himself, had sent Matt and Cahill, which surprised Matt. Where was he? What was he doing? This should be his case to lead. But Matt felt a swell of pride knowing that Smith trusted him and was confident enough in his ability to hand over the reins. He didn't delegate often.

Matt shook his head in frustration as he cleared the ground floor. Another kidnapping. Four children in seven days. This thing was out of control, the kidnappers gaining speed with no signs of slowing.

He headed outside, still not believing how effective and efficient the kidnappers were—leaving no traces of evidence whatsoever. They pulled the strings, calling the shots, but since they remained silent with no ransom demands, he felt more than a little helpless.

Cahill rounded the corner of the house and joined Matt in the backyard. "Can you believe this?" He read from his notes: Jacob Inglewood, abducted in the middle of the night. The mother found the crib empty this morning when she went to check on him."

Matt rubbed the side of his face. "Middle of the night. Someone just slipped in here while the family slept and snuck out a newborn undetected. How is that even possible? Is this guy a ghost?" He looked up at the baby's bedroom at the corner of the house, which overlooked the backyard. "What about sleeping and eating patterns?"

Cahill looked again at his notes. "He eats regularly every three to four hours. Feeding happens in the nursery, in a rocking chair. Last fed at two a.m., and when the alarm woke her at six, she sensed something wrong because she hadn't heard him wake for his next feeding."

Matt checked his watch. "What about the father?"

"Out of town on business. We're already checking that."

"She didn't hear *anything*?"

"We checked the bedroom and found the baby monitor unplugged and batteries removed."

"Smart."

"What are you thinking?"

Matt shook his head. "The kidnapper knew his eating and sleeping patterns and waited until after the two a.m. feeding, to make his move."

This showed Matt that the kidnappers were prepared and patient. Chilling.

They both examined the ground at their feet, searching for proof that someone had been there last night: a cigarette butt, a gum wrapper, a footprint. But that would have been too easy.

"I'll bet he watched the bedroom light—when it's on it means feeding time, off means sleeping time. Probably here for days, even weeks, to make sure the routine stayed true. Probably checked his watch and timed everything to the second."

"You sound like you know this guy."

"I know the type. But how did he get in?"

The lock was picked and dead-bolt chain cut—no alarm system. We found scratch marks on the inside of the keyhole. Not an elaborate setup, just your basic doorknob job."

Matt blew out a breath. "He's patient and, so far, error free." That kind of planning and execution took time, surveillance, and intelligence. "See if we can find out what tool cut the chain. Neighbors see or hear anything?"

Cahill looked doubtful. "In the middle of the night? Hardly."

Unlike the others, Matt wasn't expecting witnesses on this one, even though the kidnapper probably still wore a disguise, in case he ran into anyone. From what the Feds had seen, this kidnapper was cautious and always had a plan.

He looked around for anyone within earshot, and then whispered into Cahill's ear. "We need to continue phone surveillance in each house. We know the kidnappers won't call, but we have to give the parents hope that this is routine, and we expect a ransom demand."

They entered the house, and Matt half-leaned on a stool just inside the front door, looking over his notes. He could feel eyes on him and looked up to see Police Chief Janice Salinger eyeing him coldly.

Salinger's hatred was more than just a "local versus federal" thing. It was a "history" thing.

He shook it off and turned back to his notes but could still feel her glare as he looked down at his pad.

The kidnapper must have been in the house before, planning his route, because he'd been able to get in and out without incident, locate the bedroom, and take the baby in the dark, with the lights off.

Matt stood and strode to the window, looking out at a row of colonial–style houses. A faint morning sun did nothing to mitigate to the fierce Denver wind—the mile-high conditions that made baseball in Denver a pitcher's nightmare and a homerun haven.

The spectacle of a crime scene shortly took over—with cruisers parked hither and yon on the street, uniformed men going in and out, and crime-scene tape spread around the perimeter—disturbing this usually-peaceful neighborhood, where neighbors walked dogs, put up Christmas decorations, and tended gardens.

Did Denver know that a kidnapper terrorized their city? If not, they soon would. Local law enforcement could only keep things under wraps for so long, especially in the advent of social media. People spoke. Cops talked. This police department was no different than any other.

It was the technology-driven information age, and even Tiger Woods couldn't keep his secrets.

Thanksgiving was upcoming, but there was little to be thankful for in this house, as well as a few other houses Matt had been in over the last few days.

As he turned away, he glanced down, just outside the window. Multiple shrubs had been planted around the outside of the house. One shrub in particular caught his attention. A red twig dogwood had been dug up and then put back in place.

He knew the origins of the bush because it was a native shrub on the Colorado landscape and popular in the area. He snapped photos and made a note of the amateur job of removing and replanting it. Other bushes also looked as if they'd been removed and then replaced, while others looked untouched.

He waited his turn and then led the baby's mother, Allison Inglewood into a room toward the back of the house, that was arranged like a personal office—computer desk with laptop, filing cabinet, small shelves with books, boxes of papers stacked in the corner—and directed her to the window.

Her cheeks were red and tearstained. She was a dark-rooted blond, with wide hips, blue eyes, and a long graceful neck.

"Mrs. Inglewood, what's going on in your backyard?"

The woman dabbed her eyes. "Oh, that. We're having landscaping work done, but how did you know?" She shook her head. "They haven't started yet."

"When was the last time they came by?"

She looked at her watch. "A man stopped on Sunday to look things over."

"Do you have a business card?"

"I think so."

She rummaged through an IKEA desk. "I know they left one. Here it is." She handed it to Matt.

"Excuse me, please." He moved to the window, pulled out his cell phone, and punched in the number from the card.

"Green Thumb Landscaping," a women's voice answered.

Matt looked at the name on the card. "Roy Enright please."

"One moment."

The call was transferred.

"Hello."

"Mr. Enright, this is Agent Matt Stone with the FBI."

"Yes?" The man sounded nervous, a normal reaction to receiving a call from a federal agent.

"How long did you work at the Inglewood residence on Sunday?"

He sounded confused. "Sunday? I don't work on Sundays."

"Did you send someone to the house?"

"No."

Matt fiddled with the card in his hand. "Where can I get one of your cards?"

"You can come to the office, where there's a stack of them on the receptionist's desk."

"So, anyone can just walk in and take one?"

"Sure. Why not?"

"Thank you for your time, Mr. Enright."

"What's this all about?"

Matt hung up and went back to where the anguished mother stood. "The landscaping company doesn't work on Sundays, and they didn't send anyone over here that day."

"Oh God." She held a hand to her mouth. "Do you think it was the kidnapper?"

That's exactly what he thought. "Do you remember what he looked like?"

"I remember him perfectly. Such a nice man. Polite, told me how he loved our house and was thinking of building his own. I walked him through it... Oh my God," she gasped, looking like she might faint.

Matt took her by the arm and led her to a nearby chair. Once she was settled, he asked, "Can you describe him for me?"

Her description didn't match any of the other ten witness statements, from either case. In fact, it wasn't even close. They'd all seen men, but not the same man or the same disguise. The only similarities turned out to be the suspect's gender, skin color, and approximate age.

Matt thanked the woman and promised to be in touch. Meanwhile, as they'd done for all the victims, an agent would be posted at the house around the clock, with tracking equipment in case the kidnapper called.

He left the house and sat in his brother's '94 Prelude, arranging the details in his head, his mind in overdrive.

He removed the list from his pocket and added one more row of names.

Parents	Child
Mike and Stephanie Wilson	Allie Wilson
Mark and Tina Allen	Jonathon Allen
Peter and Liz Bailey	Mason Bailey
James and Allison Inglewood	Jacob Inglewood

The kidnappings now set the pace of the investigation.

So far, St. Anthony Central Hospital was the only link. Allie Wilson was significant because she was the first. But how did these kidnappers choose their targets? Was it random?

His papers were neatly piled and paper-clipped on the passenger's seat. He found Allie Wilson's folder, but felt bad using Jake's car as his filing cabinet on wheels. Later, back at the office, he would sign out a bureau car.

He unclipped the cell phone from his waist and placed a call.

"Special Agent Smith. It's Matt Stone."

"Agent Stone." Smith still refused to call Matt by his first name. "What did you discover?"

"Not much."

"I didn't think you would."

Matt told Smith about the business card number he'd called.

"Then maybe our guy received a business card from the real landscaper, and the landscaper can ID him?"

Matt unconsciously shook his head. "No. The guy's cards are at the front desk with the receptionist, and anyone who goes in can grab one."

"Okay."

"I'm on my way back now. DPD is done here. Any chance we can get them to send copies of their notes?"

"I've already ordered it. We might only have three chances left. Time is running out."

Matt had just put the car in gear, when there was a sharp rap at his window. Matt rolled down the window to see Cahill standing there.

"Just heard back from James Inglewood's company. He's at an annual, weeklong conference in St. Louis. Inglewood attends every year at this time. He's been contacted and is on his way back."

"Thanks."

Cahill headed back into the house. Matt inhaled loudly through his nose. More routine meant more research and planning.

He couldn't remember ever being so exhausted. Details of the case constantly ran through his mind, wreaking havoc with his sleep patterns. The handwriting was on the wall. It would be another all-nighter.

When he first signed up, he knew not every crime would be solved. But as a Fed, Matt forced himself not to think like that—instead, he chose to believe that every case had a chance. Kidnappers always make mistakes eventually, and the FBI would be there when it happened.

He looked again at the names on the list.

He and Smith had determined these suspects to be mission-based kidnappers. They wouldn't stop kidnapping children until they were caught or their mission was completed.

But what was the mission? Was it what Smith thought it was? He shuddered at the thought.

As he pulled away, Janice Salinger stepped out of the house and perched on the front steps, hands on hips, staring at his car. He watched her through the rearview mirror, feeling a chill from her glare, even as he drove away from the house.

Matt's gaze wandered around the empty precinct. Lights were off, desk lamps dimmed, and all was quiet. He wasn't planning on staying long. Jake waited down in the car while Matt made a quick stop, and then they would go out to a nice restaurant for supper. He wanted to spend more time with Jake, but now that his colleagues were in Denver, he found it harder and harder to get away from his superiors.

No leads yet on the kidnapping case. They ran it through the National Crime Information Center—NCIC—that connected missing-persons cases across the country, but so far had been unable to connect the dots.

Jake said the file was on his desk, but as Matt rummaged through the messy desktop, he didn't see it. Organization wasn't one of Jake's strong suits, but he was a good cop, and if he said the file was on his desk, then it was, somewhere. He just had to get creative and move things around.

His cell phone buzzed. He unclipped it and answered. "Yeah?"

"Janice is heading your way." Jake's voice sounded rushed and anxious.

"What?"

"She'll be upstairs any minute now."

"Damn. What the hell is she doing at the precinct this late?"

"I don't know, but you better make your exit before she catches you there."

"I can't find the file."

"It's in a blue folder."

"Jake, I don't see it."

"It's there."

Matt heard stiletto heels clicking in the hallway. He hung up and turned just in time to see the chief of police, round the corner. She stopped and stared at him.

"What are you doing here?"

Matt swallowed hard. "Just getting something for Jake."

"I saw him in the car outside. Why didn't he come in himself?"

"He was driving—just thought it'd be easier if I ran up."

"What do you want, Matt?"

"Just the file."

She let out her breath. "What do you know?"

"About what?"

"What do you know about the case?"

"As much as you guys do."

"Bullshit. The Feds swoop in here and refuse to share information. I want to know what's going on. Don't keep this department in the dark. This was *our* case. This is *our* city."

"I know. It isn't our intention to take over and leave you behind. We want to work together."

She shook her head. "Oh, don't give me that load of FBI bullshit. We both know that's exactly what the Feds do. It's all about the glory for you guys. It doesn't matter whose toes you step on or who you stab in the back."

This was going nowhere. Losing battle, time to move on. He glanced momentarily at the top of the messy desk and turned away.

"I guess I should go."

"You do that. You were always good at making a fast getaway."

He could hear her still cursing under her breath as he hit the stairwell and skipped down the steps, distancing himself as quickly as possible.

Chapter 10

"Isn't this exciting?"

Charlene yawned in the backseat of her sister's Chevy Traverse, leaning back and blowing air from her cheeks. It wasn't exactly her idea of a good time, but she could feel her mother's excitement emanating from the front seat.

Jane agreed. "It's supposed to be a great show."

They sped down the Canam Highway heading to the Buell Theatre on the corner of Fourteenth and Curtis Street. A presentation of *Mamma Mia!* wasn't exactly Charlene's "thing," but she sucked it up, an opportunity to take part in a family activity. Something they'd done little of over the last ten years.

Jane broke the thoughtful silence. "When I knew Mom was coming, Richard insisted on getting tickets. He bought three, in hopes that you would change your mind and visit. I thought this would be the perfect girls' night out for us."

The animated look on Jane's face was clearly apparent in the rearview mirror.

Turning to face Charlene, her mother said, "That was thoughtful, wasn't it, Charlene?"

Charlene gave her best fake smile. "It sure is. I'm really excited."

Jane snorted.

"What?" Charlene asked.

"You're a terrible liar."

Her mother defended Charlene. "But at least you're trying."

Jane nodded. "We'll give her an A for effort."

When they got to the theatre, they picked up the tickets at the will-call window and got sidetracked by a massive throng of people in the lobby.

"I need to use the ladies' room." Brenda headed toward the restroom signs.

"There's the bar. You want anything?" Charlene asked.

Jane looked at Charlene with a motherly gaze. "How about not tonight, Char?"

Charlene sighed quietly. "Yeah, okay."

"Thanks."

"This is gonna be painful."

Jane punched her on the shoulder. "Come on, Sis—you're tough. You're a cop."

"It's no walk in the park."

It felt good to stretch her legs during the intermission. Charlene excused herself to use the restroom, which was just past the bar. The thought of getting through the second half of the play made her temples throb.

When she returned, her family stood oddly huddled in the corner. Onlookers stared at them, and Jane appeared to be crying. Charlene hurried to reach them.

"What's wrong?"

Her mom turned around, white as a ghost. Jane's chest heaved, as if she was having trouble breathing, holding the phone away from her face.

Charlene could hear the tone and volume of Richard's voice on the phone, couldn't make out the words, but perceived the hysterics.

Jane wobbled, as if about to collapse, so Charlene grabbed her around the waist.

"Mom, help me get her outside."

The two women led Jane outside, through the crowd and into the fresh air.

Suddenly Jane said, "We have to go."

When Jane tried to step past her, Charlene put up her hand to stop her.

Charlene demanded, "What's going on?"

"It's Martina."

Charlene grabbed the car keys, already racing toward the car. "I'll drive."

Charlene saw the flashing lights before they reached the driveway. As they pulled into the lane, a group of cops rushed the car, opened the door and led the anxious women through the crowd.

Richard sat on the soft-leather couch, wrapped in a blanket, trembling and sobbing. When she saw him looking so vulnerable, it only increased Charlene's feelings of uncertainty. Officers surrounded him—some taking copious notes, others processing the crime scene.

Her eyes and ears took it all in. Her sister and mother were slumped on the couch, on either side of Richard. When Charlene's gaze met Richard's, he gave her a look that made her feel sick inside.

First and foremost, she knew she should be a good sister, but didn't know how. In fact, it had never been her strong suit. But she was a good cop—of that she was sure.

It was true that Jane needed her. But that didn't mean she couldn't keep track of the investigation.

Richard spoke rapidly while wiping tears from his cheeks. His hands and body trembled, even with Jane's arm around him. He tried to muster his resolve and keep his emotions in check, but it wasn't happening.

"I had just fed Martina and put her to bed, when I heard a knock at the door. A man stood on the doorstep because his car had broken down, and he needed to make a phone call. It's happened a few times before, so I didn't think much of it."

"He didn't have a cell phone?" Charlene interrupted Richard, and that drew stares from everyone within earshot. Even though, as a cop, interfering with the locals on their case was distinctly unprofessional, she couldn't help herself.

Richard's eyes stared blankly. "He didn't have service. He showed me his phone and I knew how it went out here, so far away from the towers of the city. I rarely get service here either." He looked back down at his hands in his lap. "When I turned around to get the phone, something hard came down on the back of my head. When I came to, Martina was gone."

The nearest neighbor was half a mile away, and the house was surrounded by trees, so they would be useless. But Charlene hoped that the Denver police had at least sent someone over there anyway.

Even though Darren Brady couldn't possibly have anything to do with this, in the back of her mind she couldn't help but think how her dream had come true. How could she have foreseen something like this? Her worst fears were realized.

Richard stopped and started through the details, answering the questions to the best of his ability. He struggled at times, his breathing coming in short, ragged gulps. Jane was quiet, motionless, looking paralyzed.

Charlene closely scrutinized the cops in the room, knowing she should consider Jane first, but in spite of her attempt to stifle them, her instincts as a detective kicked in. Unable to help herself, she studied the way they conducted their interrogation. It was pretty routine stuff.

This wasn't LA, and every city had its own way of handling investigations, but she was surprised that there was no sign of electronic equipment, no teams setting up for surveillance or monitoring, which should have been the automatic first step.

Let them do their job, Charlene. But she knew that voice would never prevail over the other voices in her head telling her to take charge and get answers.

Then she spotted a man who looked out of place, standing beside the bookshelf, his body in the next room, but leaning in toward where they sat on the couch. As was her habit, she took note of his appearance, so she could record it if the need arose.

He was handsome—not Brad Pitt handsome, but nice nonetheless. He had a lean face, bright inquisitive blue eyes, a clean-shaven jawline and short black hair.

He wore a dark gray suit that appeared custom made. He had a quiet authority about him, while staying out of the way, quietly listening in to the interview.

Charlene made her way toward him. When they made eye contact, he turned and entered the hallway; she followed close on his heels.

"Excuse me, sir."

He nodded, but didn't say anything.

"Who are you?"

She watched as his gaze surveyed the hallway, then he gestured and led her into an adjoining room. He pulled out a wallet and opened it up. "Agent Stone, FBI."

Charlene checked his credentials, which did indeed identify him as a Fed. She took a step back, hesitating. *FBI?*

She'd worked with the FBI before, as recently as the Celebrity Slayer case. She read what she could on the badge to make sure it was legit. "What's the FBI doing here?"

"Kidnapping is a federal offense. We've been called in to consult. Who are you?"

Protocol dictated that cops identify themselves to other law enforcement officers immediately. Identifying herself and the family connection might give her added leverage.

Charlene stared into his steel-blue eyes, hoping he wouldn't notice when she failed to produce her creds. "I'm LAPD, so I'm aware that kidnapping is a federal offense. But it's pretty early for the FBI to be involved."

She caught him off guard. His face showed that he was either impressed or taken aback. He hesitated as well, as if sizing her up, unsure of how much to tell her.

"Let me see some credentials?"

"I don't have my badge here. I'm on vacation." Partly true—he didn't need to know that she'd had it taken away. "I'm Jane's sister." She jerked her thumb toward the living room. "The victim is my niece. So again, why is the FBI already here?"

He eyed her up and down. "You seem to have a lot of questions."

"I think I'm entitled to them. What are *you* doing to find my niece?"

"Everything we can. Can you answer a few questions?"

"I'll do my best, but I'm sure Richard and Jane have more answers than I do. I've only been in Denver a couple of days, and we weren't even at home when the crime took place."

Charlene did her best to act like a cop, think "the case" and remain detached.

Matt rolled his eyes and sighed aloud. "Well, if you really are a cop, I have a different set of questions. Questions better handled by a cop, who can give me a different perspective on the situation. *We* see things differently than the general public. *We* see things most people don't identify with, subtle hints that might otherwise be missed."

Charlene agreed but didn't say so. Cops *did* see things differently. She still didn't trust the FBI. It had something to do with being a cop. But this guy was unlike any agents she'd ever known. It was the way he handled himself and talked to Charlene, as an equal. Not typical FBI behavior.

She had to make one thing clear. "I know what you're going to ask, and the answer is no. I know that the parents are always the first ones suspected. But there is no way my sister and her husband are involved in Martina's kidnapping, because it was like she was heaven sent."

If he was impressed with her knowledge of how an investigation worked, it didn't show. Stone nodded. "I believe you, and I don't think they're involved either."

He removed a notepad. "Have you noticed anything unusual lately, something that, as a cop, might set off your internal alarm? Or has your sister mentioned anything out of the ordinary?"

"I thought I saw someone on my run the other morning."

"Describe him to me."

She told him as much as she knew, which wasn't much. She couldn't come up with a clear physical description. In fact, she wasn't sure of anything. He sighed and closed the pad in his hand.

She tried another thread. "I'll bet Richard got a good description of the guy who hit him."

"I'm sure he did."

"That should be something to pursue."

She wanted to grab this guy by the collar and scream at him to go find her niece. She took a deep breath, trying to take it down a notch.

He shrugged. "Maybe." Charlene saw doubt in his face when he asked, "Who knew you attended the show tonight?"

She shook her head. "No idea, you would have to ask my sister. But she bought the tickets over the internet months ago, when the show was first announced."

"Huh, he might have credit card statements."

She frowned. "Who?"

The agent didn't answer, just jotted notes down on his pad. Charlene grabbed it from his hands.

He made a face. "Hey!"

Charlene held the pad away from him. "I still don't get how the FBI got here so fast. Usually, the locals get first crack. Then, if things aren't progressing, they call in outside help. This case is ten minutes old."

Charlene had seen her share of frantic parents, and even though her niece had been abducted, and she was anxious for the cops to get the hell out of the house and find her, she realized that it would be of little help if she acted out of emotion. She needed to remain strong for her family.

"Agent Stone."

Charlene turned to see a well-dressed, brown-haired woman with a pointed nose and deep scowl lines around her mouth. She stood at least a head above Charlene and was followed by a group of men in blue police uniforms. A cross look masked her face, and it was clear that there were no introductions forthcoming.

"What do you know?" Her voice was husky for a female, but low so that the conversation was only between them.

Softly, Stone said, "I just got here myself, Chief."

"Well, you seem to be faster and smarter than the rest of us, so why don't you enlighten us?"

Charlene was startled, taken back. She had never heard local law enforcement talk to a Fed that way. It was as if this female chief of police was trying to make him look like a fool in front of her men. Even though the scene was beyond unprofessional, Charlene thought she might actually like her.

"We're working together, Chief."

"Ha. That's a good one. Who is this?" She finally acknowledged Charlene.

"This is an LAPD detective."

"LA? Great. Why don't we invite half the country into our cases? They might as well be investigated by all fifty states."

Charlene had witnessed enough on-site confrontations between cops, but at least this one had a limited audience.

"Cases?" Charlene was confused, but the chief had already turned and walked away, shaking her head.

Charlene looked back at Stone. "Did she say cases? As in more than one? Multiple?"

The Fed sighed audibly and shook his head. "Go be with your sister. She needs you now more than ever. As per FBI standard operating procedure, before long we'll send over our FBI counselors for your sister and brother-in-law."

"What about setting up recording and tracking devices for when the ransom call comes in?"

But he had already turned and walked away, leaving Charlene to wonder. She hugged herself through a shiver, even though it wasn't cold, and felt the goosebumps on her bare arms. But he was right about one thing: Jane needed her tonight.

Tomorrow, however, was another story.

Book II

An Unlikely Ally

Chapter 11

She hadn't slept at all last night. She'd stayed up until well after midnight, sitting downstairs with Jane until her sister had fallen asleep on the living room couch. After covering her with a blanket, she was a ball of energy and nerves. So, to pass the time: she went for a jog, looked through pictures of Martina, and constantly glanced at the clock until she thought it was finally time to head into the city.

She had decided, from that point on, that she would be all over that department, making sure the police/feds did whatever it took to find Martina.

It was barely six a.m. when she strode into the CBI Denver office building and approached a woman clerk in a grey pantsuit, wearing a slimline headset and typing on a keyboard.

Charlene got right to the point. "I'm here to see Agent Stone."

"Do you have an appointment?"

"Tell him the LAPD detective is here."

The receptionist pressed a button and turned away as she spoke into the mouthpiece.

"He'll be right with you."

Charlene was impressed. She hadn't expected Stone to be in so early. Maybe he did take his job seriously. He kept the same long, horrible hours she did.

"Sign in here and go ahead through that door." The woman pointed to a single oak door behind the reception area.

Charlene rounded the reception booth and was buzzed inside, where a security guard had her walk through a scanner and metal detector.

Then she saw Stone crossing the lobby floor toward her carrying a Styrofoam cup, no doubt filled with the requisite steaming coffee. All cop-types drank it by the gallon.

He was well dressed, as most Feds were. His black hair was still wet from a morning shower. His eyes looked tired, with dark shadows beneath them.

During the car ride in, Charlene told herself that she would not let anything distract her from the job. Finding Martina was her number-one priority.

Stone looked young and couldn't have been long out of the academy at Quantico. His distinctly masculine voice was authoritative and commanding. Physically, he was in good shape, but she still didn't know how well he did his job.

"Detective Taylor."

He extended his hand and she shook it. He had a firm, confident handshake. How did he know her name? She didn't remember giving it to him at the house.

"Agent Stone."

"The Denver division has graciously set up a small office in the back just to accommodate our investigation."

He spoke as he walked, and she shadowed him step for step across a waxed marble floor with a large FBI logo in the center. There weren't many people in the office this early, but those present already hustled around busily.

They entered a decent-sized office, and Stone shut the door. "Please, have a seat."

He motioned toward a chair that didn't match the other two in the room, and Charlene assumed it had been borrowed from another office in this last-minute work-space arrangement.

"I don't have time to sit down. We need to get out there and find Martina." She hadn't planned to say that, but it just came out of her mouth.

"Where do you want to start?" His tone was sarcastic, and she knew, as a cop, what he meant. Then he sighed. "Easy, Detective. We have people—lots of people, qualified people who know the case—out there canvassing, following leads, tracking contacts, and doing everything they can to find your niece. Please, sit down."

She did.

He shuffled papers on his desk. "Would you like a coffee?"

"No."

He hesitated slightly. "Why didn't you tell me you were Charlene Taylor?"

She was sure her face registered surprise because Stone's words had caught her off guard. "What do you mean?"

"You're the one who brought down the Celebrity Slayer."

Charlene had never thought of it like that. To her, it was all about self-preservation, doing the right thing, maybe for the wrong reasons. She was taken aback to realize that the incident had brought her fame or celebrity status of any kind. But that's because she never stopped to think about how it looked in the eyes of colleagues and law enforcement across America.

He nodded. "Some of my colleagues who assisted your department in that case had good things to say about you."

Charlene remembered the Feds inviting her into their meetings, against her boss's wishes, because of her special connection to the killer. She had helped them narrow their search, even though they had already flown back when she took down Darren Brady, the real Celebrity Slayer.

"So you've been checking up on me." She wasn't sure whether to feel angry or honored. Did it mean that her request to be involved was being taken seriously?

Stone's face reddened slightly. He put up his hands. "Guilty. After I left your sister's house last night, I made calls and did internet searches." He held up a folder with her name on it.

She tried to look confident. What exactly was in her file? Anything from Dr. Gardner, her psych evaluation, maybe the mention of the disciplinary actions against her, emotional issues or problems with authority figures?

"So," she said, trying to remain calm and at least put on a façade of being in control. She leaned back in her chair and crossed one leg over the other. "What did you learn?"

"Charlene Taylor, born in Los Angeles. Twenty-eight years old. The younger of two daughters. Father, Martin Taylor, retired LAPD detective killed in the line of duty. Assigned to West LA out of the academy." He looked up at Charlene. "Tough beat."

Charlene nodded.

He read on. "Scored off the charts on the detective exam. Five years on the streets as an LAPD officer, trained hostage negotiator, shooting accuracy above par. Youngest woman to ever make detective with the LAPD-RH Division. Received high accolades from the department on her first homicide case, as well as the Celebrity Slayer case."

If that was all he knew, then she was satisfied, but she didn't want to hear any more. Enough chitchat. "What about this case?"

He hesitated, thinking about his answer. Then he spoke deliberately, almost calculating every word. "I was on vacation, like you, when the first kidnapping occurred. I've been following the case ever since."

"The first kidnapping?" She hadn't heard anything in the media about a kidnapping.

"This is part of an ongoing investigation, and that is all I'm at liberty to say at this time."

"Sounds like a real bureaucratic asshole thing to say." She moved her chair closer to his desk, smelling his musky cologne. "I'm a part of this."

If this was LA and an outsider demanded to work the case, she knew what the answer would be. In reality, there were a number of reasons she shouldn't be allowed anywhere near this investigation—not local, closely connected to the victim, FBI didn't like cops—but she had to stand firm.

His head jerked back in surprise. "What? Whoa, I'm doing this as a professional courtesy to a fellow law enforcement agent. I didn't say anything about—"

She stood up. "My niece it out there. I'm working this case, with or without you."

His arms came up in a defensive posture. "I need to run it by my superiors."

"I'm sure they're here, so go for it."

"Now?"

She leered. "No time like the present."

She didn't trust the FBI. Not until they proved they could be trusted. It didn't matter if the agent got the go-ahead from his superiors or not, she was on this case.

He looked doubtful. "Excuse me."

She didn't care about the response, even if he came back and denied her access. She'd already started to think of other angles. She'd develop a nonworking relationship with the agent, staying on the fringes of the official investigation, and find a source. If not Stone, then someone else on the inside to feed her information. She wasn't planning to keep Stone for a partner anyway; she just needed to know what he had.

When he left, she looked out into the lobby but didn't see Stone or anyone else watching her. She got up and walked around behind his desk, where a file lay on top.

The desk was polished to a shine with items neatly placed on top. Even Stone's handwriting was legible. Nothing hung on the walls, and only a tiny desk, chair and nondescript furniture occupied the area.

She pulled her file to the side and opened it, breathing in deeply. Her life story, printed out and placed in this folder. When she closed it, she saw her captain's phone number written in marker on the outside cover.

A photo of Martin Taylor—the sharp nose, inquisitive blue eyes—reminded her of how much she resembled her father.

A psychiatric evaluation lay hidden underneath the folder. Was this Dr. Gardner's assessment of her mental stability? Charlene was about to open it, when voices approached the office. She went back to her seat just as the door opened and Stone stepped inside, alone.

"My superiors are reluctant."

She wasn't surprised. "Why? What did my captain say to you?"

"How do you know I spoke with your captain?"

"His name and number are on that folder."

"Have you been snooping around my desk?"

"I believe I have the right, since you're snooping around my life."

"I need to know if you can be trusted. This is a sensitive case."

"What did my captain say?" She was worried that the captain might've made things more difficult for her.

"Okay, Detective, you really want to know? To be honest, Captain Dunbar has forbidden you to work this case. By no means are you allowed on this investigation. You have been given leave to support your sister, but that's it. Period."

Her face felt hot. "Why haven't the kidnappers been in contact? Why hasn't there been a ransom demand? Jane and Richard have money, but not that kind of money. Is there something more to this? Is this a personal vendetta?"

Stone blew air from his cheeks, stood, and looked at his watch. "I have a debriefing."

She stood. "I'm coming, too."

Stone stopped and turned around. "I don't think that's a good idea." He turned and left.

She ran to catch up then followed him to the back of the building and stood outside the conference room door. He stopped and turned toward her.

"Detective, you're not permitted past this point."

Over Stone's right shoulder, she noticed a large white man in a black suit standing at the far end of the hallway outside a door, his hands clasped behind his back. He was built like an NFL linebacker and stood statue still. She had seen the man somewhere before but couldn't place him.

She turned back to Stone. "The hell I'm not. I'm not leaving." She stomped a foot on the floor, as if to make a point.

He sighed audibly. "Look, I feel for you. Your niece is missing, I'm sympathetic, but I can't trust an outsider with the details of this case, especially someone so close to the inside. There's too much at stake. The Feds aren't under obligation to open an investigation to a cop."

Even though she didn't like it, she understood. It was her position. Not just as a cop but as a family member. When a case got personal, there was a thin, fragile line between being a cop first and a family member second.

"You have no idea who I am. What—you read a couple of lines in a file, so you know me?"

Stone turned away from her.

She couldn't let it go. "Then tell me what I can do—how can I help?"

They must have created a commotion because the door to the conference room opened behind Stone, and an older gentleman stepped out.

"Agent Stone, what is going on?" the man whispered. "Is this the 'loose cannon'?"

Charlene stuck out her hand. "Detective Loose Cannon, LAPD."

The man didn't smile. "Why is she here, Agent Stone?"

"She won't leave." Stone looked embarrassed, and sounded like a whiny kid.

"My niece was kidnapped last night. I'm a cop, and I can give you another set of trained eyes and ears. I have inside information on the victim. I've worked with the FBI before, and you probably know how that case ended."

The senior agent seemed to be entertaining the possibility.

Stone argued, "You know these task force meetings are confidential and closed to outsiders. You would be breaching protocol by bringing in someone from outside."

"Don't undermine my authority." The man's voice was harsh, rebuking.

Charlene stepped between them. "I can help this investigation. I'm good at my job."

Stone swiftly moved in front of Charlene. "I spoke with Detective Taylor's boss, and he doesn't think it's a good idea. From her file I see that she's in therapy. Do I have to list the reasons this woman shouldn't be here? One, she's a cop—out of her jurisdiction, two, she's closely connected to one of the victims. Three—"

The head agent stopped Stone with a halt of his hand. "As I see it, that's only motivation."

The older agent looked at Charlene, an expression of doubt mixed with feelings of anxiety written on his wrinkled face. "Will this be a problem, your niece being one of the victims? Will it cloud your judgement?"

"I can handle it. I'll stake my reputation on it."

"That's exactly what you're doing." He looked at her and then at Stone. "I'm Senior Agent Smith. You'll be paired together, working directly with Agent Stone, Detective. Now that this playground feud is done, can we proceed? I believe you have a profile for us, Agent Stone."

Stone nodded as the agent reentered the conference room.

They were just outside the door when Stone grimaced at Charlene. "Detective, you might not be prepared for what you're about to hear. I'm meeting this morning with other agents involved in this case, as well as the local Colorado police. I'm presenting a profile on the kidnappers. All of your questions will be answered in this room."

Emotion surged in her throat and her mouth went dry so she bit down on her lip. This was now real.

They stepped inside and the door closed behind them.

Charlene inspected the long mahogany conference table. Thirteen chairs were pulled up to the table, and in front of each chair, on the table, lay the usual assortment of materials needed for a law enforcement conference—pens, pencils, yellow notepads, case binders, empty water glasses, and Styrofoam coffee cups. Two jugs of ice water and two pots of coffee were situated in the middle.

She expected a crowd but nothing like this. This case had turned into a joint FBI-Denver Police investigation and it looked like all the players were in attendance.

After placing herself at the end of the table beside Stone, the briefing came to order. Charlene picked up a paper-clipped sheaf of papers from her place with the word *confidential* along with the bureau's seal stamped at the top. The covert nature of this meeting put her on edge.

Agent Smith stood. "You know Agent Stone. I'd like you all to meet Detective Charlene Taylor, LAPD. Detective Taylor has been brought in to consult. She'll be working with Agent Stone."

Charlene looked at Stone, but he didn't look at her. His face was red, unsmiling. She still hadn't dared to meet the gazes of those sitting around the table.

"We'll go around the room and introduce ourselves so that Detective Taylor can familiarize herself with us. Also, I see a few faces I don't recognize, so this will help us all."

Charlene finally looked up and scoped the table. The man on Stone's immediate left spoke first, and they went around the table.

"Bradley Jamison, lead detective, Denver Police Department."

"John Paulson, division chief, Criminal Investigation Division, Denver Police Department."

"Noreen Walters, media representative, FBI."

"Mark Murphy, coordinator, Crimes against Children Division, FBI."

"James Murdoch, deputy director, FBI."

"Special Agent Nicholas Smith, FBI."

"Janice Salinger, chief of police, Denver Police Department."

Charlene remembered her from Jane's house, where she'd confronted Stone in front of her men. She didn't seem happier now, surrounded by outsiders, and she wondered if a permanent scowl resided on what was a rather pretty face.

"Mark Easton, special agent in charge, Denver division, FBI."

"Special Agent Sam Cahill, Denver division, FBI."

"US Senator Jaqueline Bloomfield, the state of New Mexico."

Charlene froze. The senator had been hidden behind an individual to Charlene's immediate right, so she hadn't noticed her when she'd come in. Now, it felt like a dream being this close to a woman she looked up to, respected, and admired.

She wore an expensive-looking dark-colored pantsuit. In person, Bloomfield appeared younger than her forty-two years. Her skin was well tanned, a hint of makeup brought out the fine qualities of her face, and she wore her light-brown hair short, in a professional business cut. She wore no jewelry except for a wedding band.

The young senator, in only her first term, had already launched various bills and initiatives, from women's rights, to salary equality, to family well-being. She fought for women in America and paved the way for the younger generation, like Charlene, to be confident and follow their dreams.

"Randall Tinsley, profiler, Denver Police Department."

Charlene leaned forward and whispered in Stone's ear. "What's the senator doing here?"

Stone turned toward Charlene and whispered back, "She was a state senator when the kidnappings occurred in New Mexico, and very involved in trying to bring those children back. We brought her in thinking she could add insight."

"Agent Stone." Smith's voice turned both Charlene and Stone in their chairs. "I believe we're ready for you."

Stone nodded and stood. "I was asked to begin this morning's meeting with our profile of the kidnapper. I've been to every crime scene, studied the crime reports, read witness statements, and Randall and I have worked hard to come up with answers. I'll read what we've created, and I ask that you save all your questions until the end."

Charlene focused on Stone in action. Even though he looked young, she wondered about his age. He spoke with a controlled, confident voice, as if he'd led these meeting many times before, which he very well could have.

It must have been nerve-racking, at Stone's age, standing calmly in front of some of the most powerful security people in the country, knowing that each investigation depended on what he decided—they'd be following his leads. Did he feel the weight of each investigation on his shoulders? He didn't look to be one bit frazzled.

Stone opened the folder on the table in front of him and picked up the top sheet. "It will come as a surprise to most of you that I feel there is more than one kidnapper involved in this case."

Shocked expressions registered around the table. So these big-shots *could* be shaken.

Stone continued. "There's no way to determine the number of people involved, but it's definitely more than one and less than four. There's no way one person could be conducting all of this surveillance and planning by himself. It has to be a team. My guess is two. One of the two is the 'mastermind,' calling the shots. I think this is a woman."

This sudden statement brought murmurs from around the table. But Stone didn't let it slow the roll he was on.

"I say it's a woman because someone needs to be caring for these babies. What we're looking for in this UNSUB is a white female between the age of thirty and forty-five, intelligent, resourceful, patient, confident, and controlling. Probably has a high-profile job as a boss or team leader."

He let that sink in, allowing the note-takers time to finish, before going on.

"We're also looking for a white male, between the ages of thirty and forty-five. He's doing the dirty work. He's intelligent and patient. He's also weak-minded, because he's being manipulated by the leader. Look for an emotionally immature male, someone who's been in therapy, has low self-esteem, wasn't loved as a child, and is looking for acceptance. He isn't a killer but *will* do whatever it takes or whatever his partner tells him to do. Neither UNSUB has children of their own and they're probably incapable of conceiving children. They're not local, but they've been in the Denver area long enough to conduct surveillance.

"The man is good with people and has probably had a job working with the public. He's either out of work or has a shiftwork job—probably lives alone. He's a people person one on one, but in a large group, he'd seem more a social outcast. He is also good with disguises. The UNSUB drives a white unmarked van, which could be a second vehicle, so he does have a registered license." Stone hesitated, then continued. "The kidnappers are becoming increasingly more confident. The first baby was taken from a wooded park, and now the kidnappers are going right into homes. The level of trust these two kidnappers have in each other indicates they've known each other for a long time. They could be related, but this seems more like a romantic situation than a family one. They've had a recent stressor in their lives—something that triggered them before the first kidnapping occurred. In a related case, six years ago, seven babies went missing. So far, here in Denver, we're looking at a total of five. I believe we only have two more shots to catch these kidnappers. Once they get that seventh baby, they will once again disappear. I don't know why seven, but from the pattern, this is what I've surmised."

Charlene bit the inside of her cheek. *Five kidnappings. Plus seven, from six years ago.* It was a lot to take in.

"At this point, since we have one dominant and one weak link, I feel that our best bet is to separate them. We need to focus our attention on the man," he added, concluding his spiel.

Stone sat, finally lifting his head for the first time and gazing around the table. Charlene wondered what he saw. Was this the usual reaction to his profile?

People quietly shuffled papers, some took notes, others looked troubled, while others whispered among themselves. For a room such as this, their odd behavior revealed the impact this case had on everyone.

Agent Smith broke the silence. "What about a motive, Agent Stone?"

Stone shook his head. "I still haven't come up with that yet. There have been no ransom demands, no bodies recovered, and no signs of evidence or a trail to follow."

Noreen Walters broke in. "Should we release the profile to the media?"

The deputy director looked at Stone. "What do you think? It's your call."

"I'm sure many of you are aware, that in many of the cases I've worked, I suggested releasing the info to the press. In those situations, I felt that if the public knew the facts, somebody would step forward to ID someone that fit the profile. But for now, I suggest we withhold the profile. With the UNSUBs we're dealing with in this case, I don't want to tip my hand and give the kidnappers an advantage. I don't want to scare them off and lose these children."

A tense silence engulfed the space in the room. Then, Special AIC Mark Easton spoke up. "What about the parents? Statistics indicate they could be involved."

"In each case, the parents have been investigated. Alibis were checked and phone records analyzed for inconsistencies. Everything checked out. Just like six years ago, this is *not* an inside job. The parents are clean. That arm of the search has been exhausted. It's definite—we don't need another Ramsey on our hands."

Even though Charlene wasn't a Fed, she knew what Agent Stone meant. Every person who entered into law enforcement was introduced to that case.

He was referring to a 1996 case that hit close to home in Colorado—the murder of six-year-old JonBenet Ramsey. The investigation had been botched because the Boulder Police, satisfied that Ramsey's parents were the perpetrators, dropped the investigation, focusing their case entirely on the family and losing the real murderer in the process.

Charlene leaned back, biting her lip, the impact of the situation hitting her violently. She had sat and listened as Stone gave his profile of the kidnappers; now she mentally sorted through the facts of the case. Her fingers trembled as she turned the pages in her folder.

She remembered following those kidnappings six years ago in New Mexico. She'd tracked the investigation on CNN. Now Martina was potentially part of the same case. A nightmare.

She knew when walking into this room twenty minutes ago, seeing all the suits around the table, that this was more than just a simple kidnapping case. But she never imagined this.

She looked around the room, her gaze falling on the members of the committee seated at the table—a twelve-man committee: seven members from the FBI, four from the Denver Police Department, a senator, and Charlene herself—the lone wolf outcast. She was in it knee-deep now, with no turning back.

Of all those seated at the table, Special Agent Nicholas Smith appeared the most strung out. Charlene wondered if the agent had a special interest in the case, since he seemed the most anxious.

Then there was Stone—sitting in his seat, erect but relaxed, as if he'd done this a million times. When he spoke, people listened. He knew his job, and the men around the conference table respected his judgement. He took the lead when necessary, liked to be in control, and took his job seriously.

As the agents around the table discussed the cases, Charlene's gaze shifted from the table, to the wall behind them, the nucleus of the investigation. The walls were covered with newborn photos, maps, and crime scene photos. Charts had been drawn with marker writings, and card tables were set up with stacks of files piled on top. It looked as if the unit had formed a geographical profile of the kidnappers.

Two coffee machines were plugged into the wall, and a computer was turned on in the corner of the room. The conference room had been turned into a 24/7 investigation hub. Phone lines and computer terminals seemed to have been added as an afterthought.

These people—some of the brightest law enforcement officials in the country—had been working around the clock to catch these kidnappers, but so far, they had nothing to show for their efforts. Thus far, the kidnappers had covered their tracks and left nothing for the police to go on.

Charlene was abruptly snapped out of her fog by the authoritative voice of Deputy Director James Murdock. "Thank you, Agent Stone. You and your partner are dismissed."

"But—"

"But nothing. Your job was to give us a profile of the UNSUB, *assist* in focusing our investigation, and suggest proactive techniques to catch the perps. It's our job to do the rest."

The DD didn't speak down to the agent, but Charlene could perceive the hurt expression on Stone's face. His boss had delivered the order, and Stone knew enough, after the harsh reprimand, not to argue.

Charlene rose from her seat at the same time as Stone, nodded a good-bye to everyone at the table, and followed the agent out of the room.

He didn't say anything outside, appearing embarrassed. Charlene followed him to the office and stood outside the doorway. When Stone noticed, he waved her inside.

He seemed to have gotten over his tongue-lashing. "Don't worry, we're not done yet."

Stone shrugged off his suit jacket and slung it over the back of his chair. He opened a desk drawer and pulled out a stack of folders banded together with a thick rubber band, then threw them on top of his desk.

"Want a coffee? We have a lot of reading to do, and lots of reports to go over this morning. I want to get you acquainted with the case as quickly as possible. If the guys in there won't let us hear their theories"—he jerked his thumb toward the boardroom—"then we'll come up with some and generate our own momentum."

"So, you've changed your mind. You want to work with me now?" She wasn't convinced.

"I wouldn't say that, but you're all I've got."

"Lucky me."

"Take it or leave it."

"I'll take it." She leaned forward in her seat and rummaged through the files. "Why did they kick us out?"

He shrugged. "Life of a profiler. Like the DD said, we only *assist*. It's the locals who do the rest—make the arrest, conduct the interviews, etc. If they catch the kidnappers, I'll help the prosecution formulate a strategy for the trial, but mostly I'm an innocent bystander. It can be frustrating, but I love what I do. I've worked almost a hundred cases this year alone, all over the country, but when children are involved, it strikes a nerve with me."

She sighed aloud as she looked at the enormous stack of files. "You'd better get that coffee. Black."

When he left the room, she grabbed the stack and removed the rubber band. She opened the file on top and began reading through the bundle of loose papers inside. The first Denver baby, a female, had been taken in a park.

When Stone returned, Charlene closed the file and placed it on her lap. She accepted the steaming Styrofoam cup, thanked the agent, and sipped gingerly. The coffee was a far cry from a Starbucks latte, but the combination of heat and caffeine did its job. Last night's lack of sleep caught up with her during the meeting, but now, with work to do, something to follow up on, she felt her adrenaline kick into overdrive.

She waited for Stone to sit. "How do you come up with these profiles?"

He sat back in his chair, crossed his legs, and sipped the coffee. "First, I'm not a psychic. A lot of people think I am, but, believe me, I'm not. If I was, I'd be betting on the Super Bowl." He grinned. "A profile is a hypothesis, an educated theory. I've been taught by the best of the best."

"That's another thing. Why is every profile basically the same? White male, between the age of twenty-five and forty-five, medium height, medium weight, wasn't loved enough as a child, or loved too much, a loner, etcetera."

Stone chuckled, the first time she had heard him laugh. It was nice. "Maybe you should've been a profiler."

She wasn't sure whether that was a compliment or an insult.

"That *is* the basic criminal. But, trust me, profiles do change. A lot of it depends on the victim. For instance: a sexually-motivated killer always kills within his own race. It all comes with experience."

Charlene squinted at him.

He nodded. "I know, I know. I don't look old enough to have *experience*. I hear that a lot. But you'd be amazed how many cases I've consulted on. I've seen enough cases that I have a pattern in my mind of what type of person commits a certain crime before I even get to the case scene or receive the file. I collect all the evidence—photos, statements, reports, descriptions, autopsies—and then I try to get inside the head of both the criminal and the victim. I try to re-create the crime scene. But the short answer: it's what I've been trained to do."

"Tell me about New Mexico."

He closed his eyes. "I remember the case, see it in my mind as if it were yesterday. I wasn't assigned to that case, but I followed it every step of the way. Seven children, all infants, vanished into thin air in Albuquerque. To this day, none of those children have been recovered."

"No one knows anything?"

Matt opened his eyes and shook his head. "The BAU East/West working directly with CASMIRC was unable to come up with anything. My colleagues all felt helpless, like they'd let the families down. And I'm getting that same feeling all over again."

She shook her head. "This time will be different."

Stone's lips twisted. "I applaud your optimistic attitude."

They started reading the new cases first, since they were fresh, and Charlene had insisted on having Martina's file to herself. They each took half of the files and began thumbing through the enormous number of notes. When they'd finished their respective stacks, they traded folders and started all over again.

After a couple of hours of reading, her eyes burned. She was stretching her neck muscles, feeling the tightness in her back, when there was a rap on the glass office window.

They both looked up to see Senator Jaqueline Bloomfield standing outside Stone's office, looking in and smiling apologetically. She pointed at the doorknob, motioning for one of them to unlock it.

Stone scooted from his seat and stepped to the door. "Good morning, Senator."

The senator flashed a smile, one that Charlene was sure she'd practiced many times before. "Good morning." She looked at Charlene, who nodded in return.

Charlene was ready to stand, but the senator signaled for her to remain seated. She stepped inside and Matt shut the door behind her, after taking a look in the hallway.

The same dark-suited bodyguard she'd seen earlier stood just outside the office. That's why Charlene had recognized him—from the television news coverage she'd seen at Jane's house.

The senator spoke before Stone had returned to his seat. "I just wanted to thank you, Agent Stone, for your profile this morning."

"You're welcome, Senator. Just doing my job."

Charlene glanced back and forth from Stone to Bloomfield. She was impressed at how the agent didn't seem out of his league interacting with a prestigious senator.

"It's nice to have you working this case. The prodigal son returns home."

Stone raised his hands as if conceding. "I'm not exactly welcomed in these parts anymore."

Charlene wondered what the agent meant by that. From what she'd seen this morning, he was well-respected throughout the bureau, and, except for the chief of police who seemed to hold a grudge against everyone, he was well-received by the officers and staff of the DPD.

The senator nodded. "The Denver chief of police doesn't think too highly of the FBI—that's obvious. But with your resources and reach, you'll be a valuable asset."

Matt asked, "What can you tell us about the original case? How closely related is this one?"

"Almost identical." She remained stone-faced. "It's scary how this is happening all over again. A nightmare for my state, and now the people of Denver are going through the same thing."

Stone drained the rest of his now-cold coffee. "Is there anything you can add to our investigation?"

Bloomfield shook her head, looking dejected. "You guys have all of the case notes, all of the information. From what I heard in that room, there isn't much more to add."

He pursed his lips and nodded.

The senator backtracked, heading toward the door. She opened it, but turned back around. "If there's anything I can do, or any help I can give, please don't hesitate to ask. I'm sure I can get you access to anything you need to help move this case along."

Even though this wasn't New Mexico, Charlene knew that Bloomfield had a lot of clout in this part of the country. Her contacts could get them whatever they needed in terms of resources—human or otherwise.

"Thank you." Stone shook the senator's hand.

"I wish I could stay longer, but unfortunately I'm pressed for time."

"Busy schedule?"

She huffed. "My senior aide just texted my upcoming schedule. Being a politician with the US Senate means you're always on call, ready to vote, comment, or challenge Congress. I have six different offices to operate, five in New Mexico and one in Washington."

Stone smiled. "But it's all part of a greater plan, right?"

The senator winked. "Well, 1600 Pennsylvania Avenue is still miles away. But even I have to admit that my six-year term as senator has been a whirlwind so far. I'm up for reelection in a year and need to start campaigning come January."

Charlene stood and also shook the senator's hand.

"Nice meeting you, Detective Taylor. I've heard about you and your short but unforgettable career." She flashed two thumbs. "Already making a name for yourself with all of those men. Women need to take charge and not let anything get in the way of their dreams."

Charlene shivered with excitement. The senator actually knew who she was? "Thank you, Senator. And just let me say what an honor it is to meet you. I think I can speak for every woman in this country when I say: keep doing what you're doing."

"Thank you. It means a lot coming from another working woman trying to survive. I'm speaking at Colorado State University in a couple of days."

"Yes, I know."

The senator turned around and looked out into the hallway. "Morris?"

The tall, bulky head of security slipped his hand into his inside jacket pocket and pulled out two tickets. He gave them to the senator, who in turn handed them over to Charlene.

"Wait around after my speech, and we can talk more."

Charlene took the tickets. "Thank you so much, Senator Bloomfield, but I won't be able to make it this time. A lot going on."

"Yes, of course. I understand. And please, call me Jaqueline."

As the senator turned to leave, a cell phone rang. The security guard pulled a phone from his pocket and checked caller ID. He looked at the senator. "It's Ms. Lee, Senator."

Bloomfield nodded.

"Hello." Morris's deep, husky voice answered the call. He listened, a look of intent on his square face, then held out the receiver. "She wants to read the daily schedule to you."

"Tell her I'll be late for my next meeting. I'll give her time to deal with lobbyists and the media."

Morris nodded and relayed the message into the phone. Then he hung up.

With that, she waved, slid on a pair of designer sunglasses, spun on her heels, and walked briskly away. Morris followed.

Stone walked the senator to the exit. The clicking of stilettos on the hardwood floor drew Charlene's attention away in the opposite direction. She turned to see Police Chief Janice Salinger coming toward her. The chief nodded curtly at Charlene and passed the office, heading toward Stone.

A part of Charlene wanted to yell out, to warn Agent Stone, but another part wanted to watch this confrontation, to gauge the depth of Salinger's hatred for Stone and the FBI.

Salinger stood so close to Stone that when he turned around, he swung headfirst into the chief. For a moment Stone looked startled, but seeing the chief, it was as if he expected it.

Charlene stepped out into the hallway, closer to the two law officials as they stood eye to eye, so she could hear their words.

"Chief Salinger, what can I do for you?"

"What are you holding back? What was that about?"

Stone looked back at the senator as she left the building, then turned around. "The senator stopped by my office to talk about the case and offer her help."

"What did you tell her?"

"Do you think I've found something new since I left the same meeting you just attended?"

"Don't mess with me, Matt. If you know something, tell me. This is my career, my life, my future. Or do you not care about that anymore? At one time, you did."

Stone peered over Salinger's shoulder and looked at Charlene. His face was slightly flushed. "This is not the time or place, Janice."

"I want this case."

"I know you do. So do I."

He brushed past her and headed toward Charlene. The chief of police still stood there, staring at Stone's back, fists clenched.

Charlene wondered about Salinger's story.

"Let's get back to work." He half-nodded to Charlene.

"What's with her?" Charlene gestured at Salinger, who still stood in the hallway, breathing fire.

Stone looked back and whispered, "Let her cool off. It will blow over."

"You seem to know her well."

"Yeah, too well."

Chapter 12

By four o'clock, Charlene was exhausted. She'd run on coffee and adrenaline for a while, after speaking with the senator and hearing her words of encouragement. Although she didn't need any extra motivation to find her niece.

Her eyes stung. No wonder she was tired. Her brain had been working on overdrive, and she'd been breathing in the stuffy office air all afternoon. After a quick lunch of sandwiches, they'd returned to the office, where Stone had photocopied everything and they continued with their reading. She hadn't slept the previous night, and for the last eight hours, they had sequestered themselves in Stone's tiny office, studying, reading, and examining every minute detail of the case.

"What about my sister's neighbors? You must have door-to-doored them. Did anyone see or hear anything?" She heard the desperation in her voice.

Stone shook his head. "Most people, especially in a neighborhood like your sister's, tend to keep to themselves. They live outside the city for privacy. It can be a good thing, but when something like this happens, it's definitely a disadvantage."

Charlene would do whatever it took to get her niece back, but right now, she wasn't doing anyone any good running on fumes.

"I need a break."

Stone let out his breath and nodded. "I'm drained too." He checked his watch. "Go home and spend time with your family. Your sister could use you right now. I don't have to tell you that everything you heard and read today remains confidential, even if she is your sister."

Charlene nodded. She knew the routine.

"The longer this drags out, the more likely it is to lose momentum and give the UNSUBs an advantage. Let's reconvene tonight," Stone said.

She swept the bangs out of her eyes. "I don't think it's a good idea to work around here. But I do want to go over all the paperwork before I head out to talk with witnesses and check out crime scenes."

"Do you mind working at my brother's apartment? It's not exactly a precinct but it's quiet, and I'll have all the files with me."

"That works."

Charlene waited for the cab to drive away, then crossed the street and buzzed outside the door, on the slot for apartment 3B.

"Yeah?" She recognized Agent Stone's voice.

"It's me—Taylor."

Stone buzzed her into the building, where she took the stairs to the third floor and followed the hall to 3B. She stopped in front of the door, taking a moment to fix her windblown hair.

She knocked and tried to control her breathing, hearing the light rhythm of classical rock music beating from the other side of the door.

Stone's voice came from inside the apartment. "Come in."

Feeling uncomfortable, she opened the door and stepped inside. "Hello? Agent Stone?"

"I'll just be a second," his voice echoed from a back room.

She removed her shoes and followed the short hall into the apartment, a typical bachelor pad—one bedroom, one bathroom, a tiny kitchen, and a larger living room. It was much like her own back in LA, but this one lacked furniture and a feminine touch and had an odor—a combination of musky cologne and stale beer.

She smirked at the living room: a secondhand sofa in need of reupholstering, a beanbag chair, a stained coffee table with a collection of cigarette burns—and of course the thousand-dollar sound system, completed with a fifty-inch plasma TV, with surround sound and multiple gaming units attached.

She sank onto the sofa and looked around, when he appeared looking freshly showered, and clean-shaven. At their first meeting, she hadn't noticed his solid, disciplined build.

There was no mistaking it; those pecs and abs had done their time with weights. He wore a faded pair of blue jeans and a beige V-neck short-sleeved T-shirt, and his hair was dripping wet.

"I'm sorry about the mess." He scooted to Charlene's side of the couch and dug a pair of dirty socks from between the cushions. Then he was off again, picking things up. "Sorry, I just got home a short time ago and haven't had time to clean up. My brother has yet to grow past dorm living." His facial expression turned serious. "How's your sister?"

She swallowed. "She's a mess and I'm worried about her."

Stone let out a breath but said nothing. "The files are on the table."

He led her into a small eating area connected to the tiny kitchen, where a stack of boxes was piled on the counter. He heaved the first box off the top and dropped it on the tabletop with a thud.

He removed the lid and pulled out a thick brown folder she didn't recognize. When he handed over the file, his fingers lingered against Charlene's skin longer than necessary. She wasn't sure if it had been on purpose or not.

She took the folder, feeling a rush of warmth in her cheeks. She turned away so he wouldn't see. She opened the folder, spreading it across the remaining space on the tabletop.

Stone also sat and organized the information. He was so close to her that Charlene could smell his aftershave. She found herself physically drawn to him, and it made her susceptible—vulnerable—something that rarely happened, because she was usually the one in control.

Trying to regain her composure, she doggedly read through the notes, ignoring the man beside her.

"Wait," Stone said.

She looked up into his penetrating stare. "What?"

"Before we go any further, I think we should lay all our cards on the table."

Her breathing quickened and her pulse raced. "What do you mean?"

"Come on, Detective. You're a cop, I'm a Fed. I know the history. I'm not new to the Bureau, and I've been on enough cases to understand how things work. Cops don't work with Feds and vice versa. The way that locals conduct their business, the procedures, is totally different from the Feds. That's the simple truth. The two teams are out of sync and just get in each other's way."

She shrugged. "I'm not going to lie. That crossed my mind, and to tell you the truth, I'm not interested in a partner. But you have things I need. Do I think that I could have more leeway going out on my own? Hell, yes. But you're wrong about one thing, I'm not a local, and I have a hell of a lot more invested in this case than local cops. So if I for one second think that you're interfering with my investigation or getting in my way, I'll have no problem walking away from you."

He sighed aloud. "And I think that you, as an outsider, can bring a fresh new perspective to the case, and a fresh set of eyes. I wasn't on the case six years ago. I just know what I've read, so I believe your professional opinion can shed new light on the case."

"Well, then, it looks like we both need each other, for now."

"Yes. For now. Let's look over the recent kidnappings. You can check my new notes at the same time."

"Good."

She took the papers. With her lip lodged between her teeth, she read for thirty minutes, making her own notes from his.

She revisited the photos with probing investigative eyes, contrasting and comparing the various crime scenes. She perused the witness reports, the statements from the victims' parents, all with different descriptions of the kidnapper, studying everything with surgical precision.

She was in work mode, but that didn't mean she didn't notice Stone looking at her every now and then.

"Why do you keep looking at me?"

He half-grinned, the side of his lips curling. "You remind me of me, when I first started with the Bureau. I hope I haven't lost the fire that I see in you. You love being a cop, don't you?"

She nodded. "More than anything."

"Okay." He scanned her notepad. "It looks like you made new notes in here."

She could feel Stone dissecting her notes with his eyes. She placed the papers back in the folder and set it on the table, along with her own pad. She was impressed with his scrupulous notes and his ardent attention to detail.

She had an idea. "We need to look at the cases from six years ago. We're treading water right now. The new cases mean nothing unless we tie them to the old ones."

Stone nodded.

She frowned in confusion. "If they are the same kidnappers, give me your theory on where they've been for the last six years."

"I'm not sure. The majority of my cases deal with profiling serial killers, who are a totally different animal. When a serial-killer stops killing, it's usually for one of three reasons. The first is that he's committed suicide. But because the kidnappers have struck again, and the cases are so similar it's highly unlikely these kidnappers are copycats, so I think we can rule that out. Two is that he's left the area and has started killing in another time zone. But I've cross-referenced these crimes in the CASMIRC database with the last six years and have found no matches. And the third reason is that the UNSUB has been picked up and arrested for something else and has been spending time in prison. So, with that in mind, I've already run checks in the databases, going back six years, and checked the New Mexico and Colorado statistics to criminals who have been sent to jail, then released within the last six years. I've come up with no potential subjects who match our descriptions. Of course, he could be incarcerated in another state."

She pursed her lips, and drew in a deep breath, allowing her mind to work. Stone had done his homework, laid the groundwork, and had checked every angle. There was still a lot to do, but it had to be done with haste, here in Colorado. They didn't have the time or resources to trek around the country.

Stone broke her concentration. "Now that you've seen my notes, heard the details, and have formed your own beliefs, I'd love a fresh perspective."

She adjusted her pant legs, smoothing out the creases. She picked up her notepad and opened it. "The first thing we need to do is go to the hospital where all the babies were born. Could that be a coincidence? There are a lot of hospitals in Denver, so why are they all from one place?" She looked up at Matt. "And what about stores and pharmacies in the area? These babies need to be fed and changed. Has there been any splurging, any large quantities of baby supplies purchased in the area?"

"I checked on that, but I think, from what I've seen anyway, that these kidnappers are too clever for that. They would visit numerous sites and purchase only small quantities at a time. They wouldn't get caught over something like that."

She stopped—he had all the bases covered. Then she continued. "We know that the first victim, the starter, in any serial case is always the key—it's more personal. But why Allie Wilson? What makes her special? Why now? How are the kidnappers choosing their victims? Is it random? And why seven babies? Why not six or eight?"

Stone shook his head. "I hate people who quote facts and statistics, but the fact is that only about 15% of victims in serial cases are randomly chosen. There is method here that we aren't seeing."

Charlene could tell that Stone had his own questions about the case that were driving him mad. His face showed signs that he fought with something, holding out on her.

"What is it?" Charlene asked. "What are you keeping from me?"

He hesitated again, as if unsure.

"Agent Stone—"

"Please." He held up his hand. "If we're working together, call me Matt."

"Matt, I need to know everything. You have to trust me for this to work."

He stood up and turned away, then paced the small kitchen, seeming to search for the words.

"What is it?" she demanded again, her voice rising.

"I didn't tell you this before because I didn't think you were ready to hear it." He rejoined her at the table, maintaining eye contact, a solemn expression on his face. "Now I think you should know."

Charlene felt a wave of nausea hit her. Did he know something about Martina? Something about the babies? What could he possibly say that could make her feel worse?

"Because we'd been dismissed from this morning's meeting before the case was actually discussed, you didn't hear Agent Smith's take, which I tend to agree with, even though it's a frightening thought. He's worked this case for six years, and I respect his opinion. You'd better brace yourself for what I'm about to tell you next."

Twenty minutes later, Charlene was jolted back to reality when someone barged into the apartment unannounced and slammed the door. Matt had just finished his spiel, and Charlene felt a cold chill pierce her to the core.

They both grew quiet, as this intruder looked back and forth between her and Matt.

Matt said, "This is my brother, Jake. Jake, this is Charlene Taylor."

It was easy to see the resemblance. They were about the same height and weight, Jake a younger version of Matt, the age difference noticeable. Jake was cute, but not as distinguished-looking as his brother. Jake had a youthful face and probably still got carded at bars. His hair was lighter than Matt's—sandy brown, long but neatly trimmed.

"Everything okay?" Jake asked.

Matt looked at his brother. "I just told her."

"About Smith's theory?"

Matt nodded. "As much as I know about it."

She asked, "Who else knows about this?"

"Just Jake and Agent Cahill."

She exhaled loudly. She was aware, especially working with the LAPD, that the higher the number of people privy to certain facts, the greater the chance of that information getting out to the public.

"I need to go home." When she stood, her legs felt wobbly, so she grabbed the edge of the couch to regain her equilibrium.

Matt frowned. "Are you okay?"

"Fine," she snapped. "Who's taking me home?"

"I will." Matt held out his palm, and Jake handed over the keys.

She left the apartment in a trance, feeling stunned and terrified.

A baby-selling ring. History had revealed many cases of human trafficking and the selling of women for the purpose of sexual slavery, forced labor, or commercial sexual exploitation by trafficker or others. But babies?

Just the thought made Charlene feel sick. If true, and the transaction occurred before they could find the babies, the victims and suspects would be impossible to track.

The first few minutes of the ride back to Jane's house were quiet, as she mentally sorted the information. She felt horrified at the new information, but was motivated to start working the case for real.

"What else do you know about this baby-selling ring?"

Matt hesitated. "Very little. It's Smith who has been tracking and collecting information about it, searching for evidence of it, of black-market baby selling, using our informants to find info on it. We need to talk with him."

"Will he talk to us?"

"I'm not sure."

Charlene thought a moment before speaking. "So what's up with Police Chief Salinger?"

Matt shifted in his seat. "What do you mean?"

"It doesn't take a detective to see that she hates you with a passion and wants you nowhere near this case—or her."

He let out his breath. "Janice and I dated in high school."

"Come on. Are you trying to tell me that the chief of the Denver Police Department is holding a grudge after a breakup with a high school sweetheart from twenty years ago?"

"She's under a lot of stress. She's the first woman in her position, and there are men just waiting for her to fail. She's worked hard to get there and knows it will be even harder to stay there. Plus, I've heard rumors that she has higher goals."

"Like what?"

"The city attorney's office."

"So she hates you because she's stressed? No way, Stone. If you want to work as partners, then you have to be straight with me. No secrets." She stared at him, but he had yet to look her way.

He wiped his brow. "Fine." He hesitated. "We were more than high school lovers."

"Go on."

"When we were seventeen, she got pregnant."

"Yours?"

He nodded.

"And?"

"One month before the due date, complications arose, and she lost the baby."

Charlene's skin prickled, and a hollow feeling settled in the pit of her stomach.

He shook his head. "I was a kid. I didn't know how to react. Then my parents died a few months later, and I took off."

"Where did you go?"

"Drifted for a while, then landed in New York, where I went on to be a cop."

"What happened to Salinger?"

"Not sure—I lost touch with her. But I heard that she had mental health issues, and it had taken her a while to get past them. Once that was behind her, she worked her ass off for her promotion. She used it as motivation, to drive her career goals."

Charlene leaned back in the passenger seat, processing the news, and a somber silence engulfed the car.

"That was cold, what you did."

"I agree, totally. Like I said, a stupid kid. I've apologized to her over and over, told her I would do whatever it took to make it right, but she wants nothing to do with me."

"She never moved on? Had a family of her own?"

"Janice can't have children. I'm not sure all of the details, but something about the way the pregnancy ended. There have been rumors that she is seeing someone, but no one has ever seen or met the boyfriend. She's a very private person. Believe it or not, I only dated her for a short time, so I never met her family. No idea if she has siblings, because she never mentioned them at all."

"Ouch, that's tough."

Now it was Matt's turn to be quiet. They didn't speak another word until they reached Jane's house.

"You don't have to pick me up tomorrow. I'll borrow Jane's car and meet you at the hospital. Cindy Richards' shift starts at eight, and I want to be there when she gets in."

She shut the car door and headed toward the house, hearing Matt pull away and head down the road. She stopped at the doorstep and knelt, then sat on the top step, breathing in the brisk Colorado night air, and exhaling puffs of steam.

She stalled, afraid to go back into that house, especially now, with no new information to report. Could she look her sister in the eye, knowing about a possible baby-selling ring?

Salinger's hatred towards Stone made perfect sense now on a personal level. She'd been through a traumatic event and seemed to still be carrying a lot of baggage and resentment. Did it get in the way of her job?

Charlene pulled out her phone and made a call.

"Hello?"

"Captain?"

"Taylor?" His voice was raspy from smoking. "How are you holding up?"

It was after ten o'clock in Denver, so only nine in LA. "I'm fine, sir."

"Some Fed, an Agent Stone, called me this morning, asking about you."

"He told me."

"So he gave you my opinion?"

Charlene closed her eyes, remembering what Matt had told her. "Yes, sir."

"Taylor, let me say this again. You are in no way allowed to involve yourself in this investigation. Do you understand that?"

"Yes, but there is something you should know." Charlene told her captain about the Feds' theories and her niece's involvement.

He exhaled loudly. Through the phone, the theme music for SportsCenter played on TV in the background.

"Jesus. That changes everything. Okay, you are on leave, and we will explain it as time off to support your sister. You do what you can, Detective."

"Thank you."

"You know how I feel about family. You take all the time you need. If there's anything we can do on our end, just let us know."

"Yes, sir." She hung up and entered the house.

The lights were off and the house was quiet.

She removed her shoes and tiptoed across the front room and into the kitchen, where her mother sat alone at the table, with a mug of hot tea on the table in front of her.

Brenda Taylor hadn't done her hair or applied makeup today, and Charlene couldn't remember seeing her mother without it. She had even more lines on her wrinkled face today, and her eyes were dark-rimmed, tired.

She looked up when Charlene entered the room. "Any news?"

Charlene shook her head. "I'm doing what I can."

Her mother stood, approached Charlene, and kissed her cheek. "I know you are, honey."

Then she left the room. Charlene watched her mother climb the stairs with weary bones, then turned and walked toward the sink.

She filled a glass with cold water and drank it all in one pull. She wiped her mouth with her sleeve and ambled across the kitchen, getting on her tiptoes and opening the cupboard above the refrigerator—a fully stocked liquor cabinet. She sorted through the bottles, moving a few aside, before opting for a bottle of Jack Daniels.

She grabbed a clean glass and sat at the table, then poured a healthy portion and twisted the lid back on the bottle. Charlene stared at the deep-amber-brown Tennessee Whiskey that filled the glass.

She picked up the glass and swooshed it. She closed her eyes, smelling its smooth scent, imagining it deliciously burning her throat.

She felt the pull, the tug from the devil's grasp. Her heartbeat quickened, and her grip on the glass tightened.

Could she really go back *there*?

She shook her head wearily, blinking back hot tears, filled with emotion. She was staring so hard at that glass that her vision blurred. She sucked air deep into her lungs.

"I can't," she whispered, as tears trickled down her cheeks. "Not this time."

Too many people counted on her: Martina, Jane, Richard, and her mother. She could not let them down.

She had to be at her peak tomorrow when she started working the streets. She stood, left the full glass and bottle on the table, and shut off the lights.

Abigail pushed back in the recliner, feet up, a cold wet cloth folded over her eyes. Her temples throbbed.

She feigned sleep, letting her breathing come and go in a slow, steady rhythm, but she could hear Joshua rummaging in the nursery. A moment later he entered the living room.

She asked, "What were you doing in there?"

"Just checking on them."

"Joshua, be careful."

"I am being careful."

He had come a long way, and she had even told him so, but at times she still had to stroke his ego.

"Did I ever thank you for Mom and Dad?" he asked.

She took the cloth off her face and eyed him. "It had to be done."

"It won't be the same again this time, will it?"

She sat up. "No, it won't be. You can trust me." She read his eyes— he didn't trust her. "Come and have a drink with me." She held up a glass with her gloved hand and twirled the liquid. "You outdid yourself with the champagne."

Josh returned her smile, clearly proud of himself.

She got up and walked to the table. "Pour yourself some orange juice."

While on his meds, alcohol was out of the question. It only added to his headaches, and she couldn't have that.

He sat down at the table with her. "You look beautiful tonight, Abigail."

She knew he was lying. She hadn't taken the time to do her hair or makeup. "In a couple of days, it'll all be over, and we can go back to our normal lives."

He didn't say anything. He looked to be thinking, probably remembering how it had gone down last time, how he'd almost ruined things for them.

She went on. "You've been great so far. But it's not over. We still need three more, and you know why. And you know what will happen if we aren't successful." She raised her flute. "Here's to the perfect plan."

They tapped their glasses together, making a clink.

She drained the last of the champagne, and Joshua rushed to the sink where the bottle sat icing in a bucket. He refilled her empty tumbler, then poured himself more juice. When he sat back down, his facial expression was serious.

"It's nice always being one step ahead of the cops."

"I do my best."

"What about the Taylor cop?" There was a nervous, frightened tremor in his voice.

The name made her sit up straighter. "Yes, a mistake. A stupid one. An error *we* can't afford to make again."

"But I told you I saw a woman leave the house, someone I'd never seen before."

"I didn't know she was a cop." Her voice rose a decibel level.

"I told you I needed time."

"We don't have time." Now she was yelling. She drew in a deep breath. "Now this cop is working with Stone, and that could be trouble."

"Who?"

"Agent Matt Stone. He didn't work the case six years ago, but he's here now."

"Isn't he—"

"Doesn't matter who he is—he's trouble, and that's all you need to know. But I can handle those two."

"What about the deadline?" The vein in his forehead pulsated, and his shirt was soaked with sweat.

"I don't miss my deadlines. I'll get information on Taylor," she reassured him.

She had the resources to pull it off. They knew little about Detective Charlene Taylor, and that worried Abigail. And he looked more worried than she was, on the edge of cracking, which was even more of a concern. Would he hold up?

"I have to get back." She set her glass down, still half full, wiped the rim without Joshua noticing, and stood. "Make sure you wash the dishes immediately."

"I was hoping you could spend the night." There was desperation in both his eyes and his voice.

"It's out of the question. You know the rules, and you know I have to get back. People will be waiting for me. My job is important, especially now. I can't just disappear—too many questions would arise."

He nodded, looking defeated, and got up to retrieve her coat, but then turned. He inhaled deeply. "Before you leave, there's one more problem you should know about."

He's gone and fallen for the damn babies again. She was sure of it.

As Abigail steered the vehicle down the interstate, staying below the speed limit, images of the past crept into her mind. The last time had been easy—she'd been able to talk him out of his craziness. But this time, she knew, would be a different story—she could see it in his eyes.

He had grown in the last six years, not just physically but emotionally, and he was mentally stronger. Would he challenge her leadership? She couldn't control him like she did before. He had started to gain confidence, think for himself, and act on his own impulses.

She hoped it wouldn't come to this. But tonight, watching him with the babies, the realization became clear. She had no choice. Joshua wouldn't let it happen again, that she would bet on.

Well, what did she expect? Growing up with Joshua, she knew the kind of kid he was—a caregiver, and a pushover who fell in love easily. Abigail had had to protect him through school, to be the one to stand up to the bullies and to the girls when they broke her brother's heart. That's why he was sent away before they'd changed schools.

She'd raised Joshua on her own, watched him grow up, but couldn't change his soft interior. And now that was the man he was, he could easily blow her plans to smithereens.

Abigail knew how to handle it. She'd been thinking about it for the last six years. Knew the time would come when she'd need Joshua again. Now, with things so close, within reach, they couldn't afford a setback. But Joshua wasn't the only obstacle.

Abigail thought about Detective Charlene Taylor. It had been a stupid risk to take, but they'd had no choice. The deadline had to be met or else. They couldn't wait any longer. Her partners were *not* patient men—she'd found that out the last time. She didn't want to think of the actions they'd take if their demands weren't met. She shivered at the thought.

She considered again what would happen if she failed.

Abigail pulled into the deserted parking lot and stopped the vehicle in front of a phone booth she'd never used before. She got out and made the call, calling the number she'd been told to memorize.

Chapter 13

Charlene called the airlines first thing Sunday morning and cancelled their flights. Her mother wasn't leaving, and Charlene had work to do. She left the departure date open and then hung up.

Using Jane's car, she met Stone outside the Rose Medical Center Pregnancy and Childbirth Center, situated on East Ninth Avenue, not far off Colorado Boulevard, where every single kidnapped baby had been born.

Normally that wouldn't be a big deal, but because the Denver Metro Area had so many quality hospitals—from small to massive, many with great birthing options, it had sent up a huge red flag.

Cindy Richards was the day-shift head nurse on the maternity ward.

Charlene asked, "Why hasn't DPD already questioned Richards?"

She and Matt stood outside the front entrance, under the carport, shielded from the rain.

"Since the babies were kidnapped from their homes, long after any connection with the hospital, they don't suspect that the medical center is involved. Six years ago, Smith focused on the head nurse from the hospital in New Mexico, but that turned out to be a dead end."

"That doesn't mean it's not true. Even if the nurse isn't involved, she might shed light on the children and their families. Maybe they have commonalities that we can't find in the paperwork."

"Did you read Richards's bio last night?"

Charlene nodded. "Thirty-six years old, no prior arrests, married, no children, born in Denver, and has been head nurse for eight years. Not a blemish on her record—she's the ideal employee."

He shrugged. "There's no standard profile for a kidnapping suspect."

She met his gaze. "Do you mind if I speak with Richards alone?"

"I've read your bio, so I know that you have trained interrogation skills. You think Richards will open up more easily to a woman?"

"It might help."

"Good call."

They stepped through the automatic sliding front doors and entered the hospital.

Stone flashed his badge at the front desk. "Agent Stone, FBI. I'm looking for Ms. Cindy Richards."

The woman behind the counter shifted nervously. "She's with the Rose babies."

"Excuse me?" Matt looked confused.

"Sorry, that's the term we give all babies born here at Rose Medical Center. Cindy is in the Childbirth Care Center."

They were escorted down a long clean hallway, where men and women in hospital uniforms hustled from room to room.

"She'll be in one of these rooms." The lady pointed to a row of doors lining the hallway.

"Thank you."

When the woman left, Charlene opened one of the doors, only to find a new mother lying in a single bed, breastfeeding a newborn baby.

"Sorry." Charlene closed the door and continued down the hall.

Behind the third door they tried, a woman in a dark-blue nursing uniform matching Richards's description was tucking in fresh bedsheets.

They stepped inside the Labor and Delivery Suite, which was more like a five-star hotel suite: private bathroom with Jacuzzi, a place for a spouse to sleep, birth balls, rocking chairs, a flat-screen TV with DVD/VCR/CD combination unit, and internet access.

Charlene signaled to Matt. "I've got this."

Matt nodded. "I'll talk to her colleagues."

"Ms. Richards?"

"Yes?" The woman turned around.

Even though Cindy Richards was only thirty-six, the years had not been kind. It looked as if a life of stress had worn her down. Dark circles and wrinkles had made a home around the nurse's eyes, and her brown hair was pulled into a bun, revealing white roots close to the scalp. She was Charlene's height and had a smattering of freckles across the bridge of her nose.

"I'm Detective Taylor. I was wondering if we could talk." Charlene didn't have a badge, so she wasn't sure if the head nurse would even acknowledge her request. "My niece was born here not too long ago." She hoped this would make the nurse more comfortable.

"What's your niece's name?"

"Martina Gibson."

Cindy smiled. "A precious blue-eyed angel."

Was Richards guessing at Martina's eye color, or did she really recall the child? If she remembered Martina from all of those babies born over the last year, then that was impressive.

She continued, "How is Martina?"

Was this a test? Did Richards not know what had happened to the babies? It hadn't been in the news, but the Feds must have been snooping around. Matt said they had never spoken with Richards.

Then the nurse brought her hand to her mouth. "Is Martina one of the babies—" She didn't finish, bringing a hand up to her mouth.

"You know?"

Richards nodded. She walked to the window and stared outside at the rainy Colorado weather. She rubbed her arms as if chilled. "I found out a couple of days ago. A cop came by my house."

Matt said that the nurse had never been interviewed or even questioned. There was nothing on record of the DPD interacting with Cindy Richards in connection to this case.

Charlene asked, "What did this guy look like?"

"Maybe in his sixties. Tall, heavy. Curly grey hair."

Charlene mentally pictured everyone she'd seen around Jane's house, in the FBI building, and at the Denver Police Department. She couldn't place him, and he didn't fit the description given by the number of witnesses from the kidnappings, but then that man had been in disguise each time.

"Did he ID himself as a cop and show you his credentials?"

"No, but he asked questions like a cop."

Jesus Christ. Did the kidnapper visit the woman's home?

"What about his voice? Did he have an accent? Educated? What about his vocabulary?"

She shook her head. "I don't know."

Charlene took a deep breath to slow her pace. "Okay, what about a physical description? Is there anything else you remember? Any facial feature that may help us identify him?"

"I do remember he had a large mole under his left eye. I remember trying not to stare at it, but it was hard to ignore."

"What questions did he ask?"

"About the babies, about the parents. How did they act, did they get along—stuff like that. I don't know much about their lives after they leave the hospital, so I don't think I was very helpful."

"Did he speak with your husband?"

Richards hesitated, and Charlene heard the nurse's voice catch. "I'm not married."

Goose bumps popped up on Charlene's arms. Richards's file showed that she was married.

Richards twisted the ring on her finger. "My husband left me a short time ago."

"I'm so sorry."

Richards put her hand to her face and turned away. "He left after the miscarriage."

While Charlene interviewed Cindy Richards, Matt walked the hallways of Rose Medical Center, looking for anything or anyone suspicious. He'd been born there thirty-two years earlier, and he knew that Rose had an excellent reputation.

He found himself back at the reception desk asking to speak to the chief medical officer and waited while the receptionist made the call. He only waited a few minutes before a mild-mannered elderly man approached with his arm extended, flashing a practiced smile.

"Justin Wheeler, chief medical officer."

At about seventy, Wheeler had a full head of neatly parted brown hair. He was two inches taller than Matt, with a narrow chest and an angular jaw. His pale skin indicated too many hours spent indoors.

Matt shook his hand and produced his badge. "Agent Stone, FBI."

The chief gave the badge a cursory glance. "What can I do for you?"

Using a serious tone to emphasize the serious nature of the visit, Matt asked, "Is there somewhere we can talk in private?"

The chief hesitated as if to inquire, but then looked around. "Of course. Follow me."

He led Matt down the hall, where they took an elevator up to the second floor. As they walked along the corridor, they didn't speak. The aging chief walked with a tired shuffle.

With the keys jingling in his hand, he unlocked a door and ushered Matt into the office, then turned and closed the door behind him.

"Please, have a seat, Agent Stone." The chief motioned to a separate sitting area made up of burgundy leather chairs and a couch surrounding a glass coffee table.

As the chief removed his long white lab coat and nestled it on a wrought-iron coat tree, Matt observed the layout of the office. It was impressive—spacious and richly furnished.

The beige walls were covered with several framed diplomas and documents from Stanford and UCLA, and medical licenses to practice. The desk was clean—with files neatly stacked on one corner, a closed laptop resting in the middle—and four framed family photographs.

One large grey file cabinet filled the space behind his desk, and a potted plant lay dying on top. A small desk pushed against the far wall displayed 3D models of human body parts.

The doctor sat across from Matt and crossed his legs. "So, what can I do for you?"

"I'd like to speak to you about one of your employees."

"And why is that?"

"We think she might be involved in a crime."

The doctor steepled his fingers. "Year after year, Rose Medical Center has collected accolades as one of the top 'baby hospitals' in Denver. We attribute these outstanding reviews to the fact that each staff member and doctor is dedicated to creating the safest, most meaningful birthing experience possible. We follow a strict protocol when hiring, and our background searches and HR team are second to none. However, we believe that what our employees do in their personal lives is none of our business and has nothing to do with this hospital."

The speech sounded well-rehearsed, as if read from a brochure, and Matt wondered if the chief had been expecting him, and how many times he had practiced that spiel.

"With all due respect, Doctor, I'm here investigating a series of kidnappings. The babies abducted were all born in this hospital."

The doctor shifted in his chair.

"I don't plan to go to the press with it, and Rose Medical Center's name will be kept confidential, as long as I get cooperation."

That got the old man's attention. "What would you like to know?"

"Cindy Richards."

The chief stood, looking pained, as if his bones ached. He went to the filing cabinet and removed a folder. He returned to the sitting area, sat, and placed the file on his lap.

"I'm not much for computers." His face revealed a hint of a smile. He lifted a sheet from the folder, adjusted a pair of half-cut reading glasses on his nose, and read from it. "She joined us twelve years ago straight out of college, came with impeccable references, and she turned out to be a very competent nurse. She took little time to advance in promotion, becoming head nurse of the maternity ward in her eighth year. For twelve years, Cindy Richards has been a model employee."

"Have you seen any changes in Ms. Richards recently?"

The chief's expression shifted to one of sorrow. He nodded. "Cindy hit a rough patch in her personal life. Of course, we at the hospital have helped her through it as much as we could, but these things take time."

"What happened?"

"You don't know?"

Matt shook his head.

"Cindy was pregnant with her first child. We were all excited for her, because she waited such a long time for a family, and we were happy that it finally happened. Then she lost the baby."

"How?"

"You'll have to talk to her doctor about that."

"Who's that?"

"Dr. Eugene Parker. He's part of our staff."

Matt wrote down the name. "That could do a lot of harm, both mentally and physically."

"That's not all."

Matt looked up from his notepad.

"Not long after that, Cindy's husband walked out on her. What an asshole. Pardon my language."

"Do you know him?"

The doctor shook his head. "Never met him, but for any man to do that, he's gotta be a jerk."

"How did Ms. Richards handle it?"

"We begged her to take time off, but she insisted on coming back to work. Losing a baby is devastating for a family, especially for a woman who'd been pregnant eight months. But she said that being around the Rose babies made her feel better—more useful."

"Did you notice any shift in her behavior, maybe when she was around the babies?"

He shook his head. "I never noticed anything, and I haven't heard any complaints from her colleagues either. And as you can probably imagine, she has a tremendously heavy, stressful load to carry, in her position as head nurse. She hasn't cracked."

"Does she have close friends on staff?"

"I know that she's friends with another nurse named Mary Collins."

Matt wrote down the name.

"Agent," the doctor said. "If you think that Cindy Richards has anything to do with the disappearance of these babies, you're mistaken."

Charlene took notes as Cindy Richards spoke about the heartbreak of the miscarriage and the devastation of her husband's departure. At one point, she hid her face in her hands and wept, before getting her emotions under control.

"Did he give you any prior indication that he was leaving?"

Richards shook her head. "No. Ryan had always wanted children, and I guess the miscarriage was too much for him to handle. When the doctor told me that I'd never have children, Ryan was upset."

Charlene nodded.

There was a rap on the door, and Matt stuck his head inside the room. "May I join you?"

Charlene nodded and the agent entered.

After introductions, Richards sighed aloud and picked up the thread. "My work is all I have. I know they struggled to understand why I came back so soon." There was sadness in the nurse's eyes.

Charlene could relate. After the death of her father, she went back to work immediately, much to the chagrin of her colleagues and superiors.

She smiled at Richards. "Thank you for your time, Ms. Richards."

The nurse nodded, but looked as if her attention was elsewhere.

They walked to the door, then, before exiting the room, Charlene turned back to the nurse. "If you don't mind my asking, what was your baby's name?"

The woman's head jerked upward, her eyes wide with surprise. Charlene knew that expectant mothers nearly always chose the baby's name months in advance, but she guessed it was the first time anyone had asked that question.

A faint smile played on her lips. "Abigail. Her name was Abigail. Ryan picked it out."

Charlene nodded and left.

In the hallway, Matt already had his notepad out. "What did you find out?"

"Cindy Richards has been through a lot over the last couple of months."

"I heard. Definite stressors."

"She's sad for sure, but maybe she's angry too."

He nodded. "There are no alarms going off yet, but since we're already here, we might as well look into it. I have a couple of names we can check out."

"Let's go."

Dr. Eugene Parker was in surgery, so Charlene and Matt met with Mary Collins, Cindy Richards' rumored friend. Collins was fifty, single, and a native of Colorado Springs. The closest she'd ever come to marriage was a three-week engagement to a Denver man who had run off with her sister. Collins had decided late in life to become a nurse and spent two years taking night classes at Pikes Peak Community College, where she received her associate degree in nursing.

Collins frowned in confusion. "Why do you want to know about Cindy?"

The chief medical officer had asked Collins to speak with Charlene and Matt, so they expected her cooperation.

"We're just wondering about her mental state since her miscarriage."

"Well, we were all surprised when she came back to work so soon, but I'll tell you, I've never seen her more dedicated to her job. All she thinks about is the welfare of those babies. After the miscarriage and Ryan's exit, she put all her focus and attention on her work. I'm not saying she wasn't good at her job before, but now she's relentless."

"You didn't notice anything different? Any changes?"

"Well..."

Collins did little to hide her hesitation.

"What?"

"She just seemed...what's the word?"

They waited her out.

"She seemed too hands-on, overprotective."

Stone tilted his head in question. "How so?"

"It was as if she thought each baby was her own."

Interesting.

"Did you mention this to anyone?"

"Of course not. Cindy had just returned, and I knew it would take time for her to settle back in to the routine."

Charlene asked, "Do you know her husband?"

Collins shook her head. "I only saw him briefly a couple of times, and that was at a distance. I mean, she and I work well together but we've never been close friends outside the work setting. And apparently Ryan wasn't one to mix with outsiders."

Matt frowned. "I thought you were Cindy's best friend."

"The truth is that I'm one of her only friends, because she and Ryan were private people, and didn't tend to make friends easily."

Charlene checked her watch. This was a waste of time and she wanted to speak with Cindy Richards' doctor.

Wrapping it up, Charlene asked, "Where is her husband now?"

"No idea. He just up and left and never came back."

"Really? Well, thank you for your time, Ms. Collins. If you think of anything else, please don't hesitate to call." She handed her a business card and turned to go.

On the way out she whispered, "Let's go. The doctor should be out of surgery by now."

"Before I say anything, let me tell you that Cindy Richards is a wonderful person and a fine nurse."

They met Dr. Eugene Parker in a private office, near the operating room. He was still wearing soiled green scrubs when he removed the cap and wiped beads of perspiration from his forehead.

Parker was in his sixties. His skin was liver-spotted and his blue eyes tired. His jawbone pulsated, and his hair was shaved to the scalp.

They'd completed the introductions, and the doctor told them that he only had a few minutes to give them between surgeries. That's all they would need.

Matt got right to the point. "Can you tell us about Cindy's pregnancy?"

They sat around a small circular table. Parker drank black coffee from a Styrofoam cup, but he hadn't offered them any.

"I'm not Cindy's personal physician, but I got called in when there were complications. As far as I know, the early stages of her pregnancy went without a hitch, except that she didn't put on much weight, which can affect the baby's birth weight."

"So what happened?" Charlene asked.

The doctor shook his head. "I've been practicing medicine for thirty years, and this was a first for me. So strange."

"What was?"

"Cindy came in complaining of a burning sensation in her uterus. It had started the night before and she'd ignored it, but by morning the pain was so intense that she came into the ER. By the time they called me in, there was nothing I could do. Remember, every healthy woman without a personal or a family history of reproductive or developmental problems begins her pregnancy with a 3% risk for birth defects and a 15% risk of miscarriage. Keep in mind that this applies equally for all healthy pregnant women. But this was different."

Charlene rubbed her face and noticed her hand tremble. "So, what was the problem?"

"Stillbirth."

"Stillbirth?"

"The death of the fetus occurred when the pregnancy was far advanced, even before the onset of labor. If the baby had been alive, I would've done a C-section and handed it off to a neonatologist, but in this case, the baby had already died. And although it happens occasionally, there was nothing normal about it."

"How's that?"

The doctor scratched the unshaven white stubble on his sharp chin. His facial muscles tightened. "The baby was quite large so I decided we'd have to go in after it, but when I examined her organs, I discovered that her ovaries had been so badly burned that I had to remove them."

"Burned? I don't get it," Matt said. "How could that have happened?"

The doctor removed his bifocals and pinched his nose, as if entertaining a headache. "I don't know. The only logical explanation is radiation exposure."

"Like an X-ray? Had she had X-rays during her pregnancy?"

"No. She didn't have X-rays, fluoroscopy, or radiation therapy, nor was there any record that she'd taken any liquid radioactive substances. But even if she had, once she was past her twentieth week, the fetus would've been far more resistant to any negative effects of radiation. It had to be something stronger than that for it to so radically affect her internal organs, and the baby."

Charlene shook her head. "I don't get it."

"It's basically unexplainable. Cindy and I have been over it time and time again, but we've never come up with an answer."

"Let me get this straight," said Matt. "Somehow Cindy Richards was exposed to a deadly radioactive source, that destroyed her internal organs, but she has no idea how or when."

"That's correct."

Charlene asked, "What kind of radiation are we talking about here?"

"The only thing that would have such a traumatic effect is a radioactive pellet used to treat certain kinds of cancer. But Cindy was never treated for cancer, and I have no idea how she could've been exposed to that level of radiation."

Charlene leaned forward on her chair. "What about her husband? What was his reaction?"

"I'm sure he felt hurt, maybe angry. After I was certain that Cindy was stable and made it through, I broke the news to him."

"What did he say?"

"He didn't speak, didn't move. In fact, he seemed crushed when I told him that she would never be able to bear children."

"And he didn't react to that?"

"He was probably in shock. I offered to have someone from the hospital talk with him, but he refused."

"Did he leave? Go see Cindy? Make a call?"

The doctor shook his head. "I left him there, so I didn't see what happened next."

"Did you know him?"

"Never met him before. If he came to the hospital to see Cindy, I never noticed."

Charlene felt it strange that someone who had worked at the medical center for as long as Richards hadn't brought her husband around, and that none of her colleagues had ever met him.

"How was Cindy when she returned to work?"

"I don't work directly with her. But I continued to see her once a week to assess her health. Early on, she was at risk of developing blood clots but that never happened."

"Psychologically?"

"Cindy returned to work three weeks after the stillbirth, against my direct orders. Everyone reacts differently in these kinds of situations. She thought that work could help take her mind off her problems. In the end, it was her decision, and the hospital saw no reason not to allow her return."

They got up to leave, then Charlene turned to the doctor. "Doctor, where would someone have access to that level of radiation around here?"

"The only place I can think of is a radiotherapy clinic."

They sat in Jake's car in the hospital parking lot, their notepads on their laps, reading over everything they'd jotted down during the interviews.

Matt was thinking out loud. "So, she went back to work rather quickly after everything that happened. Was she ready?"

Charlene didn't mention it, but she had done the same thing, after her father's murder. Work was her comfort, so she couldn't hold that against Cindy Richards.

They talked about the odd stillbirth, the exit of Richards' husband, and the three interviews.

Matt sighed out loud. "Those are major stressors. And her actions speak volumes."

Charlene nodded. "I agree."

"You asked a lot of questions about her husband."

"Well, he lost as much as Cindy did that day. And isn't the fact that he's disappeared a little suspicious?"

"I wonder how often a husband walks out after losing a baby. I wouldn't think it's that rare, especially if he has his heart set on a child."

"I still think we should look into him. Isn't it weird that not one of her friends or colleagues had ever met the man or knew anything about him?"

"Yes, that is odd."

"I think we should go to New Mexico." She gauged his reaction. "You said one of the nurses was a suspect."

"Everything we need is here in the files."

"What if they missed something? And you admitted that you haven't looked over all of the notes—there are just too many. It will be faster if we go there and speak with those involved."

"Albuquerque is six hours away."

"Not by plane."

Matt's eyebrows arched sarcastically. "You have a plane?"

"No, but the FBI does."

"You think the FBI will give us their plane, when we aren't even supposed to be working the case?"

"I don't know, would they?"

They were quiet for a few minutes, while Matt seemed to be contemplating her suggestion.

Then she interrupted his train of thought. "I thought you told me that the Denver Police had never interviewed Cindy Richards."

He shook his head, frowning now. "They didn't."

"Cindy already knew that the babies had been taken. In fact, she said a cop showed up at her home asking about the kidnappings."

Looking concerned, he reached into the backseat and retrieved a folder. He opened it and rifled through the first few papers.

"Maybe Jake missed it?"

Matt shook his head. "Jake doesn't miss anything. He has privileges to the case files and would have mentioned it in his notes, but I don't see anything about it anywhere."

"Maybe Salinger is keeping it from Jake, since she doesn't seem to want you near the case."

He shook his head. "Janice wouldn't do that—it's not her style."

"Maybe you don't know her as well as you think you do."

"She wants to solve this case and knows that I'm her best bet."

She chewed her lip as she rolled the facts around in her head. "He was probably a detective. He was in street clothes and not a uniform."

Charlene ran down the vague description that Richards had given her, describing what the cop looked like.

"That's not a cop."

Charlene was surprised. "Not a cop? You know who it is?"

"Yes."

Matt opened his phone and called a number. He grimaced at Charlene. "Voice mail." He spoke into the phone. "Harry, it's Matt Stone. I think we need to talk. Give me a call." The agent left his number and hung up.

"What's that about?" she asked, but he was already punching in another number.

"Agent Smith, it's Agent Stone. I need the plane."

"That was smooth." She smiled as she buckled her seat belt.

"Sometimes you have to lie to get what you need," Matt replied, but he looked totally uncomfortable, as if doing something he'd never done before.

She felt mildly responsible, since Matt had lied to his superior on her behalf, but she didn't feel that bad. This needed to be done.

"So, who is this Harry guy?" She changed the subject, hoping it would put some color back in his pale complexion.

The plane's wheels had just touched off the ground, when the pilot steadied the plane. Denver to Albuquerque was a straight shot down Interstate 25, six hours by car, but less than a two-hour plane trip.

He answered, "The guy you described to me, the one Cindy Richards identified, could be a local private investigator named Harold Linden."

"A PI? I don't trust them one bit."

"You can trust this guy. He's no ambulance chaser. He's one of us— a former cop, thirty years with the Denver PD."

"Why is he a PI now?"

"He retired six years ago. Got a place out on the water to hunt and fish, but then his wife died suddenly—with cancer. Now he's his own boss and makes his own hours."

Charlene knew where this story was heading. Cops could never quit—couldn't turn off the switch. They craved the action. Just as her father had, which was why he was no longer around to enjoy his retirement and grandkids.

"He couldn't stay away. Got his PI license, joined the Professional Private Investigators Association, and started his own one-man operation. He still has a lot of contacts inside the precinct and uses every one of them."

"You think he's working this case?"

"Maybe a parent contacted him."

"Which one?"

"I don't know. But if Harry is working this case, he'll find something. He's old school—no computers or technology—but he's organized, thorough, and like a bloodhound when he catches a scent."

"Why doesn't the DPD hire Linden as a consultant on cases like this?"

"Two reasons. One, Harry likes to work alone. No pressure or having to depend on anyone else. And two, Janice Salinger hates his guts."

"Does that lady like anyone?"

Stone snorted. "Not many. Janice has her sights set on Harry for a number of issues: autonomy, resistance to authority, issues of principle. She's quite aware that Harry uses some of her men to funnel information, and like every police department, as chief, she doesn't like having her toes stepped on."

"Maybe we should think about working with him?"

"That's not a bad idea. Harry isn't a cop anymore, so he has an added advantage of not being stalled by laws or rules. PIs don't need warrants, and they don't care about people's rights. It's something to think about."

She nodded. "Let's talk about that nurse from New Mexico, Susan Harper. We need to read as much of the file as we can so we aren't going in there blind."

"Good idea. I haven't looked at it yet."

He pulled the folder out of a black leather briefcase and snapped it shut. They opened the foldout trays and placed the papers on top.

He took a sip of bottled iced tea. "These are Smith's handwritten notes. Harper is thirty-eight years old, born and raised in Albuquerque. She was hired by the Lovelace Women's Hospital right out of college. She married at twenty-eight. Jesus."

She looked at Matt and saw the blood drain from his face. She felt a chill. "What is it?"

"She had a miscarriage too."

"Really?"

"Something about Harper must have struck a nerve with Smith six years ago because he put her under surveillance."

"Anything come of it?"

"Nothing. She checked out perfectly."

"I wonder what she's been up to."

"What do you mean?"

She punched in a number on her phone, calling Information, and got the number for the police department in Albuquerque. When that call was answered, she asked to be transferred to the detective who'd been in charge of the six-year-old kidnapping case.

Charlene got lucky. Detective Bill Nicholas was still on the force and sitting at his desk. When he answered his phone, she got right to the point.

"Detective Nicholas, this is Detective Taylor. I'm working a kidnapping case in Denver that we believe may be related to your case from six years ago."

"It's about time you guys called. I wondered when you'd get around to it."

"So you know about the kidnappings?"

"I know about it. I was called a few days ago by the same FBI agent who ran the show six years ago. He had a hunch that it was related. As soon as he gave me the details, I put Susan Harper under bumper-lock surveillance."

She sighed aloud. "We're on our way to the Lovelace Women's Hospital now."

"I've already questioned her, Detective, and her alibis check out. If you want my professional opinion, she's not involved."

"I appreciate that, but I'd like to question Ms. Harper myself." She understood she was stepping on toes, and if the shoe was on the other foot... She'd be fuming if someone did that to her. But she'd made the call out of professional courtesy, hoping for cooperation and leniency.

"Feel free, but I'm telling you she's not involved." He ended the call.

She sighed in frustration, clicked off and put her iPhone away.

Matt had been listening in. "Listen, I'm an FBI agent, I don't need jurisdictional permission."

She shook her head in annoyance. "They don't know that. Plus, I wanted to see what's been going on with the case that we don't already know, since it's unlikely that we'll be given more updates. Apparently, Smith is still working the Susan Harper angle."

Chapter 14

It was after two when they got to the hospital. Since they'd called ahead, Susan Harper was waiting for them outside the emergency entrance. She led them inside and down a surprisingly quiet hallway, where only a handful of nurses stood behind a counter filling out paperwork.

Harper was all business, talking as they moved, her rubber-soled shoes squishing in the corridor.

"I can't believe this nightmare is happening all over again. Those poor parents."

The nurse was medium height and rail thin, with short blond hair cut just below her ears. Now thirty-six, Harper looked more like fifty, with wrinkles and lines that were aging her prematurely. She saw the same sadness behind Susan Harper's eyes that she had seen in Cindy Richards.

Matt said, "Anything you can add to our investigation would be helpful."

"I don't know how I can help you. I've told the Albuquerque police everything I know."

He went on, "I realize that, Ms. Harper, and I thank you for seeing us on such short notice."

The nurse's facial expression was forced and tired. "I'll do whatever I can. I just feel awful about everything that's happening. We can talk in here."

They followed her into a comfortable break room, where she closed a soundproof door behind them.

Charlene could picture an overworked on-call doctor grabbing a quick nap on the sofa after a long night of surgery. The space was sparsely decorated, but it was inviting and quiet, complete with a bathroom and a shower.

In the corner was a small table with two chairs, and a single-serve Keurig coffeemaker on top, beside a rack of assorted flavored coffee pods. The aroma of freshly brewed coffee and warm sugary doughnuts scented the air. A TV remote control was the only other item on the table.

Matt and Charlene seated themselves in padded chairs while Harper took her position on a dark leather couch that looked and smelled new.

Matt opened a folder and removed a number of photos of the Denver babies and their parents. When Charlene saw Martina's photo, her mouth went dry, and her throat tightened. She folded her hands, wrestling with the emotions building inside her.

"Do any of these people look familiar?"

Harper flipped through the photos, taking time to look carefully at each one—hesitating at a couple of them, but not for long. She shook her head. "Sorry." She handed back the images.

Matt cleared his throat. "Listen, Ms. Harper, I know you've been over this time and again, but if you could detail one more time, the events of six years ago, we would appreciate it."

"This hospital wasn't involved."

"We know, but we're also aware that you were questioned by police and the FBI, so what *do* you know about what happened?"

Harper wound her way through a story that sounded eerily familiar, almost exactly like the Denver kidnappings. Bottom line: seven babies, disappeared into thin air.

After a long pause, Matt continued, "I know that it was also a bad time for you, personally."

Harper looked away, silent.

He knew she'd rather not revisit the pain of the past. "I'm sorry to make you relive that nightmare."

"It's taken a long time to get past it. It hasn't been easy, but I found God after that. I believe that He chose me because he knew I was strong, and could handle it."

Charlene felt sad for her. "It couldn't have been easy."

Susan sighed. "It was like a double whammy, first losing the baby and then losing my husband to divorce. It didn't take long to realize that I couldn't handle it on my own, so I turned to my church for support."

"You're no longer married?" Charlene asked, while looking at Matt, who seemed to acknowledge this tidbit of information.

Harper shook her head. "I think David was even more devastated than I was. We didn't talk much about it afterward. In fact, when I look back, I think our lack of communication was probably responsible for the breakdown of our relationship."

"Are you still close to your ex-husband?"

"I haven't heard from him since. He just left."

Charlene's skin started to prickle, and she bit down on her lip. She was sure it wasn't the first time a marriage had ended due to a miscarriage, but Harper's story was just too similar to Cindy's to be a coincidence.

Charlene stood and joined the nurse on the sofa, their knees almost touching. She reached over and touched Susan's arm.

"Listen, I know this is difficult. But I need to know about the miscarriage. Can you tell me about it?"

Harper turned away, but only for a moment. When she looked back, there was something different in her eyes. Their eyes locked for seconds.

"I can't explain it."

"Please try."

Harper made a face. "It was tough, working with children every day, seeing teenage mothers who didn't want children, getting pregnant accidentally and crying on my shoulder. We were frustrated and to the point of giving up, when the Lord blessed us." Her voice trailed off, and she stared blankly at a wall-mounted television that was turned off.

In a whisper Charlene asked, "What happened?"

"I was in my third trimester when…. I felt a terrible burning sensation." She swallowed. "I tried to ignore it, but it got so bad that I couldn't take it anymore. When the ER doc examined me, he discovered that my baby had died, and they had to remove my ovaries."

She started to cry, and Charlene reached over and retrieved a box of tissues and handed it to her.

"The doctor couldn't explain it. I couldn't believe it. Somehow my ovaries had been burned so badly that they had to remove them, which effectively dashed my dreams of ever having children. A few weeks later, David was gone."

Susan took a moment to collect her emotions.

Charlene was ready to leave. "Thank you for your time. I know this was hard. It's terrible what you had to go through."

The nurse shook her head. "I guess that's what happens when you jump in headfirst. We met on the internet and married shortly after."

Charlene looked at Matt, who nodded. She got up. "Good luck, Susan."

They started to walk out. Matt left the room but Charlene stopped, letting the door shut behind him.

"What was the baby's name?"

The nurse looked up at Charlene, her eyes red and wet. "Nobody has ever asked me that before." She smiled sadly. "Her name was Abigail."

Charlene's skin tingled as she rested her hand on the doorknob. She opened the door and poked her head out.

Without explanation she said, "Get back in here."

With Harper's permission, they'd made a quick stop at the nurse's Pueblo revival-style apartment building, for a once-over, before leaving the city. Charlene and Matt hadn't said five words to each other in the car ride back to the airport, contemplating what they had discovered, letting what they'd heard fully sink in. But once they had boarded and were in the air, there was much to discuss.

Charlene held up a photo of David Harper. "So, we agree that we need to look at the husband or husbands."

Matt took the photo from Charlene and studied it. "Although he wore disguises during all the kidnappings, he fits the profile—white male, the right age, frame, and body type. But it's odd that Harper didn't know more about her husband's background. It's like this guy materialized out of thin air, swept the woman off her feet, and married her. I can't believe people do that internet dating stuff."

She put her hand on Matt's shoulder. "Never underestimate the vulnerability of a lonely woman. Some women, who dream of someday having children, will do anything when they reach a certain age. I think this guy knew that and preyed on it. When we get back, I'd like to go see Cindy Richards and ask her about her husband. Maybe get a photo and make a comparison."

"Has to be the same guy. When we get back, I'll order a full-scale check on this guy."

"Order?"

Matt raised his hands in defeat. "Well, I guess I won't be ordering anyone around. We'll be doing it together."

"Why wait?"

"Right." Matt nodded, pulling his laptop out of its bag. "We need to look into what those two nurses have in common. Have they interacted in the past? Have they crossed paths without knowing it? It could be anything, since they both had trouble getting pregnant: we'll check gym memberships, fertility clinics, adoption agencies, and doctors."

He turned on the laptop and waited.

"Susan Harper met her husband online. What was the name of that site?"

Matt checked his notes. "Lover's Lane. Call Cindy Richards."

She pulled out her phone, retrieved the number from Matt's files, and called the nurse. Richards confirmed that she had met her husband on the same dating website.

When she hung up, he had already pulled up the dating website. She studied the home page over his shoulder.

"Good-looking home page," she noted. "Professional with intricate detail. How many people are registered with the site?"

Matt shook his head. "Not sure. We'll have to get someone who can hack into the site and get more information for us."

"And what about the other thing?" It had been bothering her, nagging at her brain.

He scratched his head. "The radiation thing?"

"Yes. How were the women exposed to it?"

"You think the husband did it somehow?"

"But how? And why? From the way that both women spoke of their husbands, the men had wanted children as badly as they did. Why go to all the trouble to conceive, only to kill your unborn fetus? That makes no sense."

He raised an eyebrow. "Trouble to conceive? I'd say that's the fun part."

There it was again, that subtle flirting. She rolled her eyes. "You know what I mean."

Matt checked his cell phone messages. "I got a call when we were at the hospital. I had it on vibrate and missed it." He scrolled through the missed-calls log. "It's Harry's number."

He put his phone on speaker, tapped in his password, then set the phone down on the pull-out tray, so they could both listen in.

Harold Linden's voice was deep, hoarse. "Matt, good to hear from you. I'm glad you called. I guess you know I'm workin' the kidnappin' case. I think I have somethin' for you. Give me a call."

Matt called him back, but there was no answer. He disconnected and turned to face her. "Looks like we're going to Harry's place."

Darkness was falling and it began to rain when they left the airport in Jake's red Toyota. Now, she fidgeted nervously, anticipating a lead.

They'd been driving for twenty minutes before he turned down an unmarked dirt road, surrounded by unkempt tall grass on either side. Charlene could feel the speed of the car start to slow as they approached another turn. The vehicle finally rolled to a stop in front of a rusty trailer.

They parked the vehicle behind a dilapidated Ford truck.

"That's Harry's truck," said Matt. "He must be here."

Matt got out of the car, and Charlene, hesitantly, followed. She looked beyond the trailer to a small, calm lake with a ten-foot dock.

There a folding lawn chair was ready, near a drink holder that held a beer, awaiting a fisherman whose pole leaned against the chair. A Hibachi grill sat ready to cook the day's catch.

The wind kicked up a cloud of dust, spraying Charlene's eyes. She shielded her face and blinked her now-itchy eyes.

"You okay?"

Charlene nodded, but her eyes had already started to water.

Matt knocked hard on the door. "Harry, you in there?"

When no one responded, he opened the unlocked storm door, turned around to glance at Charlene, and then stepped inside.

Standing on a makeshift porch, she looked around the deserted land, and studied the old, rusted trailer. A string of four-season Christmas lights hung oddly against the front of the dirty, stained tin. The light blue paint was fading, and long weeds of grass hugged the sides of the trailer. The windows were too dirty to see inside, so when Matt didn't come back out, she entered.

The inside of the trailer was divided up into several sections.

Matt had turned left, heading to the front end of the trailer, while she went right, heading to the far end where the bedroom was located. A pull-down Murphy bed stood upright and rested against the wall, with a door into a small bathroom, fitted with the requisite toilet, a tiny shower and a sink crusted with dried toothpaste.

But there was no sign of Harry. Charlene headed back to the middle portion of the trailer, where the kitchen was located.

She accidentally kicked an empty beer can across the dirty, plastic tiled floor. In fact, the entire floor was littered with beer cans and dried dirt. The inside of the trailer stank of stale beer and cigarette smoke. Dirty pots and dishes littered the countertops.

Charlene opened the fridge door—two beers left from a six pack, a quarter-full jar of mayonnaise and a large can of no-name brand coffee.

"Jesus."

Matt cursed from a distant room. She slammed the fridge door and raced to the back of the trailer. The FBI agent stood at a foldout card table, where a man slumped, face down over table top.

"Is that Harry?"

Matt nodded.

Charlene stepped closer. The table was loaded with items: a paper grocery bag partially filled with processed foods, an open can of beer, a burning cigarette in an ashtray and an economy size, plastic jar of beef jerky. Beside the PI's head was a bright Nickel Colt Python .357 Magnum revolver.

A few papers were also scattered across the table with a notepad closed on top of them. She picked up the notepad but noticed that the top pages had been ripped off, and the space was far too dark for her to read what had been written there. She tucked the notepad in the back pocket of her pants.

Matt lifted Linden's head off the table, and they noticed a red, wire-thin line encircling his throat where someone had strangled him.

"He's still warm."

Linden slouched in a chair, but Charlene could tell he was a big man. Probably close to 250 pounds, with dark, olive skin and multiple chins. His dark eyes were set deep in their sockets and locked open. His hair was grey but balding on the dome. His large, hairy-knuckled hands hung down at his sides.

Then they heard a nondescript noise outside. Not loud, but enough to grab their attention. It could have been a raccoon at a trash can, but Charlene swallowed hard, her stomach tightening. Linden hadn't been dead long.

Matt had already pulled out his weapon.

She stepped to the end of the trailer and pulled back the curtain. Even though the window was grimy and partially obstructed her view, she watched as the shape of a man disappeared into the woods. Someone who had been wearing a dark-colored hoodie.

Turning to Matt, she pointed. "I just saw someone—some guy, disappear into the woods."

"Really?"

Matt turned abruptly, as if picking up a scent. "Do you smell that?"

Charlene sniffed the air. "Gasoline."

They had just entered the middle part of the trailer when the sides went up, engulfed in flames. They raced for the door and Charlene pushed on it, but it wouldn't budge.

"It won't move," Charlene yelled out, inhaling a cloud of black smoke that made her cough.

"Let me try."

He got into place and charged at the door, thrusting his shoulder into the thinly-framed trailer door. Nothing moved. Matt rubbed his shoulder but then tried again, with no success.

The place would go up fast, so they quickly scanned the area for escape routes.

It only took a second to realize there was no way they could get Linden's body out of the trailer. So, as hard as it was, they had to ignore him in the back room.

Charlene pulled her shirt up over her mouth and nose to block the smoke as much as possible when something in the corner of the trailer gave her a start. "Matt." She pointed at two twenty-pound propane tanks on the floor. They could've used one to break a window, but the small windows weren't big enough to allow their escape.

There was no back door to the trailer.

Matt tapped Charlene's shoulder and pointed to the low ceiling—a trap door. It was small, but large enough for a body to squirm through if they could get up there.

Matt, who felt hypoxic and weak turned and, using what little strength he had left, moved a folding table to the place under the trap door and held it in place, motioning her to climb. She took a second to get her balance, then rose to a standing position. She reached up, and placed her hands flat against the increasingly warm paneled trap door. Feeling desperate now, she pounded on the trap door and kept pounding until it finally gave way and flopped open.

When she gripped the lip edge of the hole and attempted to pull herself up, the sharp metal frame cut into her bare hands. As her head cleared the opening, she greedily breathed in fresh air. Hanging there, kicking her feet in midair, her arms grew weary. She didn't think she could muster enough strength to pull herself the rest of the way up and out.

Charlene's clothes were soaked in sweat, all of the air was being sucked out of the trailer and she could smell her skin starting to sear. Her eyes stung.

Then she felt firm hands push her feet upward. She used the momentum to pull herself the rest of the way, and climb out of the hole

Charlene could feel the thin metal roof begin to give slightly from her weight when she turned to glance back down inside the smoky trailer where Matt's black, soot covered face looked around anxiously.

He stepped up onto the table, balancing, but with no one to hold it, it fell over, Matt landing on the floor with it. Matt attempted to jump and grasp the edge, but he missed with each attempt and fell back down.

Charlene fell back, sitting down, taking short breaths to catch up. Her lungs burned. Then Matt's fingers emerged from the hole, his bloody knuckles turning white.

Charlene sprang to her feet and clutched Matt's wrists, pulling as strongly as she could.

With her help, Matt worked his way up through the hole where they stopped momentarily to gulp breaths of clean air. The roof was heating up fast, so, with no other options, they leaped off as far from the trailer as they could get.

They lay on their backs for several long seconds, breathing in gulps of fresh, clean air, staring up into the stars, until they heard the relentless wail of fire truck sirens.

They huddled together on a gurney, located at the back of an EMT squad, breathing O2 by mask. They watched as the trailer was quickly reduced to a charred metal skeleton.

It had only been fifteen minutes since the firetrucks arrived. The word was that a neighbor down the road had seen the blaze and called it in. Police Chief Salinger was speaking with the fire marshal and one of the arson investigators.

The fire was out and cooling in the rainy night air, when uniformed firefighters picked their way through the ash and debris. Nothing could be salvaged from the wreckage, and the rain would wash away any trace evidence.

Since the fire had destroyed any inside evidence, police teams scoured the area, collecting all debris found within a hundred-yard radius.

Charlene removed her O2 mask. "Salinger got here fast."

Stone nodded and coughed quietly.

She frowned in annoyance. "Why is she even here?"

As if she'd heard her name, Salinger turned and looked in their direction. She mouthed a few more words to the firefighter and then started walking toward Matt and Charlene. Her strides slowed, calculated, as if stalling for time before reaching them.

Matter-of-factly, she said, "You two look like hell."

He removed his mask and quipped, "I can't imagine why."

Salinger nodded. "You were lucky."

Charlene answered, "I don't feel lucky." She attempted to pull herself up into a seated position, but her muscles resisted her efforts. Salinger helped her up.

"Thanks."

Salinger pointed to the skeletonized trailer. "Harry in there?"

Matt nodded. "Murdered."

"Murdered?"

"Definitely."

"You sure?"

"Positive. Looked like he'd been strangled with a sharp metal wire."

"Shit." She pursed her lips and shook her head. "Hopefully there will be something left of Harry's body to confirm it."

"We don't need confirmation. We saw it." Matt's voice grew louder, but was halted by a coughing spell.

The chief gave him a look that said it all. "You know how this works, Matt. We need hard evidence to tie up loose ends. The arson investigators will obviously suspect foul play, but it will take a couple of days to confirm that too."

"What are you talking about? We're witnesses. We saw it all."

"I believe you. But you know the procedure—dot the I's and cross the T's."

Matt started to get to his feet, but stumbled slightly. Salinger grabbed him by the arm and steadied him, settling him back onto the stretcher.

He shook his head, resolute. "This was a deliberate attempt to destroy Harry and something he discovered. How did you get here so fast, anyway?"

"I was on my way to talk to Harry."

"Why? You hate Harry."

"Hate is a strong word. Sure, we had our disagreements, and I didn't like his tactics or methods, but he was a darn good investigator."

"Why did you want to meet with Harry?"

"He was at Police District 6 Station downtown on North Washington this morning, where I saw him but he didn't see me. I had a hunch that he was working the kidnapping case, and since we've run out of new leads, I was curious to know what Harry had. Why are you here?"

"Harry called me this morning."

"What did he say?"

"He left a message, but when I called him back, there was no answer."

"Was he working the case? What did he find?"

"No idea."

"Who hired him?"

"I don't know that either."

She looked at Matt and then stared at Charlene, who matched her resolute gaze, refusing to look away. Salinger had a curious look in her eyes, but said no more. Instead, she turned and walked away.

Charlene frowned in confusion. "Why didn't you tell her that Harry was working the case?"

"I don't know."

She grinned. "I do. You don't trust her."

He said nothing, but she was sure she saw the truth in his eyes.

She clicked her tongue by force of habit. "I wish Harry had told us what he had, over the phone."

"He was old school," Matt said. "He didn't trust phone lines, or things that could be overheard, retrieved, or stolen."

"So, we don't know if Harry was working any other cases at the time, but someone wanted him out of the way."

Matt nodded imperceptibly. "No doubt. This totally changes our perspective on the case. When we first started this investigation, we thought we were dealing with non-violent criminal offenders. Now, after this, all signs indicate that the kidnappers will do whatever it takes to accomplish their mission. This just went from a kidnapping case to a homicide investigation."

"We might find something once the fire's out."

He shook his head. "This death isn't under federal jurisdiction. Local police have jurisdiction on an individual murder case, unless we can prove it's connected to our case."

She turned back toward the charred trailer. "We need to talk to Smith ASAP."

"Remember, we're meeting with Cindy Richards at her house tomorrow morning at eleven."

"That's fine, but there's something I want to do before that."

Joshua met her at the door but she was in no mood to talk. She was incensed.

"Why are you here so late?" he asked. "I thought—"

Smack.

She caught him flush on the side of his cheek with an open-handed slap, not giving herself time to calm down or cool off. Joshua involuntarily stepped back, his eyes wide with shock. His cheek was already turning red when he touched it with his palm.

"You stupid son-of-a-bitch," she spat. "You almost killed two cops."

"Almost?"

"That's right, they made it out. Thankfully."

"I thought you'd be happy."

"Happy?" she mocked. "Do you know what killing two cops would do to this investigation? It would become a man-hunt like none other, with the cops on a mission to capture those who offed two of their own. I told you to leave Stone and Taylor alone, that I would take care of them."

"It wasn't my fault. They showed up just after I killed Linden, before I could take care of everything."

"And now they know he was murdered. You dumbass! It was supposed to look like a suicide."

"I'm sorry. I panicked. I thought the fire would destroy the evidence. I never thought they'd get out alive."

"Did you get all of Linden's notes before you left, at least?"

"I think so."

"You think so? Thinking is not your strong suit. Shit." She took off her jacket. "Now it's time for damage control. I'm getting awfully tired of cleaning up your messes."

He lowered his head, looking apologetic. "I'm sorry. Do you want to see what I got?"

"Of course, I do." Then she lightened the mood, knowing he couldn't stand the strain of criticism. "I know you're sorry." She extended her arms to him. "Come here."

He stepped into a hug. The smell of gasoline on his clothes made her shudder.

Frowning, she pushed out of his embrace. "Never mind. I don't want to get that nasty smell on my clothes. I know you thought you were helping, but next time, don't think. Just follow my orders. Now let's get you some ice for the burn on your face."

"I don't want to lose you again," he whispered. "I promise I won't lose sight of the big picture again."

She touched his face. "I know you won't."

It was close to midnight when Charlene returned to Jane's house. She pulled into the driveway to find the downstairs' lights still on. She let herself inside, careful not to wake anyone.

She hadn't seen much of her sister since Martina's abduction and couldn't even begin to understand what Jane and Richard were going through.

She relocked the door, shut off the outside light, and took a couple of the steps up the stairs when she noticed the kitchen light on, shining into the front room. She crossed the living room and entered the kitchen to find Jane sitting alone at the table.

"You okay?" Charlene asked, pulling out a chair and sitting down beside her.

Jane turned and pulled back, scrunching up her nose. "Oh my God. You stink!"

Charlene no longer noticed the stench of smoke on her clothes and skin. "Sorry." She told Jane about her near-death experience.

"Oh no. Did this have anything to do with Martina?"

"Yes. We were following a lead."

"And?" Jane looked hopeful, and it made Charlene sick to have no news.

"Nothing yet."

Her sister's shoulders slumped when she shivered. "I can't take the smell. Take off your clothes."

Charlene stripped down to her underwear while Jane retrieved a large black garbage bag from under the sink. She held the bag while her sister placed the clothes in it and put it outside the back door on the back porch, and then sat back down at the table.

Jane looked sleep-deprived, and her eyes were red and puffy from crying—an empty box of tissues was on the table beside her.

"Where are Richard and Mom?"

"In bed. I couldn't sleep." Jane turned to look outside, into the blackness of the night. "There must be something I can do."

Charlene took her sister's hands. "I swear, everything possible is being done to find Martina. I'm making sure of that."

Jane began to cry. "I just feel so empty inside."

Tense, quiet minutes passed, neither of them saying anything.

"Every day feels like a bad dream," Jane finally said. "Like I'll go to sleep and when I wake up, Martina will be back in her crib and all this will be over. But every morning I wake up to find that she isn't there."

"I know. We'll find her."

"God, I love her so much."

"I know you do."

Charlene wrapped her arms around her trembling sister. Jane dropped her head onto Charlene's chest and sobbed. It felt nice to be the nurturing sister for once.

"We have the best investigators in the country looking for her."

Finally, Jane pulled away and wiped her eyes and nose with a tissue. She looked Charlene in the eye, and saw something in her sister that she'd never seen before.

"I need to know something."

Charlene shifted uncomfortably in her seat.

"These people, the ones who took Martina." Jane hesitated, as if searching for words. "Are they...do they...*like* children?" She shook her head. "You know what I mean? Is Martina in danger, in that sense?"

Charlene swallowed hard. "From what we know, these people are *not* pedophiles. That's not their intention."

"Then what *is* their intention?" Her voice rose above the whisper she'd been using.

"We still aren't sure. But all of our resources, and the FBI has plenty of them, tell us they aren't like that. There's no reason to believe that."

Charlene told Jane as much as she could about the investigation, toeing the fine line between a police officer and a sister. She shouldn't be talking, but her sister deserved to know as much as she could.

In fact, she made a point of not mentioning the connection with the earlier abductions.

She was about to go on but began to cough, still suffering from smoke inhalation.

Jane got up from the table, poured a glass of water, and handed it to Charlene, who took a sip, allowing the liquid to sooth her dry, scratchy throat.

Jane patted Charlene's shoulder. "Goodnight, Char."

Chapter 15

Awkward. Silence.

It was actually their mother who had urged them to attend. Brenda Taylor had been married to a cop for thirty years, had endured heartache and hardships, knew about pain and suffering, and was one of the strongest women Charlene had ever known. And she knew they needed a break, even for just twenty minutes.

Matt had Charlene's number and promised to call if anything came up. He also thought this a good idea, that Charlene might have a chance to pick the senator's brain and ask pertinent questions concerning the New Mexico case.

Charlene stood backstage with her sister, behind the curtain not far from the podium where just moments earlier, Senator Jaqueline Bloomfield had stood to give a heart-felt, inspirational speech to the Colorado college crowd.

The Bloomfield campaign train was clearly gaining momentum as it moved through the country, heading toward DC, and fans, both men and women, jumped on board. The Senate election was only a year away.

When the speech came to an end, they were ushered backstage by the senator's head of security and told to wait. Normally, Charlene would have been vibrating with excitement, but today, she also felt a tingle of guilt.

Jane stood quietly, with her arms crossed, and defeat stripping the life from her normally animated face.

"Detective Taylor."

Charlene turned at the sound of the senator's voice, and saw Jaqueline Bloomfield approaching, her arm outstretched, wearing a million-dollar smile. Despite the early morning commitment, the senator looked flawless in formal business attire—a charcoal-grey skirted suit, pantyhose and closed toe pumps.

"Nice to see you again, Senator." Charlene shook Bloomfield's fine-boned, well-manicured hand. She turned and put her arm around her sister. "This is my sister, Jane."

The senator shook Jane's hand. "It's nice to meet you, Jane. I am so sorry about your daughter. My heart goes out to you and your family."

Jane gave a courteous, nearly imperceptible nod. "Thank you."

"This is for you." The senator handed them a rolled-up poster.

Charlene accepted it with a smile, removed the rubber band, and unrolled it. The poster was a blow-up of the senator, and it was also signed and personalized. Charlene admired the signature.

"Thank you, Senator."

"You're welcome."

Charlene asked, "How are Michael and Anna?"

The senator smiled. "I'm impressed. You've been doing your homework."

Charlene grinned. "I believe I told you this before, but I look up to you for all you've done on behalf of women."

"Thank you, detective. That means a lot. My husband and daughter are in Connecticut for two weeks visiting my in-laws. Last minute plans." She laughed. "I'm probably insufferable to be around these days anyway, as I'm working twenty-four-seven, on the road a lot, and I have no time to spend with them."

"Never a break, huh?"

"Probably no different than a big city cop. How is the investigation going?"

"I believe we have leads. We're hopeful."

"That's good news, for sure. So sad, all those parents without their babies."

Jane let out a squeal. "Babies? Parents?"

Charlene spun around toward her sister, who wore a genuine look of surprise. Trying to protect her family, she hadn't told Jane that Martina's abduction was part of a series of kidnappings, and linked to another case.

"Well, yes," the senator said. "Didn't you know—" Bloomfield looked at Charlene, and then put her hand to her mouth. "Oh, my God, I had no idea. I thought you knew."

Jane let out a soft cry and ran from the room.

The senator shook her head. "I'm so sorry. I thought she knew."

"That's okay." Charlene rubbed her forehead. "I should have told her. Nice seeing you again."

Charlene turned and rushed after her sister. She found Jane sitting in their car in the crowded parking lot. Jane looked out the front windshield and didn't acknowledge Charlene when she got in.

"Tell me." Jane refused to look at Charlene.

"Jane."

"Tell me." This time her voice was louder, more demanding.

Charlene relented, leaning back in the driver's seat. She took in a deep breath. Where to begin?

"Lover's Lane was established in 1999 by Ashlyn and Eric Sheedy."

Charlene and Matt met back at the FBI Denver Bureau, standing behind one of the FBI web techs, who looked over his shoulder at a computer screen. Once the FBI had contacted them and threatened to go public, the owners of the online dating site had agreed to send over an intern to help them navigate the site.

"Do the creators have a criminal record?"

The web tech replied, "Nope. Nothing. They created the site for single people who have given up on the dating scene. They get over 3 million hits a day."

Charlene asked, "What kind of screening process does the site have?"

"Not much of one. Anyone can join. It's free. Basically, you give a description of yourself: interests, hobbies, etcetera, and the site scans the millions of names in the database and finds your perfect match. Looks like it's not mandatory to post your picture."

The dating site intern nodded. "It's the same as most other dating sites." The intern, who had unshorn brown hair and horn-rimmed glasses, defended the integrity of his company, and Charlene wondered if he'd been prepped before arriving.

Smiling, Matt asked, "How do you know?"

The intern didn't respond.

Charlene leaned in closer. "Can you pull up Ryan Richards or David Harper?"

"Sure. Just let me find their usernames."

She watched his magic fingers work the keys.

"Ryan Richards' profile has been deleted. Let me try David Harper." He tapped keys nonchalantly. "Nope. Harper's profile has also been disabled."

Matt asked, "Really? Is that normal?"

The intern nodded. "I would imagine that people disable their profiles when they finally find a mate. Of course, some people forget about it and never return."

Charlene whispered, "Shit."

"No problem," said the intern. "I can go back into the archives and pull up the profiles."

She tilted her head in question. "You can do that?"

"Sure."

The intern went to work again, punching keys, and soon enough, he had both Ryan Richards and David Harper's profiles up, split screen on the monitor so they could compare the two.

There were pictures for both men.

Charlene looked at Matt. "They could be the same guy."

Matt nodded. "Definitely."

"No way," the intern said. "They don't look anything alike."

Charlene read the similar information in the profiles, only reworded to make them appear different. "Sounds desperate. Looking for a serious relationship, hoping to have a family of his own someday. Perfect bait."

"So are a million other candidates."

"When were they last online?"

"Looks like Harper was on seven years ago, and Richards three."

She asked, "Can we locate where they registered?"

The intern nodded. "Most social network sites, including this one, have GPS indicators in them to track people. Is there any chance either of them will get on again?"

"I doubt it, unless he uses a different name."

Matt chimed in. "What about targeting their other login destinations?"

"Hang on." Momentarily he leaned back in his chair. "Wow, look at that."

"What is it?"

"These guys are good. They've logged in a number of times, from many different locations using dozens of proxy servers."

"Proxy what?"

"A proxy server acts as an intermediary for requests from clients seeking resources from other servers. For instance, a client connects to the proxy server, requesting service, and the proxy server evaluates the request as a way to simplify and control its complexity."

"Ah, much clearer." Charlene rolled her eyes.

"Why would these guys do that?" Matt asked.

"If I had to guess I'd say it was to cover their tracks."

Matt scratched his scruffy chin. "Can you check to see if either of these guys contacted anyone else from the site?"

"Hold on." His fingers went back to work. "Doesn't look like it, but not because there weren't any requests. These guys each had dozens of women looking to connect with them, but they never connected."

Charlene read down the mini-profiles from the women who had sought out the suspects. "No other nurses."

"This guy's into nurses, huh? I can appreciate that."

Charlene slapped the intern on the back of the head. "Stay focused."

"Right."

She said, "So let me get this straight. Richards would surf this site, find potential desperate nurses, gain their trust, manipulate them, and then take advantage of their positions at the hospital?"

Matt nodded. "Looks like it. This guy seems good at manipulating people."

Charlene was in deep thinking mode. "What about their bank statements? Have we recovered them for each nurse at the two hospitals?"

"They've been recovered and read. No unusual, exorbitant deposits or withdrawals." Matt turned to the FBI tech. "Dwayne, print out those profiles. We'll add them to the case file. Also, run facial recognition analyses on these two profile pictures to see if they're a match." Then he turned to Charlene. "Let's go see Richards."

Momentarily, they left the parking lot.

"Before we go to the Richards house, I need to swing by Jane's place."

"Do we have time for that?" Matt asked, a skeptical look on his face.

"I have Harold Linden's notepad."

"What?" Matt almost swerved off the road.

"I forgot I had taken it last night before we got trapped in the trailer. It's in my pants' pocket at the house."

"Was there anything written in it?"

"I don't think so, but I never really looked."

"Then what good is it?"

"I have an idea."

Matt ignored the speed limit on the way to Jane's. Charlene had a feeling that he felt, as she did, that time was working against them and any second they could save would be well worth it.

He parked in the driveway behind Jane's car and left the car running while she ran inside.

The house was quiet. Richard had returned to work and Charlene found her mother seated on an oversized loveseat, reading a Nicholas Sparks novel. Her mother looked small in the oversized chair.

"Any news?" her mother asked. She set the book down, flaps open, and stood up.

"No, nothing yet. Where's Jane?"

"She went for a walk. I'm worried about her, Charlene. When Jane got home this morning, she seemed more reserved than usual. She's hardly spoken two words today and seems a little out of it. What happened with you two this morning?"

Charlene bit her lip, and ran through the house to the back door. The bag was still outside on the porch. It still stank, the overwhelming scent of smoke evident even through the plastic. She pulled out the notepad and sprinted back through the house.

"Can I make you something to eat?" her mother asked.

"I don't have time to eat, Mom. Sorry."

Charlene left the house.

She sat in the passenger's seat, with the notepad on her lap, and Matt beside her, with the car still idling. There were no notes on any of the pages, but they saw indentations remaining, indicating that he had made notes at one time.

Matt tilted his head in question. "What are you going to do?"

"I'm guessing the FBI has a forensics lab."

The Rocky Mountain Regional Computer Forensics Laboratory was located about twenty minutes from Denver. It provided computer forensics services to all law enforcement agencies operating in Colorado and Wyoming.

"This looks like the second page, the one behind the top one with the text."

The Forensic Document Examiner, a tawny-haired man with a two-day stubble, had the pad under a microscope, with a bright light illuminating its surface.

"Is that good?" Charlene asked.

"Very. I can just use photography, no need for electrostatic detection." The tech gave them a play-by-play for each step of the process.

The electro-static detection apparatus could recover indented writing three, four, or even more pages below the original script.

The tech applied oblique, glancing light, to the furrows of the indented writing. Using a digital camera to speed up the process, he took pictures, employing photography to preserve the shadowed indentation. He used a combination of multiple exposures while moving the light source around to fill in the indentations with shadow and effectively reproduced the original text.

"It's definitely not a grocery list." The examiner snorted at his own joke.

When finished, he removed the paper and handed it to Charlene, who set the paper on the counter so that she and Matt could both look at it.

Charlene glanced at Matt. "Oh boy."

Matt said, "Wow. That's a lot of text. A full page of notes written in Harry's illegible cursive handwriting."

Charlene shook her head. "That's not handwriting, that's chicken scratch. Who the hell can read that?"

The page was covered from top to bottom. Some of the words and sentences had been scratched out numerous times. There were both numbers and letters, capital and lower-case letters, full sentences and abbreviated words.

"The numbers could be a phone number, with no dashes. Any significance?" Charlene asked.

Matt shook his head. "Not to me. But I think I know someone who might be able to read this."

"Who, a nurse?" Charlene asked with a grin. "It looks like something a doctor would scribble out on a prescription pad."

"Harry's ex-wife."

Meredith Thompson lived in the City of Lakewood, a Home Rule Municipality which was the most populated municipality in Jefferson County. Lakewood was fifteen minutes west of Denver and part of the Denver-Aurora-Lakewood Metropolitan area.

Matt hopped on the Seventy out of Denver, via Colfax Avenue, the main street that ran east-west through the Denver-Aurora metropolitan area, and a straight shot to Lakewood. Then he took South Wadsworth Boulevard that ran through the heart of Lakewood.

Thompson's house was located off West Center Avenue, a charming little bungalow tucked into the corner of a predominantly WASP-like neighborhood—with beautifully manicured lawns, fenced-in yards, dogs on chains and double car garages.

Meredith Thompson, now Meredith Sturgeon since her second marriage twenty years earlier, was a friendly-looking woman in her late sixties. Her silver hair was held in a bun with a single chopstick, and glasses hung around her neck on a thin chain. She answered the door on the first knock, opening it wide to a pair of strangers, as if she'd been waiting for a visitor to help pass her day.

"Mrs. Sturgeon, I'm Agent Stone, FBI. This is my partner, Agent Taylor." Matt showed his badge.

"What can I do for you, Agent Stone?"

"We'd like to speak to you about Harold Linden."

"Of course. Come in."

She turned and they followed her into a room decorated with old but well-maintained furniture. A hoarse voice called from a back room, "Who is it, Mer?"

"It's no one, dear." She looked at Charlene and Matt. "Leonard sits in his den for most of the day. His mind plays tricks on him, though some days are still good."

Sturgeon didn't seem upset or unable to cope—just a woman who'd come to terms with the tricks the mind could play when time started to take its toll.

"Please make yourselves comfortable. Would you like tea?" She sipped from a mug, her hand shaky, but nothing spilled.

Matt smiled. "No thank you, ma'am."

He had told Charlene that the woman suffered from rheumatoid arthritis.

Momentarily he added, "Thank you for seeing us on such short notice, Mrs. Sturgeon."

She waved her hand. "Please, call me Meredith. It's nice to have company. I was upset to hear what happened to Harold. We married and separated a long time ago, but we'll always share some great memories. He was special to me." Meredith looked off in the distance for a few seconds, as if reminiscing.

"How long were you two married?" Charlene asked, bringing the woman back into the moment.

"Six years." She said with a chuckle, "It doesn't seem long, but we dated for four years before that. We were young, just having fun. It was the seventies, the era of love and drugs. We weren't ready to settle down, and when the time came, we ended it just like that. No arguing, no messy divorce, just 'adios' and went our separate ways. Neither of us had a regret or a care in the world." She looked at Charlene. "Times have changed, haven't they?"

Charlene nodded.

"You kids these days. Always in a hurry, wanting more, wanting something better. You never take the time to truly appreciate what you have—laughter, travel, life, love. Are you married, Agent Taylor?"

Charlene was taken off guard but managed to shake her head. "No, ma'am."

"Can I give you one piece of advice?"

"Sure."

"Live. Live like there's no tomorrow, and love like there are no second chances."

Charlene shifted in her seat, not at all comfortable with where the conversation was going. Changing the subject, she said, "We have something we'd like you to look at."

She signaled to Matt.

"Right." He removed the paper from his pocket. "We found this in Harry's trailer."

"What is it?" She took the paper and sat back in her seat, a reupholstered winged-back chair. She slipped her glasses onto the bridge of her nose and smiled, as if seeing her ex-husband's handwriting brought back fond memories.

Matt said, "Can you decipher it?"

"Maybe. I'm guessing you only want the information that hasn't been crossed out?"

He nodded. "Well, we'd like it all, if you can manage it."

She nodded. "Are you ready?"

Matt had his notepad out and was ready to write.

"There's a woman's name at the top. Looks like Tina something, last name starts with an 'A' and ends with an 'N'."

"Tina Allen," Matt said.

"Is that significant?" she asked.

"Very."

"That's one of the mothers," Charlene said. "So she probably hired Harry."

Matt nodded. "Please continue."

"This must be Ms. Allen's phone number."

Charlene felt hopeful. "We can cross reference that later. What else?"

"More female names, Elizabeth and Allison. And phone numbers. Then these three words circled in the corner. Not sure exactly what they are, but they all start with a 'Z.'" She looked at Matt. "I could try to spell them out for you, if that would help."

"Yes, please."

"The first word is: Z, O, P, I, C, L, O, N, E. The second word is: Z, O, L P, I, D, E, M. And this third one is…" She hesitated, squinting slightly. "Z, A, L, E, P, L, O, N."

"Could it be a code?" Charlene asked Matt.

He shrugged his shoulders. "I'm not sure."

"There are a bunch of words and groups of words he crossed out. He always leaned so hard on his pen. Then, at the bottom of the page, there are two words. Both start with capital letters, so they could be connected. They start with 'M' and 'V'. The last word looks like Valley."

"Valley, valley, valley," Matt kept repeating in a low voice.

"Does it mean anything?" Charlene asked.

Matt shook his head.

"I'm sorry, agents, but that's the best I can do. It's been a while since I've had to read Harry's handwriting. I used to tease him about it all the time."

Matt reached out and shook her hand. "You did great, Meredith. Thank you again for seeing us."

Charlene was ecstatic. "So, Tina Allen hired Harold Linden to find her child."

"It wouldn't be the first-time parents took things into their own hands. They see the cops getting nowhere and feel frustrated, and want to be proactive. Some parents even go as far to hire psychics or mediums."

They had just merged on to Colfax Avenue, heading back to Denver. Traffic was heavier, more congested than it had been earlier.

Charlene was no longer thinking about the Sturgeon interview; something else was bothering her.

"What's—" Matt was cut off by his cell phone, the ringtone of an Eminem song sounded especially loud in the quiet car. He glanced at Charlene. "Don't judge me."

He picked it up immediately. "Stone. Okay, hang on." He looked at Charlene. "It's Jake. The facial recognition analysis on the pictures we pulled from the dating website matched. Ryan Richards and David Harper are the same person."

She half-nodded. The puzzle pieces were falling into place, one at a time.

Matt got back on his phone. "Jake, go to Cindy Richards' house and pull prints from anywhere you can. She won't mind—she's been willing to cooperate so far. It's time we find out who this guy is." He listened to Jake before adding, "A search warrant isn't needed because we've already got verbal consent from the home owner."

He hung up.

Matt merged onto Valley Highway Twenty-Five. Tina Allen lived off Colorado Boulevard, located at the east end of Denver, so they had a significant drive ahead of them.

"You're quiet over there. What's on your mind?"

She laughed out loud. "You mean other than your ringtone?" She turned away, looking out at the speeding vehicles. "I'm still wondering about the source of the radiation that killed those women's babies."

"Yes, that's weird."

"Not just weird, but unusual. Not just one woman, but two. Do you know the effort it would take to make that happen? Where would someone even get access to it, and then apply it?"

Matt shook his head. "And why would they do it?"

She made a face. "You know, I'm really getting sick and tired of all these questions and no answers. How many radiotherapy clinics could there be in the area?"

"Let's find out." Matt punched in one of his contact numbers. He held the phone to his ear and waited. "Nicole, I need a favor. I need a list of radiotherapy clinics in the Denver and Albuquerque areas, and those within a 100-mile radius. Thanks." He hung up. "It's a long shot, but worth a try."

"Who was that?"

"Nicole Morton. She's our team's technical analyst back at Quantico. She's on call 24/7, and an excellent resource in the moment."

"So she's basically your Penelope from Criminal Minds?"

Matt chuckled. "I guess you could say that."

When they knocked on the door, a curly-haired boy of about four years of age answered. Charlene knelt down to speak with the boy, when a hand fell on his right shoulder and held him securely.

"This is my nephew." Tina Allen opened the door wider, and motioned them inside. "Come on in. My sister flew in from Florida and is staying with us."

They entered, following the mother who had just lost her only child. She shooed her nephew up a narrow set of carpeted stairs. The house was quiet, with no one in living room where she invited them to sit down. Tina Allen looked tired, wore no makeup, and was dressed in baggy sweatpants, with her hair pulled up in a black scrunchie.

Once they were seated she asked, "Is there anything new?"

That question had been asked a number of times over the last week, by hopeful parents. But it was clear from her demeanor that she was no longer confident that she'd ever see her baby again.

Matt shook his head. "Unfortunately, no, but we're optimistic and I believe we're taking steps in the right direction."

Allen removed the scrunchie, pulled her hair back and repositioned it. "I haven't met your partner, Agent Stone."

"This is Detective Taylor, LAPD."

"LAPD?"

Charlene nodded. "Yes, my niece—"

Matt cut her off. "Detective Taylor was here on vacation. She has expertise in the field and we thought she could assist."

Charlene had forgotten that no one knew these kidnappings were part of a series.

Tina nodded again, and then looked away.

Matt said, "We're here to talk about Harold Linden."

The woman flinched slightly, but didn't make eye contact. "I don't know who that is."

"Mrs. Allen, we know you hired Linden to track down your son."

Now she glared at Matt. "I have no idea what you're talking about, Agent."

Charlene interrupted, "Harold Linden was killed last night."

Tina suddenly sat up straight and looked into Charlene's eyes, probably wondering if she was bluffing. Then she looked at Matt, who said nothing. "Oh, my God." She covered her mouth with her hand and tears slid down her cheeks.

Charlene grabbed a nearby box of tissues and set it in front of the weeping mother, who took one and blew her nose into it.

"What's wrong? Is it Jonathan?"

Tina Allen's husband, Mark, had entered the room and rushed to embrace his wife. He settled into the sofa beside her and put his arm around her.

"Harry's dead," she gasped, whispering between sobs.

"What?"

Matt explained, "His trailer burned to the ground last night. He was in it."

"Arson?"

"We believe so, yes."

"Do you think it has to do with our son's case?"

"We're not entirely certain, but we're not ruling it out."

"Jesus."

Matt sighed then shrugged. "We need to know what Harry was working on, what leads he was chasing."

Tina Allen pulled away from her husband, wiped her nose one more time, and focused through teary eyes. "We haven't seen or even spoken with Harry since our initial interview." She looked at her husband, and took his hand in hers.

Matt asked, "Can you take us through the interview?"

The father shrugged his shoulders. "He asked much the same questions the police asked, but he questioned us together, while the cops separated us during our interviews."

Charlene pulled out the folder she had brought in from the car. "According to our report." She shuffled though the papers. "Mr. Allen, you were away, and Mrs. Allen, you were sleeping when your son was taken."

They both nodded.

He went on, "Earlier in the evening a man came to your house to conduct a survey?"

"Yes." Tina dabbed her eyes. "But we found out that was all a lie."

Charlene nodded. "So this could have been the kidnapper."

Tina nodded.

"Nothing stands out?"

"Nothing." Tina stood and walked around the couch toward the window, hugging herself, massaging her arms as if a cool breeze had entered the room. "I've been over it a thousand times in my head, trying to come up with something new, something I've missed, but I can't."

Mark got up and joined his wife, wrapping her in a hug. "It's okay, honey."

She buried her face in her husband's sweater, then mumbled under her breath, "I'm the reason Harry's dead, Mark. If I hadn't called him, he'd still be alive."

Charlene tried to comfort her. "You only did what you thought was right, Mrs. Allen. You did what any loving mother would've done."

Matt picked up the thread. "So, once you went to bed, you never heard anything more until when?"

"When Mark came in to wake me up, to tell me that Jonathon wasn't in his crib."

Mark turned to look at them. "Which is unusual because Tina is such a light sleeper. I can never even pull into the driveway without her waking up. Harry seemed to be interested in that."

Charlene checked Matt's reaction to that statement.

Tina picked up the thread. "The surveyor asked questions and filled out paperwork while we talked, and we sat at that table having tea, until he left."

Matt leapt on the idea. "You had tea with this guy? If you think back, was there ever a moment when the man was alone with your tea cup?"

She closed her eyes, as if this would help replay the events of that night. "After I set down our tea, I did go back into the kitchen, but only for a minute or so."

"Why?"

"Well, I had just baked cookies and the man mentioned how good they smelled. So I brought out a plate, which seemed to please him to no end."

A minute was all he would have needed.

"So what was the last thing Harry told you?"

"He had an idea, but he had to leave the city to follow a lead. I never heard from him again."

"Did he say where he was going?"

"No."

Charlene heard a buzzing sound and saw Matt unclip his phone from his belt. He looked at the call display. "Please excuse me. I need to take this."

He walked out of the room, and Charlene watched as he stepped outside, already speaking in low tones.

Charlene waited a few seconds. "Did Harry ever mention the possibility of more than one kidnapper?"

Mark frowned. "More than one kidnapper? Why would you ask such a thing? Do you think there's more than one person involved?"

"We're still toying with that theory. But—"

The front door banged shut and Matt reentered the living room. He signed to Charlene, then said, "Ready to go?"

She nodded.

He reached out and shook hands with both Tina and Mark. "Thank you for your time, Mr. and Mrs. Allen. We'll be in touch."

"Drugged?" It was a statement more than a question from Charlene.

"It's possible, or the kidnapper could have been really quiet when he came to take the baby."

She continued, "You know, I spent a few nights at Jane's place before Martina was taken. Babies make noise. I agree that Tina could've just slept through it, but I like the 'drugged' scenario. It makes more sense, since new mothers are usually wired to hear any little squirm or whine from their children, especially newborns. The kidnapper had a much better chance of slipping in, taking the baby, and sneaking out if the only adult in the house had been sedated."

Matt backed the car out of the Allen's driveway and headed toward downtown Denver. It was nearing supper time, in late afternoon, which meant shift workers were leaving work, and that made for serious rush hour traffic.

They moved at a snail's pace, when they moved at all. It would be stop and go for the next twenty miles.

Finally, Matt broke the silence. "Jake called earlier. They pulled a bunch of prints at Cindy Richards' house and I had him take them to the FBI Denver fieldhouse to run them through IAFIS as well as our VICAP database that checks links to homicide cases throughout the country. No matches found yet."

"This guy has got to be in the system."

"I hope so."

Charlene sighed, feeling exhaustion creep into her bones. "Let's break down what we have." This was the way she worked, usually with her LAPD partner Larry Baker. But since Larry wasn't around, Matt would have to be her sounding board.

"Okay," Matt began. "We know that Ryan Richards, AKA David Harper, is the same person, and most likely the kidnapper involved in this case. But we don't yet know who he is, because he could have a number of aliases in a number of cities.

"We have to assume these are the same guy. He strikes in New Mexico six years ago, and now in Denver. But why wait? What was he doing for the last six years? We know about his fake relationship with Cindy Richards, maybe getting information on babies from the hospital, biding his time, waiting to strike again."

"He meets women online, preferably nurses, and uses them to his advantage. Both of these women suffer from child loss, in a most unbelievable way."

She picked up the thread. "Since he impregnated them both, there's no trouble with conception. At first I thought that he could be behind the mysterious death of his children, but according to these women, this guy dearly loves children and couldn't wait to be a father."

Matt made a face. "Then who did it?"

"That takes us back to your profile, the theory that there are two kidnappers involved—one dominant and one follower. From the nurses' profile on their husband, he was gentle, tranquil and affable."

He shook his head in frustration. "Why would this guy's partner kill his kids? What would she gain by doing that?"

Charlene shrugged. "Obedience? Loyalty? I don't know, I'm just spit-balling here."

"Harry told Tina Allen that he had to leave the city to follow a lead, but we don't know what that lead was or where he was headed. Then he wrote those three 'Z' words, circling them as if they were important."

Matt's cell phone rang. Charlene couldn't believe how often it went off.

"Agent Stone. Hang on, Nicole, I'm gonna put you on speakerphone." He punched a button and positioned the phone on the console between the seats. "Go ahead, Nikki."

"I've identified 2,246 radiation therapy facilities operating in the United States, ninety-four in Colorado and New Mexico."

Charlene shook her head. "You're kidding. We have neither the time nor the resources to check them all."

"Who's that?"

"Sorry, Nik, this is Detective Charlene Taylor of the LAPD. She's working with me on this case. And she's right. We just don't have the time or manpower for that."

"Not necessary."

"What do you mean?"

"I did some digging after I narrowed my search to areas around Denver and Albuquerque, and I discovered that a technician at one of these locations was murdered. The case is still open."

"Murdered? When?"

"Six years ago, not long before the babies started disappearing in Albuquerque."

Charlene winked at Matt. "She's good."

"Thank you," came the voice over the speaker. "The agents get all of the credit for my hard work."

Charlene could almost hear the smile in Nicole's voice.

Matt looked at Charlene. "That murder can't be a coincidence, especially with the timing."

Charlene said, "Where is the clinic?"

"Aurora."

Charlene smiled. "Turn the car around."

Aurora, Colorado was a thirty-minute drive east of Denver, via West 14th Avenue. Traffic would be light, traveling away from the city.

Matt placed a calming hand on Charlene's. "It's closed for tonight. We'll go there first thing in the morning. Nicole, send me the address and also the name of the detective working that case."

"Sure thing."

"One more thing. I need you to look up three words. I'll spell them out for you."

Charlene pulled out the paper from Harry's notepad and spelled the 'Z' words to Nicole over the speaker phone.

"I'll get on it." She hung up.

"Does she ever sleep?" Charlene asked, smiling.

"I doubt it. How about a bite to eat?"

She shook her head. "Too much to do."

Matt pulled the car to the side of the road and put it in park. Cars honked, but swerved around them.

"What are you doing?"

There was no mirth in his look. "Charlene, you're not helping anyone by pushing yourself to your limit. You need food and rest. You can't work on fumes forever. Take a break, refuel and recharge."

She let out a deep breath. "You're right. I could use something to eat."

Chapter 16

She expected to go to a restaurant, order something quick and easy, but Matt surprised her by making dinner back at Jake's apartment. Jake worked the night shift so it was just the two of them.

While he fiddled in the kitchen, hovering over spicy smelling pasta sauce, Charlene took charge of the music. She browsed through Jake's collection of CDs, all heavy metal bands she'd never heard of, then set the radio dial to KQMT 99.5 FM, a local classical rock station.

With the soft music and lingering aroma of his cooking, she explored the apartment, looking at pictures of Matt and Jake as kids. She found one, of the boys on Halloween, where they both dressed as cops.

Then she found a framed photograph of Matt, Jake and two adults, presumably their parents. Matt had his father's strong jaw and penetrating blue eyes. Jake had softer features like their mother.

She had set the picture back down, when she heard his footsteps behind her. He held two glasses of red wine.

"I hope you like merlot."

She wasn't a wine drinker, but accepted the glass and sipped gingerly. A cold Corona would have been better. "Thank you."

He pointed toward the kitchen. "The sauce is ready, simmering in the pot. I just put the pasta in. Nice choice of music."

"Thanks. Jake didn't leave me much choice."

She'd spent the last three days with Agent Matt Stone, on the job, investigating, following leads and interrogating suspects, but being here with him, alone, in a more informal setting, felt different—strange.

"Are you sure there isn't something we can do? Someone to call, visit, investigate?"

He shook his head. "Relax. We need to recharge."

She felt unsure of herself. Her palms glistened with sweat and her heartbeat hammered like a drum. Maybe it was the wine, the smell of the food or the music; it was surreal, but nice.

They sat on the couch, in silence. Maybe out of exhaustion, they laid their heads back on the soft couch cushions and stared at the ceiling. Even though they could do nothing but wait, she still felt guilty about taking a break.

She was ever-aware of Matt's presence, the heat emanating from his body. He was the first guy in a while with whom she'd felt a connection, and that included her ex-boyfriend, Andy.

She didn't have the time or the energy to get back into the dating game. She just wanted to be left alone to do what she loved, and be a cop.

A small smile appeared on her lips. Here she was, on a sofa with a Fed. She knew about the unwritten rules, had lived them for ten years. Cops hated Feds. On the force, they learned not to trust the FBI. But over the last couple of days, her attitude had changed.

She set her glass on the table, and turned toward him. She hesitated, feeling tentative, unsure. Matt scooted closer to her, until he was so close that she could smell the scent of wine on his lips. His eyes danced, his lips parting ever so slightly, and she felt the warmth of his breath on her neck.

Matt brought his hand to her face, tracing his fingertip along the side of her jaw, running it under her chin, pausing along her v-shaped scar. Charlene pulled back slightly, self-conscious of the disfigurement. But he pulled her back, gently running his finger up to her mouth, parting her lips with his thumb.

She softly kissed the skin of his thumb, tasting his salty flesh. He cupped her face in his hands and moved in slowly, their lips only inches apart.

One kiss turned into two, the first one short and soft, then they yielded to their mutual desire, and the next kiss became more passionate. They embraced on the couch for several long minutes, giving in to the sexual tension that had been stirring between them.

When she finally pulled away to catch her breath, she laid her head on his chest, and felt it rise and fall with each breath.

She looked up at Matt, hoping for a response. He brushed the hair away from her face and when his eyes danced, she knew it was okay. Her breathing accelerated.

He took her by the hand and led her down the hall. She followed quietly, her body trembling. It had been so long.

They made love in a slow, tidal rhythm, satisfying her need for closeness. In fact, she had never felt closer to another human being.

As they lay under the covers, recovering from the moment, she pressed her head to his chest, releasing a soft, satisfied sigh.

Suddenly she asked, "Do you smell something burning?"

Matt ripped off the bedsheet and jumped from the bed. "The pasta."

As they perched on the edge of the bed, dressing, she could feel her stomach growling.

He asked, "You hungry?"

"Famished."

He winked. "Good, I'll put more pasta on to boil."

Matt was leaving the room when his phone rang. She picked it up and tossed it into his waiting hands.

He checked caller ID.

"It's Jake's cell phone." He answered, "What's up?"

Charlene watched Matt's facial expressions transform from a smile to a look of concern.

"Shit." He left the room in a hurry.

"What is it?" she called, trailing behind him.

"There's a press conference going on right now."

He raced to the living room and switched on the TV. He channel-surfed until he found the news conference, where a crowd filled the Bellco Theatre at the Colorado Convention Center in downtown Denver. Media, local law enforcement and curious attendees were all waiting for an announcement.

On the main stage, standing at a podium with a cluster of microphones and the curtains drawn behind them, six people had assembled, including: Peter and Liz Bailey, whose son Mason was one of the kidnapped infants, Chief of Police Janice Salinger, Colorado Senator Ethan Black, New Mexico Senator Jaqueline Bloomfield, and another woman whom Charlene didn't recognize.

"Son-of-a-bitch," Matt spat between clenched lips.

"What is it?"

"A goddamn leak."

Janice Salinger stepped up and tapped the podium microphone. She introduced the parents, and let them issue their statement.

Liz Bailey announced to the world that babies were being kidnapped in Denver. This caused an uproar, a frenzy of whispers throughout the auditorium.

She begged in desperation for the kidnappers to give her son Mason back, said that they were praying for the other children, the other parents, and anyone who suffered from the loss of these babies. She pleaded for anyone who had information to contact the local police.

Once her prepared statement ended, reporters and cameramen started snapping pictures, and yelling out questions. Once again Salinger stepped up to the mic, and addressed the assembled crowd.

"We will now take questions. I will point to one member of the press at a time. Have your question prepared. Please do not ask the same question twice. Address the person who you would like to respond directly. Do not waste our time." She pointed her finger. "You."

A reporter stood up and the room grew quiet. An attractive African American woman spoke. "Marcie Jamison, Denver Seven News. Police Chief Salinger, how long have the police known about these kidnappings and are there leads?"

"The first kidnapping occurred six days ago. There have been five kidnappings to date and we're in the process of following several leads. Of course, we can't comment on an active investigation."

More shouts from the reporters, some standing and pointing.

"Do I need to shut this down right now?" Salinger raised her voice, and it got everyone's attention. Message received. The large theatre suddenly grew silent.

"Yes?" She pointed to an overweight gentleman in the front row.

"Alex Antonelli, CBS Denver. Why wasn't the public informed of these crimes before now?"

"It was the FBI's decision. They thought that was the best action to take at the time."

Charlene could have sworn she heard a hint of bitterness in Salinger's tone. She looked at Matt to see if he had noticed anything, but he didn't react.

There was no one from the FBI present at the meeting to deny or confirm Salinger's response, but Charlene remembered Matt's profile from the first day's meeting, recommending that they keep the investigation hush-hush, to try and draw out the criminals.

Whether that would have worked or not, they would never know.

Another hand went up and a forty-something woman stepped forward to ask the next question. "Alexis Burke, KOA News Radio. This question is for Senator Bloomfield. Senator, what is your role in this investigation?"

Salinger stepped away from the microphones and Jaqueline Bloomfield strode forward. "I am here to assist in any way possible. I was present six years ago when these heinous acts occurred in my state, and I'd like to make sure the same thing doesn't happen here. I hope I can be of some comfort to the grieving parents, a shoulder to cry on, or a springboard for local and federal law enforcement."

They watched in bitter silence for another twenty minutes, as spectators threw question after question at the panel, who fouled them all away. No homeruns hit, no quick strike offense. Most of the questions were answered with the usual, "No comment at this time," or "We cannot discuss an ongoing investigation."

Every few minutes Matt sighed and rubbed his temples.

When it was over, he shut off the TV and stood up. "We need to get to the field office—now."

Charlene was quite accustomed to the everyday hustle and bustle of a police station. No station in the country, when in full throttle, was as loud or as chaotic as an LAPD precinct. In contrast, she had imagined that an FBI center would be like a library—stiff-collared agents answering phones in a serene manner, quietly tapping keyboards, sipping coffee and sending texts to family members.

But when she walked into the Denver field office, it was a mad house. With phones ringing everywhere, agents moved at a swift pace, and supervisors barked orders.

Charlene looked over at Matt who shook his head and shrugged. Business as usual.

He said, "Let's find Smith."

They didn't have to look far. As they entered the chaos, Agent Nicholas Smith hurried across the room, looking harried.

Smith looked like hell, worn down. His hair was disheveled, his thousand-dollar suit, probably hand-tailored in London, was wrinkled, and the dark bags under his eyes had grown deeper.

"We need a plan for damage control. The whole city has lost it, and we need to calm the waters. We have our PR people on it now."

They followed him through the chaos, into the conference room, where it was quiet. The heads of the departments had gathered and were talking in low tones among themselves.

The talking ceased when Smith entered and closed the door behind him, and people took their places at the table.

He made no introductions this time. Charlene and Matt found empty seats and sat down, then looked through the packets in front of them.

Smith cleared his throat. "Time is of the essence. The city is in an uproar, so we need to issue a statement immediately, and come up with a media strategy." He gestured toward Noreen Walters, the Denver FBI's local Media Representative.

She nodded. "What are we going to say?"

Smith slammed his fist against the top of the table. "They know practically everything already. That bitch."

Matt put up his hand, but didn't wait to be called on. "I suggest that we explain the reason why we withheld the information. It was my call, so I'll take the rap. And I can make the announcement if that will help. That's standard operating procedure."

Noreen Walters wrote on her notepad. "We'll need more than that to win back the public trust. The locals have snatched the case out from under us, reaching out to the parents and the public."

Charlene chipped it. "I think we need to release the profile and the photo of the suspect, to the media."

Smith cocked his head in confusion. "Photo? What photo?" Charlene had forgotten that no one else was aware of the photo match. In fact, no one knew they were even working the case.

Matt nodded. "That's good. Maybe we'll get lucky and a pertinent tip will come in, although the nut jobs will, no doubt, be out in full force as well."

Smith continued, "The local, as well as national television news will go live in an hour, so I'm giving you thirty minutes to come up with text I can review before then, okay Noreen?"

The conference room door burst opened, and Janice Salinger and Senator Jaqueline Bloomfield walked in and scanned the room.

"Senator, you're welcome here, but you—" Smith pointed a crooked finger at the police chief. "You have a lot of nerve showing your face here." His voice dripped contempt. "After the stunt you just pulled."

Salinger stared hard at Smith, not relenting an inch. "You can't talk to me like that. I'm the chief of police, not one of your lackeys. You don't run me. I do what I feel is right for this city."

Smith argued, "I thought we agreed to leave the press out of it, keeping the kidnappers in the dark."

Salinger snapped, "Without even consulting me, you've stepped up and taken over this case. But what have you accomplished so far? Nothing. So I decided it was time to spread the word and try to smoke out the kidnappers."

"You've smoked them out all right. Now they'll go into hiding because the whole city is after them."

"It's abundantly clear that they're one step ahead of you, and that's been the case from the very beginning. Hell, you've been chasing them for six years and haven't turned up a thing. Now it's time to let someone else take over."

Smith flushed a deep red, and a vein in his temple visibly pulsated. Clearly, no one had ever spoken to Smith that way before, especially in front of his team.

Charlene got Matt's attention and mouthed, "We should leave."

Matt nodded and stood up. Together they headed for the door, passing Smith, who now stood nose-to-nose with Salinger.

As they tried to slip past the feuding leaders undetected, Smith grabbed Matt by the arm of his jacket and turned him around.

"Agent Stone. We need to talk."

Salinger stepped forward and nodded. "I too need a moment of your time."

"What do you think Smith wants?" Charlene asked.

They waited in a small office down the hall, feeling the growing tension.

"It's hard to tell. Maybe he wants our opinion on what to do next."

"Does that sound like something Smith would do?"

Matt shook his head. "No. Once that profile goes out on the news, all we can do is wait for a valid lead, hoping the kidnappers don't disappear into thin air."

"I should be with Jane when that news comes out."

Matt nodded.

They could hear hurried footsteps in the hallway and Smith joined them, squeezing into the small office with a full cup of steaming coffee.

"That's why I don't like working with local cops." He looked at Charlene. "No offense."

Charlene said nothing.

"Look," Smith said. "Let's cut the crap. I asked you to sit in because I know you two have been working the case on your own."

Matt shuffled his feet. "Sir—"

"Don't bother denying it. Hell, you've been using all my resources. The private jet? Come on."

Matt swallowed. "It's true. We've been investigating."

"What can you tell me?"

Salinger stepped inside, making the room feel uncomfortably small. "Yes, I would also like to hear what he's come up with."

She looked at Charlene, who responded with a hard-core glare of her own.

Matt looked at Agent Smith, who nodded.

The agent took them through what he and Charlene had discovered over the past few days, from Harold Linden's murder, to the dead fetuses, to the photo match of David Harper and Ryan Richards.

When he completed his pitch, Smith asked Matt, "Will releasing the profile send this guy into hiding?"

"I don't think so. From what I've seen, he has an agenda and he's too confident to let anything stop him."

Smith rubbed the scruff that had grown on his face. "I was supposed to send you to Seattle today to construct a profile."

Charlene frowned. Was Matt leaving? Now? Just when they were starting to gain momentum.

Smith lowered his head in deep thought. "But that's not going to work, because we need you here. I'll send another profiler in your place."

"Thank you, sir."

Janice Salinger turned on her heels and stormed out of the office without a word.

They gave Charlene a bureau car—a four-door Chrysler sedan, to return to Jane's. She was all in now, and there would be no turning back.

She'd explained it to Matt. Charlene needed to be home for Jane, and as usual, he understood her need to be with family. And though he would've loved to be there for Charlene, he had far too much to do on the case.

When she'd gotten into the car and turned her phone on for the first time in hours, she'd noticed that she'd missed three calls from her sister. No messages, so she put the pedal to the metal.

She had no idea how Jane would've reacted to the press conference, especially the news that the earlier kidnappings had never been solved, and the children were never heard from again.

It was late when Charlene pulled into the driveway and killed the lights. Yawning, she trudged up the drive toward the front door.

The door was unlocked so she let herself in and dropped her jacket just inside the door. She eyed the couch while crossing the main floor, thinking she'd like to sink into it face first and let exhaustion take over.

But when she saw the kitchen light on, she headed toward the kitchen where Jane sat at the table, with her head resting on her arms on the table top. Though she struggled to stay awake, Charlene shook it off and returned to the living room for a pillow to slide under her sister's head.

But as she approached the table, she suddenly noticed the pill bottles.

Charlene froze, and her breath caught in her chest. She recognized the vials immediately, without reading their labels. They were her meds, prescribed by Dr. Gardner for depression.

Two of the bottles held a few pills, but one was empty. Even after wracking her brain she couldn't recall how many pills remained, but she knew she hadn't touched them since she'd arrived in town.

"Richard!"

She checked for a pulse, but couldn't find one. Jane wasn't breathing and her lips and fingertips had turned a light gray-blue. Then Charlene noticed a tiny puddle of vomit on the table beside Jane's mouth.

She shook her sister, who didn't respond. "Jane, wake up!"

Richard appeared in the kitchen. "What on earth is going on?" But when he saw Charlene hovering over an unmoving Jane, his eyes opened wide with unbelief.

"Call 911," Charlene ordered. "Tell them she's overdosed on medication. She's not breathing."

Richard ran for the phone.

"Jane, please. Jane, wake up."

Her mother stood in the doorway frowning. "What's wrong?"

"Come and help me get her on the floor."

Together they got Jane onto her back on the tiled floor where Charlene cleaned out her mouth and placed the heel of her hand on the center of the Jane's chest, lacing her fingers together. Keeping her arms straight and her shoulders over her hands, she pushed hard and fast, compressing Jane's chest at least two inches. Jane's chest rose completely before Charlene pushed down again.

"Come on, Jane, breathe!"

A thousand questions ran through her mind. How many pills had she taken? How long ago? How long had she been unconscious? How long had she been without oxygen?

Everything around her faded away, so that her entire focus was on Jane.

Exhaustion set in, and her arms grew heavy. Sweat drops poured from her forehead and burned her eyes, but she continued chest compressions.

She couldn't help wondering when help would arrive. Were they close?

Then she felt a strong hand on her shoulder and looked up to see Richard's face.

He gently pulled her away, as two men in uniform ran toward them, one carrying a defibrillator. She watched, feeling paralyzed, as if in a slow-motion movie.

Before she could move or say anything, her mom's arms wrapped around her and pulled her away.

Charlene sat at the kitchen table, feeling alone, because the rest of the house was dark and quiet. It was the middle of the night and she'd just gotten back from the hospital where Jane was alive, in recovery but not yet responding. Richard had stayed with Jane, and her mother had gone up to bed.

They had pumped Jane's stomach and used an activated charcoal cocktail to absorb the drugs she'd ingested. When possible, a staff psychiatrist would evaluate her to make sure she was no longer a threat to herself.

Charlene felt numb as she rolled the pill bottles between her fingers. How had she let this happen?

There wasn't much anyone could do but wait and pray that Jane would pull through unscathed. As a cop who had seen her fair share of OD victims, she was well aware of possible negative outcomes.

The longer a person went without oxygen, the higher the potential for brain damage. In severe cases, brain injuries from overdoses could leave people in a vegetative state.

Charlene was sure she had done everything in her power. She was a trained professional and well aware of the procedures in handling an overdose. She had followed the ambulance to the hospital, with pill bottles in hand, to make sure the doctors understood how to treat her.

She heard the front door to the house open and close but didn't turn around or get up. It was probably Richard, returning for a change of clothes. Instead, she thought about how to make this all right.

"Charlene?"

She heard the voice behind her, recognized it, but didn't turn around. If she did, she knew she would break down, and she didn't want him to see her cry.

"Char?"

Momentarily she felt his hands on her shoulders.

His voice was little more than a whisper. "How are you?"

"The pills—they were mine."

"What?"

She held up the pill bottles.

He touched her hand.

Suddenly irate she demanded, "Why are you here?"

He looked surprised. "I heard what happened to Jane and I came to see if you're all right. I'm sorry I couldn't come sooner. I should have been here with you."

He placed his hand on her shoulder but she shrugged it off. "Why are you here?"

Matt stood and stepped back. "What do you mean?"

"This is all my fault."

He shook his head in disbelief. "What do you mean?"

"I should have been here for my sister." She noticed the desperation in her voice.

"You had no idea…"

"I should have known. I should have been here for Jane when she needed me, but instead, I was having sex with you. What kind of a person am I? I'm a terrible sister and an even worse aunt."

"This isn't your fault. We're doing everything we can to find Martina."

"Don't say we, it's me. This is my family. My sister. My niece. You don't have anything to lose here. I have everything on the line and I'm mucking it up big time, letting it all slip away." She shoved her phone in his face. "I missed her call, three times. Jane reached out to me and I was too busy fucking you."

"Casting blame or feeling sorry for yourself isn't going to bring Martina back or make Jane feel better. Feeling guilty is the last thing you should be doing right now. In fact, we need to focus and work harder now than we ever have."

"Please just go."

"I'm not leaving."

She didn't say anything, but felt her body tremble. She knew what was about to happen before it did. Matt must have sensed it too because he reached out and wrapped his arms around her before she fell apart.

She tried her best to catch her breath, to stop her involuntary sobs, but had no control over her emotions. She lost the battle she had sworn never to lose again.

"Shhh," he hushed her. "It's okay. Let it all out."

Seconds later she stood up, simultaneously pushing him away.

He opened his mouth to challenge her, but must have seen something in her eyes. "I'm not giving up on you, Charlene."

He didn't wait for her to answer, but turned around and left the room. The front door opened and closed again, and she was left with nothing but silence and regret.

She wiped her face with her sleeve, then studied the pill bottles in her hand.

It was her fault.

She launched them through the air, hurling the plastic vials with all her might. The vials hit the wall and exploded, scattering all over the kitchen floor.

She hated herself.

She stumbled over to the kitchen sink breathing hard, and filled a glass with water. She held the glass to her face, at eye level, and stared at it before pouring it down the drain.

When she closed her eyes, Martina's smiling face appeared. And then that image changed to Jane on the kitchen floor, not moving, not breathing. Then she saw herself hovering over Jane's body, pounding on her chest, screaming for her to wake up.

She felt desperate enough to do the unthinkable. She headed toward the cupboard where they stored the booze. Then she pulled out a bottle and poured herself a stiff drink, hoping to drown her despair.

Book III

Forging On

Chapter 17

"Charlene."

She heard her mother's quiet whisper before she felt the woman's soft nudge against her shoulder. She rolled over and tried to open her eyes, but the sunlight streaming through the windows stung her retinas.

"What time is it?" Charlene asked in a hoarse voice. Her mouth was dry and a headache began to throb behind her eyes.

"Seven-thirty."

Charlene tried again, this time gradually opening her eyes and blinking, but her vision was blurry and her memory fuzzy.

She lay curled up on Jane's living room couch. Her mom had settled on the edge, seated with her body turned and her legs crammed between the couch and coffee table. Charlene closed her eyes, trying to recall the events of the previous night.

She attempted to sit up, but decided against it when dizziness made the room spin.

Her mother held out a glass of water and two small greenish blue capsules. "Advil?"

"How did you…" Charlene started to ask the question, but then saw the bottle of Grey Goose on the coffee table, surrounded by a handful of empty beer cans, some standing, others overturned. She accepted the pills and glass of cold water, downing them in one swallow.

Her mother put her hand on her daughter's shoulder but when Charlene looked at her, she saw sadness in her mother's eyes. She didn't know what to say to make up for what she'd done, and her mother wouldn't want to hear anything she had to say about her "problem" child.

Her mother folded Charlene's shirt that had been slung over the back of a chair. "I put on a pot of coffee."

Her pill bottles leaned on the table, put back together with transparent tape. There were also pills inside them. Had her mother picked everything up first thing this morning when she'd gotten up? Charlene was sure, after her outburst last night, those vials could not have been salvaged.

"You should have something to eat."

Charlene shook her head. "I'm not hungry. Water and coffee are fine." She could now smell the strong coffee aroma floating in from the kitchen.

Brenda Taylor nodded, stood up and headed back to the kitchen.

Charlene tried to get to her feet, stopped, then thought better of it and sat back down. She took a couple of deep breaths, waiting for her stomach to settle down before she slowly got to her feet.

Once the room stopped spinning, she took a couple of steps. She drained the rest of the water from her glass and still felt thirsty. She crossed the room and met her mother before reaching the kitchen.

She had two cups of steaming black coffee and offered them to Charlene.

"I know I look in rough shape, Mom, but I only need one."

Her mother shook her head. "Only one of them is for you."

Charlene was confused. "Who is the other one for?"

"The man sleeping in the car out in the driveway."

"What?"

Charlene moved to the window and drew back the curtain. She saw Jake's car in the driveway, parked behind the FBI-designated vehicle she'd signed out last night.

She didn't see anyone in the car, but if her mother said that someone slept in there, then it would have to be Matt.

Matt.

The memory of last night's events came flooding back to her—the ungrateful way she'd treated Matt, who'd done nothing but try to support her. She owed him an apology and an explanation, if he would even listen to her.

Charlene accepted the two mugs from her mother, who opened the door for her.

Her mother smiled. "Looks like he's worried about you."

Charlene stepped outside and the door closed behind her. The morning sun had her squinting.

She walked slowly toward the vehicle, trying to decide what to say. How could she make it up to him for her unconscionable behavior?

He was in the back, curled up on the seat with his jacket covering his upper body. The back window was cracked open and his phone lay on the floor not far from his hand. His head leaned on the driver's side door armrest, with his neck twisted awkwardly, looking acutely uncomfortable.

She rapped on the car window with her mug. Matt opened his eyes, blinked and then squinted in the dazzling sunshine as he looked up at Charlene. He sat up and rotated the kinks out of his neck, rolling his shoulders and stepped out of the car before reaching for the steaming coffee she held out for him.

She tried to manage her best, most sincere smile. "Truce?"

He nodded. "Truce."

"I wasn't sure how you take your coffee."

"Black is fine." He blew on it briefly and took a sip.

"I'm sorry," Charlene said. "I don't know how else to say it. I was a jerk."

"You have every right to be. You're going through a lot right now."

"There's no excuse. I need to do a better job of controlling my emotions. It's not exactly my forte."

"It's okay. I understand."

"Why did you sleep here last night?"

"I'm worried about you. I wasn't sure if you'd try to leave, but I wanted to be close in case you needed me."

She opened her mouth to respond when his phone chimed. He opened the door and held the phone to his nose, as if he needed bifocals.

"Shit."

"What?"

"A text from Agent Smith. Another kidnapping last night. He's at the scene and would like us there ASAP."

"Let's go."

Matt grabbed her by the arm. "You better clean up first. You're still wearing yesterday's clothes."

"Right."

In the car she handed him a warm blueberry muffin, and he nearly moaned when he took his first bite.

"Your mother is the best. How did she know we never stop for decent meals when we're on a case?"

Charlene didn't answer, because her mouth was full.

"Write the new names on this list." Matt handed Charlene a paper with names handwritten on it.

"What's this?"

"It's a list of the victims. I keep it with me at all times."

She read the list. When she got to the fifth name, her pulse skipped a beat. The kidnapping rate was speeding up while the solve rate went nowhere.

Parents	Child
Mike and Stephanie Wilson	Allie Wilson
Mark and Tina Allen	Jonathon Allen
Peter and Liz Bailey	Mason Bailey
James and Allison Inglewood	Jacob Inglewood
Richard and Jane Gibson	Martina Gibson

He used lights and the siren to speed toward the crime scene, since they'd lost time when they stopped at Jake's apartment so he could grab a quick shower and a change of clothes.

"Give me another piece of paper."

"Why?"

"Just do it, will you?"

He handed her his note pad and she ripped off a clean page.

She took out her pencil and rewrote the baby names in her own way, adding the newest victim.

Parents	Child
Wilson, Mike and Stephanie	Wilson, Allie
Allen, Mark and Tina	Allen, Jonathon
Bailey, Peter and Liz	Bailey, Mason
Inglewood, James and Alliso n	Inglewood, Jacob
Gibson, Richard and Jane	Gibson, Martina
Abbott, Wes and Mary	Abbott, Christine

Matt had been watching her. "What, my way wasn't good enough?"

She could hear the smile in his voice. "Let's just say, I have my own way of doing things."

"So particular."

There was already a collection of vehicles huddled outside a cute little suburban prefab home: police squad cars, FBI unmarked vehicles, and news media vans. They squeezed into a narrow parking spot and speed-walked toward the house, Charlene 'no commenting' the whole way there.

A well-dressed Italian woman with a Hime haircut stood with a microphone, looking into a TV camera.

"This is Elizabeth Mitrano, Channel Four News, standing outside the home of Wes and Mary Abbott, where the Denver baby serial kidnapper has struck again. Late last night..." The anchorwoman's voice trailed off as Charlene and Matt stepped inside the house.

The usuals were all there: uniformed cops, plain-clothed detectives, and suited FBI agents, doing interviews, taking inventory, dusting down hard surfaces, and checking the house for clues. Even the 'big dogs' graced their presence on the scene: Agent Smith and Chief Janice Salinger, not even attempting to get along but seeming to tolerate each other enough to at least be in the same house together.

Smith met them just inside the door, with Salinger following close behind.

Smith's eyes flashed fire. "While that shit show went on last night downtown, this guy hit again." No 'hello' or 'good morning', just straight to business. He didn't look at Salinger when speaking of last night's surprise press conference.

Salinger didn't take the bait.

"What happened?" Matt asked.

"The mother was home, husband away on an annual business trip, always at the same time of the year, same place. Some cottage on a remote lake for a team-building exercise. There's no phone service or Wi-Fi connection there, so we're still trying to track him down."

"How'd he do it?" Charlene asked.

"It's almost identical to the Allen scene. Talked his way in, probably to scope the inside of the house, then came back once the mother had fallen asleep. She didn't hear anything. Found the crib empty this morning. She didn't watch the news conference last night so she has no idea what's going on in the city."

Charlene looked at Matt, who also seemed to have picked it up. Then she looked back at Smith. "He didn't come to scope the house."

Matt added, "We're pretty sure he's been here before."

"So why come here twice? Why risk being seen before taking the baby?"

Charlene got right to the point. "We need to have the mother tested."

"What?"

"Full toxicology, blood and urine samples."

"You think she was drugged?"

Matt looked at Charlene. "That's what we believe."

"What are you hoping to find?"

"We're not sure yet," Charlene admitted. "But two women have now admitted to falling asleep and not hearing anything. It could be a coincidence, but I'm not a big fan."

Salinger was quiet, taking it all in.

Matt continued, "And we need to do it immediately, before it's too late."

Mary Abbott's toxicology report came back positive for non-benzodiazepines.

Charlene, Matt and Smith stood outside the laboratory, where Mary Abbott's blood was being drawn, along with the doctor who had studied the test results. Chief Salinger couldn't join them because she had other business to attend to.

ARCpoint Labs of Denver East, the collection site, was located at 469 S Cherry Street, in Suite 101. The MRO, Frank Russell, was a good-natured fifty-year-old black man with short salt and pepper hair and a matching beard.

"I'm glad you told me what to look for. This is the first time I've come across these drugs."

"Please go on, Doctor."

"Mrs. Abbott had a combination of three drugs found in her system—zopiclone, zolpidem, and zaleplon."

Matt and Charlene nodded to each other, and said in unison, "Harry's notepad."

The doctor continued, "We refer to these drugs on the market as 'z-drugs'. They're sedatives used exclusively for the treatment of insomnia. These compounds are notable for producing pronounced amnesia when used in large doses. Did Mrs. Abbott have trouble recalling events from the last twenty-four hours?"

Charlene answered, "A little bit, yes, and so did Tina Allen."

The doctor nodded. "The detection period for these drugs is short, so it's a good thing you brought her in immediately. It's a rare and dangerous sleeping drug. If it isn't combined in precisely the right dosage, it can cause serious side effects. In fact, we might want to hold her for observation, to make sure she has no ill effects from the drug."

That brought up several questions in Charlene's mind. "Is there any chance the perp has some kind of history with pharmaceuticals?"

"More than likely, yes."

"How long does the drug take to kick in and how long does it last?"

"These drugs usually take effect within fifteen to twenty minutes, and keep the patient sedated for two to five hours."

"Where could someone obtain these drugs?"

"You can't just purchase them over the counter at a pharmacy or a drug store, but a hospital would be a good bet."

Charlene's wheels were turning. "So a nurse could just slip some out when she finished her shift?" Charlene thought about Cindy Richards and Susan Harper, both head nurses with access and opportunity to obtain such supplies and the training to give them.

The doctor replied, "You can't find them in an ordinary hospital."

"Then what kind of hospitals are you talking about?"

"A psychiatric hospital. Doctors there use it to sedate their patients and help them sleep."

Matt turned to Smith. "I think it's time you tell us more about this 'ring' theory of yours."

Smith cocked his head to look around. "Let's go back to my office."

Matt was on the phone calling DC before they'd even made it out to the parking lot. He had the phone on speaker so Charlene could listen in. "I have another job for you, Nicole."

"Matt, I tried calling earlier. I found out what those words are you sent me. They're drugs."

"Thanks. So now I need you to follow up on that. I need a list of psychiatric hospitals in the area, in both Colorado and New Mexico. You're the best."

She steered the car down the Valley Highway Twenty-Five when her prepaid phone rang.

"Hello?"

"Abigail?"

Her pulse quickened. "I told you not to call me, ever. I call you. You don't know who I could be with. You're just lucky I'm alone, which is rare these days."

"I'm sorry." He quieted for a respectful moment, but only for a few seconds. "How did I do last night?"

She wasn't giving him compliments this morning. "We're done."

"What?"

"You've been compromised. They're starting to put things together. It's only a matter of time before they know who you are. And if that happens, then they'll find me out as well. That can't happen. I won't let it happen."

"But we're not done. We still have more."

"No, Joshua. That's it."

"But it can't be it. There has to be more. That's the way it's always been."

"I'm ending it now. No more."

"There has to be more."

"That's it," she yelled into the phone. "No. More. Do you understand me?"

The phone went dead. Joshua had hung up on her, and that wasn't like him. He had never defied her before.

"Damn." She hammered her fist against the steering wheel, and dropped her phone on the floor beside the brake pedal. "Damn it all."

She reached down, picked up the phone, and sat back up to gaze out the windshield when the tailgate of a red Chevrolet truck came hurtling toward her.

She jammed on the brake pedal with both feet, causing the car to fishtail, swerving, and sliding toward the back of the truck, as the CHEVROLET insignia grew ever closer. She cranked on the steering wheel, turning the front side of the car just in time to barely miss the truck's rear bumper.

The car swerved violently, coming to a complete stop sideways on the highway, with her driver's door only inches from the back of the truck. The smell of burnt rubber saturated the air.

Perspiration trickled down the side of her face and sweaty hands had wet the steering wheel. She rolled down the window, sucking in the fresh, cool air.

The traffic was at a standstill; apparently something ahead had caused a major jam. Nobody appeared to be looking in her direction, so she ducked below the sight line of the windshield hoping to stay concealed.

When the vehicles began moving again, she swallowed and straightened the wheel, cautiously merging with the flow of traffic. She briefly closed her eyes, which stung with tears.

She ran her fingers over the outside of her blouse, feeling the thick purplish scar. The idea of undergoing a chemical peel to have the scar minimized had crossed her mind, but it was the only piece of her past that remained. The surgery had left her unable to bear children, a thought that often depressed her and kept her up at night, but it was a disability she'd learned to live with.

Rage fueled her on.

It took a special person to survive the past she'd put behind her, before her latter high school years. She wouldn't be recognized as the kid from school. She'd returned home once, after her makeover, for one purpose, and then left that life, buying the necessary paperwork to start over fresh.

In a world where appearance was everything, minor plastic surgery had been a necessity. Just a little touch-up for concealment, and of course appearance, necessary for a female to survive in this male-dominated world—cheekbone structure, rhinoplasty, chin augmentation and lip enhancement.

Once again, Abigail Fellows composed herself, and focused on her destination.

When they stepped inside the Denver field office just before ten, a young FBI intern in a fitted-suit came speed walking over to them.

"Agent Stone, there's still no hit on the fingerprints your brother pulled from that nurse's house. It's still running through the system, but I wanted to update you."

"Thanks," Matt replied, as he and Charlene charged passed the intern and entered the department's hub of operations, heading straight to Smith's office.

Smith already sat behind a desk covered with folders and papers. "Sit down."

The senior agent sighed, rubbing his eyes, looking pressured and exhausted. He was way past needing a shave and a haircut, and his clothes had permanent wrinkles. Smith was losing it, and if he fell, he'd take with him everyone involved with this case.

They grabbed chairs in the cramped office.

Smith hesitated, then looked from Matt to Charlene.

Matt tilted his head and said to Smith, "She's okay."

Charlene felt a chill. "What?"

Smith looked at Charlene. "I didn't know how you would handle this investigation, since your niece was involved. I asked Agent Stone to keep a close eye on you."

She looked at Matt. "You babysat me?"

Matt shook his head. "We were partners, working together."

Smith cleared his throat. "We've worked with cops like you before. We heard you were a cowboy. You'll break rules, step on toes and you don't care who you run over to get the information you need."

"Then why keep me around?"

"I've been here since day one, following leads, working in the trenches, and it's cost me nearly everything. I've stayed up nights, with pictures of missing babies in my head, listening to desperate, angry parents. I seldom sleep, and I lost my family over this case, but I thought you might be just what we needed, and Agent Stone agreed."

She looked at Matt, but he didn't look back.

"It doesn't matter now," Smith interrupted. "What matters is that you're here and you need to know."

Charlene struggled to stifle the anger and humiliation she felt rising inside her. She dared not let it sidetrack her from the goal.

Smith took a sip of now-cold coffee and frowned. "Keep in mind that this is only *my* theory. I've only mentioned it behind closed doors, with only a rare few reliable people, because I don't know how deep it runs, and I don't know who to trust."

Smith removed a folder from a drawer and opened it. "Do you know anything about the American adoption process?"

Charlene shrugged. "Not really."

"The fact is that it's lengthy and incredibly costly. I've investigated the adoption process in seventeen countries, but for the sake of time, let me say that the American adoption process is complex and often misunderstood. Adoption takes many forms including closed adoption, open adoption, relative adoption, stepchild adoption, foster care adoption, and international adoption." He stopped to take a sip from a new bottle of water. "Statistics prove that there are far fewer available children than there are parents who want them, so the chances of getting a healthy newborn are quite low. The average wait time is eighteen months. Add this to the fact that the children may already be several months old when the process begins, and a year older by the time it's final. This means there is greater potential for these children to have attachment disorders and emotional problems. The average cost for domestic adoptions runs between $25,000 and $40,000, which is a lot of money for average-income families, with no guarantees. That's the big thing. Even after paying that kind of money, there are no assurances."

Charlene frowned. "Where are you going with this?"

"I'm getting to that. I started investigating this theory five years ago, a year after the New Mexico events occurred. I conducted some deep undercover work, made a few underground contacts but the people involved, for good reason, are very secretive. No new faces are allowed inside the circle, and in the end, I had to get out before my security was breached."

"Get to the point."

"The babies are being bought and sold."

Charlene felt her stomach clench with a fresh dose of horror. "You think this guy, married to Susan Harper and Cindy Richards, is the mastermind behind a baby-selling ring?"

Matt shook his head. "Not a chance."

Smith picked up the thread. "This goes far deeper than a single individual. He's only one small cog in a massive baby-selling machine. I believe he's selling them to a group, who in turn is selling them to parents desperate to adopt a child, leaving no paper trail. They're saving people money, as well as time, and they're making guarantees. A newborn will remember nothing about his family of origin, and his appearance will change almost overnight, making identification difficult, and much harder to trace. They could be shipping them all over the world."

She asked the question percolating in her mind. "When the photos of these babies are released, why does no one come forward?"

"We believe that no child is sold to adoptive parents from the same country, or even the same continent, as the ones where the babies disappeared."

Charlene leaned back, letting Smith's words resonate in her brain, and felt more frightened for Martina than ever.

Without warning, Smith added, "And once those babies cross the border, they never come back."

"Do we know if the kidnapped babies are still in the country?"

"I've been working with the RCMP and CSIS in Canada, monitoring the borders for any development. I've also been in direct communication with a senior officer with the Canadian Security Intelligence Service, and our surveillance indicates that no children have crossed the border. It's almost certain that the children are still in the United States, but we have no idea where."

Matt shook his head and squeezed the bridge of his nose.

Charlene noticed. "What is it?"

"I heard this theory a week ago, but something is bothering me about it."

"What's that?"

Matt licked his dry lips. "The theory itself is sound. It's true that it's a lengthy and costly adoption process, and that it's hard to get a healthy newborn. The baby-snatchers stand to make a lot of money. All good—except you say the babies won't be sold in the US. Instead they're being shipped overseas or to Canada. How do the kidnappers make money on that? The market for a healthy newborn is in the US. If adoption and/or the availability of babies is easier in other countries, why would parents in those countries choose to adopt an American baby, illegally?"

Charlene looked at Smith, who opened his mouth and then closed it.

Matt continued, "And how would the kidnappers make big bucks if they charge adoptive parents less than if it's done legally? Assuming the seven babies stolen six years ago were sold for twenty-five grand each, that's only $175,000. Factor in the cost of paying the kidnapper himself, buying the equipment to pull it off, paying for new documentation and flying the newborn out of the country, it becomes a very expensive enterprise, and not a lucrative crime spree, by any stretch of the imagination."

Matt sat back and let out his breath.

Smith was quiet, shuffling and rearranging papers on his desk, and stuffing them into folders. He wouldn't look at them.

Charlene said, "I know why." After a pause she added, "I don't think the money matters to the kidnappers themselves."

"What?" Smith and Matt chorused.

"Of course, I'm just thinking out loud here, and I haven't tested my theory yet. I'm not doubting your numbers, but for all we know, someone is paying this kidnapper double that for these babies. Some parents would pay unlimited money for a guaranteed healthy baby. But I don't think the kidnappers care."

Smith nodded. "Go on."

"I think this has something to do with jealousy. I think the kidnappers like seeing the parents suffer. Why else leave so many witnesses? These are intentional witnesses. He left them alive because he wants them to suffer. I think the people involved have somehow been hurt—maybe they can't have children of their own, and feel that these parents don't deserve to have children either. They want the parents to feel what they feel."

The atmosphere inside the small room grew tense.

Smith stood up and pulled his jacket from the back of the chair. "I have to meet with the press to discuss last night's kidnapping. This is going to get worse."

"We're heading to a cancer clinic in Aurora." Matt rushed to tell Smith the theory about the nurses losing their babies.

Smith nodded. "Okay, but meet me back here when you're through. From now on, the three of us are sharing information and working together."

Smith's theory tumbled around in Charlene's head as they entered the UCHealth – Hereditary Cancer Clinic – Anschutz.

The clinic was located on the third floor in the University of Colorado Hospital in metro Denver, and provided early screenings, risk assessments and education to preserve and support the health of patients with a hereditary predisposition toward cancer.

Matt showed his badge at the front counter to a young, brunette receptionist.

"Is this about Tanya's murder?" she asked.

"Yes."

"I'll let you speak with my boss." She picked up the phone and made a call.

Less than a minute later a short, stocky white-haired man appeared and strode toward them. He wore a white lab coat and sported a full beard and glasses.

"I'm Elwin Monahan." He shook their hands. "What can I do for you?"

"We'd like to speak to you about your employee's murder."

"That was a long time ago. Have you discovered new evidence?"

Matt ignored his question. "Is there somewhere where we can speak in private?"

"Of course."

He led them into the back, where on one side of the hallway each lab was surrounded by clear plexiglass. Behind the partitions, white-coated technicians worked in soundproof rooms, where a high-tech sprinkler system ran along the ceilings.

The other side of the hallway had regular-looking hospital rooms with beds and curtains that could be pulled for privacy.

"It's a shame what happened to Tanya. A damn shame." He spoke as they walked. "We can talk in my office."

"Actually," Matt said. "We'd like to see a little bit of what you guys work with here."

The man shrugged his shoulders. "Sure."

Charlene asked, "Can you tell us about Tanya?"

"Model employee, never late, never sick, and good at her job."

"What did she do?"

"Tanya was one of our cytotechnologists."

"What?"

"Tanya was chiefly responsible for specimen collection, microscopic examination of slides prepared from each specimen, as well as record keeping."

"Was she good?" Matt asked.

"One of the best. A cytotechnologist must be able to concentrate for long periods of time while examining slides with the microscope, and Tanya was one of the most focused."

"Did she have access to radiation?"

The lab tech shook his head, as if it had been an odd question. "Of course, she did—all of our employees do. But the health hazards to people working in Tanya's field are minimal. However, working in the laboratory environment and with biological material always carries risk. All cytotechnologists are trained in laboratory safety and the appropriate handling of all types of specimens."

Charlene wasn't sure how to word her next question. "Did you ever see evidence of missing radiation?"

"You think Tanya stole from us?"

"Do you?"

"Come with me," he said.

He led them into one of the labs, where a woman in a white lab coat, plastic goggles, and rubber gloves handled material through a hole in a clear plastic box. She didn't turn around when they entered.

Matt asked, "Can we be in here without protection?"

"Yes, this isn't dangerous."

He proceeded to the end of the long room and opened a door to a small shelf on the wall. He pulled out a rectangular metal box, opened it up, and showed them a collection of small, silver pebbles, each one about the size of a grain of rice.

Charlene said, "I don't get it."

"They're radioactive pellets."

Charlene took an involuntary step backward, as if she'd just been told it was an atomic bomb. From the corner of her eye, she saw Matt smile.

"If Tanya or anyone else took one of these, it would be hard to track."

"How many could someone take without it being detected?"

He shrugged. "I can't answer that."

Matt asked, "How powerful is a single pellet?"

"Extremely powerful. These pellets are used in a treatment known as high dose rate (HDR) brachytherapy. A computer-controlled machine, called a microselectron, implants a pellet which gives off radiation that damages and destroys cancerous cells."

"Would it be possible for a pregnant woman to lose her baby if she were exposed?"

"I would have to say yes, but we take every precaution here to make sure that doesn't happen."

Matt nodded. "Of course. But I have a hypothetical question for you."

Mr. Monahan appeared uncertain. "Okay."

"If someone wanted to secretly expose an unborn fetus to these radiation pellets outside of this facility, to terminate a pregnancy, what would be the best way to go about something like that?"

"That's a strange question."

"Any idea?"

"Well." The man scratched at his thick white beard. "Maybe hide it in the woman's underwear, tampon or feminine pad, but that's a weird thing to do."

"Thank you for your help, Mr. Monahan."

Chapter 18

Matt had called Agent Smith from the car but he hadn't returned from his briefing with the press, so Matt and Charlene stopped at the Aurora Police Department at 15001 East Alameda Parkway.

The station was set up much like most police departments throughout the country, including the LAPD, with detectives sharing space with their desks pushed together. Each desk held a computer and calendar.

They huddled around the desk of Detective James Remax, a young-looking, clean-cut cop who didn't look like he'd been on the job long.

Remax slapped a folder on the desk and opened it. "This one was handed down to me by Detective Charlie Hunt, who retired two years ago, and this investigation went straight to the cold case files. I put in my time, but I couldn't connect the dots."

'Put in my time' was cop jargon for following leads that came his way, but not proactively seeking, or going out of his way to find his own information.

"What do you know about Peters?"

He read from his notes. "Tanya Peters, thirty-six, Christian, single mother of two boys, employed at the UCHealth – Hereditary Cancer Clinic – Anschutz."

"Enemies?"

"Not that we know of. No outstanding warrants, didn't owe money, no problems with IRS. As far as we can tell, she was above reproach."

"What about the ex?"

"According to him, family and friends, there was no ill-will in the split. He had visiting privileges, made his payments regularly, and they split time with the kids fifty/fifty. Seems like a clean break up."

Charlene interrupted, "So what do you have on the murder?"

"Her body was found in South East Aurora, on a side street just off of Smoky Hill Road."

Matt tilted his head in question. "Really?"

The significance of the location seemed to click with Matt, who was a native, but it did nothing for Charlene.

Matt asked, "What's your take on that? She's not some junkie with a criminal record. What would a relatively young, employed, Caucasian single mother be doing in that area? Especially one who lived nowhere nearby?"

Charlene asked, "Where is that?"

The detective finger-combed his hair. "Not exactly the kind of place for a gal like Tanya Peters." He looked at Matt. "We have no reason to believe that she was a regular. When we flashed her picture at local shop owners and residents, no one had ever seen her before. There were no needle tracks or anything in her system to indicate she was a user, then or previously. The Peters family has no idea why she would've been there."

Charlene continued, "How did she die?"

"Ligature strangulation. Her purse and pockets had been emptied and her jewelry was taken. Mugged and killed. No sign of recent sexual activity, so she wasn't assaulted."

"Or someone wants you to believe that," Charlene argued.

Matt asked, "Any leads?"

"We have this."

The Aurora detective sat down and rolled his seat over to his desk, sliding in under the opening in front of the computer. The machine was already on and the case pulled up. He rolled the mouse around and clicked on an icon in the bottom corner of the screen.

A maximized image appeared on the screen. A woman stood in a long coat, holding the collar tight as if she was cold.

"That's Peters." Remax seemed ready to give them the play-by-play of the entire scene.

Matt frowned. "Looks like she's waiting for someone."

Charlene shook her head and squinted. "Why is it so hard to see?"

The recording was black and white, grainy and fuzzy and hard to follow, as if recorded by a poor-quality machine.

"This is the video feed from the parking lot behind a local pawn shop."

"Jesus, this looks like it was recorded in the eighties."

"They'd just installed it a week prior to the incident because of a break-in. They bought a cheap, second hand model off eBay. I guess it's better than nothing. Take it or leave it."

"We'll take it." Charlene didn't take her eyes off the computer monitor.

"Peters will have a visitor in a few seconds."

As if on cue, a man entered the camera frame, walking toward Peters with his back to the camera.

"Can you see his face?" Charlene asked Matt who shook his head.

The man on the screen was large. The expanse of his shoulders a good thirty inches wide. He wore a dark colored suit, but because of the poor image quality, it could have been any color. His hair was covered by a hat.

Remax confessed, "Could be any big guy."

"Definitely not our unsub," Charlene admitted.

You could change your appearance in different ways: eye color, hair color and style, lifts to add height, fake facial hair, but you couldn't hide or change body type unless you spent a lot of time and money.

The man known as Ryan Richards and David Harper was a narrow-shouldered, thin man of no more than a hundred and sixty pounds. The man on the computer screen was well over two-hundred pounds, with a thick neck and wide shoulders.

"She handed him something." Charlene's voice was animated, pointing, stepping closer to the monitor. "Back that up."

He rewound it, and they watched the exchange. Although partially concealed, the unidentified man did his best to hide the trade-off. They zoomed in as best they could without making the picture quality too blurry.

In return, the man had also handed something to Peters, which looked like a thick envelope.

Matt said, "That's gotta be money."

"But what did she give him?" Charlene asked.

They tried to improve the image quality, but the best shot only showed a small rectangular box.

Charlene looked at Matt. "Could be radiation pellets."

"What?" Remax looked confused.

"Can you email me a copy?" Matt asked. "We'll take it back and see if our A/V guys can do anything with it."

"Sure."

"When was Peters' body found?"

"The next morning. The ME said that she'd been killed the previous night, probably not long after this exchange. He pointed to the computer screen. "This guy is our only link to Tanya Peters."

"It can't be a coincidence," Charlene said. "She meets a mysterious man in a shady area of the city, makes a trade, and then is later killed. Was the envelope on her when they found her?"

"No."

"Of course not."

They thanked the Aurora detective and left the building.

As they got in the car, his phone rang, and he looked at the number. "It's Smith." He answered. "Hello." The agent listened. "We're at the Aurora Police Department but we're on our way back now."

Matt gave Smith a synopsis of what they'd learned from Detective Remax. Once he listened to Smith, he looked at Charlene. "No hit on the fingerprints from Cindy Richards's house. Apparently this guy has no criminal history."

"Or he hasn't been caught yet," Charlene corrected.

Matt spoke into the phone. "Okay, we'll be there in about twenty minutes. We'll talk to you—"

"Wait." Charlene had a thought, had been flirting with it all morning since receiving the results from Mary Abbott's toxicology report and learning about the three "z" drugs. "Tell Smith to run the prints against those from mental institutions. Pay particular attention to psychiatric hospitals in Utah, Oklahoma, Kansas, Texas, Colorado, New Mexico, and Arizona. Those are the seven states with either a related kidnapping, or are states that border the area."

In 1991, the US Senate passed a law that all patients from psychiatric institutions must be fingerprinted when registered. Because many patients committed violent crime or sex offenses, it would help keep track of them after discharge.

"You think this guy was institutionalized?"

"Yes."

Matt relayed the information to Smith and then hung up.

It was past the noon hour when they briefly stopped for taco salads and drinks. Brain power required food. You could go for a time without sleep, but you couldn't go without food.

As soon as they stepped inside the Denver field office, Smith came racing toward them. Three men in black suits followed him, along with Police Chief Salinger who brought up the rear.

Smith carried a briefcase, a laptop and a stack of folders, as if ready to move. With his disheveled hair, and tired, bloodshot eyes, Charlene couldn't help but worry about him. But Matt had assured her that Smith was one of the best in his field, and could handle the situation.

"We got a hit. We're heading to Las Cruces. I already called ahead—the jet is being fueled up as we speak."

"Wait a minute, Agent Smith. What do you think you're doing?" Salinger started jogging toward them.

Smith turned around, looking perturbed. "We've got a lead and we're following it."

"Are you seriously thinking of heading to New Mexico when we have kids right here in Denver who are missing?"

"Yes, I am. This is the best lead we've had since I started working this case. This takes precedence over anything else. Are you coming?" It sounded more like a sympathy invite than a legit offering.

Salinger eyeballed Matt and Charlene, and then acknowledged Smith. "No. I have people who need me here, in my city. I'm not chasing ghosts in Las Cruces. I'm going to do the real tracking right here."

"Suit yourself. We'll let you know what we find out."

Matt grinned at Charlene. "When he's in a mood like this, just follow. Let's go."

Trying to make himself heard over the engine sounds, Smith read from a document in his hand. "Joshua Fellows, AKA Ryan Richards, AKA David Harper—age thirty-six, from Santa Fe. He's from a devout, strict southern Baptist upbringing. Self-admitted into Mesilla Valley Hospital at sixteen, after the death of his parents. He walked away AMA ten years later and disappeared off the radar."

Charlene felt her ire rising. "Why wasn't this big news? A guy breaks out of a mental hospital?"

Smith shrugged. "It was reported, but Fellows wasn't deemed aggressive or violent. Plus, because he went in voluntarily, he could leave at any time."

Charlene pointed to the paperwork. "Tell me about the hospital."

"Top of the line. Fully accredited by JCAHO and the New Mexico Children Youth & Families Department. The hospital is part of Psychiatric Solutions, Incorporated, which offers an extensive continuum of behavioral health programs for children, adolescents and adults through ninety-one freestanding psychiatric inpatient facilities, with approximately 10,000 beds in thirty-one states, Puerto Rico and the U.S. Virgin Islands."

Matt said, "Sounds expensive. Who paid Fellows' bill?"

"Good question."

Charlene spoke next. "Does it say what medication Fellows was on?"

Smith held out a page full of documentation. "There's a whole page of drugs listed here. I can't pronounce half of these. Zolpidem, Alpidem, Saripidem, Zaleplon, Indiplon, Ocinaplon, Zopiclone, Pagoclone, Suriclone, Pazinaclone, Suproclone..."

Without meaning to, Charlene said out oud, "The three z-drugs."

"You know them?" Smith asked.

Matt replied, "We've heard of them."

Charlene said, "Did he have any family?"

"Parents committed suicide, and he has one sibling, an older sister."

"What's her story?"

"Not much in here. Abigail Fellows was born—"

"Abigail?" Charlene whispered, in disbelief.

Smith nodded. "Yeah, that's her name."

"Cindy Richards and Susan Harper both named their babies Abigail."

"Jesus," Smith said. "Do you think it was a tribute to his sister?"

Matt asked, "Where is she now?"

Smith shook his head. "No idea." He looked at his notes. "Not much in here. Never had a driver's license, never held down a job. She seems to have fallen off the edge of the earth like Fellows."

"Do you think he killed her?" Charlene asked.

Matt shook his head. "I don't think this guy is into homicide."

"He killed Harold Linden."

Charlene studied the ten-year-old hospital photo of Joshua Fellows. There was no current picture of him or his sister. Fellows didn't look anything like Ryan Richards or David Harper.

Charlene sighed aloud. "This guy never had a chance."

"Criminals are made, not born," Matt said.

Smith flipped a page. "The address given is over twenty years old and the house has been sold since then. I sent two agents over there anyway but the couple living there is in their eighties, and they know nothing of the previous owners."

Charlene leaned back in her comfortable airplane seat. Being in a psychiatric institution gave Fellows access to the drugs used to sedate the victims. Did he know how to use it to subdue the mothers without killing them, or was someone else calling the shots?

Smith broke the silence. "What are you thinking?"

His voice startled Charlene. When she glanced up, both Matt and Smith stared at her.

"My father used to say that nothing happens randomly. Random killings, or in this case, kidnappings, just don't exist. Especially with the amount of planning that went in to each of these crimes, the kidnappers must have a purpose. There's always a reason. We're just overlooking something. I think we need to take another look at the victims."

Matt said, "We've studied the victimology dozens of times."

"Then we do it again," said Smith.

They went to work, the case files divided among them. The cabin of the plane was quiet as they reviewed documents, made calls, and sent texts.

Charlene was the first one to break the silence about twenty minutes later. "Who has the Cindy Richards file?"

"I think it's over there." Smith retrieved his briefcase from another seat and returned with a file folder.

"When did Richards have her miscarriage?"

"August twenty-fourth."

Charlene held up the document. "Allie Wilson, the first baby kidnapped in Denver, was born on August twenty-fourth."

Matt said, "So that's the trigger."

Smith snapped his fingers. "He took the baby that should have been his on that day."

A hush fell over the space.

She now had motive for Allie Wilson, but the rest still made no sense. Allie Wilson was born on the anniversary of his baby's death, but how did the others fit into the whole scheme of things?

Charlene removed Matt's list and added the date beside Allie Wilson's name.

Parents	Child
Wilson, Mike and Stephanie	Wilson, Allie – 08/24
Allen, Mark and Tina	Allen, Jonathon
Bailey, Peter and Liz	Bailey, Mason
Inglewood, James and Allison	Inglewood, Jacob
Gibson, Richard and Jane	Gibson, Martina
Abbott, Wes and Mary	Abbott, Christine

Matt shook his head, in puzzlement. "So how do you think Cindy Richards was involved? She lost as much as he did that day."

Smith shook his head, but didn't look convinced. "I don't think she had any involvement. We looked at her, hard. Just like we did at Susan Harper six years ago. It led us to believe she was nothing more than an innocent bystander."

She nodded. "I think he's right. I talked to the woman and I didn't get the sense that she hid anything." After a short pause, she added, "She's been cooperative so far."

Smith sighed. "Extremely cooperative."

Charlene went on, "The Allie Wilson kidnapping makes sense, in a way, because she should have been Fellows' little girl. But Abigail had died that day, sending Fellows over the edge. He couldn't have a child, so why should anyone else?"

Matt jumped in, finishing Charlene's thought. "Fellows blamed his wife, Cindy Richards, for the miscarriage. What better way to extract revenge than to take babies that she helped deliver?"

Charlene's turn. "Richards told me how badly her husband had taken the news of the miscarriage. This was the second time around for Fellows, after Susan Harper lost his other child. When he found out Richards would never be able to have children, he lost control."

Again, the space grew quiet, everyone chewing on this new information. Thoughts screamed in Charlene's head.

Why these other babies? Where was the connection? Was Joshua Fellows planning to sell the babies for profit? Why did he need so many?

Jonathon Allen was the second baby taken. There had to be a link. Charlene had to visit the Allen home and find out what they knew. Her father always believed that nothing happened randomly, that everything had a reason behind it.

Mesilla Valley Hospital, a private psychiatric hospital, was located in Las Cruces, New Mexico, three hours south of Albuquerque, about a nine-hour trip by car; one of the benefits of working with the FBI was having access to their private jet.

Charlene had used her travel time to familiarize herself with the facts. The hospital was a free-standing psychiatric hospital that provided mental health and drug and alcohol addiction services for adolescents, adults, and seniors. It had been in operation since 1987.

A car was waiting for them when they landed. The driver introduced himself as Mark Cartman, a special agent with the Albuquerque branch who'd already been in Las Cruces for work.

Cartman was slouch-shouldered, with a square jaw and a bulbous nose. Smith prepped the New Mexico agent on the fly.

The car ride was quiet, everyone rolling scenarios in their heads, going over possible questions. With a thirty-minute drive to the hospital, Charlene sat in the backseat with Matt, with time to contemplate the case and their visit.

She had reached a point where she now trusted Matt, but the jury was still out on Smith. However, he'd been quick to join them once they had done all the leg-work.

The hospital was located on the outskirts of Las Cruces, along Del Rey Boulevard. The facility overlooked the city, and was surrounded by desert. From the outside, it looked like a high-end addiction center for celebrities, more like a country club than a hospital.

They parked at the front entrance and made their way toward the door. The desert winds kicked up just before they reached the entrance, blowing Charlene's hair away from her face.

It was early afternoon when they stepped inside the institution, where an elderly woman sat behind a desk, and a young male nurse stood over her, talking.

Smith did the talking, making his request. Charlene had seen a lot of men like Smith, superiors who had little use for those who weren't in charge.

They followed directions through a door, where a heavyset, powerhouse of a woman met them with a nod and a grunt. She introduced herself as Carla Orr, Chief Nursing Officer.

Orr escorted them down a pristine hallway, where their footsteps echoed throughout the empty corridor. They waited in a comfortable looking lounge area, while the nurse summoned someone in charge.

After only a few minutes, a tall, thin man walked toward them. He was well-dressed and impeccably groomed.

He smiled and extended his hand. "I'm Art Bromley, Leadership Team CEO."

Smith asked, "Are you the guy I spoke with on the phone?"

Bromley swallowed, and his large Adam's apple bobbed in his throat. "Yes."

"So, Mr. Bromley—"

Bromley cut Smith off.

"I understand you have an interest in one of our patients? I'm sure you understand that our records are sealed, and not open to the public. This healthcare institution is required by federal and state law—"

Smith held up his hand. "Save us the speech, Mr. Bromley."

Charlene interrupted, "Actually, he's no longer a patient."

Smith told Bromley the bare minimum about Joshua Fellows, and the former patient's involvement with their case.

Bromley seemed to take it all in, scratching his light brown hair. "Follow me."

The CEO led them through a maze of hallways before stopping outside a door where he tapped lightly.

He turned to face them. "You should probably speak with Dr. Shiam Khanna, MD, certified psychiatrist and director of our Adult Acute Psychiatric Care program."

Bromley knocked again and this time it was answered by a short, dark-haired man of Indian descent.

"Doctor," Bromley said. "These people are from the FBI and want information about one of your former patients. I've assured them that they would have this hospital's full cooperation."

Khanna shook all of their hands and welcomed them into his office. Bromley excused himself and rushed away.

They followed Khanna into a handsomely decorated office, nothing fancy, but one that exuded comfort. Agent Cartman helped himself to a handful of Skittles from a glass bowl on the psychiatrist's desk.

"Please sit down." Khanna motioned toward a conversation area with comfortable seating.

The doctor asked, "What's the name of this patient?"

"Joshua Fellows."

Khanna nodded, and punched a few keys on his keyboard.

Matt broke the silence. "What kind of treatment program was he in, Doctor?"

Khanna looked up from the computer screen as it loaded. "He was part of our acute treatment program that provides short term treatment for emotional, behavioral, psychological and substance-abuse issues. He was being treated for anxiety and depression."

Charlene asked, "How do you deal with all that?"

"We don't expect to eliminate them entirely. The goal of treatment is to stabilize symptoms, make medication adjustments and begin a plan for aftercare, so the patient can continue with treatment even after discharge."

"What was Fellows' diagnosis?"

Khanna focused back on the screen. "It says here that he suffered from a high anxiety level and bipolar disorder and struggled with panic attacks, phobias, and obsessive behaviors. Unfortunately, we only have notes to go by here."

"Why is that?" Charlene asked.

"The doctor who treated Mr. Fellows is no longer with us. Dr. Ridley passed on years ago, but all of her findings are recorded here."

Matt interrupted, "What else can you tell us about Fellows, from the notes?"

"It seems that he never recovered from the death of his parents. He's also highly intelligent, scored off the charts on his IQ testing."

Charlene said, "I'm interested in Fellows' departure. What steps did the hospital take to find him?"

"We worked with the local police but since he was self-admitted, and not violent, he didn't rank high on their priority list."

Matt picked it up there. "Who is listed as the next of kin on his intake forms?"

"Says here that both parents are deceased, and his sister is the only living relative."

"Did anyone ever meet her?"

"I have no idea."

"Did he have many visitors during his tenure here?"

"No idea. Nurse Carla would be the best source for that kind of information. I'll page her for you."

Agent Smith took the opportunity to whisper to his colleagues, "Let's divide up. Agent Cartman and I will look around while you two go with the nurse."

Khanna set down the phone. "She's in the activities room. I'll take you there."

He led Charlene and Matt down the hall. "Part of our program here includes recreation and music therapy. We find it helps relax our patients and allows them to engage and interact with each other."

The doctor held open a set of double French doors that led to a huge room filled with patients and workers. Some of the employees wore nurse's uniforms and others were in street attire wearing only name tags to identify them.

Charlene asked, "Why are some of the workers in plain clothes?"

"They're volunteers."

The walls to the activities room were painted pale yellow, with one wall containing a mural of downtown Las Cruces. Among the available activities were: table tennis, fitness classes, arts and crafts, and table games.

Three twenty-foot tables were set up, each one organized to accommodate a wide range of activities. Located in the corner by the door were floor mats, balance balls, hoops, bean bags, plastic floor hockey sticks and a net.

Charlene recognized the same nurse who'd met them at the door.

Khanna smiled. "If there's anything else I can do, please don't hesitate to ask."

"Thank you, Doctor." She turned back to the nurse. "We'd like to take a walk around the facility if it's okay."

"Sure."

They spent the next twenty minutes touring the sanatorium. Nurse Carla was a wealth of information about the institution and wasn't shy about sharing her knowledge.

Charlene began asking questions from a mental list. "What kinds of situations does the hospital handle?"

"We treat and serve both adolescents and adults. Our top priorities are: depression, suicidal behaviors, schizophrenia, bipolar disorders, alcohol and drug dependency, sexual, physical, and emotional abuse, and severe psychosomatic problems."

"Do you remember Joshua Fellows?"

"Of course I remember Joshua." She sounded as if the question was an insult. "I remember all my patients."

Charlene ignored the nurse's attitude. "What can you tell me about him?"

"Joshua had a kind soul, but rarely showed emotion because of the medication. He was sweet and obedient. The staff liked working with him because he would willingly follow directions."

Matt asked, "Who administered Fellows' medication?"

"Whichever nurse was on duty."

"Did you ever do it?"

"Of course I did, but to tell you the truth, Joshua could have done it himself. He was perceptive, and learned things easily."

Charlene changed the subject. "Any problems with break-ins or thefts?"

"What?" The nurse frowned in confusion.

"Have you ever noticed supplies go missing or had problems with theft?"

Orr looked surprised, even hesitated slightly. Charlene noticed a slight shift in the woman's demeanor.

"Of course not!" she snapped. "Something like that would have been reported."

Charlene changed directions. "How did Fellows interact with the other patients?"

"He didn't. Joshua was quiet, and suffered from bipolar disorder. You know, uncontrollable mood swings, depression. The only thing that helped was the medication. I spent a lot of time with Joshua, but the only time I ever saw him show the slightest bit of emotion was when his visitor showed up."

Matt stepped closer. "What visitor?"

"I don't know, some girl. She could've been Josh's girlfriend, though he never talked about her, and refused to answer questions when we asked, so we let him be. He was happiest when she was around."

"Did she come often?"

"At first, once a week. That lasted a couple of years. After that, we never saw her. That's when Joshua went into a funk."

"Do you remember what she looked like?"

"Oh gosh, it's been so long." The nurse pondered the question. "Skinny little thing. Looked to be just a teenager. I think she had long dark hair, and was quiet. Oh, and she had a bad case of facial acne."

"Would you recognize her if you saw her again?"

"Maybe, but it was a long time ago. She'd be an adult now."

Matt pulled out pictures of the two head nurse suspects and showed them to Carla.

She studied them closely. "This would have been twenty years ago, but I don't think it was either of them."

Matt asked, "What's security like here?"

"State of the art, for a minimum-security facility. We have surveillance cameras, top of the line alarms, and tracking devices, but we have no armed guards, and we don't allow weapons on the premises."

Matt jumped in. "Where exactly are the surveillance cameras located?"

"Both inside and out."

"The patient visiting area?"

"Of course."

"Do you think there's video tape on Joshua Fellows' visitor?"

"Not after all this time. But we do keep log-in sheets of visitors."

"Can we get copies of log-ins that apply to Fellows?"

The nurse shrugged. "Sure."

Charlene asked, "Who paid Joshua Fellows' medical bills?"

"You'd have to talk to someone in admissions about that."

Charlene nodded.

"I'll go get those log-ins photocopied for you."

Chapter 19

Charlene read from the photocopy. "The woman who visited Fellows signed the book as Becky Jacobs, though that might not be her real name."

She asked Smith, "Do you recognize the name?"

"No."

Cartman, who drove and rarely spoke, interrupted, "Could be a girlfriend."

Smith was quiet during the ride to the airport, and Charlene wondered what he thought. Did he regret letting her work this case or maybe annoyed because she and Matt had found the connection to Mesilla Valley Hospital? Was his ego bruised? The truth was that she didn't really care.

Matt said, "We caught a break with that signature. We haven't had many in this case."

Smith shifted in the front passenger's seat.

Cartman sighed aloud. "Too bad there was no video footage."

Smith said, "It was a long shot."

Charlene changed the subject. "Who paid for Joshua Fellows' hospital stay?"

"I went to see the Chief Financial Officer about that," Smith said. "He said that a money transfer came in once a month."

"They didn't ask?"

Smith shrugged. "Why would they? They got paid."

"Can we trace the transfers?"

"Not a chance. Any bank accounts they had twenty years ago are no doubt closed by now."

Charlene had a hunch. "I think the nurse is lying."

Matt nodded. "She's hiding something."

"I think she noticed that medication went missing, had no idea where it went, and since it had been on her watch, she never reported it, fearing that it would probably come out of her pocket or be held against her in other ways."

Smith blew out a breath, shaking his head. "At this point it doesn't matter anyway."

They fell into silence.

Matt's voice startled her out of her reverie. "What are you thinking?"

Charlene jerked her head up and saw Matt looking at her.

"That nurse knew an awful lot about Fellows, had spent a lot of time with him and seemed to be closer to him than anyone else. Do we know anything about her?"

Matt shook his head. "Nothing. Should we do a background on her?"

"I don't think it would hurt. She has answers to questions no one else knows."

Smith asked, "So what did she say about Fellows' visitor?"

"I showed her pictures of Cindy Richards and Susan Harper and according to her it was neither of those women, even though she agreed it was a long time ago and looks can change."

"Surgery can alter everything."

Matt interrupted, "I think we can all agree that it's not Cindy Richards or Susan Harper."

Charlene studied her notes, then read a description of Fellows' visitor.

Was it a friend or family? Was this the sister from Joshua's file? Was this Abigail?

Matt made a face. "If it was his sister, why use a fake name?"

Charlene ventured, "Maybe she was getting ready to drift away and disappear."

Smith blinked hard as if his eyes hurt. "So Fellows only had one visitor in ten years. No male friends or relatives. Just one woman every other week."

Charlene looked at Matt. "Didn't your profile indicate a second person involved in this kidnapping, and most likely a woman?"

Matt exhaled. "Yes, it did. But that's just a hypothesis."

She disagreed. "That's an educated guess."

"But it's still only a guess."

She couldn't back down. "Have you changed your mind then?"

"No."

Smith's cell phone rang. He checked the caller ID, then cleared his throat. "Smith."

Charlene followed his end of the conversation, which was short and concise. His facial expression reflected deep concentration. The respect in Smith's voice told Charlene that he spoke with someone in authority.

"Yes, sir." He hung up. "Shit."

He tossed the phone in the cup holder beside him, then stared at the open road before him. The silence grew uncomfortable. Irritation masked the face of a man who normally didn't show emotion.

Charlene frowned. "What's wrong?"

"It's over."

Charlene turned to Matt, who looked confused. "What's over?"

"The case...it's done."

Matt shook his head.

Cartman asked, "What do you mean, Agent Smith?"

"Another baby's been kidnapped."

Suddenly it seemed as if all the air was sucked out of the car.

Smith reiterated, "That's it, we're finished."

Charlene shook her head in frustration. "How can you say that? It's not over. It's just heating up."

Matt placed his hand over hers on the seat, but she pulled it away.

He said, "She's right. The public will be all over it."

Smith didn't turn around. "That was number seven, just like six years ago. The kidnappers are gone now, or have at least gone underground, as per their MO. We're running out of time and we're going to lose them."

Suddenly Charlene had trouble catching her breath. She unfolded Matt's paper and read the names over again.

Parents	Child
Wilson, Mike and Stephanie	Wilson, Allie – 08/24
Allen, Mark and Tina	Allen, Jonathon
Bailey, Peter and Liz	Bailey, Mason
Inglewood, James and Allison	Inglewood, Jacob
Gibson, Richard and Jane	Gibson, Martina
Abbott, Wes and Mary	Abbott, Christine

Speaking to no one in particular, Smith spoke in a monotone. "This was a colossal waste of time, coming all the way down here. We missed another goddamn kidnapping."

Charlene couldn't help but ask the question uppermost in her mind. "Who's the latest victim?"

"What?" Smith seemed to have been lost in his own thoughts.

"The baby taken. What's the child's name?"

"What difference does it make?"

"I want to know."

"The parents are Kurt and Leanne Idlestone. I believe the child's name is Ty."

She added the name to the list as Matt looked on.

"Nothing happens randomly," she whispered.

"What?"

Charlene glimpsed at Matt. She hadn't realized she'd said the words out loud. "Nothing."

Smith rambled on, "What are people thinking?" He paused then added, "Jesus Christ. Is every goddamn parent in Denver clueless? Are they not on high-alert since news of the kidnappings broke? They should have their babies covered in bubble-wrap by now."

They drove for the next few minutes in tense silence.

Charlene stared at the names of the babies now gone and a tear rolled down her cheek.

The mood in the car had changed. No one spoke. Moments after they left the hospital it looked like they had a break in the case, but now the whole scene had turned on a dime.

Smith fumed, while Cartman focused on the road, and Matt sat without speaking. It was as if all three grim-faced Feds were at odds, when usually nothing could have divided them. They weren't used to failure and they didn't know how to accept it.

Cartman had picked up speed, his foot hard on the accelerator. The New Mexico landscape buzzed by in a blur of snapshots. Charlene's head spun, and nausea roiled in her stomach.

Then something caught her eye and tickled the back of her mind.

She yelled, "Stop the car!"

"What?" Cartman looked at Charlene in the rearview mirror.

"Pull over."

"Do it," Matt barked. He turned to Charlene. "What is it?"

"What the hell are you doing now, detective?" Smith turned to face her, his seat belt pulling tight around his neck, the veins and chords bulging under his skin.

The car had barely come to a complete stop when Charlene bolted out of the backseat. Doors opened and closed behind her as she sprinted thirty feet in the opposite direction, the list crumpled in a fist in her hand. When she stopped, she was sweating and breathing hard.

Charlene looked up at a huge billboard advertising MADD—Mothers Against Drunk Driving. But it wasn't the message that grabbed the detective's attention. It was the layout:

*M*OTHERS
*A*GAINST
*D*RUNK
*D*RIVING

She looked at the paper in her hand, and then looked back at the board.

Smith followed her gaze. "What is it, detective?"

She looked down at the paper, reading the names again, seeing Matt, Smith and Cartman arrive in her peripheral vision.

Wilson, Allie 08/24
Allen, Jonathon
Bailey, Mason
Inglewood, Jacob
Gibson, Martina
Abbott, Christine
Idlestone, Ty

All three men were now watching her, looking at the paper in her hand.

"What's the deal, Char?" Matt asked.

"Give me a marker."

"Detective Taylor, is this necessary? Can we go now?"

"Give me a marker," she shouted.

Matt handed her a black Sharpie.

Charlene took the marker and highlighted the first letter of each last name.

Allen, Jonathon
Bailey, Mason
Inglewood, Jacob
Gibson, Martina
Abbott, Christine
Idlestone, Ty

"Jesus Christ." Smith said it in a whisper.

Charlene's voice was a monotone. "It's not over yet."

Smith was on the phone before they'd even boarded the plane. It was pressed to his ear, locked in place with his shoulder, as he lugged the rest of his bags up the stairs into the plane.

"You think this will work?" Matt asked Charlene.

She nodded. "If nothing happens randomly, we still have a chance to solve this case. Allie Wilson was the one anomaly, born on the day that Joshua Fellows was supposed to have his new daughter. Not part of the original plan."

Matt asked, "So he's spelling out his sister's name. Did he kill her? Is she still alive?"

"She must be the one who visited him at the hospital. I also think she's alive and helping him."

"How can you be so sure?"

"I'm not, but he can't be doing it alone. To pull off something like this, he has to have a partner. You suspected a woman was involved. We've studied this guy, and it's clear that he has no other known associates, so it must be her."

He shook his head. "Remember that there are no guarantees when I turn out a profile. I use evidence, crime scene information, witness testimony, and everything else the local police precinct hands over to me."

Just as the plane's wheels left the ground, Smith snapped off his phone and turned around in his seat to face them. "It's all set. I'm sending a team to the new crime scene, but we have other work to do. Everything will be at the field office when we land."

"He needs an L," Charlene said. "And he isn't going to wait long."

They sped through Denver, ignoring the speed limits, only stopping at a drive-thru for sandwiches, knowing it would be a very long night.

When they got back, a box holding various folders, stacked and banded together, waited for them on Smith's desk. He dropped the photocopied files into Agent Cahill's arms. "Divide this stuff three ways. You guys sort through them while I go and take care of priority number two."

Smith left the room and Charlene grabbed the folders from Cahill. Without counting them out, she handed a stack to Matt and a stack to Cahill, keeping the largest stack of files for herself.

After almost an hour, they'd narrowed their search. Only six babies had been born in the last six months with a last name beginning with the letter L.

"Six is too many," Matt said. "We don't have the manpower to watch that many babies at a time."

They were in agreement that Fellows wouldn't wait long to complete his puzzle. There was already a great deal of heat on the kidnappers; the word had gotten out and the risk had grown exponentially. They were as close as they'd ever been.

Matt tapped his pen on the table top. "Okay, then let's narrow down the options."

"What?" Charlene said. "We can't risk that. What if we choose the wrong one?"

"We have to. Look, it's our job. It's what we do, so let's go over the babies and their families."

"Four females and two males."

"How old?"

"One is two months, one three months, two are four-months old, and two are six months old."

Matt sighed out loud, feeling fatigued to his core. "Let's take out the six-month-olds."

"You sure?"

"Six months is the limit for infants. By then they no longer look like newborns, and their baby photos can be computer enhanced to age their appearance. Most parents want newborns if they can get them. Trust me."

Charlene stared at Matt, who looked confident. He was good at what he did, but it wasn't in her nature to trust others' opinions, especially when it came to police work.

She exhaled. "Okay." She separated those folders from the rest. "What else you got?"

"What about their families? Any of these babies have siblings?"

"That's right." She could hear the excitement in her own voice. "Every baby taken so far is an only child."

Cahill held up two fingers. "Two of these babies have older siblings."

"Take them out," Matt ordered.

"That leaves two," Charlene noted.

"Two, we can cover."

Charlene studied the biographies of the newborns. Both female. One three months old and the other four. In their previous dealings, the kidnappers showed no prejudice against age or gender.

Had one of the two already been scouted, and a plan put in place? If so, which one?

Smith had a large group gathered inside the Denver field office conference room when Charlene and Matt caught up with him. She counted six men and two women, some in suits, and others in DPD police uniforms, all focused on Agent Smith.

It was after six o'clock in the evening.

Using his pull, Smith had assembled two task forces, one for each of the two babies; each team was also set up with a DPD SWAT team sniper. Charlene had never seen a sting operation put together so swiftly and methodically. He looked frantic, moving around at a dizzying pace, making sure everything was set. The landline receiver was lodged between his ear and shoulder while he simultaneously punched numbers on his cell phone.

Smith and Cahill would lead one team, Charlene and Matt the other. This was a major sting operation, which required a twenty-four-hour detail on both houses, so the detective was flattered that the Feds trusted her enough to help lead one of the teams.

The plan was set; the DPD would work with the FBI—a joint task force. They would use two-way mics for communication. If the kidnappers arrived at one house, the other team would leave their assigned positions and head in as backup.

The only problem was that the two houses were located at opposite ends of Denver. So Charlene had suggested a third team, with only three players, to remain on guard at the halfway point and ready to move in either direction, on signal. Smith seemed pleased with the idea, even though he didn't smile, and the new team was put in place.

Each team member was given the requisite paperwork including: biographies of their prospective families, and known associates. Also, in each packet was a computer-aged sketch of the suspect, Joshua Fellows, and several line drawings of the possible disguises he'd used in the past, as well as a few he could be using now.

Smith began the debriefing. "His real name is Joshua Fellows, but he's had a number of aliases."

They distributed ten different sketches of the kidnapper in his various disguises.

Smith had just told everyone to take a fifteen-minute break, for which she was grateful, before momentarily realizing it was because he needed to take a phone call. He wasn't one to take breaks, so it made perfect sense when she thought about it.

"Fuel up," Matt whispered, approaching her from behind. He handed her a plastic-wrapped egg salad sandwich.

She unwrapped the sandwich and took a bite. She didn't know how famished she was until she realized it tasted better than she ever imagined. Looking at Matt, she smiled and mouthed the word 'thanks', as Smith called the group to get back down to business.

Salinger subtly looked their way out of the corner of her eye, with arms crossed, fuming in silence as usual. Was she looking at Charlene or Matt? Was Salinger pissed that Smith hadn't put her in charge of one of the teams? Did she want to be working more closely with Matt?

Charlene wondered if the men in the room felt hostility toward a woman who was in charge of a team, or if the FBI staff resented the fact that an LAPD detective led the charge.

She was in deep thought when something Smith proposed drew her into his lecture, and gave her pause. She felt frozen, a sick feeling rising in her gut.

When Smith finished his spiel and dismissed the group, Salinger stormed off in a huff, raging up and down in long strides, shouldering aside anyone who stood in her way.

Matt and Charlene approached Smith.

"What do you think?" Smith asked.

Matt opened his mouth to speak but Charlene beat him to it. "Why are we not alerting the families?" She knew her voice was higher and angrier than intended.

Smith spoke in a tone just above a whisper, "We need the families to follow their normal routines."

"You're using them as bait?" Charlene felt her ire rising.

"We have to," Matt said. "You've seen the crime scenes. Fellows has been researching them, knows their every move. If he sees one thing out of place, he'll run."

Matt's face showed signs of pain, as if he'd betrayed her. Yet Charlene knew his reasoning was sound. Fellows was clearly right brained, and far too organized and would sense even one thing out of place. Any sudden change in their schedules would scare off the perp, who, no doubt, had the family's routine memorized. She understood it, but she still didn't like it.

"What if something goes wrong? What if these people find out they were under surveillance without their permission? Do you understand the heat that not only the Feds will take, but also local law enforcement, politicians and officials?"

Matt shook his head—it was a foregone conclusion. "There's always a chance of blowback, but that's a chance we'll have to take."

"Answer the phone, damn it." Abigail screamed into the handset, listening to the irritating ringing in her ear.

"Hello?"

"Your cover is blown." She had the phone pressed to her ear, travelling ten miles-per-hour over the speed limit in a compact, rented car.

"What?" He sounded surprised.

"It's over. The plan ends here, now."

They didn't need the last baby, they already had the required number.

"But there's still one more."

"No. That's it. Don't go through with it. They'll be waiting for you. Do you hear me? Do not do it."

"No." Joshua's voice grew loud, angry. "It's not over. I have one more to complete the mission. I can do it."

She heard something in her brother's voice that she'd never heard before—defiance. It wasn't in his nature to disobey or talk back.

"Joshua, I'm on my way to the cabin. Don't leave until I get there."

"It's too late. I'm already gone."

She squeezed the phone inside her hand and slammed it on the car's dashboard, then took a deep breath and put the phone back to her ear. She would never change his mind, so she would adapt.

"Okay then, listen up. Change of plans. This is how you'll do it."

Chapter 20

Charlene sat in the front passenger seat and Matt behind the wheel of an unmarked DPD police cruiser. She checked the weapon, a Glock 22 pistol in .40 caliber Smith & Wesson the FBI had issued her.

They parked fifty yards down the street, and slightly above a newly-built two-story house with deep roof overhangs.

The target's name was Mariah Lance.

"What do we know about them?" Matt asked.

She had the file open on her lap. "Peggy and Nathan Lance. He sells insurance, so most of his work is conducted in the evenings when his clients are home, like this evening. She's a kindergarten teacher, but she's taken a year off to be home with their first child."

They stared at the outside of an empty house. The cops had been prepped on the details of the family's last twenty-four hours and they knew that Peggy Lance walked her daughter around the block at that time.

Charlene's team had two cars set up, with two men in the other vehicle, plus two more on foot. She and Matt were in one car, watching the house, while the other car followed the target. The two officers on foot were dressed in disguises, and stayed as close to the target as possible, without being detected.

She watched through tiny binoculars as the mother and baby returned home.

Charlene couldn't help it. "I still don't like keeping these people in the dark. We're playing with their lives."

"I know, but we need to trust Smith. He knows what he's doing."

Charlene thought about the attempts on all the children. The only two characteristics that were even remotely linked were when the mothers had been drugged. The change in pattern and MO kept the cops off balance and unprepared.

They had no idea what Fellows planned or if this was even the right house. He held all the cards.

Charlene checked out the area once the mother and baby went inside the house, making sure each team member was in position. Their other vehicle rolled into place down the street, parking at the side of the curb facing the house in the other direction.

All they could do was wait. When Nathan Lance returned from work, the team could pack up and make their exit. Fellows had never hit a house with both parents at home. Until then, Peggy Lance and her daughter were Charlene's responsibility.

She checked her watch and then looked at the ever-growing darkness of the sky. If Fellows made a move, he would have to do it soon.

Each member of her team was equipped with an ear piece and a microscopic mic for comms.

She spoke into the two-way radio. "Player A, respond?"

A man seated on a bench, at a bus stop, nodded imperceptibly.

"Player B?"

Another team member, in workout clothes, jogged by the car and gave a hidden 'thumbs up'.

"Stay alert." Charlene adjusted the frequency on her radio. "Team one, come in."

"This is Team One." Agent Smith's voice was almost drowned out by static.

"Anything, Agent Smith?"

"Negative," Smith sounded tired and impatient. "What about on your end?"

"Nothing. Stay in touch. Out."

"Ten-four. Copy that."

Why was Fellows taking so long to make a move on the house? The husband could be home any time.

Charlene looked at Matt. "Do you think Fellows sniffed us out?"

"Maybe."

"That's not what I hoped to hear."

He nodded. "I know. If we go over all of the other abductions, not one is the same. He's used multiple disguises, and taken the babies from multiple locations. We have all of the scenes memorized, the public has been made aware of what to look for, so I doubt Fellows will follow a previous method."

She made a face, biting her lip. "Maybe this isn't even the right kid."

"Maybe."

"You're not helping."

Matt grinned. "Sorry."

Silence lingered for a few minutes, and then Charlene said, "Salinger sure was pissed not to be included on this detail. I think she wanted to be close to you."

"She's the chief of police. Janice doesn't take part in the action. She's no longer hands-on."

Charlene was confident in the plan but understood that the unpredictable always lingered, especially in an operation of this magnitude.

"What's with the sniper?" Charlene asked. She looked up around the tree and house tops but couldn't spot him.

"Smith is just being cautious. A lot can go wrong, and he just wants to be prepared."

"Damn it. We need Fellows alive. He knows where the babies are. A sniper could muddy the waters."

"You think Fellows will just offer up the information we need?" Matt asked, but when he looked at Charlene, his facial expression changed. "What are you thinking?"

She smiled, as if it was a no-brainer. "Divide and conquer."

"Divide and conquer? What do you mean?"

"I had a lot of time to think about this on the plane ride back. You mentioned that these kidnappings could be a team effort, perhaps with a woman involved. I believe the person who visited Fellows in the hospital is his partner. You also indicated that one of the partners is the dominant one, and I think that it's a woman. I also think this woman had something to do with the deaths of Fellows' daughters."

"You've done a lot of thinking. So what's your divide and conquer strategy?"

"I think if we—"

She was interrupted by the squawk of her radio. "We have a visitor."

A well-dressed African-American, holding a briefcase, approached the Lance's front door. He wore a shirt and tie with a beige dress coat, and a black Colorado Rockies cap, which looked out of place with his rather formal attire.

"He's on foot," Matt said.

"Is Mrs. Lance expecting anyone?"

"Not that we know of, but we didn't talk to them, remember?"

"What's he looking at?" Charlene asked.

The man had stopped at the end of the driveway and turned completely around.

"Did he make us?"

"I don't think so. I think he's looking at Paxton on the bus bench, though."

A long red, white and blue city bus approached and stopped in front of the bench. The address: 151 via E. Colfax was displayed across the front on the digital direction schedule.

Charlene spoke into her mic. "Michaels, he's watching you. Get on that bus and get off around the corner. Find this guy's vehicle. He had to have come from somewhere."

Once the air brakes squealed and the engine roared, the bus took off, having picked up its passengers. The man watched the bus disappear around the corner, and then turned back toward the house. He walked up the paved driveway, studying the clipboard in his hand.

Night had fallen, and the neighborhood was quiet.

The man approached the door, adjusted his tie and straightened the bill of his cap. He turned around again as if to check on something, then turned back and rang the doorbell.

Matt held the mic to his lips and whispered, "Keith, use night vision to snap facial photos and send them in for comparison."

The darkness was offering visual challenges for those inside the cars. Joshua Fellows was Caucasian, not African-American. Making a move was too risky, especially if Fellows watched from the bushes somewhere. This could be a decoy, a trap or even a partner.

Peggy Lance answered the door, smiled shyly, mouthed a few words and then let the visitor inside.

"Stand down, unit two. It might be someone she knows or is expecting. Wait for my signal."

They waited, and the minutes dragged slowly on. The atmosphere in the car grew tense, the air thick.

Something's not right. Charlene could feel it deep inside, her cop's instinct, the Taylor hunch. She bit down on her bottom lip.

Her radio burst with static. "I found a black, unmarked van parked on the side street just a short distance from the Lance house. All the doors are locked and the windows are tinted, so I can't see inside."

As a street cop in LA for six years, Charlene had learned the art of canvassing neighborhoods, knowing what to look for and what was out of place. That's what cops did, and Denver police were no exception.

"Fellows was last seen driving a van."

Charlene nodded. "But a white one." She grabbed the mic. "Run the plates."

Two minutes later, his voice came back on the radio. "That vehicle was reported stolen in Arizona two days ago. It belongs to—"

Her car door flew open and Charlene hit the pavement before the dispatcher finished. She moved toward the house, weaving in and out of vehicles parked at the side of the road, staying low. Her weapon was in one hand and her mic held tight to her mouth with the other.

"Team One, move in, carefully. We don't want to alert Fellows." She motioned with her hand. "Jordan and Sanderson, you guys enter from the back. 'C' car, you're with us," Charlene ordered the car on standby. She knew that it would take them at least eighteen minutes to get to her, depending on traffic.

She charged through the bushes, gun extended, in time to see her team progressing toward the house in one, organized, collective movement. The officers on foot removed their outer garments to reveal their dark jackets with the letters DPD stenciled across the back. The street was quickly barricaded.

"Michaels, you stay with the van and cover it. Stay out of sight," she whispered into the mic.

She turned off her radio. With a hand signal, Charlene gestured to her team and whispered, "Go."

Charlene opened the door, which was unlocked, and stuck her head inside. Seeing no danger signs, she moved in farther, her gun extended in front of her.

She heard Peggy Lance's sobs before she'd turned the corner. The short, petite mother stood on the landing at the top of the staircase, while Joshua Fellows stood behind her, with his arm around her throat and a gun pressed against her head. They stood in front of the side window that looked out into the neighbor's yard.

There was no indication that he'd ever had a weapon at any of the previous crime scenes.

"Don't come any farther, or she's dead."

Charlene stopped, and aimed her gun at him. Lance's cheeks were mascara stained and she was visibly trembling. Her bottom lip quivered.

"Don't be stupid, Fellows, you're surrounded. Give it up." Charlene looked around but saw no signs of the baby.

"It's over," Matt said.

The four of them stood at the bottom of the stairs, all with their guns drawn and aimed, ready to fire without blinking. But Charlene knew they had to take Fellows alive.

The gun shook in Fellows' hand as he looked around, shaking his head.

Charlene cleared her throat. "Listen, Joshua, the truth is that your daughters didn't have to die."

He jerked his head back, cocking it as he stared at Charlene. He moved the gun from the woman's temple and pointed it at Charlene.

"What are you talking about?"

Charlene gave him an apologetic look. "Their deaths. They didn't die of natural causes. Something, *someone*, made it happen."

"What do you mean? My wives had miscarriages. *She* told me that I wasn't meant to have my own children."

"She? Who?"

"Shut up." He blinked hard, his eyes sparkling with unshed tears.

"No. Someone was behind it all. Someone who had access to your home, to your wives. Someone planted something inside them that caused your baby girls to die."

"Divide and conquer," Matt whispered to Charlene, as if it had just clicked.

Joshua's eyes flashed angrily. "You're a liar!"

"I have proof." A bluff, but he wouldn't know that.

He took an involuntary step backward, closer to the window, pulling Peggy Lance with him. He pressed the gun against the woman's skull, pushing it harder. The lady winced, and more tears slid down her cheeks.

Fellows screeched, "Not one step closer!"

"Okay." Charlene raised her hands in the air and let her gun roll around her trigger finger.

She'd holstered the gun and taken one step up the staircase when the side window blew apart and a bullet caught Fellows in the left arm, blowing a hole through his bicep. Blood splattered on the floor and wall as he dropped to a knee.

Charlene and the other officers dove to the ground as glass spewed across the staircase and spiked into the drywall. By the time they looked back, Fellows had vanished. His shoes crunched glass as he raced up the remaining stairs.

Charlene jumped to her feet and pulled her gun then sprinted up the stairs, two at a time, stopping on the first landing, where Peggy Lance crouched in a ball, shielding her face with her forearm.

"Are you okay?" Charlene asked.

When the mother looked at Charlene, her eyes were red. She nodded. "My baby is upstairs, in the room at the end of the hall."

Charlene heard a window break and followed the trail of blood that Fellows left in his wake. When they got to the top of the stairs, the hallway was clear.

Noise in the first room got their attention, which meant he hadn't gone for the baby. That removed that danger from the equation. His arm was probably of no use to him so he wouldn't be able to carry her.

The door was closed. Charlene tiptoed across the carpet and placed her ear against it, but heard no noise from inside. She took the position against the door, stepped back, then abruptly, stepped forward, ramming the door with her shoulder. Instantly, it gave and she ducked out of sight around the corner.

As she crouched low, she peeked around the corner of the door frame and saw the top of Fellows' head disappear outside the shattered window, knowing he'd jumped onto a roof overhang. She was crouched low and out of sight, ready to shoot when he stood up and fired wildly in her direction. She ducked out of view and called to her team, "He's out on the roof! I need someone out there right now!"

Then she ran to the side of the window, and staying low and to the side, she glanced through the opening.

Fellows stood at the edge of the rooftop, looking down at the ground, into the neighbor's backyard. With his back turned to Charlene, she took aim at his center, but didn't pull the trigger.

She couldn't shoot him in the back, nor go for a wound shot, because the impact of the bullet would throw him off the roof.

She yelled, "Freeze!"

Fellows turned and fired another shot, but she was able to step sideways out of the line of fire as the bullet blasted through the open frame and hit the back wall.

She popped her head up to see Fellows jump. He cleared a ten-foot high, solid wood fence that separated the Lance house from the neighbor's yard, and landed on his feet, so that his momentum enabled a perfectly-performed safety roll.

Into her mic she shouted, "Go after him! He's escaping through the neighbor's yard."

Through night vision goggles, she continued to watch as he squeezed through thick bushes and then hobbled across two streets to where an idling blue Neon waited. He limped around the back of the car and winced when he opened the passenger door. He briefly looked back up at her, before he slid inside and the car took off.

Charlene hit the radio, reporting on his progress, describing the make and model of the vehicle and the direction in which it headed.

As far as they knew, this was the first time he had a backup vehicle ready for a contingency exit.

Matt joined her at the window as they looked out to see officers finally scurrying into the neighbor's yard and out into the now-vacant street. They should have had a helicopter observation team, but that would have cost the taxpayers, and would have taken more time to implement.

The faint wail of sirens sounded in the distance, drawing closer to the house, but Charlene knew it was an exercise in futility. Fellows was gone.

They returned downstairs and met outside with a member of her team, who reported, "We put out an APB on the car."

"What the hell happened?" Smith bolted through the front swinging door of the Federal building with a serious look on his face, speed walking toward them with gazelle-like strides.

Matt frowned. "You know, it was as if he knew we were coming."

After a brief pause, he added, "Peggy Lance said that he was paranoid, constantly looking out the windows. That's not like him. Other witnesses spoke of his calm demeanor. When we stormed the house, he grabbed her."

Then Charlene chimed in, "And he had a getaway car waiting."

"A second vehicle?" Smith's eyes widened in surprise. "That's never happened before."

Matt shook his head. "It was totally out of character. From everything we learned about him, read about Fellows, we were convinced that he was always prepared, with a plan that consisted of entering and exiting the premises the same way. No need for contingency plans."

"That's why he caught us off guard," Charlene said. "Where's the sniper?"

"In the interrogation room, as you requested. Why?"

She shrugged. "You'll find out soon enough."

They entered the field office.

"Here's the file on our sniper." Smith handed Charlene a folder. "Tony Weller, twenty-six, married with a three-year-old daughter. Started with DPD and was recruited by SWAT early on. Top of his class in all classifications. He's a grade 'A' cop."

"Well, he has a lot of questions to answer."

Smith argued, "Weller has no history of insubordination or rogue behavior. He's a rules guy. He takes his orders, and follows them to the letter."

"Well then let's find out who was calling the shots." She turned to Smith. "Do you mind if I ask the questions? I mean, since I was there."

Smith looked at Matt, and then back at Charlene. "Go for it."

They entered a room at the back of the building that looked like it had once been an office. All the furniture had been removed, except for a metal table and a handful of wooden chairs.

Weller sat at the table, and a great deal of perspiration peppered his scalp. His light grey t-shirt was now dark, with round sweat stains on the back and chest.

Charlene asked the first question. "Officer Weller, we've noticed that you've racked up an impressive record since joining the DPD."

Weller looked at Charlene, and then at Matt and Smith, but said nothing.

Matt spoke next. "Why did you take that shot?"

"I had a clear view."

"Clear? The suspect was holding a hostage."

"I thought I could save her life."

Charlene looked at Smith and Matt before she finally spoke. "During a hostage situation, aren't we taught to secure the hostages first?"

Both men nodded.

Charlene looked back at Weller. "We needed the suspect alive. We all knew that."

"I saw the shot and I took it."

"Under whose authorization?"

"This guy has kidnapped babies—he's hurt a lot of people. I saw the chance to take out the scumbag so I pulled the trigger."

Charlene shook her head. "That's not your style, Weller. I've read your file, spoken to your captain. You're a rules guy." She placed her hands on the table and leaned in closer to the SWAT sniper. "Who told you to fire your weapon?"

Weller looked into Charlene's eyes. This was a man with a young family, who couldn't risk suspension or a job loss. No way had he acted on his own. At that moment he shuddered, clearly upset.

He answered through clenched teeth. "Chief Salinger."

Charlene looked at Smith. "Where is Salinger?"

Smith shrugged his shoulders. "I guess she's not back from the scene yet."

"Call her."

Matt removed his phone and punched in the numbers. He placed the phone to his ear.

Charlene heard a 'beacon' iphone ringtone drumming in the hallway just before Salinger walked through the open office door.

Matt ended the call.

Smith was clearly annoyed, if the fire in his eyes was any indication. "Where have you been?"

"I was at the scene with the mother. We saved her baby today."

"And almost got her killed." Charlene took a step closer to Salinger, trying to keep her temper in check.

Salinger nodded to Weller. "You may be excused."

"Yes, Ma'am." She didn't have to tell him twice.

Charlene held up a finger. "Wait a minute."

Salinger gave her a look. "Weller was only following a direct order. He did his job."

Matt stepped in between Charlene and Salinger. He turned to face the police chief. "How could you give an order like that? You know we need to take Fellows alive to find those babies."

Salinger's eyes narrowed, resolute. "Fellows is scum. He's hurt a lot of people, good people, good parents. He killed Harry."

Matt argued, "You hated Harry."

"Hate is a strong word. Harry was one of us, former DPD. You, of all people, should know how cops react when one of our own is killed. I knew I had a major dilemma on my hands. I had a team full of trigger-happy officers, who were closing in on a kidnapper who was terrorizing Denver... I just cut to the chase."

Smith abruptly broke the tension. "Chief Salinger, there will be consequences for your actions."

Salinger pressed her lips together in a tight line, looked daggers at them, and then turned and walked out. Charlene and Matt followed her through the department, then watched as she exited the building, got in her car and drove away.

When Charlene returned to the office, Smith hung up his phone. He looked up.

"The other sniper admitted the same thing. Salinger gave him an order to take out Fellows if he had a clean shot."

Charlene could hardly contain her ire. "How could she do that?"

"She's obsessed with Fellows," Matt said. "She's so desperate to take him down that she has tunnel vision."

Charlene argued, "But we don't know where he's keeping the babies. If he had died, so would our chances of finding them."

Matt sighed. "She's still banking on finding Fellows' partner."

Smith wiped his damp brow with a white handkerchief. "I think that should be our focus from now on. And we need to sideline Janice, keeping the facts to ourselves."

Charlene let out her breath. She was drained, fatigued beyond description.

It was after nine, but she couldn't bring herself to return to Jane's place, not after what just went down. They might never nail Joshua Fellows, and the thought exhausted her weary bones even more. Martina could be gone forever.

Chapter 21

Charlene worked at a desk in their temporary office, recounting the story Peggy Lance had told her in an interview after the dust had settled.

She put off a return trip to Jane's place, and ended up falling asleep at her desk. When she woke a short time later, she actually felt surprisingly rested, so she got back to the task at hand.

Lance had reported that Fellows was so paranoid that he'd been looking through the sheer curtains when the officers made their move on the house. That's when he pulled out the gun. The kidnapper had to have known they were there.

Had someone tipped him off?

He escaped the house from the second-floor roof, where a car had been waiting two streets over. His main goal was to get out of the house alive—survival mode.

A city-wide APB circulated on the blue Neon, but so far, there was no sign of it. Even an air unit had yet to spot the vehicle.

Fellows had been judged legally insane, but then there was a fine line between insanity and genius.

Charlene still wondered who pulled the strings. She looked at Matt. "Fellows said 'she'."

"What?"

"In the house. Fellows said, '*she*' said I wasn't meant to have babies'. He was referring to a woman."

She got up and approached a large white board secured to the wall, where notes, paper clippings and case notes were tacked up in no particular order that she could see. She skimmed the pictures of all of the women connected to the case: Fifteen mothers who had all been cleared, Cindy Richards and Susan Harper, the two head nurses, who were also cleared. Tanya Peters, employee at a cancer clinic, was dead. Only two women had yet to be cleared. Nurse Carla Orr from Mesilla Valley Hospital, and the mysterious female who'd visited Fellows.

Who was she?

They'd looked it up and there was no Becky Jacobs in the database, any database, or at least not one who matched the physical description the nurse had given them. She had to have been using an alias.

Using a red, dry erase marker, she circled and drew lines on the board, trying to link the players.

What now? Fellows and his partner would surely disappear with their mission incomplete. They'd hideout for a while, and then reappear in another city at another time and try again.

But they would have to deliver the babies they already had.

As if sensing her exhaustion, Matt said, "How about we go get a coffee?"

Charlene shook her head. "Go ahead. I'm not leaving."

"Char…"

"I'm not leaving."

Smith said, "Come on. I'll go with you."

They grabbed their jackets and headed toward the door. "You want something?" Matt asked.

Charlene didn't look his way, just shook her head, biting her lip as she studied the white board. She heard the door shut when they left.

She felt like crying, like breaking down and just letting go. All the pictures, words, numbers written on the board suddenly became little more than a jumble of red and black.

Charlene rested her head on the desk, and it finally hit her. The exhaustion in her body was overwhelming, had been for days, and she had no strength to fight it anymore.

She closed her eyes, wondering if she'd ever see Martina again. She trembled, fighting the temptation to doubt.

The Feds had every border covered. If Fellows or the babies tried to leave the country, they'd be stopped. The local police had every exit out of the city barricaded, for every means of transportation. Every vehicle was to be inspected before it was allowed to pass through. And yet, Fellows hadn't been found. Had he even left the city? Where had he been staying all this time?

They'd checked hospitals, pharmacies and doctor offices. Fellows had been shot, was probably bleeding badly, and would no doubt need medical treatment. But if he was shacked up with a nurse….

She opened her eyes, her head still resting on her arms, on the desktop. Her gaze scanned the top of Smith's desk, glimpsing the printout of Joshua Fellows' entire bio that Smith had obtained from Mesilla Valley Hospital, a fifteen-page history of the criminal's prior life.

Focused now, she flipped through the pages, having read most of it already. She reached the third to the last page and stopped. She sat up abruptly as a thought came to her. A long shot, but it was worth a try.

Charlene jumped out of the seat just as Matt reentered the room.

"What's up?"

"I just thought of something. Where's Smith?"

"On the phone."

Charlene parked herself at one of the computers in the room and logged onto the Internet. She googled newspapers in Santa Fe and discovered a link for the Santa Fe Times. She clicked on it and was transferred to the newspaper's home page.

"What's the date that Fellows' parents committed suicide?"

Matt put a pastry in his mouth and rifled through the papers, yelling out the date.

She followed the site archives and read the article on the suicide, and then turned to Matt. "I need the FBI to grand me a high-level security clearance."

"What do you want?"

She told him, then got up and let Matt sit in her seat to punch in multiple, high-level passwords.

"I'm in." Matt stood up.

Charlene settled back into the seat and started punching keys and scrolling around with the mouse.

"The printout showed that after Fellows' parents' died, the family house and real-estate sold within months of being put on the market."

Matt said, "Remember that Smith already checked their old house. The new residents have no connection to Fellows or this case. No babies, no Fellows."

"Got it."

"What?"

Matt stood behind Charlene's chair, reading the screen over her shoulder. She could feel his presence, smell his cologne.

"Fellows' mother's family is listed as title holders to real-estate in Denver. It wasn't under the Fellows name, so it never came up in the database search. On this property, a log cabin was built in the thirties and never sold. The cabin is still registered in his mother's maiden name."

There was an aerial shot of the log cabin.

Matt said, "I don't recognize that address."

Charlene Google-mapped the city of Denver but couldn't locate it either.

There was a wall-sized map of Colorado on the wall adjacent to the white board. They walked over to it and stood in front. Calculating the address, they studied the chart. In the end, using GPS coordinates, it took them fifteen minutes to pinpoint the location of the cabin on a dirt road that wasn't listed on any map.

Charlene looked at Matt and, as if they had ESP, they nodded in unison. "Let's check it out."

Joshua slumped at the kitchen table, with pools of blood puddled around his chair. He'd removed his left shoe and sock, and rolled up his pant leg to reveal a swelling knot the size of a tennis ball on his ankle. It had already started to discolor.

"I parked the car in the back. It doesn't look like anyone followed us." Abigail walked toward him, pulling down her glove to check her watch. "How is it?"

He looked up, swallowing hard. His face was pale and covered with beads of sweat, after taking a bullet to the upper arm. It wasn't fatal, but it was still bleeding profusely.

He pleaded with her. "I need a doctor."

She cupped his face in her gloved hands. "You did good, baby."

"Is it over, now?"

"It's over." Abigail turned around and walked toward the window.

"You didn't tell me there would be a sniper," he said, sounding upset.

His words stopped her. "I didn't know."

"How could you not know? You knew everything else."

"I swear, Joshua, I didn't know. Why would I send you if I did?"

He lowered his head, and stared at her, his gaze unflinching. "I don't know, why would you?"

She paced the room in annoyance. "What is wrong with you?"

This wasn't like him. He'd always been weak, a follower, but not now.

"The lady detective told me that my babies didn't die from natural causes."

"What?"

"She mentioned that someone killed them. The cop said it wasn't my fault."

"What are you talking about? Your wives had miscarriages."

"You told me that I wasn't supposed to have kids, and that it was God's way of showing me."

"It was."

"She told me she had proof."

He screamed, spitting from the mouth, and lunged at her from his seat, shoving her against the nearby wall, pinning her against the decorative wood paneling. Even from his seat, having lost a great deal of blood, rage motivated him as he put his good hand around her throat as if to strangle her.

"Joshua," she whispered, her anxiety rising to a fever pitch. "What are you doing?"

"Why did you do it?" he yelled. "Why did you kill my babies?"

"I did nothing of the kind. Please."

A tear slid down her cheek just as he released his hold on her neck. Trying not to overreact she took a deep breath and rubbed her neck, stunned that he could be so out of control.

She shook her head. "I would never do a thing like that to you."

"She has proof."

"Proof of what? It was a trick—a complete fabrication. She just said that to get you to turn on me. I love you."

He no longer looked convinced. "You do?"

"Of course, I do."

She wrapped her arms around him, caressing his head, playing with his hair, hearing his heavy breath in her ear.

"It's just the two of us. That's the way it's always been. You're my baby brother. Who took care of you growing up? Who rocked you, sang you to sleep when you were scared? Who protected you? Who's always loved you when no one else did?"

"You?"

"That's right. Me. It's us against the world."

"So, what do we do now?"

She smiled, relieved to have him back. "We need to get ready to move the babies. But first, we need to remove that bullet."

"So, can I keep one, like you promised?"

"That was before you screwed things up. We have a contract. The buyers want a certain number and we promised to deliver them. What do you think they'll do to us if we don't hold up our end of the bargain? You know who we're dealing with."

His face flushed red and his eyes flashed anger. She knew all his trigger points, things that set him off, and she knew she had little time to extinguish what would be an inevitable explosion.

"But that's my baby. I deserve it." He ground his teeth, the sign his tension was at its peak.

"We've already received half the money up front. Don't you know what will happen if we don't deliver?"

He opened his mouth to respond when he suddenly slapped his flat hand against his right temple. His migraines had returned with a vengeance, as they always did after a tirade.

It came to her then; she wasn't going to win, not this time. He was hell-bent on keeping that child, had generated his own plan. His eyes told the story. It was over.

She spoke in a soothing tone. "Oh, sweetie, I can see that you're in pain. Let me help you get rid of that headache."

Just as she always did, she reached over and began to massage his temples with soft, circular strokes.

"Is that better?"

"Yes." She could tell he was de-escalating.

As she massaged, she wondered, where they had gone wrong. She'd been careful for six endless years. Who had solved the puzzle? The local police certainly weren't bright enough to figure it out, and Smith and the FBI had been chasing down leads for years, with no success.

From the start she knew the LA detective would be trouble. They should never have kidnapped the woman's niece. That had been dangerous, but necessary. The harsh truth was that they should have eliminated Taylor when they'd had the chance.

She knew what had to be done.

"Okay, Josh, you can keep a baby."

Smiling now, he took her hands and squeezed them. "Really? You mean it?"

She nodded and smiled. "Of course. Now let's remove that bullet." After a brief pause, she added, "I'll get you a drink to make it easier."

"Really?" His face opened wide in surprise. "You're going to let me have a drink? You never do that."

She struggled with ambivalent feelings. It couldn't end well, but there was no other option. "You won't want to feel anything when I plunge the tweezers into that hole in your arm. Plus, it's a celebration."

"What are we celebrating?"

"The end."

She turned and unlocked the cabinet door and took out his favorite bottle, Jack Daniels, and poured a healthy portion into a glass of ice cubes. Then, behind his back, she added a few drops from another smaller bottle and then stirred it with her gloved fingertip.

When she turned back to the table, he smiled, excited about the prospect of a rare drink.

"You're not having one?" he asked.

She shook her head. "There will be questions if I show up with booze on my breath."

"Good thinking. That's why you're the brains." He held up the glass as if to make an imaginary toast. "I love you, sis."

He took a sip, then two, then downed the whole glass of whisky in one swallow. Joshua closed his eyes, looking dreamy and contented.

Abigail bent over and whispered in his ear, "I love you too."

Without warning, he frowned, as if noting a bitter after-taste. He looked inside his glass, and then traced his finger around the rim. His eyes were already glazing over.

"How could you—"

He tried to strike out at her, but instead he grabbed his throat and his body convulsed before his eyes rolled back in his head. His upper body slumped over the table top, and his breathing ceased. It was over.

She sat at the table, staring at her brother. Finally, she put her hand to his wrist. He was gone.

She had just started cleaning up when a buzzer sounded; the motion sensor alarm in the path had been activated. Only the weight of a vehicle could set it off.

The sensor was planted one mile from the cabin so, depending on the speed of the vehicle, she had only minutes to escape.

"Let's stop here and walk." Charlene put her hand on Matt's arm as he slowly drove the car down a winding dirt path, enclosed on both sides by woods.

"Why?"

"The cabin can't be far. If he's there, we'll attract his attention when we arrive. Let's move in on foot, just in case."

Matt pulled the car over slightly, as much as he could since the tree line was so close to the road on either side, and shut off the engine. The car blocked over half of the access road.

The cabin sat back in the woods, hidden in a secluded area that no one had ever purchased, at least on paper. The perfect location for a hideout. No neighbors and lots of privacy.

"No wonder we couldn't find this place on a map. There are no roads."

It was colder when they exited their vehicle, zipping their coats up against frigid air that reflected the higher elevation.

They stayed just inside the tree line, not far from the path, but followed it around a curve hidden by bushes to where the cabin was visible in front of them.

The exterior of the building looked old and dilapidated, with much of the outside wood rotting. It had clearly been upscale when it was new, with two stories and a wide wraparound porch.

"Look." Charlene pointed to the far edge of the trees, just across from the house. A subtle cloud of dust kicked up. "Looks like someone just is either coming or going, but they can't get past our unit unless they find another way out."

"I don't see a vehicle."

"They probably parked it out of sight."

They continued to move, careful not to make noise that would arouse suspicion.

As they approached the cabin, they stayed in the bushes, but saw no signs of movement from either inside or outside the structure.

Then they heard a gas-powered generator humming from a little shed in the back.

Matt pointed his flashlight to a place behind the building. "There's a car."

The blue Neon was parked under a stand of trees, well hidden from view, but close enough that Fellows could easily escape if the need arose. As he moved his light around, he saw a white van—the other of the two vehicles they'd been hunting.

Neither vehicle would have been visible by aerial surveillance.

Her heart was beating hard in her chest when she said, "Let's go."

She stepped out of the bushes and felt Matt's strong hand on her shoulder, pulling her back, almost knocking her over.

Charlene looked at him. "What are you doing?"

"No, the question is, what are you doing?"

"I'm going in there."

"No, you aren't."

"Oh, yes I am. Martina could be in there."

He shook his head. "The blue Neon confirms our guy is here. That means the babies are probably here, too. If we go in and he sees us coming, there's no telling what he'll do to those babies. He'll be like a cornered animal."

She knew it was a great argument, but she didn't want to hear it.

Was Martina in there? She couldn't let her mind go there, or she wouldn't be able to wait.

"Hang on, baby girl," she whispered.

"Let's call Smith and circle around front, where we can keep an eye on the house and wait for backup."

It took less than a half-hour for Smith to arrive with a team and a plan, though it seemed like forever to Charlene.

Smith hadn't notified DPD SWAT this time around. In fact, he'd told Charlene that he hadn't even consulted with Janice Salinger. That lapse would create some serious backlash.

They couldn't risk SWAT's "search and destroy" mentality, especially with babies inside the cabin. Instead, Smith had summoned the FBI's Hostage Rescue Team to be in charge of this tactical situation.

The night had turned frigid, and her breath was visible even against the darkening night sky. The cold had worked its way through her thin jacket.

She and Matt huddled together, behind one of the FBI's dark-colored SUVs.

Through lighted, high-powered binoculars, Charlene inspected the cabin. It didn't look the same as it had on the computer screen.

Clearly there would be no negotiation, a one-shot deal. The EHR Team would storm the house. She didn't like the plan because it put the babies at risk, but it wasn't her call so she kept her mouth shut.

When Smith walked by, she followed him.

A dozen or so men waited for the order to advance. Most of them looked fresh out of Quantico.

Smith approached a man who scoped the cabin through a FLIR Scout PS24 Heat Sensing Thermal Imaging Camera, attached to a tripod.

There hadn't been time to get a search warrant, and in 2001, the United States Supreme Court ruled that performing surveillance of private property using thermal imaging cameras without a search warrant by law enforcement violated the Fourth Amendment's protection from unreasonable searches and seizures. But they had no other choice.

An HRT member said, "We have a warm one."

Smith asked, "What do you see?"

"One person, sitting on a chair. Haven't seen any sign of anyone else."

"What about the babies?"

"Nothing yet."

"Keep looking."

Charlene nudged Smith. "We can't wait forever."

Smith stared at Charlene, opened his mouth, and then closed it again. Then he turned and strode away.

When Charlene turned around Matt smiled at her. "What?"

He shook his head. "Nothing. Let's go."

They joined Smith in one of the cars, the heater turned up high.

"We ready?" asked Charlene.

"Yes," said Smith. "Just waiting for one more confirmation."

She asked, "Is the medic here?"

Smith nodded. "Yes, she's here. It's a good idea, since we might need to use force to take Fellows."

"I don't give a shit about the perp. I'm more interested in the health of the babies."

As if on cue, a sharp rap hit the window, and Smith rolled it down.

"One adult in the kitchen. He hasn't moved since I spotted him. I see seven, smaller forms in another room, all lying down. No other life forms detected."

"There should be two adults," Charlene said.

"Only one adult in there now, ma'am. Looks like a man."

Matt said, "It's gotta be our guy."

Smith put his hand to his mouth, talking on his earpiece. "Move in."

Charlene stepped out of the car and quietly closed the door. Matt got out and walked around to stand beside her, while Smith stayed inside the warm vehicle.

The tactical team had already been in position, setting up an inner perimeter around the cabin, awaiting the command.

She held her breath, closed her eyes, and mouthed a silent prayer.

The car's interior light came on, startling Charlene, as Smith stepped out of the vehicle. He held an iPad, following the video feed from the helmet-cam of one of the tactical unit members, and handed it to Charlene, which surprised her.

On the helmet-cam, the front door lock was picked and the team entered. The man's breath clouded in front of him as he moved.

One by one the teams cleared the rooms. The man with the video-cam joined other team members who had entered the cabin from other locations.

They turned a corner and the video stopped on Joshua Fellows, sitting at a table, not moving.

No gunfire. No screams. No eruption of chaos. No dramatic final shootout. Nothing like you see on cop shows.

Then a voice came over Smith's radio. "We're clear."

Smith looked at Charlene. "Let's go."

Charlene sprinted from the vehicle and entered the cabin, bumping into an officer on his way out.

"Where are the babies?" Charlene asked, hearing the desperation in her own voice.

"In a room in the back."

She jumped past the man and ran down the hall, passing Fellows without a second glance.

"The babies are in here," someone yelled from the back room.

Charlene followed the voice and found a room that looked to have been an add-on, lined with cribs. Seven cribs held seven babies. There was only one adult in the room, a woman, with a stethoscope in her ears—the medic.

She looked up when Charlene reached the doorway. "From what I've seen so far, it looks like they're okay. Of course, we'll have to get them back to the clinic and run tests, but they look good at first glance."

Charlene stepped into the room, and paced to the end, glancing in each crib. She recognized the tiny infant who lay squirming inside the second to the last one, and her breath caught in her throat.

"Oh my God," Charlene whispered. Tears slid down her cheeks, and she trembled as she lifted Martina from the crib. "Oh, baby girl, I've missed you so much."

She hugged Martina, as if she'd never let her go.

Martina felt warm, and Charlene breathed in the soft baby smell while cradling her niece gently, having forgotten how it felt to hold her. Then she laid her back down, opening her onesie, looking for bruises, scratches, or any other signs of physical abuse, but saw nothing.

The medic asked, "Can I check her out?"

Charlene nodded.

The woman blew warm air on the end of the stethoscope and then placed it on the baby's uncovered chest. Martina squirmed slightly.

Momentarily the medic said, "It looks like she's fine."

Charlene snapped up the onesie, wrapped a thick receiving blanket around Martina and hugged her to her chest.

Matt came into the back room. "How is she?"

Charlene nodded. "She's good. They're all good."

"Thank God." Matt exhaled loudly. "Do you want to see Fellows?"

"Absolutely."

"I'll take her." The medic held her arms out.

Charlene looked at the doctor and held the baby tighter. "I think I'll hang on to her."

Matt nodded a silent "okay" to the medic.

Charlene entered the hallway with Martina, and opened a door across from the nursery.

It was a large walk-in closet loaded to the ceiling with baby supplies including crib sheets and blankets, diapers, wipes, creams, lotions, baby powder, cans of formula and jars of pureed fruit and vegetables, everything that a baby could possibly need.

Charlene followed Matt down the hall and into the eating area, a small room just off the kitchen.

The focal point of the room was the dinner table, where Joshua Fellows sat, his lifeless body slumped in a chair, and a glass on the table in front of him with only a few drops of a light brown liquid remaining. Blood had pooled on the floor around his chair.

Magnetic and fingerprint powder covered every hard surface to enhance fingerprints on both polished and non-polished surfaces.

An overweight woman with red curly hair was examining his body.

"No vital signs. He's gone." Smith picked up the glass, swirled it, and then smelled its contents. "Looks like poison."

"Suicide?" Matt asked.

"Could be."

Charlene asked, "Is there a note?"

"Haven't found one yet. He probably would have bled out anyway." Momentarily she added, "He hasn't been dead long. The blood still hasn't had time to congeal."

Fellows didn't look anything like his pictures, and Charlene didn't think she would have recognized him, except that he still wore the same clothes he had on at the Lance home.

His head had been shaved to the scalp, making wearing a wig much easier to do. The dark makeup he'd worn to look African American had been smeared by sweat.

An HRT member came out of the kitchen. "There's a bottle of Jack Daniels on the kitchen counter."

Smith said, "Bag it as evidence."

Charlene added, "And dust it for prints." She stepped closer to Matt and whispered in his ear. "I don't buy it. Fellows didn't commit suicide. This should be listed as a 'suspicious death', or at least homicide/poisoning."

Matt nodded.

Charlene asked, "How long has he been dead?"

The red-headed ME still worked on the body. "Rigor mortis hasn't set in yet, so less than two hours."

"Remember the cloud of dust we saw when we first got here?" She motioned to Matt. "We just missed her. Someone had to be driving that getaway car." To the medical examiner, "Any chance of pulling prints off the victim's body?"

She looked at Matt, who nodded. "I'll have to get him back to the lab for a soft-tissue x-ray to answer that question."

Matt gestured to Charlene. "Let's check out the rest of the cabin." She followed him and Smith into another adjoining room, a ten-by-ten area that had been used as an office, but with a tattered couch pushed against the wall. She still held the sleeping baby in her arms.

As soon as she entered the room, Charlene recognized the scent. "You smell that?"

Smith sniffed the air. "Smell what?"

Matt answered, "Women's perfume."

Charlene nodded. "*Expensive* women's perfume." The scent tripped a memory. She'd smelled it before on someone she knew. She just couldn't remember who.

She inspected the room. The walls were plastered with maps, blueprints, notes, and pictures of the targets. The victims' houses had been photographed, inside and out and pictures scattered on the desk, along with a dated timeline of the victims' routines. She skimmed through the papers, noticing flight plans and credit card receipts from the fathers who'd left town on business.

She found a myriad of "how to" books lining the bookshelves, from tapping into phone lines to picking locks. She also made note of a toolbox and tool belt, as well as an empty briefcase and used her phone to photograph everything.

Uniforms for local cable, phone and landscaping companies hung on hangers in the closet. On the floor, piled beside the shoes, were half a dozen sets of lifts that Fellows had used to alter his height.

With the amount of precise detail the kidnappers had gone to, to pull off their nearly-perfect crimes, she realized it had just been a matter of dumb luck that they'd recovered the babies at all.

She studied the tacked-up posters. Scribbled red lines crossed the maps, highlighting the victims' homes.

Her spine tightened when she saw a photo of her and her sister, with Richard and Martina, tacked to the board. It had been taken the day they went shopping.

She had seen someone that morning while jogging. He had been there, watching, studying their routines.

Smith handed Charlene a paper—a printed copy of the credit card receipt Richard had used to purchase the tickets for Mamma Mia at the Buell Theatre.

An agent walked into the room holding a full garbage bag, which she held open for them to see. "There was a mini pharmacy locked up in the kitchen, full of pill bottles and prescription drugs."

Charlene asked, "The Z drugs?"

Matt nodded. "Looks like it."

"We also found a gun." The agent held up a bagged weapon.

"Probably the one he used today," Matt said.

They dusted the cabin for fingerprints but found only a single set. Charlene presumed they would belong to Fellows, who wasn't wearing gloves when they found him. Chances were good that the person calling the shots would be too savvy to leave prints on anything.

They went back to Fellows, where only one glass rested on the table, and it had no lipstick marks. In fact, there was no evidence that anyone else had been in the house with him at all. Charlene felt sick. Who had been driving that car?

Smith bent over and stared at the perpetrator's face. Charlene was close enough to hear Smith whisper.

"I got you, you sick son-of-a-bitch."

For the first time since she'd met him, Smith smiled slightly, a tight-jawed, almost reluctant grin that suited the strung-out agent. He straightened, and turned around.

Charlene argued, "It's not over yet."

Smith looked at her.

"Someone is still out there. We don't have his partner yet."

Smith looked away from Charlene and acknowledged Matt. "I'll see you back at the field office. Tomorrow, we'll get packed up and head back to Washington."

Charlene looked at Matt, who wouldn't look back at her, averting his gaze.

Officers scoured the grounds outside, many uniforms still moving in and out.

The night was brisk, so she snuggled Martina deep inside her jacket. Charlene pulled out her cell phone and punched in the number.

"Hello?"

"Jane, it's me. I have Martina."

Chapter 22

She gingerly opened her eyes. The sunlight filtered in through the partially closed blinds. It took a second to gather her thoughts.

As she sat up in her bedroom at Jane's house, the events of the previous night flashed back. She smiled and relaxed remembering the relief she felt when the babies were found, unharmed.

She had never felt so overjoyed as she had last night when she handed Martina to her parents.

The medic had wanted the babies to stay in the hospital overnight, but the parents wanted them home, which was to be expected. Jane and Richard had scheduled Martina for a quick check up at the clinic that afternoon.

She expected to feel great, but her body felt beat up and in physical pain, aching in places she didn't know she had. Then she realized that something was missing. They had yet to find the perp's accomplice, and she knew she wouldn't be completely satisfied until that part of the puzzle was solved.

She heard everyone downstairs, sounding giddy and content, while preparing breakfast. Charlene looked at her phone; it was after ten. She was surprised, unable to believe she had heard nothing since she'd laid her head on the pillow. In fact, the combined stress, worry and lack of sleep had taken its toll, so that she hadn't moved at all during the night.

She had needed that sleep for both her physical and mental well-being. She'd been ignoring the warning signs and knew she had to start taking care of herself. Hers was a dangerous game, one she'd played before, but she wasn't really surprised, because she'd never learned to stop when met with a challenge. She sighed, knowing that would have to change.

She couldn't help but smile when she heard the sweet sound of her mother laughing in the kitchen. From the top of the stairs she could smell coffee and hear bacon sizzling. Her stomach growled.

She tiptoed down the steps, enjoying the sights and sounds of a happy family. It was important to appreciate the things most people took for granted: family, safety, togetherness.

It was a complete one-eighty from the way this house sounded and felt over the last week, and it felt great.

Charlene stopped just outside the kitchen, watching her family. Her mother was fully dressed, with her makeup and hair done, while Richard and Jane were still in their pajamas and robes.

A day after Joshua Fellows' death, the media had a field day; city officials were content to have the crime solved; the DPD and FBI would receive citations for a job well done.

Fortunately, Fellows' first escape from law enforcement hadn't been leaked to the media. No one knew that he'd evaded them with the help of a getaway car driven by a second perp. The public was purposely being spoon-fed information that would make them feel safe again.

Her mother smiled. "Charlene."

Everyone turned and smiled, and even Martina let out a delighted giggle. At that precise moment, Charlene wished she'd had her camera to capture the moment.

Her mother rushed over with a mug of steaming black coffee. "Here. Come and sit down."

Jane asked, "How are you feeling?"

"A little tired, but good."

"We didn't wake you, did we?"

"No."

Charlene picked up one of Martina's rattles and shook it in front of the baby girl. Martina giggled and reached out for the toy, and Charlene set it in her tiny hands.

Jane gave her a look. "So when are we going to meet this Matt guy?"

Charlene shrugged. "I don't know."

Her stomach was growling when Richard brought over plates filled with pancakes, eggs, bacon, fried potatoes and toast.

Charlene surveyed the huge spread that covered most of the table. "This is a lot of food for the four of us."

Jane smirked, an ornery grin that wasn't her sister's style. "Well, you never know who might show up."

Charlene squinted at Jane, but her sister looked away.

Before Charlene could say another word, the doorbell rang.

Jane stood and headed for the door. "I wonder who that could be."

Charlene frowned. "What are you up to?"

Jane raised her hands. "Don't look at me."

Charlene turned around and looked at her mom. "What did you do?"

Her mother smiled at Matt. "Good morning, Agent Stone."

She looked at her mother again, but Brenda shrugged. "I had to invite the guy for breakfast. He helped save my grandchild."

A total set up.

Charlene stood up and looked in the wall mirror behind the table. Her sandy blond hair was tousled, her blue eyes bloodshot, and the 'v' shaped scar on her chin looked redder than usual. So basically—a complete mess.

No time for makeup. She finger-combed her hair and rubbed the sleep from her eyes.

Richard winked at Charlene. "Oh yeah, he's just another cop."

Charlene gave him a look that said it all.

She pointed toward their guest. "Everyone, this is Agent Stone."

He was showered, shaved and dressed in a freshly pressed dark suit with a light blue tie. "Please, call me Matt."

Jane answered, "Matt, this is my husband, Richard."

Richard came over, wiped his hands on the most feminine apron Charlene had ever seen, and shook hands with Matt. "Thank you for everything."

Matt smiled and nodded.

Jane introduced their mother. "This is my mother, Brenda."

Matt walked over to their mother and shook her hand. "It's a pleasure to meet you, Mrs. Taylor."

"And I think you already know Martina."

He smiled. "We met last night." Turning toward the baby, he said, "Hey, squirt."

Charlene shook her head. "I see that my family has already seduced you into their web."

"What can I say? I never heard a word after 'bacon'." He grinned, and Charlene felt her knees quiver.

Jane asked, "Are you hungry?"

Matt nodded. "Starved."

Richard held up the coffee pot. "How do you take your coffee, Matt?"

"Black," Charlene answered, before Matt had a chance to say anything. She felt her face flush. "Sorry."

"Yeah." Richard nodded. "Just another cop…"

After breakfast they retreated to the living room, where the family peppered Matt with questions, many that had nothing to do with the case, which embarrassed Charlene to no end. She felt like a teenager whose prom date got the third degree from her overprotective father.

Without preamble Matt suddenly asked, "Listen, do you mind if we watch the press conference?"

Richard frowned. "What press-conference?"

"The case has been solved and the babies are safe. The public will want to know the end of the story, and of course, our superiors will expect credit for a job well done."

"I forgot about that." Richard nodded in agreement and turned on the local news station.

The press conference took place at the Bellco Theatre, as it had a few days earlier. That press conference had caused an uproar and started the whole FBI versus DPD debate.

Janice Salinger stood at the podium, dressed in a designer outfit. "Today is a special day and one that I am proud to be a part of. Not only have we brought down the man who single-handedly terrorized the good folks of this city, but we have also made families whole again, by returning their loved ones, safe and sound. This city won't be bullied. When terror strikes, it will only bring us closer together as a community. We are strong…Denver strong."

The gathered crowd exploded with applause. Cameras flashed, and media heads shouted questions. Salinger stepped away from the podium and approached the few parents who had attended, standing on stage with their infants. Most hadn't bothered to show up, probably weary of the media attention.

Salinger hugged the mothers, shook hands with the fathers, and kissed the babies, already prepping for the next election.

Once Salinger stepped off screen, Senator Jaqueline Bloomfield stepped forward, hand-in-hand with her daughter, Anna, and her husband, Michael. Her husband hugged her and her daughter kissed her on the cheek, before the senator stepped up to the cluster of microphones.

Jane smiled at her sister. "There's your girl, Charlene."

The senator spoke. "This is a great day for Denver, and I'm proud to be here. But I'm here to tell the people of New Mexico that I will not stop looking for our babies. I know they're out there, and I won't rest until I have answers. You can take that to the bank."

Again, the applause thundered. The senator stepped down, took her family's hands, and raised them over their heads. Salinger and the parents also stepped up to the edge of the stage, standing beside the senator's family, and raised their hands, much like a boxer who had just won the heavyweight championship of the world.

Charlene looked at Jane. "Did you know about this press conference?"

Jane nodded. "Police Chief Salinger called us this morning and asked if we wanted to be part of it. But we've had enough of the spotlight."

Brenda asked, "Would anyone like anything from the kitchen?"

Jane answered, "I think we're good, Mom."

"Okay, then I'm going upstairs to lie down."

Jane said, "We're heading out, too. Richard and I are taking Martina for a walk, making up for lost time. Then after lunch we'll take her in for her checkup."

In a matter of minutes, Charlene and Matt were alone.

She couldn't help but ask what was uppermost in her mind. "So, what happened last night after I left?"

"We gutted the place. Of course, DPD showed up to hog some glory. Together we inspected it from top to bottom, and found not one personal item, not even a picture. There was no indication that Fellows had acted with a partner, let alone a woman."

"When do you fly back to Washington?"

"We fly out tonight."

Charlene nodded, staring at the TV, but not hearing a word.

She had a million questions for Matt—only her questions were of a personal nature. Was this a relationship or a one-time thing?

Matt asked, "What about you?"

"My captain has given me a few extra days off and I can return to full duty when I get back."

"That's good news."

"I guess so, yeah."

Again, silence.

Charlene realized that for all the families involved, nothing would ever be the same. Parents would be overprotective, seeing every stranger on the street as a threat. It would be a long road back, but Charlene would help Jane and Richard every step of the way.

Except for mild dehydration, the babies hadn't been physically injured in any way. They would all move on to live normal, happy lives. The parents would suffer the most. They would remember.

Charlene said, "Last night, I noticed that you didn't share Agent Smith's enthusiasm."

He looked down into his lap. "It's hard to feel good about them, when there are so many more out there."

"The other babies?"

"I'll never stop looking for them, and I doubt Agent Smith will either."

"You think we'll ever hear from the partner?"

He shook his head. "You mean if there is one?"

"I believe there is, and I think you do, too."

He nodded but looked unconvinced. "If there is, she got lucky, escaped justice, and won't risk it again." He looked at Charlene. "You can't let it go, can you?"

"No. It's not in my nature. And I think you feel the same way."

He shook his head, got up and retrieved a leather briefcase from the floor just inside the front door.

"What's that?" Charlene asked.

He opened it to reveal the case files. "I'm not leaving until tonight."

They spread the papers out on the coffee table.

"Fellows scored off the charts in his IQ testing, but there's no way he planned these kidnappings in such precise detail by himself. It's true that he was a master of disguise, and had a keen sense for detail, but he was no leader."

"The woman has to be the key." Charlene got out the paperwork from the mental hospital and studied it until it blurred before her eyes.

When she finally focused, she scanned the page again, but this time something caught her attention. At first she wasn't sure what it was, until her gaze fell on the signature, which was somehow familiar. Her psyche was trying to tell her something.

Then it hit her. "Oh no."

Matt tilted his head in question. "What?"

She set the page on his lap and then stood, then retrieved the poster and returned to the couch. She unrolled it, covering the papers that remained on the table.

"What are you doing?"

"Becky Jacobs signed the hospital login sheet."

"So?" He gave her a weird look.

"This poster was signed by Jacqueline Bloomfield."

"Okay?"

"Look at the signatures."

Matt did. "I'm not a handwriting specialist."

"Neither am I, but those look very similar. The 'J's' and the 'B's' are identical. Both letters have a similar slash at the end."

He shook his head in disbelief. "Are you saying it's the same person? Are you kidding?"

"No, I'm not." And at that moment, she puzzled, realizing that the puzzle pieces were right before her eyes, but she hadn't connected the dots. What was she missing?

Matt stood up, turned away and then turned to look back at her. "I thought you believed that the 'woman' involved was probably someone who's been hurt, who probably can't have children of her own? Senator Bloomfield has a daughter."

"Anna is adopted."

"What?"

"Senator Bloomfield's daughter is adopted."

"Really?"

Charlene nodded. "It was front page news years ago. Most people think it was a publicity stunt, but the senator and her husband adopted a little girl when she ran for her first term of office. She'd married quickly and adopted a child, creating a family, exactly what every person in America expected from a female senatorial candidate. Some people say she did it to get the sympathy vote."

Matt stared at the floor, uncertainty still tracing his face. "Charlene, we're talking about a United States Senator here."

"Think about it, Matt. Who's been around since the beginning, even in New Mexico? She's been there every step of the way, even involving herself in the investigation."

"Char—"

"You guys must have a handwriting specialist at the office."

Matt exhaled loudly. "It's called the Questioned Documents Unit (QDU) in the FBI Lab. They're known for their handwriting analysis."

"Will you take it to them?"

"This is a sitting Senator of New Mexico."

"Who had inside knowledge of our investigation. Just take it in. If there's nothing there, then I'll let it go."

Matt snatched the papers out of her grasp. "Fine."

He walked toward the front door and opened it to see a blond female DPD officer he recognized. Her metal name tag read Officer Cripps.

She smiled. "Hi, Matt."

"Paige? What are you doing here?"

She held up an old, rusted metal box that looked like it had been burned in a fire. "Jake told me to bring this to you."

"What is it?"

"Not sure, but your name is on it."

Matt accepted the box. It smelled like charcoal. "Where's it from?"

"The fire marshal said it was buried in the rubble of Harold Linden's trailer. Jake was there when they found it and, since they saw your name on it, they gave it to him."

"Thanks, Paige."

"No problem."

Matt closed the door and carried the box over to where Charlene sat unmoving.

"Screwdriver?" Matt said.

Charlene returned momentarily with a flat-headed screwdriver that she handed to him, eager to see what was in the box.

The smoke smell from the box stirred her memory of another scent, the scent of expensive perfume, and suddenly she knew who wore it, but she said nothing, not wanting to interrupt his examination of the box. Then she changed her mind. "Listen, about that expensive perfume I noticed at the cabin? Well, I just remembered that it's the same scent the senator wears."

"You're kidding? That's one more nail in her coffin."

He turned his attention back to the box, turning it over and around. The box was old, dented and the paint was worn thin, in places that hadn't been scorched by fire.

"It's light." Matt shook it but it made no noise.

He set the box on the coffee table and attempted to pry open the lid, but it refused to budge. On the second attempt, the top popped open, and papers took flight, then landed on the floor.

At least a dozen papers had been folded inside the box, and Matt and Charlene bent to pick them up, then began to read.

Seconds later Charlene felt dizzy, as if her legs would give out. Neither of them spoke. Finally she looked at Matt, and could see tension in his face.

"You'd better check that signature."

Then the other shoe dropped.

After comparing the documents, handwriting examiners deemed that they were 98.3% identical. They had a match.

Charlene and Matt took notes in the backseat of an unmarked SUV, while Smith sat behind the wheel but turned toward the back, bringing them up to speed. They had to go over their options and decide which way to proceed. It was a delicate matter that had to be handled with the utmost discretion.

The FBI Deputy Director had suggested an elaborate sting, with wire taps and informants to trap the suspect. But Smith had pleaded for urgency, demanding that the suspect be taken down before she fled the country. And this time they couldn't afford any leaks.

They'd decided to execute every search warrant simultaneously, so evidence couldn't be destroyed by a phone call. At that moment, cops all over the US carried out searches in the senator's five New Mexico offices, her Washington office, her two homes and three vehicles.

"I can't believe what I did, keeping her in the loop," Janice Salinger shook her head in the front passenger seat.

Matt said, "It's okay. You didn't know. None of us knew."

She repeated, "I let her follow the investigation, giving her all the details from day one."

Matt repeated, "It's okay."

Salinger shook her head. "She's the one who told me to give the snipers the green light to take the shot at Fellows. She said he needed to be taken down, that Colorado and New Mexico would be indebted to me, and that I'd be fast-tracked to the top." She was breathing hard when she added, "I filled her in at every step of the investigation."

Charlene sighed aloud. "She had us all fooled."

Salinger refused to look at them.

It was all in Harold Linden's little tin box. Linden had helped nail Jaqueline Bloomfield from the grave, and the Feds had uncovered the rest after an in-depth computer analysis. But it was Harry's notes that pointed them in the right direction.

It had taken them over two days, using the sharpest hackers in the country, to unearth sealed information on Senator Bloomfield, better known as Abigail Fellows. The techies spent hours digging into deeply hidden confidential files. Ms. Fellows had spent a lot of money, and gone to great lengths to bury her past. Many of the blanks still remained in question.

The whole process had to be dealt with using the utmost care and speed. Only a handful of outsiders were allowed access to the information. Bloomfield was admired and well liked, and they had no idea who was on her payroll. The fewer people involved, the less chance there would be of a leak.

"How did this Harold Linden find out so much?" Smith asked.

Charlene answered, "My father used to call it the 'Triple S Threat'. Someone, somewhere knows something."

Matt nodded. "Looks like Harry found that someone."

Smith shook his head, wild-eyed with fury. "Just look at this thing—the whole file on the senator, her life, her past—it was all a lie—all of it."

Jaqueline Bloomfield was a member of the Democratic Party. She was the first woman to be elected to a US Senate seat representing the state of New Mexico and one of only twenty women serving in that position.

She earned a B.A. in Economics from Georgetown University and then a JD degree. She was a member of Pi Beta Phi sorority, clerked for an associate justice of the New Mexico Supreme Court, and then hired on as an associate at a law firm.

"Everything in here is bullshit," Salinger said. "Bloomfield must have hired the best computer geniuses in the world to build her backstory."

Then they spoke about what they'd found hidden deep in the archives of the internet. The dark web.

Jaqueline Bloomfield had been born with the name Abigail Fellows. She'd gotten pregnant at the age of fifteen, but lost the baby at six months after her abusive alcoholic father pushed her down the stairs. Doctors tried to save the baby by way of a cesarean section, but to no avail. There was no record of the identity of the child's father. It could have been Abigail's father, brother, or someone else.

After the miscarriage, Fellows' parents died in what had been ruled a murder-suicide. The death of their parents hit Joshua hard, sending him over the edge. Abigail had her brother commit himself and then she cut all ties with him.

It was only speculation, but they assumed that Abigail started a new life, using the remainder of her parents' life insurance money to hire reliable computer wizards to cover her tracks. She paid for new personal documentation, changed her name and her looks, moved to a new city, and used her charm and intelligence to climb the ladder.

Salinger asked, "But what was it all about? Why kidnap babies? Where are the babies from New Mexico?"

Nobody in the car answered the police chief, even though they all had their theories.

They'd used six agents to sift through all the evidence found in the cabin. There had been no mention, no sign of anything to do with a baby-selling ring. The senator's bank accounts had been checked, and hidden through transactions and overseas bank accounts was one large, current deposit that couldn't be explained.

Denver law dictated that no arrest was needed to subpoena evidence. But with someone like a US Senator, no judge in Colorado, New Mexico, or the rest of the country would grant warrants or allow access to her possessions on a hunch, or on circumstantial evidence alone.

They'd kept the files confidential, releasing no names. They wanted to make sure they had everything they needed on the senator, before making an arrest. The DA still didn't have enough concrete evidence to implicate her directly, but they did have enough to bring her in for questioning. Charlene could feel the depth of their disbelief—an almost tangible thing, right there in the car.

She looked at Smith. What was he thinking? How was he feeling? He'd been chasing this case for six years, been through an endless number of sleepless nights, comforted suffering parents, and tracked every lead, phone call and tip.

While they were investigating, they'd tracked the senator's movements for the last forty-eight hours.

She'd spent the night of the cabin raid in a hotel room, in the top floor penthouse suite, before spending the weekend at a house on Hayden Lake, outside Boulder—a house that belonged to her husband.

Now Bloomfield was alone, with no husband or daughter. As Charlene looked around the quiet, serene lakefront property, she understood why the senator would choose such a location—a chance to get away from the hustle and bustle of her busy personal life. The quietness of the outdoors, the nearest neighbor seven miles away, gave Bloomfield much needed time to herself.

Though she was less than a year away from re-election, with much campaigning to do, Bloomfield had called in sick to her office. Charlene wondered if Bloomfield knew just how much they had on her.

Smith pointed toward the house. "There she is."

Bloomfield emerged through the large, custom front door to the stone-fronted ranch-style lake house. Clouds of mist floated around her head when she breathed. She looked fit, an avid runner who regularly jogged.

But Bloomfield wasn't alone. When the senator stepped down from the top step, she was followed by the same thick-necked, linebacker look-alike guard that had accompanied her to the field office in Denver. He looked to have on the same suit as he wore that day, too.

Salinger spoke, breaking the silence. "She's got a bodyguard."

Smith sighed aloud. "Looks like there's only one. She must be paying him out of pocket."

The bodyguard whispered something to the senator, who nodded, and then pulled a set of earphones down over her ears. Then Bloomfield took off jogging at a slow pace, with her bodyguard following along behind, easily keeping up.

"Let's go."

"Senator."

They emerged from the car with their badges drawn, walking as the senator jogged toward them. Smith was in the lead.

Bloomfield slowed her jog when they stepped out on the trail, and then stopped completely. She pulled off her headphones.

Smith said, "Senator, FBI."

"I know who you are, Agent Smith."

The guard reached into his jacket pocket.

Charlene, Matt and Salinger simultaneously drew their guns from their holsters.

"Whoa." Smith had his hands in the air. "Let's just take it easy."

The guard paused, his hand still inside his jacket. Charlene could make out the form of a gun and shoulder holster, through the thin fabric.

They now had three guns aimed on the senator and her guard, taking no chances. They fanned out to form an arc, with Salinger and Smith in the middle, and Charlene and Matt anchoring the ends.

The gun felt heavy in Charlene's hand, as she aimed her weapon at a woman she had so admired.

Smith barked, "Not like this, Senator!"

Bloomfield looked at her guard, who hadn't given an inch, and then stared back at them with confidence etched across her face.

The senator asked, "What do you want?"

"We would like you to come to the office to answer some questions. That's all."

"Questions about what?"

"Joshua Fellows."

When the guard glanced at Bloomfield, his hand was still inside his jacket, his fingers flirting with the butt of his revolver.

"The man who kidnapped those babies in Denver? Why do you want to ask me about him?"

"We think you already know that."

The senator's eyes narrowed. "Agent Smith, can you please tell me what you're really doing here? I'm not coming to the office to answer questions about a deranged kidnapper. That man has put us all through enough."

"You mean your brother?"

Bloomfield paused, clearly uncertain. She looked to be calculating her odds, and Charlene thought the senator probably wondered if this was a bluff, or if they really knew about her past.

Smith pulled out a paper. "We also have a search warrant for this property."

This time, the big guard used his tree trunk of an arm to move the senator behind him.

When he pulled out his gun, the senator turned and took off, heading for the path behind the house, hidden by a thick forest of trees.

Without warning, the bodyguard opened fire, and the first shot reverberated through the air.

Charlene returned fire.

The guard was hit three times before going down to a knee, but still managed to get off another round before a final bullet took him all the way down. His white shirt was coated red from blood, after taking hits in his abdomen and chest.

Matt yelled, "We have a man down." Charlene turned to see Janice Salinger, face down on the ground, not moving.

Matt shouted, "You two go after Bloomfield!"

He swiftly moved toward Salinger, then rolled her over. Her blue blouse was stained with a red dot that blossomed, and her face had lost all color.

Charlene and Smith took off at a full run. She felt an adrenaline rush push her harder, as she ran.

As she rounded the corner, she spotted Bloomfield, a good thirty yards in front of them. The senator was quick, agile, and knew these woods—a distinct advantage over her pursuers.

Charlene checked her peripheral vision and noticed that Smith was lagging behind. She herself had been running for years, and could no doubt catch Bloomfield, or at least keep up. But Smith had had a desk job for the last twenty years, and Charlene doubted that he had seen the inside of a gym in recent history.

The lake was on her left and a pine forest on her right as they followed the shoreline. Under any other circumstances, this would have been a great place for a leisurely run, but not today.

She kicked it up a notch, pumping her arms and legs faster as the sun beat down on them. The chill that had once been in the air had disappeared and Charlene could now feel the sun's heat through her heavy jacket.

She could no longer see Smith behind her, as, inch by inch, she gained on the senator.

She looked up ahead, trying to peer past the senator to get a glimpse of the path. It appeared to veer right, away from the water and deeper into the forest. The question was…would Bloomfield follow it or go off-road?

Charlene took a chance.

She left the path, ducked into the woods, dodging through trees, her feet grinding and squishing through layers of pine needles on the ground. She smelled sharp, intense resin, like the remote outdoors in the mountains. She plowed through in a straight line, trying to cut the senator off at the path they'd been following.

The senator passed her just as Charlene left the tree line behind, and landed back on the path, but now she was only a few feet behind her.

Charlene's breath came hard now, and sweat slid down her face and burned her eyes.

She could feel herself start to slow slightly, and knew that the intensity of the situation, and the stress of the run were taking their toll. Was the senator slowing also? It didn't look like it.

Soon, Charlene knew, she'd be toast, so she had to make her move now.

She launched her body at the senator, reaching out for her in midair. When she wrapped her arms around Bloomfield's legs, taking the woman down, all of Charlene's weight landed roughly on Bloomfield's right ankle.

The impact of the hard landing forced an "oomph" out of the senator, who was breathing hard. Lying on her stomach, sprawled out, Bloomfield wasn't moving. Then she reached for her ankle, which was oddly twisted.

Charlene had taken the senator's heels to her gut, which knocked the wind out of her. She bent down, grabbing at her abdomen, gulping deep breaths of air.

The senator tried to stand but her ankle gave out, and she fell back to the ground, letting out an ear-shattering scream.

Charlene grabbed Bloomfield by the bottom of the pant leg. She got to her knees, caught her breath and pulled a set of handcuffs from the back of her belt. "Senator Jaqueline Bloomfield, you have the right to remain silent."

Chapter 23

After being treated for a badly sprained ankle, Bloomfield spent two days in a holding cell while the cops searched her homes, offices, and vehicles. There had been no way to keep such news from the media.

The warrants had been a time-consuming process, but it was even more of a challenge to find judges to sign on the dotted line.

When the news was released, chaos broke out. The senator's expensive team of lawyers did all they could to have her released. They talked to the media about the outrage and injustice of prosecuting a sitting senator. Everyone pointed fingers, and local law enforcement was under fire. The senator's press team worked on damage control.

The police and FBI engaged in a kind of competition. The FBI Special Investigative Division was brought in and scurried to find enough evidence to hold her until trial.

But as hard as they tried, no one could come up with a motive. The senator was incapable of having children of her own, so unless they received an admission that Bloomfield hated mothers who could bear children, they had no motive at all.

Time was of the essence, since search warrants were only good for twenty-four hours after a judge signed them. On the second day of the search, the FBI and the DPD thought they had a breakthrough.

In a hidden safe, under a cut-out group of floor boards in the library in the senator's lake cabin, they found maps with areas circled and code words written across the area. The positions could have been drop-off points, and had agents frantically trying to break the codes. The circles on the maps indicated positions just outside El Paso, near the Mexican border.

The Feds were sure they had enough on the senator to take her down, or at least hold her and hope she broke. Just before the deadline they finally had enough evidence for the case to go to trial. Senator Jaqueline Bloomfield would be tried as an accessory to kidnapping fourteen babies, and as an accessory to the murder of Harold Linden.

America was rocked.

Janice Salinger was on life support at the University of Colorado Hospital. She'd been shot in the chest, with major damage to one lung and her chest wall, which caused massive hemorrhaging. She'd undergone successful surgery but was still not out of the woods. Infection was a major concern.

So, accessory to attempted murder was also added to the list of Bloomfield's charges.

Bloomfield's head of security, Morris Chamberlain, had been pronounced dead at the scene. Using Chamberlain's physical description, Charlene and Matt identified him as the suspect in the Tanya Peters video, the exchange that had taken place outside the pawn shop in Aurora. One of the pawn shop employees even identified Chamberlain from a photo.

When they'd searched the man's house, they found the box he'd received from Peters. It was empty, but they had a good idea of what it had contained. Chamberlain was no longer around to deny or confirm it, and it would be impossible to find out who had killed Tanya Peters, but they had the whole scenario pretty well laid out.

Bloomfield had paid Peters to sneak out the radioactive pellets and Chamberlain was there for the trade. Later on, Bloomfield had someone kill Peters to silence her, maybe Chamberlain himself. It was all hearsay though, and Bloomfield would never admit to it.

But the truth was that Chamberlain never acted unless ordered to do something.

Smith said, "That's not good enough."

Matt and Charlene joined Smith, the FBI Assistant Deputy Director and an attorney with a special prosecution section of the DA. They'd come to celebrate the news of the trial, but what started out as a celebration, had turned into a heated debate led by Smith.

Charlene looked out the office windows and saw a group of personnel who had stopped and watched Smith go off alone into the tiny office.

Matt closed the blinds.

"Keep your voice down, Nick," said the ADD.

Very few people knew about the baby-selling ring theory, and there was little evidence to back it up. The ADD tried his best to redirect attention away from the angry shouts and wild accusations taking place inside his office.

But Smith wasn't after the senator, who was only a middle man. Smith wanted the big Kahuna, the person or people responsible for the whole operation. He'd been chasing his theory for six years. The senator was as close as he'd ever come.

"So what do you suggest?" the ADD asked.

Smith had his sites on a bigger goal. "A major product makes her a major player. Let's cut her a deal."

"What?" Charlene leapt up from her seat. "She kidnapped fourteen babies and you want to let her go free?" She had trouble keeping her voice modulated.

"I'm not saying she should go free, but there's a bigger picture out there. This will continue to go on across the United States, even internationally, if we don't cut the snake off at the head. We need to take it down from the top, and then the rest will come crumbling after. The senator is just a minor player."

So that's why someone from the DA's office was there, to finalize the approval of the 'deal' Smith was considering. Charlene sat back down, looking at Matt for support.

He leaned in close to her. "He's right, Char. This is bigger than we think."

The tension was thick enough to cut with a knife. Charlene felt alone. She understood where the Feds stood and why, but what about the babies, especially Martina, and the parents who the senator had put through hell?

It *did* make sense, but she just couldn't let Bloomfield go unpunished.

"Okay, I'll get on board, under one condition."

They all looked at her.

"That I'm in the room when we make the deal."

The ADD and Smith looked at each other. Smith nodded. "Alright, fine. But don't try to be a hero."

Charlene held up her hand. "Before we go in, tell me all about this baby-selling racket. How does it work? Who do you think is involved? If we can get a better sense of their motivation, we can use that."

Smith stood with his arms crossed. "If I knew who was behind it all, I'd have arrested them already."

"You don't even have a theory?"

Smith hesitated, looking each one of them in the eye. "As a matter of fact, I do."

The tension in the air rose even higher.

He continued, "In 1995, the Russian government enacted legislation that would allow the adoption of infants and children by foreign families. Most of their major cities have several orphanage-type facilities called baby houses that house children from birth to approximately four to five years of age. Older children ranging from five to eighteen years of age are frequently held at boarding schools or orphanages. Infants and children from age six months to fourteen years old are available for adoption. Most families want a child 'as young as possible.' Realistically, 'as young as possible' means the child will be between nine to fourteen months when families bring them home."

Charlene shook her head in confusion. "So what does all this mean? Russians?"

Smith wore a worried look. "This goes a hell of a lot deeper than you think."

Charlene looked at Matt, who met her gaze. Then they both nodded at Smith.

"We don't know for sure, but I suspect the Russian government has their hands in the pot. We think they're getting a percentage of the funds."

"How does it work?"

"Easy. The government has a group they trust to handle the negotiations, and they contract it out to them. This group takes care of everything. The first thing they do is network, all over the world, looking for parents. I'm talking desperate parents who have been through the process and tried everything, with no luck. Then the group looks for people to help carry out their scheme. The group promises the kidnappers wealth, as well as safe, happy homes for the babies. Once the negotiations are finalized, they meet with the kidnappers, probably somewhere safe, but just inside the Mexican border because it's easier for Americans to cross than Russians or Mexicans, and they make the exchange. The money is handed over and the babies are taken to their new homes. That way there's no paper trail. Sometimes requests are made in advance, such as gender, race, hair or eye color, etc. From all the intel I've collected, I have no idea who is behind it all. Abigail Fellows is our best lead, our only lead. This could be our one shot to stop it forever."

"So you think there are more American kidnappers?"

"Could be, but they don't hang on to the babies for long."

Charlene felt sick. "I've heard enough. Let's do this."

They entered a meeting room at the Denver County Jail, part of the Denver Sheriff's Department on East Smith Road, where Bloomfield and three attorneys waited. The senator, in a bright orange jump suit and uncuffed hands, slumped at the table with two men and a woman.

Bloomfield wore no makeup, because she no longer had a team of beauticians at her beck and call. In fact, she looked much older, with deep stress lines on her face, and her lip was still swollen from the takedown. At that moment her cold stare was fixed on Charlene, Matt and Smith. The senator's swollen ankle was wrapped in an ACE bandage.

Smith spoke first. "Good morning, Senator."

The senator didn't reply.

Smith carried a folder with the typed agreement inside. It had taken them three hours of shouting and hair-pulling to come up with a deal that satisfied law enforcement, both at the local and federal levels.

From beside the senator, a dark-suited man spoke. "I'm Brett Sawyer, Senator Bloomfield's attorney." The other two didn't introduce themselves.

"Okay, Agent Smith, we're here," said Sawyer. "You've called on us for a good reason, I hope, and not just to waste our time. As you can see, my client is cooperating."

"Yes, it's funny how warrants will do that."

The lawyer pursed his lips, but didn't comment.

"Look, Senator, or should I call you Abigail? Which would you prefer?"

When the senator didn't reply, Smith continued.

"We have all we need on you. We know your background. We have an eyewitness who put you at Mesilla Valley Hospital to meet with your brother, who's been identified by the parents as the kidnapper, and now, we have the maps with the drop-off points that we discovered under the floorboards at your lake house."

It wasn't exactly a bluff. Nurse Carla had seen the senator there, but she would never be able to identify her because she'd changed her appearance so much. But the senator didn't know that.

The attorney cut in, "Are you accusing my client without due process? Those maps don't prove anything. They could be maps of anything. Maybe the senator and her family planned a vacation. When we're done with you, agent, we'll have sued the FBI, the DPD and anyone else responsible for such malicious accusations, and for ruining the reputation of my client."

Charlene understood the drill—the guilty ones put everyone else on trial.

"We know that as a teenager, you lost a baby. Whose baby was that?"

The senator didn't look at Smith. She stared straight ahead, poised, as if eye contact would trigger something in her.

"Then you acted on the hate you felt afterwards, killing your parents, and then taking your anger out on innocent children to help finance your campaign."

Charlene realized at that moment that the lawyer would be challenging them every step of the way.

To that end, he railed, "Do you have proof? The senator's parents' deaths were ruled a murder-suicide."

Bloomfield didn't budge. She stared straight at the wall in front of her, wearing a noncommittal expression.

"Agent Smith," the attorney started again. "Let's face it. You have nothing on my client. All these false accusations won't get you a verdict. You have nothing concrete. So what if she had a heartbreaking childhood? We all have something we're ashamed of. There's no proof of her involvement in any of this."

Rising from his seat, Smith shouted, "She had a private investigator killed." When Matt calmly touched his arm, Smith sat back down.

The lawyer's red face betrayed his ire. "Where's your proof my client was involved? Do you have fingerprints, hair fibers, or DNA? Anything that links my client to this case? Maybe Joshua Fellows committed these murders and kidnappings, but that has nothing to do with my client. She hasn't seen or spoken to her brother in years."

He was using the disassociation game as a defense mechanism. Smith leaned back in his chair, crossed his legs and pulled at his tie, stroking and flattening it out.

That was all it took to fuel the enemy's arguments. "Exactly. You have nothing. How the judge allowed this case to go to trial is anyone's guess. Because your profiler says there were two kidnappers involved, and one of them a woman—oh, please," Sawyer snorted.

Matt blinked in anger, took a couple of deep breaths, leaned back and then said, "The chief of police is fighting for her life. When she comes out of it, she'll testify that she fed you information throughout the investigation, and you ordered her to have your brother killed, to shut him up."

"My client never ordered her bodyguard to shoot. He did all of that on his own. And as for having her brother killed—well, you're way off base."

Charlene had had enough. "Mr. Sawyer, does your client know that kidnapping is a death penalty offense in the state of Colorado? The length of time between verdict and death in the United States is approximately ten years. So she could live to enjoy life in prison until her early fifties."

The senator still refused to make eye contact and the attorneys weren't talking either. So Charlene went on.

"What do you think the jury will see when we open up about Abigail Fellows—especially when we can place her in both cities where the kidnappings took place? When we discuss the senator's brother, the lost baby, and the father of that baby? How she lived off her parents' insurance money after their deaths, and the rush to cover her past, change her name, identity, and her very life?"

The lawyer flashed a smile Charlene didn't like. "I beg to differ. They'll see a successful, confident leader who had a terrible past that she wanted to put behind her. They'll see a woman, against all odds, with a mentally insane brother and parents who committed suicide, overcome those odds and succeed in a position which, in the past, were only occupied by men. When it's over I'll have the jury feeling so sorry for my client that they might reelect her without a vote."

There was a slight twinkle discernable in the senator's eyes.

Charlene resumed her questioning. "Why did you kill Joshua's daughters, Abigail? They were your flesh and blood too. Your nieces. And then to kill your own brother?"

The senator turned and looked at Charlene. She appeared deadly calm when she opened her mouth to speak. Sawyer put his hand on her arm to silence her.

"Remember, we discussed this. You only speak when I tell you."

Sawyer looked at Charlene. "What are you talking about? Last time I checked, American Senators have power, but they can't play God, they can't magically stir up miscarriages. Now you're grasping. Joshua Fellows committed suicide like his parents—it's genetic. Everyone knows that."

Brett Sawyer stood up and buttoned his jacket.

"Sit down." Smith's voice rose. "We're not through yet."

Sawyer sighed and sat down, unbuttoning the jacket that was uncomfortably tight around his middle.

"There is the little matter of a large, unidentified deposit in one of her offshore bank accounts."

"The senator receives campaign contributions all the time, sometimes more than she can even keep track of. With the proper amount of time, we can get to the bottom of every cent in every account in the senator's name. She has people who take care of that for her."

"And under which name would that be?" Charlene asked sarcastically.

"We have another theory about that money." This time, *Smith* smiled.

"Really," Sawyer mocked. "I can't wait to hear this elaborate new FBI theory."

"We know where that money came from and why it was deposited in her account. Should I continue?"

Charlene thought she saw something in Bloomfield, a twitch, or at least a nervous fidget. The senator whispered something in her attorney's ear.

The attorney shook his head at the senator, but then looked at Smith. "We're listening."

"Just think about the people who gave you that money, Senator. What are they going to think when you don't hold up your end of the bargain?"

That caught the senator's attention.

He went on, "I'm just a law-abiding FBI agent, but I know how I would feel if I paid someone a great deal of money in advance to do a job that didn't get done. We've subpoenaed all her bank records. She won't have access to that money for a very, very long time—if ever."

Charlene picked up the thread, addressing the senator herself. "But that doesn't mean you don't have options. You can look over your shoulder for the rest of your life, what's left of it anyway, wondering where or when it will come. Or, you can opt for protection."

Smith dropped the folder on the table with a thud, for dramatic effect.

The senator shifted in her seat, looking uncomfortable. She paled slightly, and swallowed hard.

Sawyer stood again. "I think we've heard enough."

But the senator grabbed him by the expensive jacket sleeve and pulled him back into his seat, to his great chagrin. Once again, she leaned over and whispered in his ear, and her other attorneys leaned in to listen.

They had a short conversation, in whispers. Even though Charlene couldn't hear their words or read their lips, she could read their general facial expressions. The lawyer was distraught and the senator adamant. It looked like a huddle on a pitcher's mound, the manager trying to pull a reluctant starting pitcher.

Sawyer spoke first. "I just want it on the record that I am against all of this." He looked at Bloomfield and then back at Smith. "My client would like to speak."

The senator all of a sudden looked small, fragile, even meek. The woman Charlene remembered from TV, debates and live public appearances, was long gone.

"Can you guarantee my safety? Witness protection?"

"That can be arranged, if you give us what we're looking for."

The lawyer whispered in the senator's ear. But she looked at the agents. "I have what you're looking for and I'll give it to you."

She turned and murmured something to her lawyer, and he mouthed something back.

"What's the deal?" the lawyer asked.

Smith picked up the folder from the table, opened it slowly, and removed a single piece of paper. He slid it across the table, and the lawyer picked it up and read it over.

Smith explained, "The way I see it, without this, your client is being charged, and *will* be convicted of two counts of conspiring and accessory to murder, and fourteen counts of kidnapping."

"We know what the 'trumped up' charges are, agent. We want to know what the deal is." The attorney sounded impatient.

"We'll drop the death penalty if your client pleads guilty, and gives us the information we need to track the people involved. And that's only if we catch them. And she'll get twenty-five years in a *minimum*-security women's penitentiary."

This was followed by another heated whispering session that lasted several long minutes. The top man shook his head several times, but the senator was resolute, and would not back down. The other two attorneys said little or nothing.

Then, Sawyer spoke. "If my client leads you to the men in charge, her life will be in grave danger, even in prison."

Charlene didn't like where this was heading.

The attorney argued, "No prison time, and my client enters the witness protection program where she will be given a new identity and a new life in a country of her choice."

"Absolutely not," Charlene said. "Your client is guilty of murder, kidnapping and putting helpless infants in danger of bodily harm."

"Allegedly," the attorney corrected her. "You need us more than we need you. Isn't that right, Agent Smith?"

Smith rubbed his stubbled face. He looked tired, with pronounced bags under his eyes.

Charlene looked at Smith, unable to believe what she was hearing. "You're not going to do this?" But she could read the look he gave her.

Charlene leaned back in her seat. This time bile rose in her throat.

The room was quiet for several minutes before anyone spoke.

Smith rolled his head around on his neck. "Fifteen years in minimum security. The senator will still be under sixty when she's released." He was almost pleading now. "That's all I'm permitted to offer."

Sawyer shook his head. "Her life is in danger. No matter where she goes, she'll live in constant fear that will never end, unless you grant her a new identity."

Smith shrugged his shoulders and did not back down. "She put herself in this position."

Bloomfield whispered something else in her lawyer's ear and all four of them stood up.

Sawyer announced, "We need time to think about it. We'll be in touch."

Charlene sat with Matt at a table for two at the Venice Ristorante and Wine Bar, an extravagant Italian restaurant in downtown Denver. Today's meeting had exhausted them both.

She shook her head. "Smith is going to give in. He all but begged them to take that deal."

"He wants these guys as badly as you do, and will do whatever it takes to get them."

"I can't let that happen. She can't walk away from this."

"There's nothing we can do. It's out of our hands."

She abruptly changed the subject. "How's Janice?"

"They think she's going to make it. She got lucky."

"That's good."

Their food arrived.

She knew Matt would be leaving for Washington and she would be on her way back to fighting crime in LA. Where did they stand? They had spent one night together, one special night, but what they had, what they'd been through, had been more than just sex. At least she thought so.

The fact that he had asked to stay in Denver on the case longer, when he could have hightailed it to another city and another case, meant more to her than any words.

He wasn't a quitter. He made a commitment to something and saw it all the way through, and that's exactly what she wanted—a man who wouldn't let her down.

Could they try the long-distance thing?

She would never give up her job as an LAPD detective, and could never ask him to leave his job in Washington. Their relationship wasn't yet at the place where one of them would leave the job and relocate for the other. Who knew if it would ever come to that? Her job meant everything to her and she understood that he felt the same way about his.

She looked into his eyes and the feeling of their romantic interlude at Jake's house came flooding back. They'd acted on impulse, letting the heat of the moment overcome good sense. Could that fire remain burning strong?

She grabbed a warm baguette from the basket and broke off a small piece, popping it into her mouth.

After taking a sip of his water he asked, "So, what did you think of the interview?"

She still had a hard time seeing Abigail Fellows as Senator Jaqueline Bloomfield, even after everything she'd read in the file. She had been following the senator's career for so long, modeling herself after the woman's example that she felt betrayed just thinking about it. She was a fraud, living a double life—a lie.

She swallowed a sip of water before speaking. "She was certainly rattled when we mentioned her unpaid debt."

"Do you think she'll take the deal?"

She thought about it for a few brief seconds. "Yes."

Matt poured them each a glass of red wine. Charlene didn't know the first thing about wine—didn't usually drink it at all. He had ordered a California Pinot Noir. Charlene sipped at it.

"It's good." She watched Matt taste his, then asked. "So, be honest, what did you really think when you first met me?"

He eyed her over his wine glass. "You sound like you have doubts."

"Let's just say I'm not a real 'people person' and not much for trusting first impressions."

He grinned. "When you confronted me at Jane's house that first night, I wasn't sure what to think. Your blue eyes danced, with something in them. You meant business. You didn't act like the average California blond. You had a surprising air of confidence and authority about you."

She lowered her chin and smiled. "At least I didn't scare you away."

"Because I know what police work can do to anyone, I appreciate women in the field. LA is a tough city, and a woman detective who can handle herself in that environment, especially in the Robbery/Homicide Division, is impressive."

"Oh, keep going, you sweet talker, you." She took another drink.

"As an FBI profiler, I'm in the habit of profiling everyone I meet, and I had you pegged right away: Caucasian female, average height, between the ages of twenty-five to thirty-five, single, never willing to be held back by any man. Tough exterior, to prove you could make it in male-dominated industry. A perfectionist, who always had to be in control, the best at everything you do. Your concern for your sister proved that you were very family-oriented, and your love for police work was a family trait. I saw you as a competent, confident detective whose attention to detail made you an excellent investigator."

She pondered his words. 'Never to be held back by any man'—was that how het really saw her?

"Not bad for a first impression."

He gave her a nod. "But remember I've been watching you work for a week."

She tapped her fingernail on the wine glass. "Okay, enough profiling."

"Sorry, it's my nature."

"How did you become a profiler?"

"Good question. I guess it's my turn now."

Charlene raised her glass in a mock toast.

"I grew up in Denver, but I knew I had to get out. I always wanted to be a Fed—I guess it was all those cop movies I watched as a kid. But first I had to do my time in the trenches. I started out as a cop in New York. I worked six years with the NYPD and at age twenty-six I was approached by the FBI. After training at Quantico, they assigned me to Organized Crime. But that didn't last long. A year later, a guy from the Behavioral Science Unit came to me, and admitted they'd been watching me since I graduated from training. I didn't know much about the BSU then, because it was a relatively new program and not well-respected around the Bureau." He chuckled, "Guys in the bureau referred to it as the BS division—guess that's why they changed its name to Behavioral Analysis Unit. But I saw an opportunity so I took it."

She could see the glint in his eye when he talked about his work, about how it felt to help bring cases to justice. The passion he had for his job was evident; it was as if she was listening to herself talk about being a cop.

She changed the subject. "What about your family?"

"Both my parents died in a car accident when I was eighteen, hit head on by a drunk driver, and Jake is my only sibling. Our Aunt Ellen took us in. We owe her everything."

"That must have been hard on you."

Matt nodded. "It was, but at eighteen, I was old enough to handle it, whereas Jake was only eight."

"Wow."

Matt paused. "That was fourteen years ago." He swallowed, and blinked, clearly uncomfortable venting his feelings. "I didn't try hard enough for Jake. I knew it crushed him when I left for New York, but I was only thinking of myself. I knew he was in good hands with our aunt. Jake eventually accepted the decision, but it took a while, and we didn't speak for several years."

It was almost a carbon copy of Charlene's relationship with Jane.

"But you chased your dream. A profiler for the FBI. And he's a cop, just like he always wanted to be. It worked out for everyone in the end."

Matt nodded. "I'm proud of Jake's strength, and the man he's grown to be."

After a pregnant pause, she said, "You know, he looks up to you."

"I know. He's a good kid, a good officer, and a devoted policeman. He wants to be a Fed someday. I'm glad I can be a role model for him." Matt put up his hands. "Your turn now. What did you think of me the first time we met?"

She shrugged her shoulders. "The usual, an FBI asshole."

Matt laughed so hard that other diners turned to stare at them.

"Thanks, for your honesty," he said. "So, tell me, how did little Charlene Taylor come to be Detective Charlene Taylor of the LAPD?"

"You mean you don't know that, after calling my captain or reading my bio?" She gave him a look of amusement, and he flashed a guilty grin.

She gave him the short version—growing up in LA as the tomboy daughter of an LAPD detective, then following in her father's footsteps. She briefly detailed her college life at NYU, her days as an officer, and her first case, which he already seemed to know about.

"The Celebrity Slayer—pretty amazing work, Detective Taylor."

"Why, thank you."

They clinked their glasses together.

He was smiling when he asked, "What is your ultimate first date?"

"Dodgers. Hot Dogs. Beer."

"What? And I bought wine. Damn."

They both laughed.

He steepled his fingers together and looked her in the eye, growing serious all of a sudden. "What would you be doing if you weren't a cop?"

No one had ever asked her that before. She didn't know anything else, never thought of anything else. In all honesty, she couldn't see herself doing anything else.

She shrugged. "I don't know."

She couldn't remember ever feeling so comfortable talking to a man.

Finally, she asked, "So where are we going with this?" There it was, the million-dollar question.

Matt opened his mouth just as his cell phone rang. He raised a finger and checked caller ID.

"It's Smith."

He picked up. Charlene listened in on Matt's end of the conversation.

"Good evening, Agent Smith." He paused. "Are you going to accept that? Okay, we'll be there first thing in the morning."

He hung up and looked at Charlene. "Brett Sawyer called. They want to make the deal. The senator will tell us everything we want to know about the men she worked for. We're meeting with them first thing in the morning."

"Just like that?"

"Well," he stalled. "They do want to add stipulations to the deal."

"Like what?"

"The senator wants to be cleared of all wrong-doing. Witness protection for her and her family. When it's all over, a statement will be issued declaring that the senator and her brother worked with the FBI to help bring down the criminals."

"And he took it, didn't he?"

"He jumped at it." Then he added, "This is a good thing, Char."

She sat back in the comfortable, leather chair, breathing in the garlic and peppers, feeling ambivalent. It should have been the perfect night—having dinner with a great guy with whom she loved talking, and tomorrow they would get a confession and the lead the FBI had been waiting six years for.

They held up their wine glasses, and he said, "To happy endings."

She still wasn't sure.

Chapter 24

Charlene awoke the next morning to the sound of a cell phone chiming. She looked around the room in a daze, the remnants of last night's wine leaving her mind a blur. They'd finished the first bottle and ordered a second, reveling in the thought of taking down Senator Bloomfield, and the information she'd give them.

She'd had one of the soundest nights' sleep of her life. She had heard nothing during the night, but even more importantly, she had no nightmares.

She leaned over the edge of the bed, reaching for the floor and fumbled with her jacket, lifting the iphone from the pocket. She checked the time—it was very early. Her phone was silent, and not vibrating.

She rolled over and nudged Matt, who snored beside her, the hair on his chest rising and falling with each deep breath, even though his cell phone continued to ring.

"Matt, it's yours."

He sat up and looked at her. When Matt smiled, it warmed her. "Always on call," he said.

Moments later he rolled off the bed, landing on his feet, and retrieved his phone from the dresser top. Her eyes blinked wide open now, appreciating his well-developed abs.

She leapt out of bed, threw on one of his shirts and tried to slip out of the room. But she was pulled back in by a tug on the back of her shirt, and spun on her toes, as he wrapped an arm around her waist and then tugged her down and kissed her on the lips.

She closed her eyes and kissed him back, tasting his lips, still smelling the fruity richness of red wine. She finally pulled away, against her own will, and headed toward the bathroom.

From the hallway, she could hear his end of the phone conversation.

"Sorry, Agent Smith, I had a problem with the phone."

Charlene snorted and closed the bathroom door behind her. She ran water in the sink and looked at herself in the mirror. Her cheeks were flushed from the kiss.

"Get a hold of yourself," she whispered.

She couldn't deny it; he had that effect on her, even after such a short time. She'd never felt like this about a guy.

She felt like a teenager again. He brought out something in her that had her acting unlike herself, and it felt good. She splashed water on her face and dried it with the hand towel.

She brushed and flossed, and then turned off the tap and wiped her mouth with a clean towel. She tucked her hair behind her ears and exited the bathroom.

Matt slumped on the edge of the bed, still in his boxers, with his head in his hands, looking down at the floor.

"What is it?"

He looked up, and she saw something in his eyes. Fear. "That was Agent Smith. The senator's dead."

"What?" Charlene felt sick.

She sat down beside him.

"They found her this morning in her cell, on the floor in a pool of her own blood. Her carotid artery had been severed."

"I thought she had protection? What happened to the guards on duty?"

He shook his head. "Bloomfield died instantly, unable to cry out. Apparently, no one saw or heard anything. We'll investigate it."

Charlene paced the room. "We know who did it, but how did *they* know she wanted to meet us?"

"They know everything. Apparently, they knew she'd give them up. Paid her up front and when she couldn't supply the goods and deliver on her part of the transaction, they took matters into their own hands. They made sure she wouldn't talk, ever."

"Now what?" Charlene tried to swallow, but her mouth was dry.

"That's it. We have no leads. We have no idea who the senator worked with. Smith is pissed. He's ready to fly back now. He's ordered the jet to be fueled up, as we speak."

"What about the attorney?"

"Smith can't reach him and he's not in his office. Smith is on his way to his house now."

She was thinking out loud. "So, there's a chance that the senator told him something. Maybe she told him whatever she was going to tell us. Chances are they would have discussed it, even written it down, to determine how much she would reveal and what to hold on to for a better deal."

"I guess there's a chance. That's all we have to cling to right now."

"Sawyer won't be tied to attorney/client confidentiality and he'll work his ass off to make whoever did this pay."

The mood was tense, and when Matt's phone suddenly rang it startled them both.

She said, "Put it on speaker."

Matt answered. "Agent Smith, what did Sawyer say?"

"Sawyer's dead."

He announced it so matter-of-factly that when Charlene met Matt's eyes, she didn't believe him.

"What do you mean?"

"Same thing as Bloomfield, throat sliced in his kitchen, while he ate at the table. Blood everywhere. Someone is sending a message."

"Jesus."

"There's a team here working the scene but I'm not optimistic. That's our last witness, our last lead. If Sawyer knew anything at all, we'll never know. We'll go through all of his files to make sure, but I'm not counting on anything."

"What now?" Charlene asked.

"Nothing. We're heading out at noon. See you at the plane, Agent Stone. And Detective Taylor?"

"Yes?"

"It was great working with you. I'd be happy to do it again."

"Thank you, sir."

Matt hung up and they sat quietly, holding hands for several long moments.

After a long pause, she sat up and finally spoke. "Either they have someone on the inside, or they just knew she'd break to save her own ass. They must have thought Bloomfield told Sawyer something and needed to silence that threat. These people will stop at nothing. No one is untouchable to them."

"Those people are still out there, Matt. They could, and probably will, strike again."

"I know."

Once again, he wrapped his arms around her, and it felt good being in his embrace. She felt safe with him, as if nothing could hurt her there. They were still sitting there an hour later.

Epilogue

Sleeping Ghosts

After hours of discussion, Matt and Charlene decided that they weren't ready to part ways. They would attempt to make a long-distance relationship work. She would live her life, and he would live his, and when they could, they'd visit and spend time together.

She had no idea how or even *if* it would work, but he was worth the effort. He seemed on board, and actually believed they could do it. She had no idea when they'd see each other again, but he had insisted they would do everything they could to make it happen.

As tough as it was leaving Denver, when she stepped into her apartment it felt as if she'd been gone a long time, when, it had really only been a few weeks. It was good to be home.

The way the case had played out, still had her bewildered. She recognized that without Harold Linden's investigation, the police would probably never have found out about the real Senator Jaqueline Bloomfield, or uncovered enough information to convict her.

She thought about the woman she had all but worshipped. What she couldn't understand was why the senator had done it. Jaqueline Bloomfield had the world in her hands, a powerful woman with a bright future, on her way to the top.

But in the end, like most of the criminals Charlene brought down, the senator couldn't hide from her past, and it eventually caught up with her. She'd lost her life over her greed and lust for power, but also out of hate.

She hated her life, her family, and most importantly, herself, and couldn't go on without acting on that loathing.

Charlene thought about Jane, Richard and Martina, as well as the other families who'd had their worlds turned upside down. Would they ever be the same? Would their wounds ever heal and allow them to live a normal life? Only time would tell.

She gave a great deal of thought to law enforcement. All the different agencies who worked together, had put their differences aside, and worked as one unit to find the kidnappers.

Janice Salinger would survive, but would she ever work as the chief of police again?

Susan Harper and Cindy Richards had their lives upended because of their involvement with Joshua Fellows. Jackie Bloomfield had killed their daughters just to keep Fellows by her side, and now those nurses could never have children of their own.

But she couldn't help think about the parents from the first case, and her heart sank. She'd lost Martina for only a few days, and it had crushed her. Those parents had lost their children for six years, and maybe forever.

Then Charlene thought about Matt—his motivation, his drive, and his investigative talents. His profile had helped catch the kidnappers and return the children to their parents.

She had doubts that their relationship would work because they were both so focused on their careers. They thought of the job first and foremost. He would always be on call as a consultant, living out of a suitcase. And that would make his part of the relationship a challenge.

But now, at this moment she felt hopeful as she stood at the front of the tiny classroom, looking out at the smiling faces of children looking back at her—the curiosity in their eyes brought her a sense of peace and tranquility. It was their youthful innocence that motivated her to do her job, to provide safety and security for the public, and allow these children a chance to grow up in a nonviolent environment.

The teacher stepped up and smiled. "Thank you, Detective Taylor."

Twenty-one second graders cheered and clapped until their teacher finally gave them a dirty look.

Charlene turned around and looked at the teacher. "Thank you for having me."

"Well, I'm glad that Lauren suggested it."

Charlene turned back and winked at little Lauren, who sat in the front row, wearing a wide toothless grin. Ever since Charlene had stepped inside the classroom twenty minutes earlier, Lauren had been the class rock star, with everyone crowding around and wanting to sit beside her.

Knowing, or suspecting, what Lauren had been going through in her life, with a drug/alcohol addicted mother and an abusive stepfather, Charlene felt gratified to have made a difference in the little girl's life, even for a brief moment.

In fact, the kids had sat quietly, mesmerized, and hanging on her every word as she explained what it was like to be an LAPD detective.

Charlene turned back to the teacher. "I can take a few questions if you'd like."

When Charlene turned back toward the students, twenty-one flapping hands flew into the air.

"We'll take two questions. Is that understood?" The teacher leaned against the wall, watching.

"Yes, Mrs. Valleau," the class echoed.

"Marcus." The teacher pointed to a freckled-face, red-headed boy in the back row.

"My dad said that cops are jerks."

The teacher was flushed when she scolded him. "That's enough, Marcus." Ms. Valleau looked at Charlene. "I'm sorry." She turned back to focus on Marcus. "That's a comment, not a question. And an inappropriate one at that. Remember the difference between a question and a comment, class. Jasmine."

An African-American girl with pigtails and big dimples asked, "What's your favorite part of the job?"

Charlene smiled. "That's a great question, Jasmine. My favorite part of the job is helping people, and keeping them safe."

"Okay, one more question. Jeremy."

A tall lanky boy with longish blond hair wrinkled his nose. "Have you ever shot anyone?"

The class was silent, hanging on her every word.

"Yes, I have."

"That's so cool." One boy grinned. "Can I touch your gun?"

The class got loud.

"Boys and girls." The teacher stepped in front of Charlene and used a stern voice to quiet the group which had grown giddy. "Thank you for coming by today, Detective Taylor."

"You're welcome."

"Class, what do we say?"

"Thank you, Detective Taylor."

Charlene walked down an aisle, patting Lauren on the top of the head as she passed the girl's desk, and left the room. Out in the hallway, the cell phone in her pocket started vibrating.

She pulled it out and answered it. "Taylor."

"Charlene."

"Hey, Larry. What's up?" Charlene hadn't spoken to her partner since she'd returned to LA last night.

"You just get in?"

"Last night. Why?"

"It's Brady. He's awake."

THE END

If you enjoyed this book, please consider writing a short review and posting it on your favorite review sites. Reviews are very helpful to other readers and are greatly appreciated by authors, especially me. When you post a review, drop me an email and let me know.

Luke

luke@authorlukemurphy.com

Dear Reader,

Thank you for picking up a copy of Rock-A-Bye Baby. I hope you enjoyed reading this novel as much as I did writing it. My goal was to take these characters to another level. I hope I succeeded.

I had always hoped to write a sequel to Kiss & Tell, I just didn't know it would take so long. I really missed the characters in this series, and it felt great getting back inside their heads. I had so much fun revisiting this cast that I can definitely see another book in the future.

This is a work of fiction. I did not base the characters or plot on any real people or events. Any familiarities are strictly coincidence.

I can't believe how many comments I've received from readers, how much you all fell in love with the Charlene Taylor character. She is definitely a woman with whom people can relate—she is so real. Writing from a female point of view is always a challenge, and many women in my life had to undergo questioning to help me fill in some blanks. I had to make her tomboyish, a little bit athletic and tough, to help me along the way.

Although I've never visited the city of Denver, I have been to Colorado Springs, and I fell in love with the state. The Internet is quite remarkable for research purposes.

For more information about my books, please visit my website at www.authorlukemurphy.com. You can also "like" my Facebook page and follow me on Twitter.

I'm always happy to hear from readers. Please be assured that I read each email personally and will respond to them in good time. I'm always happy to give advice to aspiring writers, or answer questions from readers. You can direct your questions/comments to the contact form on my website. I look forward to hearing from you.

Regards,

Luke

Books by Luke Murphy

CALVIN WATTERS MYSTERIES
Dead Man's Hand
Wild Card

CHARLENE TAYLOR MYSTERIES
Kiss & Tell
Rock-A-Bye Baby

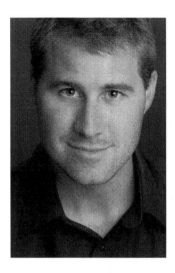

Luke Murphy is the international bestselling author of Dead Man's Hand (Imajin Books, 2012), Kiss & Tell (Imajin Books, 2015), and Wild Card (Imajin Books, 2017).

Murphy played six years of professional hockey before retiring in 2006. His sports column, "Overtime" (Pontiac Equity), was nominated for the 2007 Best Sports Page in Quebec, and won the award in 2009. He has also worked as a radio journalist (CHIPFM 101.7).

Murphy lives in Shawville, QC with his wife and three daughters. He is a teacher who holds a Bachelor of Science degree in Marketing, and a Bachelor of Education (Magna Cum Laude).

Rock-A-Bye Baby, a sequel to Kiss & Tell, is Murphy's fourth novel.

For more information on Luke and his books, visit:
www.authorlukemurphy.com

'Like' his Facebook page: www.facebook.com/AuthorLukeMurphy

Follow him on Twitter: www.twitter.com/AuthorLMurphy

Be the first to know when Luke Murphy's next book is available! Follow him at: bookbub.com/authors/luke-murphy to receive new release and discount alerts.

Made in the USA
Lexington, KY
15 June 2019